RANDOM
HOUSE

LARGE
PRINT

CLIVE CUSSLER'S
DARK VECTOR

CLIVE CUSSLER'S
DARK VECTOR

A Novel from the NUMA® Files

GRAHAM BROWN

RANDOM HOUSE
LARGE PRINT

Copyright © 2022 by Sandecker, RLLLP

Published in the United States of America by Random House Large Print in association with G. P. Putnam's Sons, an imprint of Penguin Random House LLC.

Cover art by Mike Heath
Title page image by Yasemin Yurtman Candemir / Shutterstock.com

The Library of Congress has established a Cataloging-in-Publication record for this title.

ISBN: 978-0-593-55620-7

www.penguinrandomhouse.com/large-print-format-books

FIRST LARGE PRINT EDITION

Printed in the United States of America

1st Printing

This Large Print edition published in accord with the standards of the N.A.V.H.

CAST OF CHARACTERS

CHINA 1808

ZI JUN CHU—Owner of a three-masted junk plying trade routes in the East China Sea
CAPTAIN OF JUN'S SHIP
CHING SHIH—Pirate queen whose fleet dominated the South China Sea in the early part of the nineteenth century

PRESENT DAY

Water Rats (Pirate Group)

LUCAS TENG (TENG KUNG-LU)—Leader of the band of thieves calling themselves the Water Rats
VINCENT UHR—Second in command of the Water Rats
CALLUM ZHEN—Member of the Water Rats

Hong Kong

KINNARD EMMERSON—British expatriate
and leader of a Hong Kong–based
criminal organization

GUĀNCHÁ (THE WATCHER)—Emmerson's
lieutenant and most trusted assassin

YAN-LI—Nautical historian and former dive
specialist for the PRN, her academic discipline
underwater excavation

DEGRA—One of the leaders of CIPHER,
a notorious cybercrime organization based
in China

FERRET—One of the hackers working
for CIPHER

National Underwater and Marine Agency (NUMA)

KURT AUSTIN—Director of Special Projects,
salvage expert and boating enthusiast

JOE ZAVALA—Kurt's assistant and best friend,
helicopter pilot and mechanical genius

RUDI GUNN—Deputy Director of NUMA,
graduate of the Naval Academy, runs most
of the day-to-day operations at NUMA

HIRAM YAEGER—NUMA's Director of
Information Technology, expert in the
design and function of the most advanced
computers

PAUL TROUT—NUMA's chief geologist, graduate of Scripps Institute

GAMAY TROUT—NUMA's leading marine biologist, also graduated from Scripps

WINTERBURN—Executive officer of the NUMA yacht **Sapphire**

STRATTON—NUMA engineer specializing in the operation of sub-surface drones

Naha, Okinawa—U.S. Navy Weather Station

LIEUTENANT CALLIE BAKER—Sonar specialist working at the Naha Weather Station

LIEUTENANT COMMANDER AARON STEWART—Senior officer at Naha Station

Washington, D.C.

ANNA BIEL—Presidential adviser and director of the National Security Agency

ELLIOT HARNER—Deputy director of the CIA

REAR ADMIRAL MARCUS WAGNER—Head of Naval Intelligence for the Western Pacific

ARTHUR HICKS—U.S. Cyber Command

Taiwan R.O.C.

STEVEN WU—CIA liaison officer in Taipei

Hydro-Com Corporation

SUNIL PRADI—Founder and CEO of Hydro-Com
   Corporation
SABRINA LANG—Chief of Digital Security at
   Hydro-Com Corporation

CLIVE CUSSLER'S
DARK VECTOR

PROLOGUE
THE CRIMSON FLAG

SOUTH CHINA SEA
SEPTEMBER 1808

Jun Chu stood on the deck of a three-masted junk given the auspicious name **Silken Dragon.** The ship was a feast for the eyes, with an emerald green hull, golden adornments and sails dyed a resplendent blood orange hue.

The ship sat at anchor in a tranquil bay. Clear aquamarine water lay beneath the hull, while a steep mountain peak rose from an island beyond.

The peak had given them some morning shade. But the sun was now high above and the temperature had soared. If not for the breeze blowing in from the west, the heat would have been unbearable. As it was, an odd sulfur-like smell could be detected. The source of the aroma baffled Jun, but he had bigger issues to worry about.

He pulled a brass telescope from a leather case. The beautiful instrument was polished and gleaming. Engraved characters on the casing reminded him that it had been given as a gift, from the powerful pirate queen Ching Shih.

The captain of the vessel moved up next to him. "What do you see?"

Jun gazed through the spyglass. His face turned grim. "It seems our escape from Macau did not go unnoticed. Three ships are approaching."

"This is a trade route," the captain reminded him. "Many vessels ply these waters. Do not assume danger where there is only the company of other travelers."

"I assume nothing," Jun said. "Take the spyglass. You'll see that I'm not wary without reason. Those ships fly the red banner of Madam Ching. They're hunters sent to slay us or bring us to Macau for punishments that I choose not to imagine."

Jun focused on the nearest of the approaching ships. It was a larger vessel than the **Dragon.** Four sails to his three and a topmast adorned with banners red as blood.

The other ships in the squadron were farther back, too far to see any details, but they tracked the same heading.

The captain offered a hopeful suggestion. "It's said Madam Ching will spare a ship's crew if the master surrenders their cargo without a fight."

Jun lowered the telescope. Ching Shih had indeed created a code of honor among her pirates, but such considerations would not be extended to Jun. "Her code will not apply to us. We are thieves and traitors, not honorable adversaries."

There was no need to say more. The treasure in their hold had been pirated by Madam Ching's ships once already, but instead of being turned in to the collective and disbursed fairly, a rogue captain of hers had set much of it aside. He'd sold it to Jun, assuring him the truth had been hidden.

"Your friend must have been caught short," the captain said.

Jun shivered at the man's fate. "To withhold captured plunder is punishable by death," he said. "To steal it outright . . . Beheading would be the best fate such a man could hope for. No doubt he's been killed. Though not soon enough to keep him from speaking our names."

"We cannot outrun them," the captain said. "Each of her ships are larger and faster."

"Then we must fight," Jun said. "We have cannonades we bought from the East India Company. We have crossbows and harquebuses."

"We'll be outnumbered five to one."

"They cannot come all at once," Jun said. "And her large ships will not be able to cross the reef. If we remain here, they will have to come in small boats, hoping to climb aboard using ladders and grappling hooks. In my experience, **grenadoes** and flaming arrows are quite effective at such a range."

The captain's face began to soften. "You hope to bleed them one small group at a time."

Jun nodded. It was truly their only hope. "And when they've bled enough, they'll depart from us and return to Macau, where they'll tell Madam Ching we burned the ship rather than surrender and face death."

The captain's face was inscrutable. He took the spyglass back, gazing at the red-flagged ships as they turned toward the bay. "You have a silken tongue, Master Jun. You almost make me believe we might survive."

As the men aboard the **Dragon** steeled themselves for battle, Ching Shih's fleet approached the reef and pulled back. Small boats were called for and the better part of each ship's complement prepared to sail forth.

Each of Jun's predictions had so far proved accurate, all except one. There was no condition under which the small fleet would return to Macau with a false story to tell their master, since Madam Ching was aboard the largest of the ships and her fury had been stoked like a bonfire.

Zheng Yi Sao, or Ching Shih as she was known, walked the deck before her men. An average-sized woman with broad shoulders and piercing eyes, her face remained as beautiful as it had been when she'd been taken by Lord Cheng as a wife.

Together they'd built a dynasty, ultimately controlling the towns and waters around Macau with iron fists. After Cheng's death, Ching Shih had assumed full control, building the empire ever larger, making allies out of conquered people, creating order out of chaos.

A large portion of that order stemmed from the code she'd put forth. It required fair treatment of crews, captives and concubines. It punished officers who mistreated their men. It demanded swift and ruthless retribution upon anyone who betrayed the collective good of the red-bannered fleet.

With these rules in place, she became the de facto governor of a sprawling region and the most feared and therefore respected pirate lord in all of Asia. One did not steal from her and live to tell the story.

Striding resplendently across the deck in a shimmering gown of lilac and gray, she commanded the full attention of every man on board. A red scarf adorned her neck, a black three-pointed hat rested on her head. Not a sound emanated from the hundred men standing before her as she climbed the steps to address them.

"These traitors have not stolen from me," she said, "they have stolen from you." She allowed that to sink in and then asked them a question. "What is the law of the plunder?"

They replied in unison. "What is taken must be presented. It must be shared by all."

Her pride grew as they spoke. "And what is the punishment for stealing?"

"Flogging and death."

She was pleased. Her fleet was disciplined. Her men, a well-trained army. Knowing they would suffer heavy losses, she made a promise. "All who go forth shall receive a double share. All who are wounded shall receive triple. All who die today will have their family's prosperity secured for the next generation."

They stood still. The air silent and hot.

"And whoever brings me the living body of the traitor," she finished, "shall be rich beyond the dreams of an emperor."

The men cheered loudly, chanting her name repeatedly, their minds and bodies ready for battle.

"Go," she said. "Retrieve what is yours."

Sixty-four men climbed down the ladders into four boats. Eight additional boats were launching from Ching's other ships. In each boat half the crew worked the oars while the other half stood ready to fight, either armed or waiting to throw ladders and hooks up.

Jun watched the fleet of small craft as they crossed the reef and continued toward him on the strength of the oarsmen's arms. Twelve small boats. Perhaps a hundred and eighty men. He had only seventy-five. But he stood aboard a floating castle.

"They're coming," he shouted. "Be ready!"

Warnings were called out from bow to stern. Jun's men swarmed the top deck of the junk, carrying weapons of every kind. The first group went to the rail carrying crossbows and muskets. Other groups stood behind them ready to fill in the gaps. They opened fire as soon as the approaching boats came within range.

The muskets were inaccurate at any sort of range and, aside from the noise and smoke, mostly ineffective. The crossbows, on the other hand, were lethal. The first flight of darts pierced several men in the leading boats. Several oarsmen took bolts to the back. They slumped forward or writhed in pain. Two men holding a ladder were hit in the chest. They toppled into the sea.

In the second boat several men were hit in the legs and pinned to the wooden planks beneath them. As they shrieked in agony, the fleet kept coming.

With the leading boats decimated, the men in the following boats opened fire from their longer range, hoping to force Jun's men back.

Jun ducked as musket balls whistled overhead, but this return fire was more sound and fury than danger. The rocking boats and the inaccurate shots from firearms made for a wild spray of lead that passed without hitting a single crewman.

Subsequent volleys were more effective, and for

several minutes the crews traded fire, with each side losing men in the exchange.

It was a war of attrition, one that Jun's men were winning, but with each passing second Ching Shih's men sailed closer. Soon they'd surrounded the **Dragon,** with half of the small boats within reach of the junk's hull.

"They're splitting up," Jun called out. Several boats had rowed across to the port side. Others were making for the bow. "They plan to take us on all sides. Disperse the men."

The defenders fanned out, attempting to protect all sections of the ship at once as the pitched battle resumed.

"Our ability to concentrate fire has been sorely compromised," the captain said.

Jun pulled out his flintlock pistol and cocked the hammer. "They still have to get aboard."

That task was already underway. Grappling hooks had been thrown up on the port side. Rickety ladders on the starboard.

"Push them back," the captain ordered.

Jun's men attacked with axes, raising them high and hammering down with vicious blows. Their targets were not the men but the hooks and the lines. The vicious blows cleaved the ropes in two and dug into the ship's painted wooden rail.

On the other side of the vessel, ladders were forced backward with long poles. They were pushed hard until gravity took over and the men climbing them tumbled into the sea.

The pirates attacked with covering fire overhead, using a barrage of arrows, gunfire and even spears to keep Jun's men from rappelling. For each grappling hook cut and ladder knocked loose, Jun lost a defender, or two, or three. And still Ching Shih's men came.

Additional hooks were thrown up and the first invaders reached the deck. The attackers were smaller men—renowned for the speed with which they climbed. They raced up the side of the jade green hull and vaulted over the rail, firing pistols and slashing wildly with swords at anything within reach.

Expecting exactly this type of attack—and knowing the first wave of men would often climb with bare feet for better speed and traction—Jun had covered the deck in crow's feet: sharp barbs of twisted metal designed to impale the soles of the men who leapt over the rail.

But Ching Shih knew all the tricks. Her men were shod in thick boots. The crow's feet did nothing to slow them. They rushed forward, short swords and daggers in hand.

Jun blasted one of them with his pistol, sending the man to the deck with a bloody chest wound. A crossbow took out the second arrival. And the captain dispatched a third with a slash of his sword.

But others were climbing up behind them. Both sides of the ship were now in question, while a score of Ching Shih's men had come aboard near the bow, which was closer to the water and more easily accessible.

The combat became hand to hand. Pistols could be used but not reloaded. Muskets were useless except as blunt instruments to parry a sword or cave in an attacker's skull.

Jun's men were forced back on all sides, pushed inevitably inward from the rail and back toward the raised stern, where they would make their final stand.

Another flight of crossbow bolts went forth, thinning the number of attackers, but still more boarders came up the ropes and ladders.

"They seem willing to empty their boats to the last man," the captain shouted.

Jun was shocked by this, but the captain was correct. Several boats could be seen drifting near the stern with no one aboard but the injured or the dead.

"Form two lines," Jun shouted.

The crew did as ordered, but the lines didn't hold for long. The survivors were forced to retreat even farther, relinquishing space on the bloodstained decks.

They retreated up the stairs and onto the sterncastle. Fewer than thirty men survived, with twice that number coming their way.

Ching Shih's pirates massed for a final charge,

rushing the stairs and surging toward the top. They came forward shoulder to shoulder, a wall of men and swords. At the last moment, Jun shouted an order with all the breath in his lungs.

His forces spread to the sides and dropped to the deck, revealing four cannonades and an equal number of harquebuses standing at the ready on their mounts. The weapons weren't aimed outward against seaborne attack, but inward and down. Their yawning barrels pointed toward the stairs, now jammed with attacking pirates.

The cannonades went off with a deafening explosion of black powder. The sound was loud enough to throw any man to the deck, but the devastation came from the munitions inside.

The smoothbore barrels were packed with chains, broken blades and other fragments of metal and glass. They sent this hail of shrapnel flying into the onrushing force of men. It spread out as it flew, the chains whipping in a circular motion, the glass and metal acting like a hundred musket balls fired simultaneously.

In an instant, the attacking force was cut in half. Of those who survived, half again were injured. Even the untouched fell back in stunned disbelief.

The swivel guns fired next. Not as deadly or destructive, but effective enough to reduce the pirate forces further.

"Finish them," Jun shouted.

The captain rushed forth with his sword. The

surviving members of the crew charged alongside him, a fury of hacking and stabbing.

Jun stood where he was, gloating over his master-stroke. By waiting to employ his greatest weapons until Madam Ching's soldiers were massed together, he'd slaughtered most of them in a single instant.

With his men counterattacking, Ching's pirates were forced off the boat, diving over the rails into the bay. Some swam for the safety of the island, others toward the drifting boats or even toward the reef beyond.

Rushing to the aft rail, Jun pointed through the smoke at one of the departing boats. "Swing the guns around," he shouted. "Destroy the boats so they can't attack again."

A pair of his men worked to turn one of the cannonades. A third crewman packed it with powder and solid projectiles. But before they could light the fuse, a deafening blast rang out. It shook the bay, louder than any cannon or clap of thunder, or anything Jun had ever heard or felt.

The shock wave knocked him to the deck, threw several men off the ship and snapped one of the masts in half. The **Dragon** itself shuddered, leaning and threatening to roll over in the bay.

Facedown on wooden planks, Jun felt fingers of heat dancing on the nape of his neck. A wave of hot air burned his nostrils and dried his eyes. He rolled over, fearing himself on fire and trying desperately to stamp out the imaginary flames.

He wasn't burning, just being buffeted by three-hundred-degree winds and pelted by small rocks falling from the sky. Looking up, he watched the sun vanish behind a cloud of darkness.

Only now did he understand. The mountain had exploded, its upper third pulverized by a volcanic explosion. A mushroom cloud of ash could be seen bulling its way upward. Boulders the size of houses flew across the sky like birds. Trees and bushes, most of them in flame, rose alongside them. Lightning caused by static charges rippled through the maelstrom above.

"My god," Jun whispered.

All fighting stopped. The battle no longer mattered; the treasure no longer mattered. A single thought obsessed every mind. Get away from the island or die.

"Flare the sails," Jun shouted. "Cut the anchor loose."

The men rushed to do the work. Out beyond the reef, the red-bannered ships were leaving their stations, abandoning their rowing comrades to certain doom.

Boulders and rocks began to fall, towers of white water erupting from the bay as they landed, drenching the ship and everyone on board.

With the anchor gone and the remaining sails catching the wind, the ship began to move.

Ash began to fall around them, coating the deck with gray snow. Looking back, Jun understood the good fortune that had kept them alive so far. The eruption had been concentrated on the far side of the island. The force of the blast had been to the east, outward, away from the bay. The ash and pumice were spreading more widely, but the constant breeze of the trade winds was propelling the cloud eastward as well. Even the **Dragon** was picking up speed faster than he'd imagined it could.

"Perhaps the **Dragon** still favors us," Jun said.

The captain, wounded in one leg and limping, shook his head. "The bay is emptying," he said.

Jun stared through the falling ash. Large heads of coral were emerging from the bay, rising from the water like a barricade of dripping teeth. Stretches of wet sand were appearing, leaving pools of water between them, filled with desperate fish.

"What's happening?" Jun asked.

"The island is rising," the captain said. "The eruption isn't finished."

The ship ground to a painful stop, planks in the hull breaking against the reef.

They settled in what was left of the water, sinking lower and tilting over on one side as if they were careening the ship on a beach at high tide.

Another tremor hit and the gases and magma stored up in a chamber below the island were released all at once.

The remnants of the peak were obliterated. The ground beneath the ship collapsed and the sea rushed back in. At the same exact moment, a pyroclastic flow of fire, ash and mud surged down what was left of the mountain. The two surges collided over the sinking ship, crashing together like a pair of gigantic hands, erasing the **Silken Dragon** from view and from history.

CHAPTER 1

The **Canberra Swift** sailed through the night, heading north from Taiwan. She was a midsized cargo vessel, with a high beltline and an aerodynamic shell covering the front half of the ship. Her bridge emerged from this shell near the middle of the ship, while twin funnels, raked sharply backward, extended aft.

A leading nautical magazine described her as unattractive in nautical terms, suggesting a Japanese bullet train and seagoing ferry had borne a child together. But the strange shape had a purpose.

The ship had been designed to carry oversize cargo in a roll on/roll off configuration, much like a ferry. Freight and equipment were loaded on the ship at the stern, using a ramp wide enough to accommodate six lanes of traffic. It would be parked or stored inside, in a vast, unbroken cargo hold that ran the length of the main deck from bow to stern. Upon reaching its destination, the cargo was simply driven forward and off the ship on another ramp at the front.

Because of her size, shape and speed, the **Swift** had been used to transport everything from the fuselage sections of large aircraft, to rocket parts, and even nuclear waste, which traveled in sealed, lead-lined containers. If a war ever broke out, she was already committed by an option contract to be pressed into service carrying oversize military equipment to bases near whatever combat zone arose.

Jobs like these fell to the **Swift,** not only because she'd been designed to carry unique cargoes but also because—as the name implied—the **Swift** was one of the fastest cargo ships ever built. She could make forty knots in a sprint and travel at thirty-five all day long. She could cross the Pacific in seven days, a third of the time required for the average containership.

Standing on the bridge, the **Swift**'s captain studied the radar. There were no vessels near enough to be a bother. "All ahead full," he ordered. "There's a storm heading down the Canadian coast from Alaska and I'd very much like to beat it to San Francisco Bay."

The helmsman acknowledged the order and, using the computer panel in front of him, ordered the gas turbine engines to maximum output.

With the engine room answering, the captain was satisfied. He turned to the first officer. "The ship is yours. I'll be in my quarters if you need me."

The first officer nodded as the captain left the bridge. Expecting a peaceful night, he took a seat in the command chair as the **Swift** put on more speed.

Clinging to the outside of the ship with magnetic hand and knee pads, Teng Kung-lu, known to his men as Lucas, did not appreciate the additional speed in quite the same way. The electromagnetic force holding him in place was substantial, but every additional bit of velocity increased the gusting slip-stream that threatened to break the magnets' grip.

He pulled himself close to the hull, doing all he could to prevent the air from getting between him and the ship. Turning his face away from the wind, he looked to the side and down. The eight men of his team were doing as he was, clinging to the ship like barnacles. Each of them dressed in black, their submachine guns held tight under Velcro flaps.

He could see the strain in their arms and the tension in their faces, as this part of the heist had gone on far longer than intended.

Looking up, he counted the seconds until finally the main lights of the ship went dark. Third watch had begun. Using his thumb, he triggered a pin-point light in the magnetic pad under his left hand. Three dots constituted an order to begin climbing again. They needed to get up and inside before the wind blew them off the hull.

With his right thumb, he pressed down on a button connected to the gauntlet wrapped around his right arm. It disabled the power on that magnet, allowing him to pull it from the hull and move it upward. Stretching as far as he could, he released the button.

The electromagnet switched on instantly and his arm was pulled back to the steel plate, where it locked into position. Pressing a second button, he was able to move his right leg upward. He then repeated the procedure on the left side, slowly but surely crawling toward an awaiting hatch.

His men did the same, following him up. A trail of human ants, heading for the sugar inside the ship.

Reaching the hatch, he risked detaching his left hand long enough to pound on the metal plating. Nothing happened. He hammered it harder, using the metal part of the gauntlet to elicit a metallic clang.

This time he heard something, a latch releasing, a wheel—which was sometimes called a dog—spinning inside. Thank god, Lucas thought.

The hatch, large enough to set a gangplank on and load ship's stores, swung inward as it opened. A crewman wearing the shipping line's uniform appeared. He had black hair with an odd white streak down the middle. He made eye contact and offered a gloved hand.

Lucas took it, released the other magnets and was pulled inside.

The crewman moved back into the shadows as Lucas helped his men through the hatch and into the shelter of the small compartment.

All went well until the last man. The man disengaged his magnets a moment too soon. His leg slipped and he dropped.

Lunging forward, Lucas grabbed the strap of the submachine gun. The weapon wedged up under the man's shoulder and held tight, even as Lucas was pulled to the deck and nearly dragged out the hatch.

"Callum!" Lucas shouted. Despite their Chinese ethnicity, the members of the group chose Western names when they joined. Each knew the other by no other name, so that in the event of capture they could not give up any of their comrades.

"Reengage!" Lucas shouted. "Use the couplers."

Realizing that Callum was frozen with fear and concerned that he might be pulled over the edge, Lucas engaged his own magnetic system and locked himself to the deck.

"Climb over me," he shouted.

The man looked up.

"Hurry," Lucas said, "before you pull my arm out of the socket."

With several of the other men now crowding around to assist, Callum pulled himself up using Lucas like a rope ladder. As soon as they could reach him, Callum's comrades grabbed him and hauled him inside.

Lucas relaxed and disengaged the magnets, pushing back from the edge. Callum offered a hand and helped him to his feet.

Rubbing his shoulder and stretching, Lucas moved closer to Callum. "That was foolish," he said, glaring at the man who'd almost fallen. "Get sloppy again and I'll let you die."

The words were harsh, but the men knew better. Lucas was the leader of a band of brothers, pirates who looked after their own. Unlike the famous pirate code of old, Lucas had never left a man behind.

Callum dropped his head and looked away, ashamed. As he stepped back, Lucas turned to the man who'd let them in. "You were late."

"Couldn't be helped," the crewman said. "The captain stayed on watch thirty minutes later than usual. He's gone to bed now."

Lucas nodded. "Anything else we should know?"

The crewman shook his head. "The security systems are disabled. You should have no problem getting into the engine room or the communications suite."

"Good," Lucas said. He sent three men to the engine room and two others to the communications center, where the satellite receivers, multiband radios and controls for the various automatic beacons lay.

Turning to the **Swift**'s crewman, he made a

change. "Take one of my men and go to the captain's quarters. Wake the old man up and bring him to me."

"I thought you'd want me to lead you to the bridge," the crewman replied.

"That, we can find on our own."

The various groups left the compartment, heading in opposite directions. Lucas took Callum with him. They went forward toward the nearest stairwell.

Moving calmly, Lucas raised the Velcro flap covering his belly. Without breaking stride, he removed a QCW-05 submachine gun that was strapped diagonally across his chest. He slung it into place and screwed a cylindrical compressor into the barrel.

The Chinese QCW fired a subsonic 5.8mm round made of hardened steel instead of soft lead. It was compact and well suited for close quarters combat. The shell could punch through a quarter-inch steel plate.

Lucas had trained his men to use them to lethal effect, but if things went as planned, they wouldn't have to fire a single shot.

Reaching the bridge, they found the **Swift**'s first officer and a pair of crewmen at the helm. Avoiding the theatrics of bursting into the compartment shouting threats, Lucas stepped quietly over the threshold, clearing his throat to get everyone's attention.

The men on the bridge reacted with glacial speed. Their collective surprise at the appearance of armed men in commando gear was so complete that they froze in confusion.

"Get down on the deck," Lucas said calmly, "if you'd rather not be shot to pieces."

The two crewmen did as ordered. The first officer seemed stuck in his chair. Finally he spoke. "We have cash in the safe," he said, raising his hands, easing out of the seat and dropping to one knee. "It's unlocked."

"Of course it is," Lucas said.

The lack of resistance and an unlocked safe were marks of the modern state of piracy. An unspoken agreement had arisen between the world's various pirates and shipping lines whose vessels plowed the seas.

Pirates came aboard vessels where they could. Usually in tight coastal waters near poor, unstable countries. Instead of fighting them off and risking death and destruction, officers and crew often hid in safe rooms, or **castles,** that the pirates could not access, but allowing them time to search the ship for cash or valuables. Safes were left open and supplied with a modicum of currency. Just enough to give the pirates an easy score and incentive to get off the ship as fast as possible. At times, cell phones and laptop computers were used to augment the bribe, left out for the taking like cookies for Santa Claus.

The deal was simple. Pirates didn't injure or kill the crews, they didn't steal cargoes worth millions or damage the ships and, in return, the shipping lines didn't fortify their vessels with armed guards, ex–special forces members or former Mossad agents.

The system was more akin to bribery or a protection racket, but it worked for the most part. Except when it didn't.

As he stared down the barrel of the gun, the first officer realized this would be one of those times. He studied Lucas and his comrades, studying their clothing and weapons and considering the stealth with which they'd come aboard. "You're not here for cash," he said, "are you?"

Lucas ignored the question. "Call your other officers to the bridge," he instructed. "Make no attempt to alert them to our presence. We know your code words for security threats."

The first officer stood slowly and stepped to the console. Setting the PA system for shipwide, he made the call. "This is First Officer Crawford speaking. All officers report to the bridge for general briefing. We have new orders to review."

As the sound of his voice was relayed over the ship's speakers, Crawford looked at Lucas pleadingly. "I had to give them a reason," he said, justifying his extra words.

Lucas nodded. "At least you didn't lie."

CHAPTER 2

BRISBANE, AUSTRALIA

Jonathan Freeman sat at the communications desk of Canberra Shipping & Logistics in the early hours of the Australian morning. He was covering the overnight shift for the third week in a row and the hours had begun to wear on him. Yawning and checking a clipboard, a rather quaint backup for all the computer screens in front of him, he confirmed for the third time in an hour that he'd cleared all the assigned check-ins and had nothing left to do but sit there until six a.m. when his relief would arrive.

He hoped they'd bring breakfast. Steak and mushroom pie with a basket of hot cross buns would be delightful.

"There you go again," he said to himself. "Now you're hungry."

Looking for something to take his mind off

breakfast, he glanced down at the monitor that tracked the firm's ships via their AIS, Automatic Identification System, beacons. On different screens he could see them plowing the various oceans of the world, doing just what they should be doing. All of them, he realized, except one.

Tapping the screen, he zoomed in on the western Pacific, where what had been a green line was now flashing amber.

"What have we here?"

Tapping the screen again, he brought up the ship's identifying information.

"Canberra Swift," he said. "Not moving so swift anymore, are you?"

The information on-screen showed the ship slowing from its previous speed of thirty-five knots to less than ten and still dropping. Freeman watched as it dipped down to 9.2 and held steady.

Using both feet to propel his rolling chair, he slid to the right, stopping in front of the satcom station. Essentially a second computer, he tapped this screen to life and dialed up the correct prefix to contact the **Swift.**

"Canberra Swift, Canberra Swift," he said. "This is Operations, how do you read?"

He spoke into a slim white plastic microphone.

"This is First Officer Crawford," a voice called back over the speakers. **"Go ahead, Operations."**

"We show you slowing. Plot has you at a speed of 9.2. Is anything wrong?"

"**Plot is correct,**" the voice replied. "**We've had an issue with the fuel pressurization system for the gas turbine. We're running on the diesel backup. Engineering is looking into the issue. They inform me the main engine should be back up and running in about an hour.**"

Freeman was always amazed by the calmness of the various captains and crews. The previous month he'd helped shepherd a vessel through a Force 5 gale, complete with waves that were crashing over the deck and a balky rudder. Judging from the captain's tone, it had sounded more like a minor inconvenience.

"Will note that," Freeman said, writing down the information. "Do you need me to alert San Francisco and amend the expected time of arrival?"

"**Negative on that, Operations. We'll make the distance up once we get the problem fixed.**"

Freeman noted the directive on his clipboard and jotted down the time. "Confirmed," he said. "Give us a shout if things change."

The first officer signed off politely and Freeman rolled his chair back to the main computer console, where he typed in the details of the conversation.

He was still at his desk an hour later when the signal from the **Canberra Swift** vanished from the screen.

At the same moment, eight thousand miles away, the captain of the South Korean freighter **Yeongju** was taking a break on the port wing of his ship's bridge. A world traveler who preferred Indonesian cigarettes for their deep flavor, he smoked slowly and methodically, getting every speck of pleasure out of his chosen addiction and passing as much time as possible.

He took one last drag and flicked the butt over the rail, sending it out into the night. The tip glowed orange for an instant with the rush of wind but then vanished like a burned-out flare.

He was about to exhale when a double flash of light lit up the horizon to the north. It was soundless and brilliant. It had an odd bluish white hue.

It neither flickered nor faded. It was simply there one instant and then gone.

The captain stared after it for a long time, aware that the flash had been bright enough to spot his vision green. Feeling a wave of pressure in his chest, he realized he'd been holding his breath. He exhaled a cloud of smoke and then stepped back inside.

"Any weather to speak of?" he asked the helmsman.

"No, sir," the crewman replied instantly. "Nothing until tomorrow afternoon."

Curious, he thought. Perhaps it was heat lightning. At times, the atmosphere played strange tricks. "Make a note in the log," he said. "Large-scale double flash to the north of our position. Range unknown. Origin unknown."

CHAPTER 3

M.V. CANBERRA SWIFT

On the bridge of the darkened ship, Lucas Teng counted the minutes—it was easier than counting the hours. Two hundred and thirty-one minutes had gone by since they took the ship. One hundred and seventy since they'd gone dark and changed course. One hundred more and he'd be in position for the rendezvous and the largest payday of his life.

Twenty million dollars, split between himself and his men. After expenses, bribes and payoffs to employees of the shipping company who'd given him inside information, it was still more than enough to get him out of the criminal life.

What would he do then? he wondered. Live a little. And spend the money quickly. He knew himself well enough to know it was the thrill of the hunt that grabbed him, even more than the money. But both temptations would lure him back. It might take a year or two, the money would go, life would get boring. But one way or another, he'd find himself back planning another job.

Another glance at his watch showed the counter had lost a full digit. Ninety-nine minutes to go. Time to walk the ship.

"Keep us steady on," he said to Callum. "Change the watch every twenty minutes. I don't want the boys getting tired."

One of the men stood at the wheel; two others stood on the ship's bridge wings, watching the horizon with night vision binoculars. The seas were calm and the winds almost nonexistent, but cruising at top speed meant the resulting gust was howling across the ship. Having shut down every system that emitted light or radio waves—even the weather radar and collision warning system—posting a pair of old-fashioned lookouts had become necessary. The last thing Lucas wanted was to run across another ship.

Lucas grabbed a radio and held it up for Callum to see. "I'll be back in fifteen minutes. Alert me if anything happens."

Leaving the bridge, Lucas made his way through the empty ship and down toward the cargo hold. He had the captain's key card, a list of codes and a loading manifest. Reaching the main cargo deck, he stepped out into a vast open space that looked more like a warehouse or an airplane hangar.

Walking among the oversize cargo, he came to a temporary wall that had been placed in the center of the hold. The thin steel wall was designed to protect the ship's most precious cargo if the weather got rough or if anything broke loose.

Checking the manifest and the code number he'd been given, Lucas waved the captain's card in front of the reader. The device glowed pink. Using the keypad, he punched in the code. The pink light turned green and the electronic lock disengaged.

Lucas opened the hatch and stepped across the raised sill. A swath of lights came on above him, illuminating the space in sterile fluorescence.

The hold didn't look like anything on a normal cargo vessel. The walls were white plastic, scuffed in places but still glossy and reflecting the lights above.

Large racks inside held a group of long octagonal cylinders. Stepping closer to the first one, Lucas found an inscription.

HYDRO-COM CORP.
VECTOR 1-001-04
Warning: Container is pressurized with nitrogen
to five atmospheres.
Depressurize before opening.

"So, this is what Emmerson wants," he whispered to himself. "I would have expected weapons or uranium yellowcake. This is so much more palatable."

"And profitable," a voice said from behind him.

Lucas wheeled around. He saw a figure in the doorway. The crewman who'd let them into the ship. He was holding a weapon.

"What are you doing here?" Lucas demanded. "You're supposed to be with the rest of the crew, pretending to be captive."

The man trained the gun on Lucas. "I got tired of pretending," he said. "So I released myself from captivity and then I shot them all dead."

Expecting the same treatment, Lucas dove to the side, attempting to use the server housing as cover.

The man fired rapidly, squeezing off several shots. Two went long, one hit the server, but the fourth caught Lucas in the calf, tearing through the muscle and shattering his shinbone.

He howled in pain as he hit the deck but scrambled forward in a desperate attempt to save himself.

"You should have brought your weapon," the man said, walking slowly. "But then, I guess you thought you didn't need it."

Lucas was crawling now, dragging his injured leg and leaving a smear of red blood along the white plastic floor.

Pulling the radio from his belt, he called for help. "Cal," he called out, "I need help. We've been double-crossed."

Releasing the talk switch, he listened for a reply, but all he heard was the sound of dead air and soft footsteps shuffling along behind the server units. He pressed the transmit button again. "Callum?"

"It would have done you some good to familiarize yourself with the ship before you came aboard," the stalking man said. "You see, this hold is a temporary oasis for these machines, designed to protect them from any form of electromagnetic radiation. No radio waves can get in or out, meaning your call for help is trapped in here, just as you are."

Lucas continued to crawl, ducking behind another one of the servers, as the man appeared at the far end and capped off another shot. This bullet hit Lucas below the knee, causing further pain in his damaged leg.

Pushing himself back against the wall, Lucas reached down and tore a strip from his pants, starting at the leg where the first bullet hit. It showed him the extent of the damage to his shin. Exposed muscle and protruding bone. Even if he survived, he would probably face amputation.

He tied a tourniquet mid-thigh, cinching it as tight as he could. "You're not a part of the crew," he called out. "Who do you work for?"

"I'm afraid that's something you'll never know."

Another shot rang out. This one punched a hole in the wall.

"You're a dead man," Lucas shouted, squeezing in between two of the servers and inching his way along. "Even if my men don't kill you, Emmerson will hunt you down."

"Emmerson will never find me," the man said, sounding farther away. "Even if he does, I will certainly outlive you."

The voice sounded distant now. A moment later, the hatch slamming shut told Lucas why. He forced himself to look. It was closed and locked. He'd been sealed up inside the hold.

Seconds later a low rumble shook the hull. It came in bursts, traveling forward from the stern.

Lucas recognized it as blasting charges set off in rapid succession, similar to the method a demolition expert would use to bring down a large building.

As he tried to figure out the logic behind this latest surprise, alarms rang out. The ship was taking on water.

The hull had been blown open all along the waterline. The man who'd shot him was sinking the ship. Lucas couldn't fathom why, but as the ship began to list and the floor increasingly sloped, he was certain the vessel would be going down.

Escaping from his hiding place, he dragged himself to the hatch. It would not budge, not even as he pulled on it with all his might.

He tried the radio once again. "Callum," he called out. "Callum."

Water began leaking through tiny gaps on the sides of the hatch and dribbling in through the bullet hole in the wall.

The water had to be rising fast if it was already two feet up on the outside of the compartment.

Forcing himself to stand on his one good leg, Lucas threw himself against the door to no avail. He grabbed the handle as he fell back, pulling with all his strength and hoping the water on the outside would help push the door in. The lock held, so he pulled once more.

The door creaked and the frame bent inward. Both gave way all at once.

Lucas threw himself to the side, trying to get clear, but the rush of water caught him as it blasted through the gap. He was swept off his feet and dragged along like a piece of driftwood caught by a crashing wave.

He hit the far wall and was washed along the length of the room. Swirling water hitting the far end pushed him under and then brought him back up again. Gasping for air as he surfaced, he grabbed for the metal frame protecting one of the servers. His grip was firm and he pulled himself forward, wrapping both of his arms and legs around it like he was clinging to a tree.

By now, the ship was tilting noticeably backward. The stern had blown first. She was going to go down with her bow in the air.

Lucas pulled himself higher as more water poured in. But he knew it was a losing battle. He hoped the room would reach equilibrium and allow him to swim out, but as the water climbed his strength ebbed.

A resounding metallic bang echoed behind him as some piece of machinery or improperly tied-down cargo broke loose and slammed into the adjoining wall.

Seconds later the lights flickered and went out.

Lucas felt the cold soaking him to the bone. He no longer fought to keep above water. No longer imagined he could swim to the next deck and find a way off the ship.

He clutched the framework around the server, his fingers going numb, as his mind seethed, wondering who had beaten him, who had betrayed him. And then, not willing to let those be his last living thoughts, he focused on better things, his wife and children, lost to him because of the life he'd chosen, but out there somewhere safe and warm in a world far different than his own.

His grip weakened, he slipped from the framework and sank downward. In the dark, he noticed two sources of light. The first was the blurred face of the watch on his wrist, still counting down the minutes to success. The second was the glow from the panels on the octagonal casing of the server in front of him. Despite the chaos and the shooting and the flood of frigid water, the machine was still running.

CHAPTER 4

Two figures in wetsuits swam at a depth of thirty feet. Sunlight streamed down through the clear water, dancing in patterns where it hit the living reef below.

Kurt Austin studied the changing patterns of light and darkness, drifting lower, while looking past a small group of bright yellow fish and out into the bluer regions beyond.

He was head of special assignments for the American organization NUMA—the National Underwater and Marine Agency. He'd spent over a thousand hours of his life underwater on various dives. Probably three times that in submersibles of one kind or another. In all that time he'd never tired of the beauty of the sea, nor chosen to underestimate its danger.

"Butterflyfish," a voice said. The name came through a tiny speaker in his full-face helmet.

Kurt glanced over at the diver beside him. His diving partner was a woman named Yan-Li, a nautical historian from the People's Republic of China who'd once been a dive specialist in the People's Navy. Her wetsuit and helmet were the same red as the Chinese flag. Her air tank was a yellow aluminum cylinder and she wore matching yellow dive fins.

In contrast his gear was industrial and workmanlike. Dark blue wetsuit, scuffed steel oxygen tank, black fins, boots and gloves.

"I've often thought fish get a raw deal," she continued.

"If you mean as in sashimi," Kurt replied, "I'd have to agree with you."

Kurt grinned as he spoke, the wrinkles around his eyes accentuated by the way the helmet pressed tight against his face. He was pushing forty these days, but a life at sea and in the sun had given his face more character than most. Tufts of steel gray hair added to his look, giving him an older, even more weathered appearance.

"I mean," the woman explained, "in the naming regimens we use for aquatic species. So many of them are named after other things. Butterflyfish, parrotfish, lionfish. Earlier today I saw a pineapplefish. And if we look hard enough, we might even find a garlic bread sea cucumber around here somewhere."

"You're making that last one up," Kurt said,

turning his attention to the deeper water beyond the reef once more.

"I assure you, I'm not," she replied, using a helicopter stroke to remain in position.

Kurt focused his gaze on a shadow in the distance. It had come up from the deeper offshore waters and then circled out beyond view. It was back now, gliding closer, the sunlight filtering down, accentuating the subtle stripes on its back.

"I suggest we drop down toward the coral," Kurt said. "Another one of your unfairly named creatures is coming this way. Tiger shark. Fifteen-footer."

Yan's posture stiffened a bit, but she gave off no sense of alarm. Releasing some air from her buoyancy compensator, she dropped alongside Kurt into a gap in the reef.

Kurt knew she could take care of herself. They'd spent the last five months on the trail of a mythical treasure, working together in a sort of unsanctioned international partnership. They'd been shot at, chased through the mountains, even forced to leap off a bridge when cornered in a remote part of Cambodia. All because of a diary belonging to the famed pirate Ching Shih and the vast treasure she recorded in it as being stolen and then lost in the South China Sea.

Still, there was a difference between brawling in an alleyway and fighting a thousand-pound shark.

Dropping slowly toward the reef below, Kurt

kept his eyes on the shark. It swam toward them and then turned to the north. Just as it looked like it might be leaving it turned back, accelerating and arching its back.

"Aggressive posture," Yan said. "Not good."

The shark swam in toward them, surging forward like a torpedo in the water. Kurt grabbed on to a large outcropping of brain coral, pulled himself downward and dragged Yan down with his free hand.

Dropping behind the island-like obstruction, they avoided the shark's first pass. It crossed above them, its square nose and white belly near enough to touch.

Kurt spun around to track it, his flipper breaking off a tree of stag coral in the process.

"Big fish," Yan said.

"I wish he was bigger," Kurt joked. "Sharks with full bellies are less dangerous. This guy looked like he might have been on a diet."

The tiger shark swam into the shallows and began another turn.

"Look at this," Yan said.

Kurt had no intention of taking his eyes off the big predator, but at Yan's insistence he glanced down.

There at the base of the coral formation was a blackened stretch of reef that ran in a perfectly straight line. "This isn't coral," Yan said. "It's a growth of corallimorph."

Corallimorph was an invasive species that thrived on iron, sometimes causing what was known as black band disease.

Kurt understood the significance, but it would do them no good if they were chewed up by the tiger shark before they could examine it. "Unless it's a plate of tuna we can offer to our lunch guest, I suggest we worry about it later."

The shark swam wide, circling back toward the deep with a casual motion. It seemed as if it was done with them, but tigers were slow swimmers, lazy almost, right up until the moment they shot forward and attacked.

"He's leaving us," Yan said.

"Don't be so sure," Kurt replied.

Yan aimed her dive light on the corallimorph, wafting away the surrounding sand and sediment with her free hand. A three-foot-long tube was exposed, connected to a hand grip, complete with a trigger guard and the slightest remnant of the trigger itself. Protruding bits of coral covered the rest of the weapon, including two metal plates that would have been used to attach the barrel to a bipod-shaped stand.

"It's a weapon," she said.

Having spent time as a collector of dueling pistols and rare antique weapons, Kurt recognized it instantly. "An harquebus. Muzzle-loading. From the early eighteen hundreds."

"The logbook described four such weapons on board the **Dragon,**" Yan-Li said.

"They were common on ships of the day," Kurt said, "one of the best ways to repel boarders."

He strained to see through the water. The shark was now out beyond visual range, but that didn't mean it was gone. He turned from quarter to quarter. And suddenly it was there.

"Look out."

He pushed Yan behind the coral while swinging his camera toward the face of the charging shark. It hit square on the snout. The shark reacted by flinging its head from side to side. The flashing strobe seemed to confuse it. The beast chomped down on open water and then lunged forward and bit into the coral.

Not enjoying the taste or texture, it jerked away, swiping Kurt with its powerful tail.

Yan was a bit shaken now. And Kurt wasn't feeling so happy himself. "If this was a great white, I'd expect him to move on," he said. "They're not really fond of eating people. But tigers are more aggressive. They'll chow down on anything."

He expected at least one more pass and the mangled camera was not going to be enough for a second round.

"Keep your eye on it," Kurt said.

"I am," Yan replied.

Kurt switched channels and called out to their

surface support. "**Sapphire,** we have a problem. Hungry tiger shark looking to make a meal out of us. Need you to bring the boat in where we can make a quick exit. I'm releasing a beacon."

"**Thought I saw some stripes in the water,**" a voice replied. "**Be there in sixty seconds.**"

Kurt pulled a small device off his dive harness. It was the size and shape of an electric shaver.

"Tell me that's shark repellant," Yan said.

"Locator beacon," Kurt said. "At this point I'd rather not swim for the ship if we can make the ship come to us."

He twisted the top ninety degrees and released the device. It floated upward, its strong positive buoyancy drawing it rapidly toward the surface as its tiny strobe light flashed. It had a stubby, rubber-ized antenna on the side, which broadcast a signal that would be detected by satellite and relayed to the **Sapphire** the instant the device hit the surface.

"Joe had better get here quick," Yan said, pointing into the distance. "The shark is coming back."

Kurt dropped down beside her. "Any chance you could pry that harquebus from the coral? It'd be nice to have a long iron bar to jab at this shark with."

"Nope," she said. "It's completely embedded."

Looking around for another weapon, Kurt found a colony of black and purple sea urchins with three-inch spines. He carefully plucked the largest one from the bottom, broke a few of the spines off so he could hold it and then spun around.

The tiger was coming in slowly, trying to figure out how to get at them around the large pillar. It moved closer and closer, circling them as they moved around their shield of coral.

With astonishing speed, it turned and shot downward. Yan shoved the dive light toward it, Kurt arched his body to the side and slammed the sea urchin in the shark's face. It hit near the snout and the shark snapped from side to side, once again trying to bite anything it could get its teeth into.

The sea urchin came loose, the shark gobbled it with a snap and then took off, several of the long spikes sticking out of its nose. This time it hustled off into the deep water, showing no signs of coming back.

"Now," Kurt said, removing a painful spike from one hand, "we just need it to stay away for a minute or so."

CHAPTER 5

Joe Zavala stood on the flybridge of a ninety-foot motor yacht named **Sapphire.** His tanned skin and short dark hair contrasted with the pink linen shirt and white shorts he wore. Polarized sunglasses protected his eyes, while tight-fitting boat shoes with no socks covered his feet. All in all, he looked more like a model in the midst of a photo shoot for a yachting magazine than the mechanical genius, mechanic and former boxer that he was.

In truth, his steely gaze was more an act of concentration as he brought the multimillion-dollar vessel around the perimeter of the deserted island, cutting as close to the reef as possible while dividing his attention between the changing color of the water and the sonar display. Both of which told him the bottom was not far below the keel.

Cruising offshore, the yacht appeared like any other plaything of the rich and famous, but belowdecks it had been repurposed for nautical exploration.

The luxurious master suite had been reworked as a storage area for diving and excavation equipment. The main salon had lost its wet bar, leather-upholstered sectionals and gleaming wooden furniture in exchange for a satellite communications system, other forms of electronics and enough computing power to fuel a video game convention. The aft deck had been widened and stiffened to accommodate a landing pad for small helicopters, while the stern sported winches and cranes to deploy sonar arrays, magnetometers and other types of **fish** used to hunt for objects hiding in the depths.

One thing that hadn't been sacrificed were the powerful engines that Joe had used to the fullest while circumnavigating the island. He'd made a full survey of the island's perimeter in the forty minutes since Kurt and Yan-Li had left the boat.

Easing back on the twin throttles, he allowed the yacht to bleed off some speed and then rolled the wheel to the right. The sharp turn to starboard brought a grunt from the **Sapphire**'s usual helmsman, a long-term NUMA specialist named Winterburn.

"I shouldn't like it if you scratched my hull," Winterburn said.

Winterburn considered the ship his personal property. The small crew his men. It had taken Joe a solid week to convince Winterburn to let him at the helm.

"Better than Kurt and Yan being the main course on that shark's lunch menu," Joe replied.

"Hmm . . ." Winterburn grunted. "I suppose."

The yacht curved around to starboard, slowing and easing into the bay through a groove in the reef. Joe dropped the throttles into reverse and brought it to a stop right next to the flashing locator beacon.

With the **Sapphire** now stationary, he lifted a handheld radio off its charger. "In position to retrieve divers," he said, sounding awfully official. "That is, assuming you two are done splashing about."

Kurt's voice came back moments later, sounding tinny and flat over the small speaker. **"We have you in sight. Let the stairs down, will you? No telling where our fine finned friend went off to."**

Joe flicked a switch on the panel beside the wheel. In response, a swim platform with a pair of ladders descended from the aft end of the yacht.

"Ladders in the water," he said, "coming to help."

Joe turned the helm over to Winterburn and raced to the stern. He grabbed a boat hook as he neared the platform just in case he had to fend off the hungry shark.

He reached the platform as the two divers broke the surface. Yan-Li was the nearest of the two. She tossed her yellow flippers onto the deck and began climbing the ladder without the slightest hesitation.

As she neared the top, Joe offered a hand. He pulled her forward to help balance the weight of the tank on her back.

She pulled off her helmet. "Thank you, Joe. Helpful as always."

Joe grinned. Glad to be appreciated. Before he could turn back to the ladder, a second pair of fins came flying over the transom. He ducked to avoid being hit. Kurt was out of the water and halfway up the ladder.

"Nice throw," Joe said, referencing the fins. "You missed again. Wide right."

Kurt released the seal on his helmet and pulled it off, exposing a wet tangle of silver hair. "Those long-lost boxing reflexes of yours must still be working."

Joe had been an amateur boxer during his time in the Navy. He still sparred on a regular basis. "**Long-lost**? I could go back into the ring tomorrow if I wanted to."

"In that case it must be my aim," Kurt said. He pulled off his glove; three broken spikes from the sea urchin remained embedded in his hand. His palm and wrist were red and swelling.

"You're going to need vinegar and pliers," Joe said.

"Not to mention something for the pain."

"We're all out of rum," Joe said, finding a set of needle-nose pliers. "But there's plenty of scotch."

"That'll do," Kurt said.

As Kurt plucked the needles out of his hand, Yan slipped out of her dive harness and exhaled. "That was wild," she said, more excited than scared. "And thanks to that shark, we ended up in the right place."

"You found something?" Joe asked.

"The remnants of a nineteenth-century swivel gun," Yan said. "No sign of a ship yet, but there's no other reason for a weapon like that to be here on this uninhabited island. Did you find anything in the bay or outside the reef?"

"No. I circled the entire island. Nothing on the sonar or either of the mags."

"They may have used stone ballast," Yan said. "And the treasure was mostly objects of gold, silver and jade. All of these are nonferrous materials. We wouldn't pick any of that up on a mag even if the ship were here."

"Sounds like you were more successful," Joe said.

"If you considered getting skewered and nearly eaten alive successful," Kurt replied, grinning. "Actually, once we're sure that tiger has moved out of the area, we'll go back down, run a portable magnetometer over the area and excavate that harquebus. Even though many ships of the day carried similar weapons, the guns on the **Dragon** were known to be ornamented with silver and pearls. It could prove she was here."

Joe shook his head. "Sadly, I have the duty to inform you that the folks in D.C. sent us a message while you were down on the reef. Recess is over. A situation has developed that requires our attention."

Aside from a slight tightening of his jaw, Kurt's face betrayed little emotion.

Yan-Li was a different story. "You're kidding me," she said. "We're so close."

Joe felt for her. She'd been on a personal quest to find this ship for nearly three years. Long before the Chinese government attached a monetary prize to the discovery.

"Sorry," Joe said. "There's a helicopter on its way to pick you up and fly you back to Da Nang. You can catch a flight from there to Hong Kong."

"You're not taking me?"

"We're headed the other way. East to Manila, where we have to link up with another NUMA vessel. Won't even know our orders until we get there."

Yan sighed in resignation.

"We'll put a pin in this," Kurt said. "Whatever our new assignment is, I doubt it'll take long to handle. Probably a lost dolphin or something. When we're done, we'll come find you and pick up where we left off."

Joe reached over the side with the boat hook and plucked the locator beacon out of the water. He snapped it shut and tossed it to Yan. "And if you need us in the meantime, just twist the top and throw it in the water, Kurt and I will come running."

Yan grinned and tucked the beacon away as a memento. Ninety minutes later, a NUMA helicopter touched down on the **Sapphire**'s landing pad. The pilot kept the power up, ready to make a quick departure.

Yan-Li stood nearby with a duffel bag at her feet and a backpack over her shoulder. "I've never been one for long good-byes," she said. "How about 'Until we meet again'?"

"Works for me," Kurt replied.

He gave her a quick hug and then stepped out of the way. Joe followed suit. Hugs completed, she grabbed her things and climbed into the helicopter. The side door slammed shut and the craft flew away.

After watching it move off, Kurt turned to Joe. "Since we don't have any ships operating in the Philippines, I'm going to assume we're not heading to Manila."

"Nope," Joe said. "Northwest toward Taiwan."

"Anyone tell you why?"

Joe shook his head and then glanced at his watch. "But considering we need to be on a satellite call in five minutes, I'd say we're about to find out."

CHAPTER 6

A large and important ship has gone missing."

These words came from Rudi Gunn, NUMA's Deputy Director of Operations, who was appearing on a high-definition screen in the **Sapphire**'s communications suite.

Rudi Gunn stood no more than five foot six, but like many actors of shorter stature, he had presence about him that made him seem bigger. It was noticeable enough in person, but on the video conference he filled the screen like a young Brando or Newman. Albeit with horn-rimmed glasses and no evidence of a sneer.

"The **Canberra Swift**," Rudi continued. "She was just beginning a run between Taiwan and San Francisco."

Kurt glanced at a fact sheet they'd downloaded and printed out. The paper listed what NUMA knew and didn't know. Sadly, the second list was much more extensive than the first.

He saw that the **Swift** was a modern, fifty-thousand-ton vessel with a crew of twenty-six. A disappearance like that would normally be all over the news.

"Why haven't we heard about this?" Joe asked from the seat next to Kurt.

"Because the NSA and the Pentagon want it that way," Rudi said bluntly.

"Here we go," Joe whispered.

Rudi picked up the whisper and called Joe out for it. "What was that, Zavala?"

"I said . . . good to know." Joe was grinning from ear to ear as he spoke.

"Sure you did," Rudi replied. "Just a heads-up. The microphones on the yacht are much more sensitive than the old ones in our other ships. Best if you watch what you mumble under your breath. Wouldn't want your boss to know what you really think about him."

"Also good to know," Kurt replied, laughing. "Back to the missing ship. Why is the NSA covering up the disappearance of a random freighter? What was she carrying?"

"Eight of the most advanced server units ever produced," Rudi said. "Designed by Hydro-Com Corporation out of Silicon Valley, assembled in Taiwan and on their way to the West Coast. They call them Vector units, but they're basically incredibly powerful computers, the size of a Volkswagen bus, and capable of handling billions of transactions per second. More importantly, they're banned from sale to Russia, China, Iran and at least a dozen other countries."

Rudi tapped a key and an image of the Vector units came up on-screen. They were black or dark gray and roughly cylindrical, but with flat sides that turned the cylinder into an elongated octagon. They had built-in screens on the sides and multiple ports for fiber-optic cables and other connections at each end.

"Under normal circumstances," Rudi continued, "these machines would never be shipped out of American waters, but this is the twenty-first century and for reasons that are anything but strategic, computers designed in the U.S. are built elsewhere and shipped back home for installation."

Kurt began to see why the power brokers in Washington were so concerned. "Leaving aside the madness of building your top secret computers a hundred miles from your biggest adversary's shore, what's the point of involving us? Surely we have military units in Japan that could conduct a search-and-rescue mission more effectively."

"There's no SAR play here," Rudi said. "We've picked up no emergency beacons or calls for help. The ship just vanished in the middle of the night. We ran a satellite pass this morning and the Navy sent a recon aircraft over the same section of ocean.

There are no lifeboats out there, just a mile-long oil slick and small amounts of what might be wreckage but could just as easily be trash."

Kurt was a little surprised by the information. He ran his hands through his hair. "That doesn't make any sense. Ships aren't like planes, Rudi. They don't vanish in balls of fire or break up upon hitting the water. When they have problems, they usually come to a stop, drift with the current and call for help. Even when they do sink, it's pretty rare not to get off a distress call or leave plenty of survivors bobbing around in little orange lifeboats. You're telling me there are no survivors?"

Rudi didn't flinch. "No survivors. No distress calls, no EPIRB signals or lifeboats. And as far as the ball of fire is concerned, this ship may have vanished in exactly that fashion."

"How's that?"

"The **Swift** is a specially built fast freighter," Rudi said. "It uses a pair of high-compression gas turbine engines and runs on liquefied natural gas. As you probably know, rupturing an LNG tank can result in a catastrophic event."

"Which is why they are manufactured to ridiculously strong safety margins," Joe said.

"Anything to indicate they ruptured a tank?" Kurt asked.

"Shortly after two in the morning the ship slowed from thirty-five to nine knots. Seas were calm, wind nonexistent. A report to the company ops center in

Auckland indicated a problem with the gas turbines and a switchover to the diesel auxiliary. About an hour later, just as they expected to be resuming normal operations, the ship vanished from radar. At roughly the same moment, the captain of a South Korean ship reported an intense, unexplained white flash on the horizon."

"That doesn't sound good," Kurt said, turning to Joe, who was the engineering expert.

"Not good at all," Joe seconded. "If an LNG storage tank ruptured, it would be like setting off the powder magazine of an old warship. There wouldn't be much left to escape from. And there certainly wouldn't be time to get off a distress call."

"That appears to be what happened," Rudi said.

"Which begs the question," Kurt replied, "why send us up there? My heart breaks for the crew, but we can't help them now. As for these computers, if the ship blew itself apart, what does the NSA have to worry about? Even if the explosion just blew off the top half of the vessel and the rest of the ship broke in half and went down, those machines would be crushed by the depth, corroded by the salt water and almost certainly mangled and burned by the initial explosion. Can't imagine them being much good to anyone at that point."

Rudi sat back, grinning and nodding. Kurt realized he'd been set up.

"One would think that," Rudi began. "Having wiped out my old laptop with nothing more than an overturned bottle of water, I'd normally have to agree with you. But these computers are different. They've been developed from the get-go to operate underwater. They're encased in pressurized shells of carbon fiber. Bulletproof, shockproof, waterproof for certain."

"Why would anyone build a computer designed to operate underwater?" Joe asked.

"Because the more powerful these servers and computers become, the more heat they generate," Rudi explained. "Seventy-five percent of the energy used by current server farms and supercomputers is applied directly to the cooling systems. Powerful fans and heat sinks in low-tech systems. Nitrogen pumps and liquid cooling packs in higher-end units. By some estimates, the world's computers now use more electricity than the cities of New York, London and Abu Dhabi combined just to keep from melting down. From what I'm told, the larger the system, the more cooling it requires. It's an exponential relationship. Double the power of the system and you need to drain four times as much heat. Quadruple the power and you need sixteen times as much cooling. You can see that this becomes a process of diminishing returns."

"You reach a point where it's costing so much to cool the computer that increasing the power isn't worth it," Joe said. "Growth limit."

Rudi nodded. "Hydro-Com gets around this problem by designing their servers to be immersed in deep, cold-water currents. Having swam in cold lakes and seas, you two know that water transfers heat much better than air, twenty-five times better in fact. Because of this, Hydro-Com units can run at peak speeds twenty-five times faster than the competition and they can keep it up for extended stretches."

Kurt folded his arms across his chest. "I can see where this is leading. What depth are these containers rated to?"

"Five thousand feet," Rudi said. "With a twenty percent safety factor on top of that."

Kurt glanced at the nautical chart showing where the **Swift** vanished. Joe did the same. The shipping lane from Taipei to San Francisco was a looping route that began on a northerly track up toward Japan before turning west. This great circle cut a thousand miles off the journey when compared to crossing the Pacific directly—or what looked like a direct path on a flat, two-dimensional map. In terms of depth, it was like traveling the razor's edge. Shallow waters and an abyssal plain stretched out to port, while depths of six and seven thousand feet dominated a few miles to starboard.

"If we're lucky, she turned left before she went to the bottom," Joe said.

"Doubt we can count on luck," Rudi replied.

Kurt didn't like to count on luck, he hoped to hold it in reserve for the rare moments when it was truly needed. "Assuming we do find the wreck, how, exactly, are we supposed to salvage eight telephone-booth-sized computers on our own?"

Joe nodded his support, adding, "To paraphrase the immortal words of Martin Brody in **Jaws,** 'We're gonna need a bigger boat.'"

"You don't need to salvage them," Rudi said coldly. "Just find them and confirm that they've been crushed and mangled beyond repair."

"And if they're still in one piece?"

"You have explosives on board," Rudi said. "I trust you know how to use them."

CHAPTER 7

Seven men sat on the deck in the aft section of a massive cargo plane. They shivered in sodden clothes, their ears assaulted by the scream of jet engines just outside the thin aluminum walls. Sunburn and the beginnings of saltwater sores could be seen on their faces.

They stared off into the distance or sat with closed eyes. When their gazes did meet, they exchanged a look. At least they were alive.

Standing away from the others, feet spaced apart for balance as if he were riding in an unstable subway car, Callum Zhen—the man whom Lucas had saved from falling into the sea—wondered how long that reprieve would last.

They'd been advanced a great deal of money to accomplish the hijacking. And they'd failed utterly.

The man they worked for was not known to forgive that type of failure.

Having harbored these thoughts for quite some time alone, Callum was glad to see another member of the group stand and come his way.

"All your twitching and tension is making the men nervous," Vincent Uhr told him.

Uhr pointed to the strap that Callum clung to. It was now twisted so tightly it was cutting off the circulation to his fingers.

Callum relaxed his grip. "I'm sorry," he said. "I'm worried. Laoban is going to demand an explanation."

Laoban was slang for the bossman, the director. In this case it was a reference to Kinnard Emmerson, the leader of a criminal syndicate based on the mainland. Emmerson had hired them to take over the **Canberra Swift** and deliver its cargo. The ship's sinking was not part of the plan.

Uhr did not respond immediately. He seemed lost in thought. This made Callum even more uncomfortable.

"We'll be back home soon," Callum prodded. "You need to be ready. Now that Lucas is gone, you're number one."

With Lucas missing and presumed dead, each of them moved up a notch in the pecking order. That was the way of the group. That would normally be a profitable change, especially for whoever took over the top spot, but not when the first act of the new leader was to explain the disastrous loss of the ship and cargo.

Callum was thankful that task wouldn't fall to him. "What are you going to say?"

When Uhr spoke next, his voice was cold and measured. "Whatever I need to," he replied cryptically. "Whatever happens, keep quiet. We'll only get through this if we stick together."

An additional set of bulbs flickered on in the dimly lit metallic tube. A door leading to the passengers' compartment near the cockpit unlatched and swung open.

Several armed men came through the doorway, one carrying a pistol, another with a submachine gun. Two others menaced with poles they gripped in their hands. Callum saw they were cattle prods. Suddenly, he wished he'd kept his own weapon, but none of them had the foresight to hold on to the guns or heavy magazines while they were treading water and trying to stay alive.

Behind the armed men, he saw Emmerson. He was a well-built figure of average height. He had wide shoulders and an overly large head for the size of his body. It gave him a forward-leaning look as if he were top-heavy and always in motion.

Known for his expensive handmade suits, in this instance Emmerson wore a green flight jacket over a black cashmere sweater. He had a noise-canceling headset over his ears. It did little to disguise him.

The bulldog stance, the slicked-back hair, the broken, flattened nose that turned slightly to one side—these features gave him away.

Callum stiffened as Emmerson approached. "Laoban has come to pick us up personally. Is this good news or bad?"

Uhr replied without hesitation. "I'd wager on bad."

Emmerson took center stage, removing his headset and running a hand through his dark hair. "This is not the glorious reception I intended to give you."

No one replied. They hadn't been asked anything yet.

"I gave you a million dollars up front," Emmerson continued. "I gave you all the help you needed and, in return, you sink my ship and deprive me of my cargo."

Uhr took a deep breath and stepped forward. "It had to be sabotage," he said. "We had the ship. The crew was subdued and locked belowdecks. All was going according to plan until . . ."

"Until what?" Emmerson asked.

"Explosions," Uhr said, his voice firm but strained. "A series of small blasts. Immediately followed by the general alarm. Someone must have scuttled the ship."

"You just told me the crew had been secured."

"They were," Uhr insisted. "There may have been a hidden security team. One or two men could have easily accomplished the task."

Emmerson looked disappointed. "This is what you come up with? Hidden saboteurs? Why would they sink the ship instead of call for assistance? Why not free the crew and retake the vessel?"

"I . . . I . . . That, I can't explain," Uhr said. "But scuttling charges are the only explanation for how fast the ship went down."

Emmerson did not seem to agree. "The **Canberra Swift** was a cargo vessel, not a man-of-war. It carried no hidden security team or scuttle switch ready to send it to the bottom. You insult me with this nonsense."

"We did hear explosions," Callum added, trying to back up his new leader.

Emmerson looked at Callum with a brutal stare. He did not speak to underlings.

As he turned back to Uhr, Callum felt like he'd just escaped death. He vowed to remain silent.

"The water came in fast," Uhr said. "What else could it be?"

"Yes," Emmerson said, looking skeptical. "What else indeed." He looked over the group, scanning each of the faces. "Where is Lucas Teng?"

"He went down with the ship."

Emmerson appeared incredulous. "Why on earth would he choose such a thing? Was he that afraid to face me?"

From his position as spectator, Callum could see threads of suspicion beginning to intertwine. In his caution, Uhr wasn't being clear and Emmerson had begun reading the vague statements as if they were deliberately deceptive.

"He didn't **choose** to go down with the ship," Uhr said. "He was trapped."

"On the bridge? At the highest point on the ship." The expression on Emmerson's face could best be described as disgust. "You must take me for a fool."

"He was belowdecks," Uhr explained. "He'd gone to do an inspection."

"Of what?"

"I don't know."

"Did you see him drown?"

"No, but . . ."

Emmerson looked up at the ceiling as if looking to the heavens for strength. "Let me get this straight. Lucas left the bridge to inspect some other part of the ship for reasons unknown **and then** these explosions shook the ship and then the ship went down. Is that the order of things?"

Uhr clammed up. It was better than tripping over his tongue.

Emmerson waved two of his men forward. One of them slammed a baton into Uhr's stomach, doubling him over. The other hit him with a jolt of electricity from the cattle prod.

Uhr's muscles tensed in a painful spasm. He flipped backward onto the deck, landing on his side. A second jolt sent him writhing like a fish out of water while filling the cabin with the smell of burned hair.

The man with the cattle prod looked to be going in for another jab when Emmerson called out for him to stop. "Not all at once," he said. "We want him to remember his name."

Callum looked at Uhr in horror. Partly out of compassion, but also if Uhr died, Callum would become the leader and bear the brunt of the questioning.

As Emmerson's men backed off, Uhr slowly recovered. He uncurled from a fetal position and managed to get to his hands and knees. He was breathing hard and drooling a mixture of blood and spit where he'd bitten through his tongue. He looked down at the deck before tilting his head up toward Emmerson.

"I'm waiting," Emmerson said. Presumably, he meant for a better explanation.

Uhr said nothing.

Emmerson shook his head and wafted a hand in front of his face. "Let some air in here," he said to one of his men. "It stinks."

The man with the cattle prod stepped toward the tail end of the fuselage, where a set of controls waited. He disarmed the lock, released the safety lever and pulled the main handle down, moving it from closed to open.

The sound of hydraulics filled the fuselage and a crack of light appeared in the aft section of the cabin. It widened on both sides as a pair of clamshell doors opened.

The sound of jet engines and the howling wind doubled in intensity. Air currents whipped into the fuselage, swirling through the cabin and tugging at the men standing there. The man at the controls stood firm, his pant legs and shirt snapping.

When the doors had opened to the full width of the fuselage, they locked in place. A ramp slid into position and tilted downward until it was secured between the doors.

Callum squinted as the harsh light poured in. When his eyes adjusted, he saw the early-morning sky and the dark ocean roaring past beneath it. They were no more than sixty feet off the water, traveling at three hundred miles an hour.

Emmerson moved closer and crouched down beside Uhr. "I assume you understand what's about to happen here, but to ensure there's no doubt let me offer you a demonstration."

He stood up and snapped his fingers, pointing to one of the injured pirates. Two of his men rushed toward the man, lifting him from a makeshift bed.

"No," Uhr shouted, finding his voice again.

Similarly alarmed, Callum lunged forward hoping to intervene. He was immediately knocked to the deck and held down by one of Emmerson's men. With a knee in between his shoulder blades, Callum fought to see what was happening.

By the time he craned his head around, the injured man had been dragged to the back of the aircraft, lifted to his feet and heaved forward. Out and over the edge.

He disappeared beneath the tail ramp, dropping out of sight for an instant, only to reemerge as he hit the water. Instead of plunging instantly to the depths, his body skipped and tumbled grotesquely. He fell behind them rapidly, bouncing a second time and then skidding and vanishing in a small ring of foam.

"There was no need for that," Uhr insisted.

"On that, we disagree," Emmerson said. "The purpose was to get your attention. From the look on your face, I sense it worked. Now, I'll ask you one more time—and if you don't explain it to my satisfaction, I'll throw you from the aircraft and move on to the next man. And then the next. And then the next. I will have the truth or I'll run out of people to question. Do I make myself clear?"

Uhr nodded slowly. And when he'd finished, Emmerson asked his question again. "What happened to your leader? And where has he taken my ship and my cargo?"

Watching from his spot on the deck, Callum finally grasped the problem. Emmerson didn't believe the ship had gone down. He thought Lucas and the other pirates had double-crossed him, stealing the vessel and the cargo for themselves.

Uhr looked up. "I've told you all I know."

Emmerson looked away, disgusted. "Hook him."

Another of Emmerson's men came forward. He wrapped Uhr's hands with several loops of duct tape around which he hooked a large carabiner. The carabiner was latched to a substantial length of nylon rope, which lay coiled on the deck in a figure eight.

The far end of the rope was tossed out into the wind. There was no weight on it, just the plastic tip covering to keep the strands from unraveling. Still, the friction with the wind began to pull on the cord and slowly but surely the figure eight began to uncoil.

Uhr's gaze darted from the hundred-foot coil of rope to the gaping doorway at the back of the aircraft.

"The longer the rope gets, the more drag the air will place on it," Emmerson explained, "and the faster it will unwind. When it reaches the sea, it will spool out even faster. And once enough of it is wet and heavy, it will stay in the water. At that moment, you'll be pulled from where you stand as if ten men were tugging on the other end."

Emmerson turned to the rope as another layer vanished. "By my estimation, you have sixty seconds."

Uhr was jolted into speaking. "I'm trying to explain," he said. "The ship sank. Someone booby-trapped it."

The rope was stretching out farther, whipping from side to side like a streamer.

"You've told me that lie," Emmerson said. "Now, give me the truth."

Callum could wait no longer. "I know where the ship is," he shouted.

Emmerson held up a hand and the man nearest the rope stepped on it, stopping the exodus.

"Say your piece," Emmerson advised.

Callum squirmed under the weight of his captor, struggling to get the words out. "I was at the helm when the explosions hit. We were fifty miles northwest of Miyako-jima. An underwater feature called Ryukyu Ridge runs between that island and Okinawa a hundred miles away. The depth in that area varies, but readings of five hundred feet are not uncommon."

Had he seen the chart, Emmerson would have scarcely believed how fortunate he was. Ryukyu Ridge was a narrow geologic feature that ran diagonally in front of one of the world's great drop-offs. Had the ship sank thirty minutes earlier, it wouldn't have hit bottom until it had traveled three miles straight down.

Still, he looked at Callum suspiciously. "You seem quite sure of this information. How is it you know so much about these underwater features?"

"I spent four years in the People's Navy," Callum said. "My training was in navigation. It's second nature for me to track position and depth. My first instinct after the explosion was to note our position in case we needed assistance. Of course, I didn't call for help, but the old practice happens naturally."

"Fortunate for you," Emmerson said. "Can you find this location?"

Callum nodded. "Within a mile or two."

Emmerson considered his words, his mind lost in calculations. Finally, he turned toward the man whose foot was on Uhr's rope. "Release him."

Callum breathed a sigh of relief, but it was short-lived. Instead of cutting Uhr free, the man took his foot off the rope. It began to unspool once again.

"No," Callum called out.

Uhr was panicking now, digging in against the inevitable pull. "Callum told you the truth," he shouted.

"Yes," Emmerson said. "He told me."

"No," Uhr said as the last few coils unspooled.

The far end of the rope hit the water and bounced. Seconds later it hit again, this time stretching taut, before emerging like a flying fish and springing forward. Uhr was yanked toward the door, landing facedown and sliding several feet.

When the pressure released—as the rope sprung up and forward—he spun his body around, jamming his feet against the lip of the ramp and bracing for the next pull.

This position gave him enough leverage to fight. He shouted to Emmerson, "Let me loose. You've made your point."

The next impact hit so hard that it felt as if Uhr's arms would be ripped from their sockets. One foot slipped, the other knee bent and buckled under the strain. With no room left to spare, he begged Emmerson once more. "Please," he shouted. "Lucas is gone. I'm the leader."

"Actually," Emmerson said. "I have someone else in mind."

The rope caught the ocean again and Uhr was snatched from the aircraft in a blink. Any cries or shouts he might have uttered were lost on the wind.

Callum turned away. He could neither look out the door nor at the other men across from him.

Emmerson, on the other hand, seemed eminently satisfied. He signaled for one of his men to raise the ramp and close the door. As the hydraulics came to life, he turned to Callum. "You'd better not be lying," he said, "or your fate will be worse than his."

Emmerson's aircraft raced onward, flying beneath the radar coverage of the nearest Western countries. But the East China Sea was home to other pairs of eyes besides the observers on large ships or at shore-based stations. A thousand tiny fishing boats plowed these waters.

A group of men in one such vessel happened to be working their nets as the howling sound of an aircraft caught their attention. Looking up from the morning's work, they saw a craft unlike any other traveling low and fast just above the horizon.

It had six jet engines mounted up front on pylons near the nose. Thick, stubby wings sprouted from the middle of the fuselage, their tips equipped with extendable floats. Its tail soared high at the aft end of the fuselage, but instead of a single fin, it ended in two outward-slanting blades that sprouted in a Y formation. Its engines were older models, louder, higher pitched and less efficient than those on modern airliners. They left thin trails of brown smoke in the sky behind them.

"**Guaiwu,**" the older fisherman said.

The word meant monster in English. It was a joke, of course, but closer to the truth than the man would ever know.

CHAPTER 8

HONG KONG

The sight of a red taxi pulling to the curb told Yan-Li she was finally, truly home.

Her flight from Da Nang had been smooth and uneventful, her arrival and processing through customs handled in typically efficient style. But the Hong Kong Airport reminded her of a dozen other airports around the world—efficient and indistinct, clean and sterile, with the same bland style as a modern oversize mall. The red taxi, on the other hand, was a unique symbol of old Hong Kong. She'd been riding in them since she was a little girl.

She settled in the back, enjoying the familiar sights as they traveled across Stonecutters Island and through West Kowloon. The route offered slightly less traffic and an incredible view of Victoria Harbour.

Leaving Kowloon, they went down through a

tunnel, under the bay and onto Hong Kong Island proper. Here the road traveled upward, snaking through the hills and into an area known as the Mid-Levels.

Hong Kong University sat at the foot of these hills, while thirty-story apartment buildings sprouted from the greenery at various heights along the slope.

The red taxi dropped her in front of her building. She took the elevator to her apartment on the tenth floor. After it had been buttoned up for several months, she'd expected the air inside to be musty and stale. Instead, it smelled fresh, with the scent of spring rain.

She wondered if her mother had come over to air the place out for her return.

Stepping into the tiny foyer, she dropped the duffel bag filled with her diving gear by the door. She moved past the compact kitchen and into the living room.

There she paused, noticing that a gauzy curtain between the living room and the balcony was wafting in the breeze. "Mother," she called out, stepping toward the bedroom.

A man appeared in the open doorway to the small room. He stood with his arms folded but made no move to attack her.

She stepped back and turned for the outer door.

Too late.

A second man, taking a similar stance, was now blocking her path.

With little choice in the matter, she held her ground. The men might be from the government, she thought. Hong Kong was not as free as it used to be. That and the fact that she'd spent the summer working with Americans was likely to bring questions at some point.

"Who are you?" she demanded.

Neither brute answered. Instead, a third man appeared, stepping through the curtain from the balcony. "No need to get angry," he said, "we're not here to harm you."

She noticed immediately that he was Caucasian and dressed in an expensive suit. Not from the government, she decided. His accent was some form of British. He'd never make high tea with the Queen, but the UK was clearly where he'd learned to speak. Staring at him, she had the odd feeling she'd seen him somewhere before.

"Then what are you here for?" she said, responding to his promise.

"To make you an offer," the Caucasian man said. "A lucrative offer at that. My name is Emmerson. I'm an associate of your ex-husband's."

Recognition came to her suddenly. She had seen him before. Years ago, having dinner with Kung-lu, in the days before the truth about his criminal life had come to the surface.

"I haven't seen Lucas in years," she insisted, using her husband's better-known nickname. "Whatever business you have with him has nothing to do with me."

The man shrugged. "I think you'll feel differently once I explain."

Yan-Li had faced danger before—searching for lost ships filled with treasure tended to bring out certain types of confrontation—but there was something odd about this interaction. As if the man was waiting to see what she might do.

He glanced around like an appraiser. "Expensive place, this," he said. "Two bedrooms and a balcony, up high in the Mid-Levels. Not much of a view, of course, unless you like to stare at the back side of another building, but it has a full kitchen. How much did it run you? A million at least."

"I don't really know," she replied defensively. "The university owns it. I get to live here as long as I teach and publish."

"Ah," he said. "Tuition dollars well spent. Work with me and you'll be able to buy a place like this . . . for cash."

"I'd rather go live in Sham Shui Po."

Sham Shui Po was the poorest district in Hong Kong. Crowds upon crowds piled atop one another in tiny tenements.

"Your husband came from there," he reminded her. "He wasn't so keen to go back."

"Lucas wasn't keen about a lot of things," she

snapped. "Truth and honesty among them. You're not the first person he's let down. And you won't be the last."

"On the contrary," the man said, "I will be the last. One way or another."

He leaned toward her, his eyes pinched and searching, his lips stretched taut across feral teeth. "Your husband is either dead or has betrayed me, in which case he's as good as dead. But in either case he owes me a debt. And since he cannot pay, that debt falls to you . . . and your children."

Stepping back, Emmerson pulled the curtain aside, revealing the balcony. Two more men stood there. In front of them, on their knees, were Yan's young children and her diminutive mother.

Their mouths had been taped shut, their hands zip-tied in front of them. Tears streamed down their terrified faces.

Yan-Li lost all composure at the sight. Her knees almost buckled, but instead she ran forward. The Englishman grabbed her by the arm and kept her from reaching the balcony.

"No," he said, shaking his head. "No, you don't touch them. Not until you agree."

She wanted to fight, wanted to spin around and plant her elbow in the Adam's apple of the bastard who held her arm. But it would just set the tragedy in motion.

Her son and daughter were both small and light for their ages. It would take just a second for the thugs on the balcony to lift them and toss them over the rail. It would mean nothing to them and the end of everything for her.

She found a sudden and icy calm. The same calm that had eventually given her the strength to get away from the man she'd loved.

A deep breath followed and after looking into her son's brown eyes she chose strength and iron instead of weakness and fear. She stepped back, pulling loose from the Englishman who held her. After putting a few paces between them, she glared back in his direction. "What is it you want me to do?" she asked bitterly.

He smiled, his face suddenly soft and rubbery again. "It's quite simple, really. There's a ship out there with a very special cargo on board. A cargo that Lucas was supposed to bring me. You're going to retrieve it for me."

Of course, she thought. Piracy. Her ex-husband's stock-in-trade. If he wasn't looting the treasures that she led him to, he was hijacking ships outright and stealing their cargoes.

"And if I do as you say, you'll release my family?"

He said nothing, instead waving his henchmen inside. The children and their grandmother were brought into the living room and allowed to sit.

"Ready to help?" Emmerson asked.

She nodded. What else could she do?

"Grab your gear," Emmerson said, pointing toward

the dive bag and the hallway beyond. "You're going to need it."

"Why?" she asked.

"Because the ship is sitting at the bottom of the East China Sea."

CHAPTER 9

EAST CHINA SEA

Kurt leaned over the edge of the **Sapphire**'s swim platform with a long boat hook in hand. Stretching precariously, he looked along the side of the ship as floating debris slid past its gleaming hull.

"What's it look like?" Joe asked from a position behind Kurt.

"More plastic garbage," Kurt said.

As the debris neared the stern, Kurt stretched the full length of his six-foot-two frame, hooking a corner of the plastic and pulling it close. Lifting the waterlogged mess out of the water was harder than it looked and Kurt had to lean back and use every muscle in his body. Swinging around, he dumped the catch on the deck.

Joe stepped in behind him, using a make-shift skimmer to scoop up smaller pieces, which were added to a growing pile at the center of the swim platform.

Kurt bent to examine the find. Cloth, plastic and a few bits of Styrofoam. Nothing to suggest it came from the missing ship. "For all we know, this stuff could have been dumped off a cruise ship."

"Or swept down to the sea from a landfill," Joe replied, placing the skimmer down and stretching his back. "Be easier to do this if we could stop the boat."

Kurt felt the soreness in his own muscles. "If we stopped every time we spotted floating junk, we'd have covered about two miles in the last five hours. We need to keep moving so the towed array will scan as much of the seafloor as possible."

Joe knew this, but he had no interest in wrenching a muscle or being dragged off the platform while trying to haul garbage aboard the ship as it sped past. "If you say so, but don't be upset when you get the bill from my chiropractor."

The radio squawked to life beside them. **"New target,"** Winterburn's voice called out. **"Five degrees to port. I'd say about a thousand yards out."**

"A thousand yards," Kurt said. "The kid's got good eyes."

"He's using the LiDAR system to look for debris," Joe said. "Pretty smart of him."

LiDAR stood for Light Detection and Ranging. The system used a pair of high-definition cameras with zoom lenses to scan back and forth. Because the cameras were placed a wide distance from each other on the forward deck, they got a stereoscopic view of the world that a computer examined for recognizable shapes.

The system was supposed to be capable of observing a small raft at ten miles and an average-sized trawler out to the horizon. Using it to look for debris in their path was playing into its strengths.

Kurt admired the ingenuity. He grabbed the radio and pressed the talk switch. "Turn toward it. Take it down the starboard side if you can. That way, Joe can pull a muscle on both sides of his back."

Joe laughed. "Surely you jest. But if I get hurt, you're doing the work on your own."

Good point, Kurt thought. He pressed the talk switch again. "And chop the throttle a notch. No reason to be hasty."

The **Sapphire** changed course, easing onto a new heading and slowing just a bit. Kurt and Joe switched to the other side of the platform. As the object grew closer, they were able to make out details with the naked eye.

Joe was up front this time. "Does that look like international orange to you?"

Kurt nodded. The color was dull and tarnished, but definitely the standard shade of emergency equipment.

As the object came closer it seemed to grow larger. It bumped against the hull at one point, spinning in the yacht's slipstream.

"All stop," Kurt called out over the radio.

The vibration from the engines died away and the **Sapphire** slowed. The floating object continued to bump and whirl until it was almost even with the swim platform.

Joe caught it in the net and pulled. Kurt latched onto an exposed section with the boat hook. Together they pulled the object up against the platform and held it there. When the yacht came to a stop, they hauled it in.

Like fishermen with a prize catch, they'd captured something almost too large for the deck. Six feet long and several feet across, it had the shape of a giant puzzle piece. It was twisted and scorched in places. Lifting it over the transom, Kurt would have guessed the weight at nearly a hundred pounds.

Joe rapped his knuckles on the object. "FRP," he said. "Fiber-reinforced plastic."

Kurt was examining the cross section. "It's a sandwich of two layers with a hollow center filled with waterproof foam."

"This came from a lifeboat," Joe concluded.

Kurt nodded. The gravity in Joe's voice matched the concern in Kurt's mind. Modern lifeboats were designed to be virtually indestructible. The fact that they'd found only a small chunk was bad news.

Joe knelt down and found part of it was covered with oil. He used his hand to wipe it clean. The name **Canberra Swift** and the ship's ID number were stenciled there in faded letters.

"Well," Joe said, looking up, "at least we know we're looking in the right place."

Kurt studied the fragment up close. He found cracks radiating along its entire length as if it had been bent backward before breaking loose from the rest of the lifeboat and snapping back to its original shape. He found the texture of the melted plastic to be rough and barbed, with jagged little hooks protruding from the previously smooth surface. "Thoughts?"

"Flash heat and shock cooling," Joe said. "This thing flew out of the frying pan but not into the fire. I'd say it hit the cold ocean and its melting plastic froze in whatever weird shape it had curled into."

Kurt trusted Joe's analysis. The explosion theory was looking more likely with every passing second. And yet something was out of place. For the moment, Kurt kept that thought to himself.

Standing up, Kurt scanned the horizon. The sun was getting low. It was turning the water dark while painting the surface with streaks of gold and platinum. He found it hard to look west, even with his best polarized sunglasses on.

"We're losing the daylight," he said. "I'll clean up out here, you go store that somewhere safe, check with Stratton on the sonar scan. That's going to be our best hope of finding anything now."

As Joe dragged the orange slab of wreckage inside, Kurt grabbed the radio. "Winterburn, you see anything else on the horizon?"

"**Nope,**" the ensign replied. "**I mean . . . negative, sir.**"

Kurt laughed. He wasn't a stickler for detail. He cared more if people got the job done than whether they followed any communication protocol. "Get us moving and resume our original course. Best speed you can manage without degrading the sonar signal."

As the yacht began to move, Kurt gathered up the rest of the debris they'd found, stuffing it into large plastic bags. He stored them in the aft dive locker and raised the swim platform before making his way toward the forward compartment.

He arrived to find Joe talking with Stratton, the other NUMA crewman on board. Stratton was a sonar specialist and underwater drone expert. He'd spent the last four hours monitoring the moving images from the **Sapphire**'s towed array and a trio of underwater drones that were traveling in formation with the yacht.

"Anything new?" Kurt asked.

"Bloodshot eyes and an empty coffee mug," Stratton said, holding up the oversize cup for Kurt to see.

"I was referring to the search."

Stratton shook his head.

Kurt checked a computer screen displaying the search area. He saw four vertical swaths that ran parallel—with the exception of the **Sapphire**'s course deviations to retrieve floating debris. In six hours, they'd covered about three hundred square miles altogether. Normally, that would be a drop in the bucket, but with a detailed location provided by the last beep of the **Swift**'s AIS beacon and the flash seen by the officer on the Korean freighter, they were working in a relatively small area. Another day or two, there would be nowhere left to look.

"I'm going to grab some chow," Kurt said. "You guys want me to bring something back from the galley? By that, I mean the microwave."

Joe didn't answer right away, which was odd considering the subject was food.

"Stratt?" Kurt asked.

He noticed now that both men were leaning closer to the screen.

"Do you see that?" Joe said quietly.

"I do," Stratton replied. He tapped the keyboard, enhancing the image they were staring at.

"There's definitely something there," Joe said.

"Hold your applause," the sonar specialist replied. "It could be junk. Or a shipping container. I've found three of them in the last hour. One had at least a thousand pairs of expensive sneakers pouring out the back end. Do you know what we could get for those if we salvaged them?"

"We're not here to rescue footwear," Joe said. "But talk to me later."

Kurt moved closer, looking over their shoulders and remaining quiet. All thoughts of food were now forgotten. Or at least postponed.

"It's at the edge of the scanning field," Joe said. "We need a better image."

"Let me reroute the drone for another pass," Stratton replied. Tapping the keyboard, he took command of the torpedo-shaped vehicle, maneuvering it out of the formation and back toward the distorted image it had picked up.

As the drone lined up on the new course, Stratton switched from side-scan sonar to a bottom-scanning system.

"Let's get a visual," Joe said.

Stratton switched on the drone's camera and high-intensity lights. At first, they revealed nothing but the barren plain of the ocean floor thirty-six hundred feet down. Then little shards of debris appeared, some of them sitting in the little craters they'd excavated as they hit the mud.

"Getting a strong reading on the mag," Joe said.

Kurt shook his head softly. "We couldn't get this lucky," he said, "not in a million years."

"Speak for yourself," Joe replied.

Several twisted lengths of metal appeared and then the lights found something more impressive.

"Is that what I think it is?"

"Engine block," Joe said. "Large diesel, by the look of it."

Kurt studied the image, nodding silently. He could see the sleeves for the pistons clearly. "Need I remind you the **Swift** ran on gas turbines?"

"She also had a diesel backup for low-speed

maneuvering and a couple APUs that ran on heavy fuel."

"Fair point," Kurt said, folding his arms and leaning against the bulkhead. He was doing his best to withhold judgment, but something felt wrong.

Finally, another shape appeared. This one larger than the engine block they'd seen earlier. It began to take on color as it filled out the screen. Dull brown at first, brightening to international orange.

"Lifeboat," Joe said. "Or part of one."

"Where's the rest of it?" Stratton asked.

"One part is in the dive locker," Kurt noted.

What they'd found was the pointed bow of the craft. It lay on its side like a three-dimensional triangle or a tent that had been blown over by the wind.

"Get in closer," Joe suggested.

Stratton took the drone down and held it in place against the current. The aluminum framework to which the high-strength plastic was attached could be seen now. It had been bent and twisted outward by a tremendous force. Scorch marks and more of the rapidly melted and cooled plastic could be seen.

It was all very telling, Kurt thought. And misleading. "Hate to tell you, gentlemen, but we've been had."

CHAPTER 10

WASHINGTON, D.C.

It fell to Rudi Gunn to deliver the bad news.

After alerting his counterpart in the NSA, Rudi arranged a briefing at NUMA headquarters. By five a.m. the main conference room was filled with the representatives from various Washington-based agencies and a few members of the NUMA staff.

Joining Rudi was NUMA's Director of Information Technology, Hiram Yaeger. While Rudi was clean-shaven and squared away—even at this hour of the morning—Hiram wore faded jeans and a black pullover sweater. He was also in need of a haircut, or at least everyone in the office thought so, but for now had his graying hair tucked back under a vintage Washington Senators ball cap.

Hiram's style was not a function of the early wake-up call. Like many computer experts and IT directors, he dressed in a very relaxed manner.

In Hiram's case, a fondness for comfort, Harley-Davidsons and classic rock bands tended to inform most fashion decisions.

Taking his first gulp of the dark, unadulterated coffee, Yaeger turned to Rudi. "If we're going to keep having meetings before the sun is up—or Starbucks is open—I'm going to need NUMA to install a cappuccino machine."

Rudi grinned. "You do know that cappuccino has less caffeine than an ordinary cup of coffee, right?"

"Well aware of that," Yaeger insisted. "But I could drink six cappuccinos and still consume less liquid. Which becomes important"—he raised his eyebrows—"later on."

Rudi laughed and made his way over to the conference table, where several outsiders were reading over the report Kurt and Joe had sent in.

Front and center sat Anna Biel, one of the President's advisers and the director of the National Security Agency.

One seat over he saw Elliot Harner, deputy director of the CIA. There was the only true civilian in the group, Sunil Pradi, the CEO of Hydro-Com, the company that designed the missing computers.

And finally, looking less than happy at his inclusion, Rear Admiral Marcus Wagner, an old friend of Rudi's and the current head of Naval Intelligence for the Western Pacific.

"Not really sure why I'm here," Wagner said to

Rudi, "but this better be good. Otherwise, I'll be inviting you to some of our early-morning meetings."

"Wouldn't bother me," Rudi said. "I'm up at four without an alarm."

Rudi was a former Navy man. He'd graduated first in his class at Annapolis and had a full career in the service before joining NUMA. That background brought him a great deal of respect with the Navy brass and also the type of familiarity that made them treat him like he was one of their own. That could be good or bad, depending on the circumstances.

"I bet you are," Wagner replied smugly.

Rudi sat down. "I suppose you've all read Kurt's report. What do you think?"

Anna Biel spoke first. "If I understand this correctly, he's suggesting the explosion and the loss of the AIS signal was a ruse designed to make us think the ship had gone down in deep waters. When it was, in fact, still afloat and proceeding at full speed toward some unknown destination. Assuming he's correct, this is basically our worst-case scenario. Quite frankly, I'm hoping he's wrong."

"Not likely," Rudi said. "First of all, Kurt's a very measured thinker. And second, the data is anything but inconclusive. The stress points on the lifeboat show that it was blown apart from the inside, not damaged or crushed by a larger exterior detonation. In addition, the fiber-reinforced plastic—which the lifeboat's shell was made of—displays distinctive signs of flash heating and melting, but, once again, only on the interior surfaces. This is completely opposite of what we'd expect if the lifeboat was thrown from the **Swift** in a cataclysmic blast that took out the entire ship. Finally, there's the little item on page three. In my opinion, Kurt has buried the key."

Everyone turned simultaneously to page three.

"Please direct your attention to number five on the list of items recovered from the bottom," Rudi said.

"AIS transponder," Rear Admiral Wagner said, reading aloud. "So what? All lifeboats carry them."

"Except this one was found jury-rigged to an odd section of the lifeboat's hull," Rudi replied. "You might expect that on an older vessel plying the coastal waters of a Third World nation somewhere but not on a state-of-the-art lifeboat hitched to a modern freighter."

"Then there's the size," Yaeger chimed in. "That unit is an NJX 1700 model. It draws a larger current and puts out a stronger signal than what a lifeboat normally carries. The antenna has been torn off in the explosion, but you can see clearly that the attachment point is designed for a longer, heavier aerial."

"Meaning what, exactly?" Ms. Biel asked.

"It belongs on a larger ship," Rudi replied. "In this case, the **Canberra Swift.** Kurt's theory is that it was taken from the freighter and attached to the lifeboat to simulate the **Swift**'s continuing on course. The only thing they couldn't do was simulate the **Swift**'s incredible speed."

Yaeger jumped in. "Which necessitated the message they sent to the operations center indicating trouble with the fuel system and a switch to the diesel auxiliary."

Rudi nodded. "A hardworking lie, since it did double duty, covering up the lifeboat's limited speed while suggesting the possibility of a massive explosion based on one of the liquid natural gas tanks rupturing."

Ms. Biel looked perturbed by this news, but she was the type to follow the evidence where it took her. "So, we all watched the AIS beacon on the lifeboat while the freighter itself went dark and took off in a different direction, is that it?"

"Sleight of hand," Rudi said. "Or sleight of ship, if you prefer."

The room fell quiet as the various individuals pondered the meaning of this news. The CEO of Hydro-Com looked almost apoplectic, given this idea. A sunken ship and destroyed computers were one thing. Stolen technology and all that came with it was something else entirely. "But they've found wreckage."

"A very small amount," Rudi insisted. "A sinking ship the size of this freighter would have left a trail of floating debris miles long. An exploding ship would scatter it like confetti."

"And the oil slick?"

"Staged or from the lifeboats."

Pradi took this in, but as a man used to arguing with board members and shareholders, he wasn't so easily dissuaded. "Mr. Gunn," he said. "Your men have covered almost three hundred square miles of the seafloor. Quick work—and admirable, I admit—but there's still an entire ocean out there to search. Many ships and planes have vanished over years never to be found."

"I'm sorry, Mr. Pradi," Rudi said, "it is a big ocean. But if the **Swift** did explode where the AIS track ended and the Korean captain saw the flash, the wreck would have to hit bottom somewhere close by. Such a calamity would not allow the ship to continue sailing for miles and miles before eventually sinking. Certainly not unseen by other vessels or their radar. That limits the search area to a relatively small area. And Kurt and Joe have now covered that area thoroughly."

Elliot Harner, the CIA rep, stirred to life. Like a good spy, he'd blended into the background to the point he'd almost been forgotten. "Well," he said calmly, "if it makes you feel any better, my people have found nothing to indicate this was state sponsored. The Chinese seem to grasp that something has happened, but they don't appear to know the significance or care all that much at this point. I'd call it 2.5 on the Richter scale, not felt anywhere above middle management."

"What about the Russians?" Ms. Biel asked. "Or the North Korean and Iranian factions?"

"The Russians are asleep at the wheel," Harner said. "They have limited assets in the area and are simply not a significant player at the moment. That could change, of course, assuming word gets out. As for North Korea and Iran, they're nonfactors."

Ms. Biel seemed reassured by this, but she needed more info. "You've ruled out all the major suspects, Elliot. Tell me you have someone to replace them?"

"Not at the moment."

Yaeger offered a suggestion. "What about other corporations?" he asked. "This technology is extremely advanced. It could even be called disruptive. How many billions would it be worth to another company? How much time would stealing it save over trying to develop a competing line?"

The CEO answered. "Billions of dollars and years of intense research. But we have deals in place with most of the legitimate competitors, licensing agreements and joint manufacturing plans. As for the smaller firms . . ." He shook his head after considering it. "No, no, no. To come out with something similar to our product would just get them sued. We would block them at every turn. And even with the physical architecture, they'd still have to develop their own source code and AI procedure to operate efficiently. It would bankrupt a smaller rival and our larger competitors already have a piece of the pie. They'd be sabotaging their interests. If this is piracy, the thief has to be some nation's government. No one else would truly benefit."

Rudi saw the conundrum. While he agreed with Pradi's logic, he also knew how deep Elliot Harner's sources went, especially in China and Russia. If Harner said those nations weren't factors, Rudi would accept that until it was proven otherwise.

"Most likely, there's something we don't know," Ms. Biel said calmly. "It wouldn't be the first time. Regardless, we must assume the ship has been hijacked and the Vector units stolen."

"Except for one thing," Harner replied. "If you hijack a ship, you have to park it somewhere eventually. Our satellites have scanned every port and river within a thousand miles of the ship's last-known location. It's not docked anywhere nor is it tied to a riverbank. In addition, we've got high-resolution scans of every vessel in the search area that's still at sea. All of them have been positively identified and the **Swift** isn't among them."

"What about dry docks?" Wagner suggested. "Or under a construction blind? The Chinese build some of their larger ships that way to keep our eyes off them."

Harner shook his head. "We have observers stationed at every major Chinese port and construction facility. There's no sign of the **Swift**."

"Maybe they've piled it high with containers,"

Pradi suggested. "Thrown a slapdash paint job on it or hidden it under a throng of cranes."

Rudi answered that one. "Here's where certain facts work against them. The **Swift** has a unique profile. It's designed to be fast and aerodynamic on the water. From above, it looks more like an elongated blimp or an overinflated bullet train. No matter where you put it, it would stick out like a sore thumb."

"What about a rendezvous?" Ms. Biel suggested. "They could swap the cargo to another ship and send the original carrier to the bottom."

"Can't rule that out," Rudi admitted. "But it would be difficult to accomplish, given the **Swift**'s configuration. She's an RO/RO vessel—roll on/roll off. Great for moving cargo when the ship's docked at a nice concrete pier, but much less efficient when trying to transfer cargo at sea."

"It can't have happened," Pradi said, cutting in.

"What do you mean can't?"

"The Vector units cannot have been transferred from ship to ship," he explained. "If they had been, we would know about it."

"Explain," Ms. Biel said.

"The machines are designed to communicate by satellite with our control center in San Francisco," he said. "Had they been transferred from the **Swift** to another ship, they would have linked up with the satellites in a process called a handshake. The connection would be automatic and nearly instantaneous. Location and operational data would have been uploaded instantly. The fact that such a linkup hasn't occurred tells us they haven't left the hold of that ship."

Ms. Biel grew frustrated. "I report back to the President in two hours," she said. "Telling him we have no earthly clue what's happened, who caused it to happen or why it happened isn't the message he's going to want to hear. I need something. If the ship isn't in port or upriver or still out at sea, where the hell is it?"

"The only place it could be," Rudi said. "On the bottom."

"But your man said it didn't sink," she replied sharply.

"No," Rudi corrected. "He said it wasn't found where the facts led us to believe it would be. That doesn't mean it hasn't ended up on the bottom in a more accessible spot."

A look of innate understanding appeared on her face. She leaned back. "Our original fear comes back to haunt us. The ship going down in the shallows where the computers would remain intact and easily accessible. Is that what you're suggesting?"

Rudi nodded.

"Now I see why you brought me out here," Wagner said. "You need Navy assets to handle the search."

"No," Rudi replied. "NUMA was tasked with this for a reason. You send a bunch of battleship gray salvage ships into the East China Sea and you'll be telling the whole world that we're looking for something. Our team will find the ship. What we need from the Navy is a little bit of information, which you've got hidden up your sleeve."

Wagner looked suspicious. "What information might that be?"

"You have a listening station at Naha," Rudi said. "On the southern tip of Okinawa. It's officially listed as a weather station and supposedly manned by civilians, but rumor has it Naha is the control center for a subsurface listening operation using powerful hydrophones designed to track Chinese submarines in the shallows of their own waters."

The Rear Admiral cleared his throat before speaking. "You hear a lot of rumors, Gunn, but go on . . ."

"Considering that continental shelf extends out from China to Okinawa and that the flat, shallow areas of the shelf would be the best place to put the ship down if someone wanted to salvage the computers, it's highly likely that your listening system would be in a perfect position to hear the ship being scuttled and settling to the bottom. You give us the location of any such signal and we'll go find the ship and the missing computers, all before the Chinese and Russians even get out of bed."

Wagner was stoic but Ms. Biel was already nodding her approval. "I like this plan. I'll inform the President and get his authorization." She snapped the file shut in front of her before adding to this directive. "Don't wait on my answer to get moving. I can't see any circumstance where he might object to this course of action. But I want to implement it immediately."

Rear Admiral Wagner looked as if he'd been bushwhacked, but he nodded respectfully. "I know of no such weather station," he insisted. "But I'll let you know what they've heard."

CHAPTER 11

NAHA, OKINAWA

Lieutenant Callie Baker pulled to a stop at the outer gate of the Naha Weather Station in her 1975 Ford Bronco. The red and white vehicle was an absolute classic, though this particular version was fighting a losing battle with the salt air of Okinawa.

The Bronco had been on the island more than forty years, passed down from one Navy serviceman to the next. It had dents, rust and over a hundred thousand miles on the odometer. It had no roof—thanks to a buzz saw after an unintended meeting with a large tree branch during a typhoon.

Even with all that, the vehicle remained a sought-after item among those Americans based on the island. This was partially because of tradition, but also because a Japanese law had prohibited import of U.S.-made vehicles since 1976.

Looking over the vehicle with a jealous gaze, the guard made Callie an offer that he'd made several times before. "You ever let me restore this thing, I can promise you a six-figure sales price."

"How much to do the work?" she asked.

"Five figures," he guessed. "High five figures."

"That's what I thought," she said. "I'll pass."

He shrugged, raised the gate and Callie drove on through. She pulled up in front of an unassuming one-story building, parking on the gravel beside a hedge of tropical bushes.

Stepping out of the Bronco, she made her way toward the front door. She wore khaki shorts, a sleeveless top and dark sunglasses. Her feet were clad in comfortable sandals and her hair was pulled back in a ponytail to fight the heat and humidity. She looked every bit the civilian worker she was supposed to be, but she was all Navy and often couldn't wait to get to work.

Entering the station, she ran into her boss, Lieutenant Commander Aaron Stewart. He wore shorts and a blue and yellow Hawaiian-print shirt. His hair was curly and certainly not regulation, considering how much it covered his ears.

"Morning, Aaron," she said. Because they were supposed to be civilians, they referred to each other by their first names, a practice that had been hard to get used to.

"Morning, Callie," he said. "Glad you're here

early. We got a strange request from the brass. Need you to go back through the logs from three days ago and look for an odd signal. They think a ship went down somewhere between here and the Chinese coast."

"Haven't heard of anything," she said. "But I wouldn't put it past the Chinese to keep something like that secret."

"It's not a Chinese vessel," he said. "That's all I can tell you."

She took a file, left the office and skipped her usual morning trip to the vending machines.

Settling in at her desk, she used the computers to run through the recordings of the previous three days. It took a couple hours.

She found nothing of interest near the coast, but out of an abundance of caution she checked the other regions covered by the hydrophone network.

Soon enough, the computer picked out a signal that she listened to several times. When the background noise was eliminated, it became clear. Five minutes later, she was back in Stewart's office.

"A series of minor explosions," she explained as he listened to the tape. "Followed by the sound of venting air. There's no mechanical breakup and no sign of internal structural failures. The closest audio match we have comes from a ship we scrapped and sank intentionally several years ago as part of an exercise to build an artificial reef."

"A controlled event?" he asked.

"Could be," she said. "Whatever it is, it went to the bottom in one piece."

"Do you have a location?"

"The coordinates are in the file."

He took the report, leafing through it for a moment. Callie stood there, waiting.

"That's all, Lieutenant," he said, no longer using her first name.

Officially dismissed, she turned and left. She couldn't help but feel mildly disappointed. One reality of the job was being just a small cog in a large wheel, which usually meant not getting a peek at the bigger picture.

Too bad, she thought. She wondered who would scuttle a ship in the Ryukyu Channel and why no one in the world seemed to know about it.

It started raining as a sudden tropical downpour hit the building. Within seconds, the rain was pounding the roof and rattling the windows.

Forgetting about the missing ship, Callie ran outside to pull the tarp over the top of the Bronco and save what was left of the tattered seats.

CHAPTER 12

RYUKYU CHANNEL

There she is," Joe announced.

Kurt and Joe stood in the **Sapphire**'s wheelhouse, their eyes locked on a flat-screen monitor relaying the sonar signal that Stratton was watching downstairs. The image on the screen could only be the **Canberra Swift.**

"Tip of the cap to the folks at that Navy 'weather station,'" Kurt replied. "They took us right over the top of the ship."

"Scarily accurate," Joe agreed. "If they forecast a typhoon or a tsunami, I'm out of here."

Kurt grinned, his eyes still on the screen as the image of the ship unfurled in three dimensions. Viewed like this, it didn't look real, more like a toy at the bottom of a pool. "She's sitting upright. Like she's waiting for us."

"Waiting for somebody," Joe qualified.

Kurt agreed. "Good point."

It was just past six p.m. local time. Since getting the information from the Naha station, the **Sapphire** had run west at flank speed, cutting through the waves as the evening approached. They'd been going nearly nonstop since Rudi's initial message and, at this point, finding the ship brought a feeling of relief rather than celebration.

Kurt tilted back in his chair, allowing himself a moment of rest. But the job wasn't done. He turned to Winterburn, faithfully at the helm. "Take us southwest for a mile and a half and cut the engines. We'll drift back over the wreck with the current and deploy the submersible."

"Southwest for one-point-five," Winterburn replied, turning the wheel and adjusting the throttle.

"You don't want to wait till morning?" Joe asked.

"I'd rather get this done before anyone knows we're here."

As the **Sapphire** began to turn, Kurt and Joe left the bridge. They made their way down to the bottom deck, where a compartment that once held Jet Skis, inflatable water toys and a sixteen-foot runabout had been redesigned to hold a small submersible and the torpedo-shaped drones they'd used the day before to search the deeper water.

"What's the plan?" Joe asked, following Kurt into the deployment bay.

"Cut into the ship, go inside, place the charges,"

Kurt said. "We'll need the **Scarab** for that. I'll get it ready while you figure a way for me to carry the explosives."

Kurt climbed into the **Scarab,** a tough one-man sub that NUMA often used on short-endurance deep dives. It was nicknamed that because it looked something like an armored beetle, especially when its robot arms were extended like antennas. The small craft was maneuverable and fast for a submersible, an attribute that had come in handy more than once.

Sitting in the cramped cockpit with its bubble canopy over him, Kurt ran through a checklist and powered up the submarine's systems while Joe carefully placed a set of rectangular blocks into a locker at the front.

"Putting the bombs in your little bicycle basket," Joe said.

"What are we using?" Kurt asked, pulling a headset on and adjusting the microphone.

"I'm loading you up with fire sauce," Joe said.

Fire sauce was a two-stage compound explosive made of RDX, Research Department Explosive, and thermite, a material that burned at extremely high temperatures.

"Will that be enough to get through the protective casing?" Kurt asked.

"The thermite will go off first," Joe said. "That'll create a four-thousand-degree jet of flame, which will instantly burn a hole in the outer casing. A half second later the RDX will detonate, blasting the superheated gas down into the container, where it'll spread out with the shock wave. What isn't melted will be fractured into a thousand pieces. Trust me, the fire sauce will do the trick."

Kurt activated the sub's robotic arm to ensure it was operational. Playing with the controls, he manipulated the grasping hand into a thumbs-up to confirm he'd heard what Joe told him.

"Very funny."

Kurt switched the robotic hand into a flat, outward-facing palm. "High-five?"

Joe obliged, slapping the robotic hand and moving to the launch controls. Flipping a series of switches, he released the **Scarab** from the deck and powered up the conveyor that carried it to the outer compartment door.

At the edge of the compartment, it stopped on an elevator platform that swung out over the water.

"Going down," Joe announced.

The elevator's hydraulic system came on and the platform dropped slowly toward the water. As it dropped, waves began washing over the platform, rocking the sub. Eventually, the **Scarab** drifted off the platform.

Clear of the elevator, Kurt powered up the thrusters and kicked the rudder to the left, pulling away from the yacht.

Like all submarines, the **Scarab** was designed to operate best underwater, a fact that made it unstable and uncomfortable wallowing in the swells on the surface.

With all the lights on his board glowing green, Kurt opened the valve to let the air out of the ballast tanks. Air hissed out of the tanks, replaced by the water, and the **Scarab** grew heavy.

Kurt watched as the water climbed the plexiglass canopy until it covered the top. A moment later, the submersible broke free from the surface tension and began its long fall.

After adjusting the dive planes and setting his course, Kurt glanced upward. The **Sapphire** was a long, flat silhouette in a glowing orb of light. One that was dimming and shrinking rapidly.

Kurt tested the radio. "You guys reading me okay?"

"Loud and clear," Joe said. **"We show you reaching the** Swift **in six minutes. You want us to hold station?"**

One thing the **Sapphire** did not have was the fancy station-keeping thrusters that allowed large salvage vessels to hover over a spot on the ocean floor despite changing wind and currents.

"Negative," Kurt said. "Just let her drift until you get a couple miles past the wreck, then fire up the engines and loop around again for another pass."

"Will do," Joe said.

"And keep an eye out for trouble," Kurt added.

"Whoever put this ship down here is probably watching it like a hawk."

"According to Rudi, there isn't a vessel within thirty miles of our position."

"Ships can move," Kurt pointed out. "Keep your eyes on that radar."

CHAPTER 13

After buttoning up the launch bay, Joe returned to the bridge and relayed Kurt's orders. With the yacht drifting to the northeast, Winterburn took a seat and put his feet up for a few minutes.

While he rested, Joe looked over the radar screen and set the LiDAR system to small craft search mode. Set like this it would scan the horizon continuously, picking up what the radar might miss.

That done, he grabbed a pair of marine binoculars and made his way toward the ladder that would take him up to the flybridge.

"No faith in these fancy electronic systems?" Winterburn asked.

Joe shook his head. "I've fixed too many of them that were broken and adjusted plenty more that had blind spots. I'd rather confirm that we're alone with my own eyes."

Emerging onto the **Sapphire**'s upper deck, Joe

found the evening air pleasant and humid. The sun had just set but the twilight lingered.

Raising the binoculars, he scanned the horizon in every direction, just as sailors had done since the beginning of time. To the west, a thin strip of orange clung to the horizon, above which rested a layer best described as aquamarine. To the south, thunderheads from an isolated storm, pink where they caught the sunlight that still reached their crowns, gray, with flashes of blue, lower down. He found nothing of interest to the north. And back to the east, he saw only the deep indigo of the coming night and a smattering of stars.

Focusing the binoculars on a dark spot there, Joe found it was filled with a dozen points of light. Stars too dim to be seen without help.

It was a reminder, he told himself, that there was often more to this world than what could be seen with the naked eye.

Four hundred and sixty feet below, Kurt would have agreed with Joe's assessment. He was traveling in a pitch-black void of his own, punctuated by the occasional microbe or other speck of life reflecting the **Scarab**'s lights.

The depths of the ocean were as dark as space. Darker, actually, since seawater absorbed all light after a few hundred feet, while space allowed it to travel unimpeded for billions of light-years.

Only through the systems built into the **Scarab** did Kurt have any clue as to where he was, where the surface and the **Sapphire** lay and where he was supposed to find the sunken cargo ship.

Nearing the bottom, he slowed his descent. The lights of his craft lit up the seafloor and he continued west, keeping about thirty feet between himself and the bottom. It would take only a minute before his lights began to reflect off the side of the **Swift**'s hull.

"**Scarab** has arrived on-site," he said, speaking calmly into the microphone.

"**Roger that,**" Joe replied. "**How's it look?**"

"Like a giant placed it down here by hand. It's sitting even-keeled and the bow is undamaged."

"**Looking at the design schematics,**" Joe said, "**the best entry point is from the stern. Cut through the aft door and you'll hit the main deck. It's wide open. Like the interior of an auto ferry.**"

Adjusting the controls, Kurt turned to the left, heading along the side of the ship and toward the stern.

Resting on the sediment, with only five or six feet of the hull stuck down in the mud, the **Swift** sat up taller than it would have on the sea. At least fifteen feet of red-painted steel were visible that would normally be hidden below the waterline. Here and there, Kurt saw the ruptured plates where the explosives had gone off. They were evenly spaced and large enough to cause a sudden inflow of water while not destroying the entire hull. "Professional scuttle job," he announced. "Cleanly done."

"Find out who did it," Joe said. **"We could hire him next time we have to sink something."**

Easing past the tail end, Kurt swung around to face the stern. There he saw the first obstacle. "Aft end is damaged."

The hull plating was bent and crushed upward at the bottom, the aerodynamic shell broken and cracked where it had been fitted to the hull. It hung down in front of the wide cargo door.

"That looks pretty bad from up here," Joe said, watching the video feed.

"Looks worse in person," Kurt said. "She must have landed tail end first. Not sure I want to cut through this tangled mess. Where else can we go?"

"Stand by," Joe said. **"Let me look at the plans again."**

While Joe was taking a look at the ship's schematics up above, Kurt backed off to a point where he could float in neutral buoyancy and conserve power.

The current at the bottom was almost nonexistent. It made for little drift and clear waters. It also made things quiet enough that Kurt could hear his own breathing and heartbeat. And . . . something else.

Cocking an ear, he listened intently. A thrumming noise had arisen in the water around him. It was indistinct—but unmistakable. "Are you guys on the move already?"

"Negative," Joe said. "**Drifting on our back like a sea otter taking a nap.**"

Kurt held his breath and listened further. The sound was still there, slightly louder now.

"What about other traffic?"

"**We checked six ways from Sunday,**" Joe said. "**Nothing moving up here. Not for thirty miles.**"

Kurt's jaw tightened. If the sound of spinning propellers wasn't coming from a vessel on the surface, it had to be coming from something down below.

"I hate to say this," he said, "but we've got company."

CHAPTER 14

Sitting in the **Scarab,** Kurt reached over and shut off the exterior floodlights. In their place a strip of low-intensity LEDs came on. They put out just enough light to kiss the edge of the sunken vessel, making it appear like a shadow.

Drifting in the dark heightened Kurt's senses, but he still couldn't tell where the sound was coming from or how far away it might be. A fact that was more annoying than surprising.

Water had a way of playing tricks with acoustics. Not only did sound travel much faster through water than air—nearly three thousand miles an hour—it also traveled much farther. Under the right conditions, whale songs and other low-pitched noises could travel hundreds, even thousands, of miles, deflecting off layers of water with different temperatures and salinity, like a bowling ball traveling down a lane lined with walls instead of gutters.

And yet, the sounds he heard were higher pitched.

They had to be coming from water jets or small propellers spinning quickly close by, not large ones turning slowly in the distance.

Flipping another switch, Kurt activated a night vision setting on the monitor in front of him. On the screen, the shadow of the **Canberra Swift** resolved into a bright green monolith, the seawater in the background painted a dim gray world.

Kurt wasn't interested in the freighter anymore. He wanted to catch sight of anything that might be coming his way. Nudging the thrusters, he backed away from the wreck. And the farther back he went, the wider his view became. Soon he could see down both sides of the ship and over the top.

The new position offered better acoustics as well, the approaching sounds growing louder and more distinct.

"There's definitely something coming this way," he whispered.

"Maybe you should get out of there and return to the surface," Joe suggested.

"And miss finding out who's coming to dinner? Not on your life."

"I'm worried it may be on yours," Joe said. **"Whoever put that ship on the bottom has either been watching it or is coming to pick up the computers stashed inside. Either way, they're not going to be happy when they find you there."**

"In that case," Kurt said calmly, "I won't let them find me."

He killed the last strip of lights, plunging himself into total darkness except for the green hue of the screen and the colored pinpoints of the illuminated instruments around him.

"And what do you want us to do?" Joe asked.

"Keep drifting and watching for trouble."

Joe's acknowledgment was not all that clear, probably because he'd muttered it under his breath as a complaint. Neither one of them liked being passive and Joe was probably unhappy being stuck on the surface when things were about to get interesting down below.

Still adrift, Kurt made slight adjustments to his position to see if he could localize where the propeller sounds were coming from.

"Loudest to the west," he said, holding position.

He gazed out into the black water, seeing only the reflections from inside the **Scarab** on the glass. Turning his attention back to the night vision monitor, he saw a flicker of light appear. It slowly resolved into several oval-shaped orbs that spread out as they grew closer.

The light was still too dim to see with the unaided eye, but on the screen it was obvious that several submersibles were nearing the ship.

"New friends showing up at the dance," he told Joe.

"Did they spot you?"

"No," Kurt said. "I'm running dark, but I'm

sitting aft of the ship. Looks like they had the same idea we did, to cut into the wreck at the stern."

Backing off a little farther and trying not to stir up too much sediment in the process, Kurt watched as the dim points of light became visible, changing from a deep blue to a yellow-green hue as they moved closer.

Still relatively weak, the lights seemed as if they were far off in the distance, but at this point they were only a few hundred feet away.

Kurt switched off the thruster. If he could see them, it wouldn't be too long before they would be able to see him, something that got easier if there was a floating cloud of sediment around him.

"Contact with three . . . make that four submersibles," he told Joe. "One mini-sub about ninety feet in length and three smaller craft, possibly one-man vessels or ROVs."

"I don't suppose you see a Chinese or Russian flag on any of them?"

Kurt stared. He saw no identifying marks of any kind, but the machines looked familiar just the same. The larger vessel, which he'd referred to as a mini-sub, was about ninety feet long, but instead of being cylindrical like most submarines, it was long and rectangular. Wider than it was tall. It had a gray-white paint scheme and a raised orange docking collar. It reminded him of an older Chinese rescue sub.

The smaller units were definitely ROVs. And as he examined them more closely, he came to think he knew their origin as well. "No markings of any kind. But these little machines look like the Russian pipeline welders that we encountered last year in the Caspian Sea."

The Russians had spent decades building pipelines under the Baltic, Caspian and Black Seas. During that time, they'd come up with a plethora of specialized craft to work underwater, some guided by men and women in other ships, some completely autonomous. NUMA had studied every single design.

With a half dozen floodlights on the mini-sub pointed at the stern of the wreck, the "pipeline welders" took up position. Moments later, acetylene torches blazed as the three craft worked to cut through the hull.

"They're cutting on the stern now," Kurt said. "By the look of it, they want a space large enough to drive a bus through."

As the new arrivals worked on the ship, Kurt considered his options. The **Scarab** was maneuverable but not all that fast. The only weapon he had at his disposal was the explosive charges and they had to be placed by hand.

Even the **Hunley** had a spar, he thought.

The welders continued slicing the hull plating, cutting a line that would be the bottom edge of a wide rectangle and moving upward, creating two vertical incisions on either side. With only the top cut to make, one of the welders drifted out of the way, moving up over the top of the wreck and out of view, while the two remaining craft continued to work, moving slowly from each side cut toward the center.

When the last bit of steel was burned through, the welders pulled away. The rectangular section dropped, jamming itself against the lower edge of the incision for a second and then toppling over.

It fell in slow motion, clanging against the bottom of the keel and pancaking onto the seafloor.

The impact sent a huge cloud of marine sediment billowing outward like a dust storm. The surge hit the **Scarab,** obscuring Kurt's view and pushing him out of position.

He activated the thrusters to keep the submersible from tumbling. The last thing he needed was to end up mired in the sediment.

With the **Scarab** under control and the sediment dispersing, Kurt turned his attention back to the underwater heist. It had grown darker near the stern of the freighter. Only the mini-sub remained on station.

Kurt assumed the smaller machines had gone inside, but he saw no light coming from the dark interior of the cargo hold.

If they didn't go inside . . .

He never finished the thought. The **Scarab** was hit from behind. Kurt was nearly thrown from the seat as the impact pushed the submersible forward and down.

Kurt swore as he grabbed for the throttle, twisting it to full power and pulling back on the attitude controller. The **Scarab** pivoted upward, but it remained in the grasp of the attacking sub.

"What was that?" Joe asked, reacting to the curses. **"Didn't quite copy."**

"Bad words," Kurt grunted. "But completely appropriate for the situation."

The combined thrust of Kurt's sub and the pipeline welder caused the two craft to begin circling, like planets orbiting each other, in an accelerating death spiral.

They whipped around once, then twice. By the third pivot, Kurt could no longer tell which way was up or down.

He switched the floodlights on, hoping to blind whoever had attacked him, but the cockpit of the other vessel was empty. Now he understood the rationale behind such a reckless style of attack. His opponent was unmanned, probably being controlled remotely from the larger sub.

As the two craft continued to pinwheel, Kurt fought against the g-forces. He stretched to reach the controls that worked the robotic arm.

Raising the arm, he tried a karate chop, hoping to knock the attacking sub's pincer loose. Several blows did him no good.

"What's happening?" Joe asked.

"I'm being attacked by an ROV on steroids," Kurt replied. "Next time you build a robot arm, give it some muscle."

Kurt needed another plan. He retracted the arm and went back to the thrusters, shutting them down. The spinning slowed, but that was only a welcome side effect. Switching the controls to the opposite side, he went to full throttle again.

The **Scarab** lurched sideways and the pincer grasping it slipped a few inches. Kurt shut the power off again and flipped the thruster around the other way before applying full throttle once more.

The pincer slipped farther, its metal claws scraping over the hull.

"One more time at the village gate," Kurt said, yanking the controls back in the opposite direction.

This time the strain was too much. Though the pincer gripping his craft didn't let go, the arm itself bent. Kurt saw a diagonal crease appear in the aluminum of the frame. He moved the controls back the other way one more time and the metal arm failed, twisting and snapping off.

It hung on briefly, still attached by virtue of its wiring harness, but with a burst of power the **Scarab** pulled away, ripping the arm off as it went.

Inside the mini-sub, several figures watched this battle with concern. Closest to the action was the ROV operator, who had his eyes glued to the screen while his hands raced over a keyboard and worked a joystick.

Standing behind him, hunched over in the cramped space and alternating their attention between the jerky video image and the view out the clear window, were the two people in charge of the operation.

It was Yan-Li who had spotted the submersible lurking off the stern quarter. It was she who had ordered the ROV to move in under cover of the sediment cloud and attack the interloper. But as the two craft locked together and began to spin, she noticed something that gave her chills.

The pipeline welder's camera remained locked onto a single spot on the other submersible's hull. The image revealed a logo, a name and a flag.

"It's not a Chinese craft," the ROV operator said. "It's American."

She could see the American flag on the metal flank of the sub. The nearby logo was obscured by a shadow, but letters spelling out the name of the agency that operated the submersible were clearly visible.

The ROV operator saw them too. "N . . . U . . . M . . ."

"NUMA," she said before he could finish. A feeling swept over her, like the proverbial rug had just been pulled out from under her. She leaned closer to the screen, hoping to look inside the submarine and see who was at the controls. There wasn't enough light for her to see anything.

It didn't matter. She knew who it was, who it had to be.

Damn, she thought, how could they be here? They were a thousand miles away when she'd left them.

"Destroy it," the man standing beside her ordered. "Use the torch."

"No," she countered. "Run it into the seabed. Leave it damaged but intact."

"You're taking a huge risk," Callum said. "The kind that could get us all killed."

"Lucas would never take a life if it wasn't necessary," she said, invoking the name of her ex-husband, their former leader. "These men are explorers," she said, "not military."

Callum, sucking air between his teeth, nonetheless said nothing.

"Once we have the computers, it won't matter that they've seen us," she insisted. "We're unmarked. This submarine and the ROVs belong to Emmerson. There's nothing to connect this back to any of you."

On-screen, the tumbling battle continued until suddenly the view changed as the grasping arm of the ROV bent and snapped off.

"Well, that didn't work," Callum noted sarcastically. "Now what?"

"Send in the other ROVs," Yan ordered.

"This time use the torches," Callum insisted.

Yan stared at the screen. The NUMA submersible was not fleeing to the surface as she might have hoped.

The ROV operator glanced back at her for confirmation. Her heart seized as the choice weighed on her, while her lips chose not to form any words.

And then she thought of her children and what would happen if she failed Emmerson. She nodded to the ROV driver. "Send in the others. Use the torches."

Free of the first machine, Kurt stole a glance out into the dark to look for the other welders. He saw both of them coming for him, spread wide as if to prevent him from getting away. Looking behind him, he saw the machine with the broken arm still following him as well.

"Sapphire," Kurt called out over the comm system. "I have a problem. I'm outnumbered three to one. And these ROVs don't play well with others."

Up on the **Sapphire,** Joe was already moving. He wasn't the kind to sit around and be a spectator. Especially not when his best friend was in danger.

"Start the engines," he called out to Winterburn. "Take us back around."

Winterburn fired up the power plant and rolled

the wheel to starboard as the propellers dug into the sea. With froth churning at the stern, the **Sapphire** began to move. "Underway," he reported. "But what, exactly, are we going to do?"

Joe was already heading for the lower deck. He shouted back anyway. "We're going to even the odds."

CHAPTER 15

Racing toward the **Sapphire**'s deployment bay, Joe slid down a ladder and almost collided with Stratton.

"What's going on?" the sonar operator asked. "I'm picking up all kinds of chaos down there."

"Kurt's in a dogfight," Joe said. "We need to help him out. Come with me."

With Stratton following close behind, they ran the length of the ship, arriving at the deployment bay, from where Kurt had launched in the **Scarab** twenty minutes earlier.

Joe burst into the compartment and flipped on the lights. With the submersible gone, the bay was positively roomy. He scanned it for options.

To his left sat an ROV the size and shape of a large refrigerator, while over on the right the torpedo-shaped drones sat in their cradles on a rack, their pointed noses aiming toward the outer door, their stubby wings all but begging to take flight.

"Get the drones ready to launch," Joe said.

Stratton stepped over to the rack without a word, rushing to remove the safety straps that held them in place. "They're only at sixty percent."

"That should be fifty-nine percent more than we need," Joe said.

After unlocking and opening the bay door, Joe tapped the intercom button and called out to Winterburn. "Anything new from Kurt?"

"Just a few curse words used in new and imaginative ways. Sounds like he's still in the fight though."

"Tell him to keep ducking and weaving," Joe said.

The bay door locked in place. The gray horizon and dark sea appeared beyond. As the **Sapphire** picked up speed, the bow generated a wave that kept most of the swells away from the launch bay. But waves were never perfectly predictable and every third or fourth swell slapped at the ship, dousing the bay in a spray of foam.

Putting his hand on the elevator control, Joe realized they had a problem. The drones were designed to be launched in the same fashion as the **Scarab.** One at a time, using the platform, while the ship was in a stationary position.

Not only would that take far too long, considering the current circumstances, but stopping would leave them open to attack if the people Kurt was tangling with had the means to go after a ship on the surface.

Another wave hit the hull. This one clipped the edge of the compartment and sent a flood of sea-water into the bay. Stratton got soaked, and Joe was doused pretty well himself.

"New plan," Joe told Winterburn. "Turn the ship to starboard. Hard enough to give us a good lean. And keep us going that way until I tell you otherwise."

"Aye," Winterburn replied. **"Hang on."**

As Winterburn spun the wheel to the right, the twin rudders at the tail end of the **Sapphire** deflected until they were locked against the stops. The nose of the yacht swung around to the right, but because of the vessel's size and displacement it actually rolled in the opposite direction, leaning over like a mid-seventies Cadillac.

Joe's view turned from the rolling sea to the twilight sky. Balancing himself against a fifteen-degree list, he moved into position to help Stratton pull the safety straps from the drones.

"You're not going to try what I think you're going to try?" Stratton asked.

"It's the only way to join the fight before the final bell," Joe said.

"Oh . . . my beautiful drones," Stratton said, as if kissing a prize orchid good-bye.

With the full collection of cotter pins and cords in hand, Joe hit the intercom button. "How far around are we?"

"Fifteen seconds from a full circle," Winterburn said.

"When we hit the original course, swing the boat around in the opposite direction," Joe ordered. "Hard to port this time. As hard as you can."

Stratton grabbed a handhold, anticipating the sharp turn. Joe positioned himself to give the drones a shove. The yacht returned to its original heading, rolled level for a second or two and then answered the helm, snapping hard in the other direction.

The sudden change sent the drones sliding off their cradles and out the open door.

The drone on the top rack made it all the way to the water without a problem, flying off the rack and plunging through the surface like a kingfisher looking for a meal.

The second drone was right behind it, launching from the middle tier and clearing the lip of the compartment by a few inches.

The third drone wasn't as fortunate. It was too low on the rack to catch much air. It hit the deck and slid toward the opening like a penguin on a glacier. Just as it was about to topple into the sea, a passing wave barreled into the side of the ship, shoving the drone backward and flooding the compartment with a torrent of seawater.

Joe leapt over the drone as it swept underneath him, while Stratton dodged it by stepping nimbly to the side.

The drone slammed into the inner bulkhead, coming to a rest with its propeller spinning wildly.

Stratton flipped a switch on the control panel, cutting the power. The propeller jerked to a stop as the water drained away over the compartment's outer sill.

"Two out of three ain't bad," Joe said.

Stratton didn't share his joy. But considering what Joe planned to do next, he'd probably be happy that one of the drones had remained behind.

Kurt would have been thrilled with any help whatsoever. Anything to make it a fair fight. But with the robotic welders circling like mechanical sharks, he decided discretion was the better part of valor.

Feinting the **Scarab** one way and then rolling it in the opposite direction, he made a run for less crowded waters. It was not successful. The pipeline welders were smaller and faster. They tracked him like hounds on the trail of a wounded fox.

"Note to self," he said. "Build faster submersibles."

As the unmanned machines closed in, he turned hard, attempting to cut inside them.

The move worked well enough the first time, but they soon swarmed around him again. Dropping toward the seabed, he ran as close as possible to the sediment. Deploying the **Scarab**'s vacuum hose, he switched it on, sucking up large amounts of silt.

The sediment poured out the back end of the hose, creating a smoke screen of sorts. With the cloud billowing out behind him, Kurt lifted the **Scarab**'s nose and began a climb toward the surface.

Rising upward, he looked back. He could see the cloud illuminated from within by the lights of the pursuing ROVs. One of them emerged from it and continued moving in a straight trajectory. A second ROV peeled off to the right and began to circle back.

Try as he might, Kurt couldn't spot the third machine.

Suddenly, he remembered an old adage he'd heard from a fighter pilot. If you can't see the enemy, it means he's on your six.

He turned his craft to the left to get a better view, but it was too late. The impact from behind told him all he needed to know. The welder had locked onto the back end of the **Scarab.** The flashes of blue light could only be coming from the acetylene torch.

Checking an exterior camera view, he saw the torch cut into the thruster housing. This was bad news. If they destroyed the power plant, he was dead in the water. And probably dead in every other way as well.

He began the left-right dance again, but this attacker was clamped on much more securely than the first one had been. He considered using the explosives, but at such close range and such great depth, the explosion would probably just destroy both craft.

"**Sapphire,**" he called out. "Now would be a good time . . ."

The metal on the thruster housing began to melt and flake off. The only thing slowing the destruction was the flow of water across the **Scarab,** which was diluting the power of the cutting torch.

Kurt put the thruster to full and dove toward the bottom, picking up speed. It helped, but not much. Any second, something important would burn, melt or fail.

Sudden movement distracted Kurt for a second. A gray sharklike object flashed into view. He saw it for just a second before a new impact sent the **Scarab** tumbling.

"**Direct hit,**" Joe called out over the radio. "**Or as we like to say back at Dillon's Pub, bull's-eye.**"

Righting the **Scarab,** Kurt looked down through the nose bubble. He saw the welder sinking to the bottom, its hull bent and broken. The NUMA drone fared no better. It was still under power but circling downward, with a crushed nose and a missing wing.

"Best use of a million-dollar drone ever," Kurt called out. "How many more darts you have in that quiver of yours?"

"**Just one,**" Joe said. "**And we'll have to put Stratton in therapy once we use it.**"

"Tell him the bill's on me," Kurt said. "Now, see if you can keep these folks busy while I head back to the freighter."

"To do what?"

"Finish the job."

CHAPTER 16

Seizing the opportunity to act, Kurt switched off all the lights once more and raised the dive planes. He went up high, climbing to a spot where he could look down at the wreck. Its stern remained lit up by the floodlights, the name **Canberra Swift** still visible under the jagged cut. He could see the mini-sub holding station near the recently carved opening.

"Nice of you to leave a light on for me."

Glancing back farther aft of the ship, he saw the remaining NUMA drone was still chasing around the two pipeline welders. Exactly who was chasing whom was open to interpretation, but it mattered little to him. This was the moment.

He crossed over the mini-sub, perhaps a hundred feet above, then dropped straight down like a spider on its thread. He hoped to duck into the wreck without being noticed, but the floodlit area was too brightly illuminated for that hope to be realistic. He sped through the jagged opening and into the hull of the **Swift** with little doubt that he'd been seen.

A stark change took place the moment he crossed the threshold. The well-lit white hull plating of the ship's stern gave way to a dark cave-like environment. Kurt had no choice but to power up the lights again.

As they came on, he found himself in a cavernous space, every bit the size and shape of an aircraft carrier's hangar deck. As a roll on/roll off ship, the **Canberra** was originally designed to carry full-sized military equipment. Abrams tanks, F-16s and Chinook helicopters had to fit inside. There was plenty of space for the smaller **Scarab** to maneuver with ease.

"Now I know what it's like to be a little guppy in a big pond."

Moving deeper into the hold, he came across a pair of earthmovers many times larger than the **Scarab** and a trio of large cranes. All of them brand-new and covered in gleaming yellow paint. They sat on deflated tires, crushed by the pressure at this depth.

Initially, Kurt was surprised that the cargo had remained in place, but passing the earthmovers he spotted the monstrous chains they'd been tied down with remaining firmly in place.

Next, he came to a row of cargo containers. On the far side, he arrived at what the shipping line had called the temporary storage corral. Aiming the

Scarab's lights at the base of the wall, Kurt could see fresh welds and hastily erected footers designed to hold the wall in place.

A garbled communication came over the radio. "**. . . hurry, amigo,**" Joe's voice was telling him. "**. . . have left the fight . . . heading your way . . .**"

Lighting his own acetylene torch, Kurt began to cut into the partition. It turned out to be thin and light, whatever alloy it was made from melting at a relatively low temperature.

Moving up, down and over, he cut a square just large enough for the **Scarab.** Finishing the job, he rammed the weakened section and knocked it inward. It fell away, flattening out and gliding to the metal deck like a leaf falling from a tree, back and forth and then down.

He dropped down to the deck and scanned the compartment with the lights.

"**You inside?**" Joe asked.

"I am," Kurt said, looking around. "One small problem. There's nothing here."

CHAPTER 17

Kurt stared in utter surprise at the emptiness of the vast compartment.

More static came over the comm system and then Joe's voice. **"Make sure you're in the right spot. Amidships . . . station number three."**

Painted on the wall ahead of him was a large yellow 3. Impossible to miss. He was in the right spot, but the compartment was empty.

Or almost empty.

Several fish darted by and then an octopus. As they vanished, the **Scarab**'s lights brushed something else in the corner.

Kurt turned and focused on the ghastly sight of a drowned man floating in the water with his arms out and his dark hair wafting in the current. His skin was white but not yet bloated. He had marks on his hands and face where the fish had gnawed him, but no major damage had yet been done.

Kurt noted that he wasn't dressed in a crewman's

uniform and that one of his pant legs had been ripped off above the knee. Looking closer, Kurt saw a tourniquet had been strapped tight across the thigh. The lower leg was a mangled mess where a bullet had hit and shattered the bone. As Kurt watched, a small fish swam up and took a bite.

Fish . . .

Kurt had done enough wreck diving that the presence of fish swimming inside a sunken vessel didn't surprise him. But it should have. How had sea life, he wondered, already gotten into a compartment that he'd just cut his way into?

He turned back toward the opening he'd made. The view beyond was brightening, like a dark road at the approach of a semitruck.

He'd run out of time.

"This may be a mistake," he called out, "but I'm gonna blow the compartment anyway."

"Make sure you get out first," Joe suggested.

"That would be too easy."

Using the robot arm he set one of the magnetic charges against the floor and a second one against the wall.

He was setting the timer for sixty seconds just as one of the pipeline welders swept into the hold above him. It cruised overhead like a manta ray, turning and dropping toward the deck.

Kurt used the vertical thruster to maneuver the **Scarab** straight up, intending to exit the compartment and leave the welder behind. He reached the opening, turned toward the second ROV and slammed headlong into it.

The impact was enough to knock the **Scarab** back into the temporary hold.

"I really need to start listening to you," he called out to Joe.

Getting control of the craft, he maneuvered around in a circle. Now he had a real problem. One ROV was sitting in the opening, blocking his escape, while the other was moving in behind him.

The second ROV hit him with a glancing blow, knocking Kurt's submersible into the wall directly into one of the large 3s. The partition dented with a loud metallic clang but showed no signs of giving way.

Kurt turned the **Scarab** away from the dented wall, figuring he'd have to battering-ram his way out. When his lights painted the far side of the compartment, he saw both the answer to his earlier question about the sea life and the path to safety and escape.

Whoever had taken the computers had cut into the ship from the side, leaving a gaping hole that led out to the ocean beyond.

Kurt checked the timer. Twenty-six seconds, he saw. Plenty of time.

Charging forward, he raced through the gap and out into the open water, catching only a single

exterior light on the edge of the bulkhead. The fix-
ture broke off, bathing the scene with a brilliant
blue flash, but the **Scarab** never slowed.

Clear of the ship, Kurt pointed the nose upward
and opened all the compressed air valves, forcing
the water from the ballast tanks. Rising rapidly, he
used the submersible's engine to assist in propelling
him toward the surface.

Checking the timer, he saw the count fall into
single digits.

Nine . . . eight . . . seven . . .

Aboard the mini-sub, time had come to a standstill.

For Callum, it was the shock of seeing an empty
compartment that should have been filled with the
high-tech servers. "This can't be right," he said. But
he saw the numbers on the wall and he knew that
it was.

For Yan-Li, it was a different surprise. There,
floating in a watery grave, was her ex-husband. A
man she hadn't seen in years but who even in death
couldn't hide his handsome features.

"Lucas," she whispered.

"What?" Callum muttered.

"They killed him."

Callum now saw what she saw. The man who'd
saved his life, only to disappear when the ship went
down. He saw the face and the eyes. Saw the arms

and hair wafting in seawater. Lucas almost seemed to be beckoning.

A blinding flash filled the screen.

The shock wave billowed out through the gap in the side and at the stern. It hit the mini-sub on the flank, rolling the ninety-foot vessel hard over onto its side.

Callum was thrown from his spot, but Yan-Li remained standing, her hands locked on the console with a white-knuckled death grip. She continued to stare at the screen even though it had gone dark.

With their official leader frozen, Callum gave the order. "Get us out of here," he said. "As fast as possible."

Kurt felt the shock wave on his way to the surface. It shook the **Scarab** and rang his ears, but all things considered, was mostly contained within the hull of the freighter.

He had no doubt that the attacking ROVs were now gone. Nor did he doubt that the mini-sub was still around and unaffected. He surfaced a mile downrange and waited for the **Sapphire** to come pick him up.

Joe put the elevator platform in the water and brought the **Scarab** up and into the deployment bay. Kurt threw open the hatch and popped his head out.

"You all right?" Joe asked.

"Been worse," Kurt said. "Any sign of that sub?"

Joe shook his head. "The explosion pretty much scrambled the sonar picture," he said. "Stratton tried to follow it with the surviving drone, but it pulled away. Too fast to keep up with. Think they'll give us any more trouble?"

"Not at the moment," Kurt said. "They saw what we saw, an empty cargo hold. No point sticking around when the prize you're after has been hauled off by someone else. The question is, who took it?"

"Not just who," Joe replied, "but how? We found this ship in record time," he pointed out. "Whoever you just fought with down there found it just as quickly. So, how did someone beat both of us to it?"

As usual, Joe spoke volumes with just a few words. Kurt had no idea how to answer that question, but something told him the dead man, shot and drowned in the cargo hold of the freighter, had something to do with it.

CHAPTER 18

VICTORIA HARBOUR, HONG KONG

A pair of tugs pushed a gray dredging barge along the channel in the outer section of Victoria Harbour. The barge was little more than a giant hopper, designed to be filled with dredged sediment. But at the moment, it held a different cargo—the rectangular mini-sub and the crew that had commanded her.

The sub rested in the bowels of the barge, covered by tarps to keep it from prying eyes. Yan-Li and the other members of the crew stood beside it, wondering about their future.

There was little visibility on that front, she thought. And little visibility in real life. Looking around, she could see only the gray metal walls of the hopper and a rectangular swath of sky directly above.

"Feels like a prison," she said.

Still, even with the limited view, she knew where

she was. She could hear the horns of various ships, the seagulls calling overhead, the clamor of heavy cargoes being loaded and unloaded on the docks.

"Prison might be better than what Emmerson will do to us," one of the men suggested.

The dark mood was omnipresent. They'd failed Emmerson twice. They'd seen his response to the first disappointment, so they rightly feared what might happen now.

"I have to go see him," she told them. "He has my children. But if you like, I can go alone. You men want to escape, this is probably your best chance."

They looked at one another in the silent gloom. Then Callum spoke for them. "Where would we go that Emmerson couldn't find us?"

He had a point.

"Running is still better than dying," she said.

He laughed cynically. "Haven't run much in your life, have you?"

She shook her head.

"Trust me, it's not that much better. I ran all my life until Lucas took me on. I owe him. Every one of us owes him. Not four days ago, he saved my life. It wasn't the first time. For that, I'll stay with you."

A couple others nodded. One voiced his agreement.

Yan was almost overwhelmed by this. She felt so alone. Torn between anger and grief for her ex-husband and fear for her children. Her lasting thought was that Lucas had been nothing but a con man and a criminal and that he'd somehow burdened her even in death. It never dawned on her that he might have had his own code of honor.

"You talk about him like he was an honorable man," she said.

"He taught us to steal without killing, to act without hate," Callum continued. "What does that tell you? When Zho stabbed a security guard on one of our jobs, Lucas took the injured man with us and found a doctor to operate on him and save his life. When one of our brothers died on a job that went bad, Lucas got money to his family. He made sure they were taken care of."

"Wish he'd shown our children the same level of compassion," she said bitterly.

"He was what he was," Callum said.

The barge shook as the tugs pushed it up against a concrete jetty. Yan-Li turned away from Callum, fighting back the tears that were welling up in her eyes.

CHAPTER 19

GOVERNMENT HOUSE, THE PEAK

Two hours later, she and Callum were guests at Kinnard Emmerson's compound in the hills above the city. The historic home sat cliffside in an area known as the Peak, where the cool mountain breeze caressed the slopes and one could look down at the heat and the steam of the city.

The Peak had been the place to live ever since the British first occupied Hong Kong back in 1842. Over the years, various governors and power players had built summer homes up there. The climate was one reason, but there was a psychological advantage to it as well.

Staring down at the inhabitants of the city from on high, one couldn't help but feel a sense of power and superiority. While those looking up at the big houses from below never doubted just who ruled whom.

Yan-Li recalled her ex-husband promising to buy their family a place up on the Peak one day. It was a silly dream, but it was part of his desire to be the one gazing patronizingly downward instead of enviously upward.

Escorted by two of Emmerson's men, Yan was brought around the side of the home and out onto a spacious veranda at the back. In one corner she passed, hidden from everything else, was a wire cage the size of a large suitcase. Inside were a dozen or more rats. Some alive. Others dead and half eaten.

The sight surprised and sickened her at the same time. "Rats in a cage," she said. "Cruelty seems to be your stock-in-trade."

He was unmoved. "Fond of rodents, are you?"

"Not really," she said. "But I prefer to deal with them humanely."

"Ahh," he said in a mocking tone. "Yes, I suppose I could poison them and let them die, convulsing in pain. Or perhaps smash them in spring-loaded traps that rarely kill them instantly, but I prefer to give them a sporting chance. And it gives the men a bit of light entertainment at the same time."

He rattled the cage and sent the rodents scrambling.

"See how some of them are marked with dye?" he said. "While others have their ears clipped? Wagers have been placed to see which one will survive the longest."

As she expected, more cruelty.

"It's a surprisingly slow process," he assured her. "When we first put them in the cage, they do all they can to get along. They even work together looking for ways out and searching for water or food. After several days, they become withdrawn. After a few more, they turn hostile and begin attacking one another, fighting to the death and resorting to cannibalism."

He shook the cage again and laughed at the sport of it.

"Eventually," he explained, "only one of the animals is left alive. And the wagers are paid."

"And you release the survivor?"

"Of course," he said. "When you're in my business, you become a big fan of parole."

The men around him laughed. Yan-Li tried not to cry. She doubted any of the rats were ever released just as she doubted he'd ever release her or her family.

They left the caged rats and walked across the veranda to a glass railing. As a servant brought Emmerson a tumbler filled with gin and tonic, Yan gazed over the railing. The godlike view awed her, as she could see half the city below her and yet she would have felt safer down below, wrapped in the embrace of the towering buildings and busy streets.

Whatever Lucas had wanted in his hilltop dream she didn't share. She was a creature of the lowlands, the dominated rather than the powerful. She knew this to be true.

With a deep breath, she turned Emmerson's way. "Why have you brought me here?" she asked. "You've seen the videos from the ROVs, you know the computers were already gone. None of that can be blamed on us."

Emmerson tilted his head. "I'll be the judge of who can be blamed for what. And let me be clear. Despite my calm demeanor, my anger is barely held in check. You're here because I want to know about the Americans. Did they retrieve the cargo?"

"I don't think so," she said.

"You don't think so?"

"I can't prove it one way or another," she said desperately.

"So, make your best argument," Emmerson demanded. "Information is what matters. Data is the key. Facts. What you know, what you don't know. These are the things that count. Not vague assumptions or conclusions."

She felt light-headed and weak. She told herself she was not made for this. But if she didn't speak, no one would. "If the Americans had recovered the servers, there would be no reason for them to risk life and limb fighting with our ROVs," she began. "They could have surfaced and escaped with ease. If they had the servers, there would have been no reason for the pilot of that submersible to enter the wreck and set off explosive charges. The evidence suggests they were as surprised by the disappearance of the servers as we were. These facts tell us the Americans don't have them."

"Better," Emmerson said. "What else?"

Emboldened, she spoke further. "Lucas was murdered on that ship. He'd been shot twice and drowned. You've seen the video evidence of that too. That fact proves he did not betray you. Therefore, neither I nor my children remain in your debt. You should release us immediately."

The eyebrows went up, the gin and tonic came up to his lips for a moment. "And you were doing so well." He took a sip.

"Have I misstated anything?"

"You conflate one truth with another," Emmerson said. "Your ex-husband did not betray me. Yes, apparently this is true. But his debt is not erased. He was paid to deliver a cargo, which I still do not have. You will continue to lead my effort to recover these machines until I have them. If you fail, your children will pay the debt by working a lifetime in my service."

Her hand balled into a fist with an instinct so pure it could barely be controlled. She willed herself not to do anything foolish. "I don't see how I can be of further help," she said stiffly. "My skills no longer fit what you require."

Emmerson placed the drink down and stepped

toward her. "You're capable of more than you give yourself credit for. Most people are. Take me, for instance. I'm the bastard son of a British diplomat. Abandoned twice. First, when I was left to the streets. And again when the Crown turned the colony back over to the Chinese."

"Not only that," he added, "they advised me not to return home." He shrugged. "I admit, I abused the small amount of patronage I was able to claim. But really, who wouldn't, given my position."

Kinnard Emmerson laughed as he spoke. Laughter directed inward at some private joke for which only he knew the punch line.

Yan-Li found it impossible to feel sorry for him. "You seem to have done well enough."

"Only because I exceeded my station," he insisted. "Only because I learned the most important lesson in life, the value of information, which I covet and hoard like the finest platinum and gold."

She listened intently.

"I possess what they cannot allow to be made public," he continued. "The truth about secret dealings, the pictures and videos of many who suffer at the hands of the government and many more who suffer from their own vices and predilections. These weapons are more potent than any gun or bomb. With information like this in one's possession, there is no need to fight. Indeed, some enemies will end up praying for your health—lest the poison pill of truth come out upon your death. So let me sum up—weapons make you dangerous, information makes you untouchable."

Yan listened, convinced that he was intoxicated on gin and tonic or power or both. The bravado had loosened his tongue.

"I was able to collect all this information," Emmerson said, "because no one believed I was capable of such grand things. Now I live here, in the house of the governor. So who is the bastard now?"

She didn't know how to respond. The man was grandiose and full of himself. Perhaps fawning would be helpful, but she couldn't bring herself to do it.

"Not everyone can transcend her station," she said.

"You'll adapt," he insisted. "Or, like all creatures that fail to do so, you'll die."

She was ready for the word games to end. She kept her next question simple. "What is it you want me to do?"

"I'm sending you to Taiwan," he said. "As it happens, I've learned two additional facts since you returned from your mission. One of great interest to me. The other should be of great interest to you."

"I'm listening," she said.

"I've done some digging since you reported the computers missing from the ship. It turns out a competitor of ours learned of my plan, waited for Lucas to act and stole the machines out from under us."

As Yan-Li listened to him she found herself growing angry. Forcing her to explain her supposed failure at the wreck was just another game to him, just more sport, like torturing the trapped rats. His silken words and civilized tone could no longer cover up the truth that he was barbaric and cruel.

She found she couldn't control her tongue. "How is it you missed the actions of a competitor if you possess so many facts?"

He backhanded her across the face. Yan was knocked to the ground.

She looked up to see not only an angry man but an angry man who seemed pleased to have struck a blow.

"We all have competition," he said in a low voice. "In my case, a devious, unprincipled group known as CIPHER."

Her cheek throbbed. Her lip bled. But the blow seemed to clear some mental cobwebs. Any doubt that she was going to have to fight her way out of this situation vanished.

"I'm sorry," she said.

"You're forgiven," he replied. "This time."

She got back to her feet. "CIPHER?" she asked cautiously. "What are they . . . a gang? Like the triads?"

"More modern," he said. "Cybercriminals. Hacking and extortion mostly."

She dabbed at her bleeding lip. "What am I supposed to do against a group like that?"

"You can be the figure they underestimate," he said. "You see, they plan to hold an auction where they'll be selling my computers to the highest bidder. You will attend this auction."

"And do what?" she asked. "Surely you're not going to purchase the computers from the people who stole them from you?"

Her words came quickly and with an edge to them. The idea that someone would get rich off murdering her husband was like rubbing salt in the wound. If anything, she hoped Emmerson might exact revenge on the men who'd murdered Lucas.

"No," Emmerson said. "I'm going to make them pay for what they did, preferably in blood. But to do that I need to get someone inside the room. My people are known to them, you're not. You're an enigma. And with a little manipulation of the facts, I can create a false persona for you that will have them drooling to invite you in."

"And then?"

"And then I will put a metaphorical bullet through CIPHER's collective heart while you get the opportunity to put a real bullet in the man who killed your husband. A detestable human being who calls himself Degra."

Yan-Li froze, not because she was gripped with fear but because the idea of vengeance greatly appealed to her. She felt a wave of heat flush across her skin, a surge of adrenaline. "You're saying this man killed Lucas?"

"It was on his orders."

That made it no better. She tried to remain in control. "Revenge is just a bitter fantasy," she said. "It holds nothing for me."

"I find it delectable," Emmerson replied with a shrug. "At any rate, you're going to Taiwan, where you'll be the instrument I use to inflict pain on CIPHER. How much pleasure you take from the act? Well . . . that's really up to you."

CHAPTER 20

There had always been a certain hierarchy at the meetings that took place in Washington, D.C., especially when they involved intelligence agencies or higher-level figures in the executive branch.

If the CIA invited someone to Langley, it meant they felt like they were in control of the situation and were willing to dole out a tiny piece of compartmentalized information they felt they could safely share.

If they came knocking on another agency's door—as Elliot Harner had on NUMA's five days earlier—it meant something had slipped and the agency was looking for answers without much regard to where those answers came from.

And when some important figure invited various parties to their home or a casual social function, it usually meant things had gone off the rails and everyone was scrambling to grab some small lever of control.

A surprise request to attend a hastily arranged brunch at Anna Biel's Maryland home told Rudi things had indeed gone off the rails.

Escorted through the breezeway to the garden behind the house, he found two acres surrounded by twelve-foot ivy-covered brick walls. Colorful flowers sprouted from raised beds around a gazebo in the center of the lawn. A small group of guests were sitting around a wrought iron table painted a gleaming white.

Anna got up and met Rudi halfway. "Mimosa or Bloody Mary?"

Elliot Harner and another member of the CIA were already sipping maroon-colored cocktails.

"I haven't had my vitamin C yet," Rudi replied.

"Mimosa it is."

A pitcher filled with a swirling yellow liquid was produced. Rudi's glass was filled to the top. He took a sip.

"How is it?"

"A little tart," he admitted.

She shrugged. "It's still the sweetest thing you'll taste this morning. Find yourself a chair."

Rudi took a seat and leaned back in the sun, waiting for their host to take her place. "What gives?" he asked once she'd sat down.

"Good news and bad," she said. "Turns out your man Austin was right. The dead body in the cargo hold was an important clue. We've identified him as Lucas Teng, the leader of a pirate group known as the Water Rats. He's a known associate of Kinnard Emmerson, the head of a ruthless Hong Kong–based criminal organization. Emmerson is a man who's anything but subtle; his family motto is **Semper magis.** Always more."

"You think Lucas Teng was hijacking the **Swift** to deliver the computers to Emmerson," Rudi surmised. "So what happened, why'd he end up shot and drowning on a sinking ship?"

"Because the worm has a way of turning," she told him with a grin. "For the last several months, Emmerson has been at odds with another group called CIPHER. The CIA has intel suggesting CIPHER got someone into position to double-cross Lucas. Killing him and taking possession of the ship and, we assume, the computers."

"So, the Hydro-Com servers aren't in Emmerson's hands, they're with this group CIPHER," Rudi said. "Is that a good thing or a bad thing?"

"Six of one," she replied, before turning it over to Elliot Harner.

Harner leaned forward, pulling a pair of sunglasses from his face. "The thing is," he began, "we have no idea what Emmerson planned to do with the Vector units, but CIPHER's intentions are clear.

They've broadcast info to a wide array of players, suggesting they'd be willing to sell the computers to the highest bidder."

Bad news, Rudi thought, but not completely unexpected. "It was only a matter of time before word got out. Who are they bringing to the table?"

Harner went down a list of the usual suspects. "Russia, China, North Korea, Iran," he said. "Not to mention a couple anonymous bidders."

"Sounds like quite an operation," Rudi said, understanding the sour mood around the table. "Bad enough to lose these machines to one competitor, worse if they end up in the hands of three or four. That said, I've never heard of CIPHER before. Who, exactly, are they?"

The other man at the table spoke up. "Arthur Hicks," he said, announcing his name. "U.S. Cyber Command."

Rudi raised his glass.

"CIPHER is a hacker group based in Southeast Asia," Hicks began. "They're known mostly for extortion and other internet-based criminal enterprises. They've also been known to steal technology and hack into accounts filled with cryptocurrency. Last winter, they shut down several gas and electric utilities in Europe, demanding ransom payments to release the hacked systems. We see them as opportunists, mostly, working their scams anywhere technology intersects with crime."

The NSA director jumped back in. "The odd thing is, they're not usually connected with hardware theft. They prefer to work on the digital side. Codes and digital files are easier to steal and transfer than physical objects."

"Are they a front for someone else?" Rudi asked.

"We don't think so," Hicks replied. "More likely, they saw an opportunity to strike another blow in this feud with Emmerson and they took it. Regardless, we can't let them sell the technology to any of the groups we just mentioned."

Rudi got the picture. It was the same as earlier, except with more detail and a better idea of how bad the disaster was going to be if things didn't get straightened out.

"You said these guys at CIPHER are into digital theft. Sunil Pradi told us the computers wouldn't be much good to anyone without the source code for the operating system."

"And that's partly where you come in," Anna said, taking over the conversation once more. "We want NUMA to link in with Hydro-Com. Shouldn't be too hard, as their CEO seemed to take a liking to your IT director, Hiram Yaeger."

"They talk the same language," Rudi noted. "And by that, I mean ones and zeros."

"We'd like to get them talking that language in person," she replied. "Have Yaeger fly out to San Francisco so he can poke around the security precautions at Hydro-Com. Have him act as a fresh set of eyes to see if there's a weakness someone could exploit."

"Why not send someone from Langley or Cyber Command?"

She looked at him as if the question answered itself. "No one likes the CIA or NSA looking into their computer systems. Too afraid we'll steal something or leave some type of Trojan horse behind."

Rudi laughed. "You said that's partly where NUMA comes in. What else do you need?"

Before she replied, Anna looked over at Elliot Harner for one last confirmation. He nodded. Whatever it was, it had already been arranged.

She looked Rudi's way again. "How good are your men?" she asked. "Austin and Zavala. Are they as capable as they look on paper?"

"Better," Rudi insisted. "Why?"

She didn't hesitate any further. "Because we'd like to send them into CIPHER's lair as our representatives."

Now Rudi understood. For the moment, he remained silent.

"Obviously, it's a hell of a risk," she added. "Do you think it's one they'd be willing to take? More importantly, do you think they'd stand much chance of success?"

"I'll let Kurt and Joe answer the first question," Rudi said. "As for the second, if they agree to go in, you can plan on them coming out the other side with everything you asked for and a stuffed bear from the gift shop to boot."

She nodded respectfully and turned to Harner. "Pull your strings," she said. "Get us an invite to the dance. And let's hope Austin and Zavala pick up more than a stuffed bear on their way out the door."

CHAPTER 21

NORTHERN CALIFORNIA

Hiram Yaeger arrived in California aboard a Gulfstream G700 owned by Hydro-Com. The eighty-million-dollar aircraft brought him across the country in speed and style, cutting over an hour off the trip in comparison to a nonstop commercial flight.

It touched down at Moffett Field, south of San Francisco. In comparison to the bustling commercial hubs at San Francisco and Oakland International, Moffett looked positively deserted. There were no glitzy terminals or fleets of gleaming aircraft from nations around the world, just a few military planes in unassuming gray, some unpainted whitetails parked here and there and a giant building that looked like an upside-down bathtub.

"What in the world is that?" a woman seated across from Hiram asked.

Gamay Trout and her husband Paul had been sent along with Hiram as part of the team. Though he didn't object to the company, Hiram wondered what they would do while on-site.

"That's Hangar 1," Yaeger said. "It was built in the thirties to house airships like the USS **Macon.** NASA uses it now."

Gamay's interest waned rapidly. She brushed her red-wine-colored hair back, craning her neck to see past the offending building. "A blimp hangar is not exactly sightseeing material. Was hoping to see the Transamerica Pyramid, Nob Hill or the Golden Gate Bridge on our way in."

"They're a long way from here," Yaeger explained. "We're at the south end of the bay. Closer to Silicon Valley."

"There goes your trip to Fisherman's Wharf," her husband said.

Paul sat in a row of his own. He had his feet stretched out into the middle of the aisle. Even then, his six-foot-eight frame was folded into a seat far too small for a man his size.

"Been there, done that," Gamay said. "I'm much more interested in Muir Woods and the old-growth redwoods. Or," she added with a grin, "a side trip to Sonoma."

Yaeger cleared his throat. "Might want to focus on the task at hand. We have hours and hours of looking at security protocols ahead of us. Just testing their firewall system is going to take half the day."

"For you," Gamay said. "I can barely operate my laptop without calling for technical support. And Paul . . ."

"I'm still using a Commodore 64," Paul said, jokingly recalling the first computer he'd ever owned.

"Very funny," Yaeger replied. He knew they were joking. But in all honesty, it made little sense for them to be along for the ride. Gamay was a marine biologist and Paul was a geologist with expertise in deep-sea rock formations and plate tectonics. They usually spent their time out in the field, often assisting Kurt and Joe in some far-flung region of the earth. "Why did Rudi send you with me, again?"

"To keep you company," Gamay said. "And to keep the venture capitalists from stealing you away."

Paul concurred. "Should anyone utter the words **stock options** or **advisory shares,** we've been authorized to sedate you and transport you out of state."

Yaeger had to laugh, a bit of pride welling up inside. He was something of an iconoclast in the computing world. A brilliant designer of both hardware and software, he had over a hundred patents to his name. At least once a month he got a call from a headhunter or a Silicon Valley firm looking to lure him away. He thought they might have learned by now that he wasn't leaving NUMA, but they kept trying.

Truth was he had no reason to leave. Every day he earned royalties from design features in common use. He had enough money in the bank to last ten lifetimes even if he spent like a drunken sailor. Lusting for more held little interest for him, while working for NUMA gave him something additional wealth couldn't match—a challenge.

"The only company you might lose me to is Harley-Davidson," he said. "Or possibly . . . Ben & Jerry's."

Picking up a car, they drove ten miles south to the Hydro-Com design center. From a distance, the building was nothing special, but up close it turned out to be an architectural masterpiece. The curving, low-profile compound was constructed of natural stone, tinted glass and purposely rusted steel. The property was crisscrossed with man-made canals, with fountains spouting in various spots, and waterfalls cascading off the roof of the building itself.

After parking in the shade of some well-manicured paloverde trees, they walked to the main entrance on a path that took them up across a canal on a cantilevered bridge. From the center of the bridge the compound resembled an underwater city emerging from the sea.

"A little bit of Atlantis in California," Gamay said.

"These companies spend a lot of money on appearances," Yaeger replied, sounding grumpy.

Sunil Pradi had just come out the front door to greet them as Yaeger spoke these words. He'd overheard him. "Actually," he said, "the water flowing across the roof keeps the temperature in the buildings down in the summer and up in the winter. It cuts our cooling and heating costs. And since sunlight penetrates shallow water, we've placed solar panels beneath the surface to generate electrical power. The cooling effect of the water makes them more efficient. On a sunny day, we make twice the electricity we consume. And in the winter, the water keeps our buildings warm and the humidity up."

"Green," Gamay said.

"Positively chlorophyllous," Pradi replied with a smile.

Yaeger nodded. He admired ingenuity as much as any other trait. "Very clever," he said.

Pradi grinned at the compliment. "If you like this trick, wait till you see our aquarium."

They followed him inside the building, passing through two security checkpoints. The first included metal detectors and required them to relinquish their cell phones and all other electronics. The second was a millimeter wave scanner like those used at airports.

"We use this to make sure no one is smuggling zip drives or other data storage devices in or out of the building," Pradi said.

"What about hacking?" Yaeger asked.

"Our most sensitive systems are protected by an air gap."

"Air gap?" Paul asked.

"It means they're physically disconnected from the internet and the rest of the computing world."

"Like your old Commodore 64," Yaeger joked.

"What about Wi-Fi?" Gamay asked.

"No Wi-Fi or cellular in here," Pradi said. "There are jammers set up around the building. And the rusted metal and water you saw creates an additional barrier, similar to what's known as a Faraday cage. No electronic signals can get in or out of the building."

"How do your systems communicate with one another?"

"Fiber-optic cables," Pradi said. "More efficient and more secure than radio waves."

Hiram nodded. "At first blush, your security seems formidable."

Pradi handed them brightly colored badges. "I assure you, it is," he said. "Follow me. I'll show you more."

They moved down a hallway, the walls lined with industry awards and blowups of flattering magazine covers proclaiming Hydro-Com as the next big thing. At the far end, they stepped onto an escalator that was moving downward in a curving spiral.

"Another neat trick," Paul said.

"Normal escalators take up too much space."

As Hiram was riding in a slowly descending circle on the only spiral escalator he'd ever seen, the sense that this was a start-up company with billions to spend on appearances returned to him, but this time he kept the thought to himself.

Gamay felt otherwise. Looking around at the

high-tech workstations and glass-walled offices, she was thoroughly impressed. "Feels like I'm in an electronic version of Willy Wonka's chocolate factory."

On the lower level, they made their way into a sprawling lab. Technicians inside were busy constructing the prototype of some new machine using lasers and other devices. On the far side of the lab stood a wall of blue-tinted glass. It allowed in a soothing aquamarine light, while holding back the waters of a million-gallon pool.

Unlike the pools at NASA, which were wide and relatively shallow, this one was a tall cylinder, with the surface fifty feet above the lab level and its bottom another thirty feet below.

As everyone's attention turned inexorably to the pool, a diver in a hard suit descended from above.

Gamay broke the silence. "When you said aquarium, I thought you might mean a large tropical fish tank."

"No fish," Pradi said. "Just men and machines. Inside you'll see a mock-up of our entire system."

They moved closer, looking through the glass wall at the diver in the hard suit. He passed their level, heading lower, while a trail of bubbles floated upward from his regulator.

Thirty feet down sat an octagonal pressurized cylinder, identical to those that had been on the **Swift.**

"You see the K-shaped tool he's carrying?" Pradi asked. "That device will link the fiber-optic cable to the server. Once applied in the right position, it does everything automatically. With this device, a job that used to take hours can be done in twenty minutes."

"Why is the diver in a hard suit?" Paul asked. "The water isn't that deep."

"It's a training exercise," Pradi explained. "Our staff will need to use hard suits in the real world because the servers will be placed at much greater depth. That being the case, it's best that they practice using them from day one."

"Don't your other employees get distracted by the goings-on?" Gamay asked.

"Not at all," Pradi boasted. "It's a very calming backdrop. We've seen a significant increase in productivity and reported well-being since the day we filled the tank."

Gamay leaned close to Hiram. "You won't get that at Ben & Jerry's."

Yaeger smiled. "Free tubs of rocky road will do the same thing."

As Gamay laughed and Yaeger turned toward the lab beside them, Paul stepped closer to the tank, drawn in by the live training session. He looked upward toward the dappled surface and down toward the diver nearing the bottom. He saw the octagonal mock-up of the server and the snaking fiber-optic cables, wrapped in their thick rubber coatings.

The diver reached the bottom, moved himself into position and began aligning the K-shaped tool Pradi had spoken about.

Despite the simplicity Pradi had boasted of, the diver seemed to be having some difficulty. After several attempts he dropped the tool altogether. Instead of picking it up, he jerked backward and over onto his side. He shook one way and another like a landed fish.

"Something's wrong," Paul said.

"What?"

The others had turned their attention elsewhere.

"Something's gone wrong in there," Paul insisted, getting the CEO's attention. "Your diver is in trouble."

CHAPTER 22

Paul's words cut through the room and got everyone's attention. Pradi, Gamay and Hiram all gathered at the wall of glass, straining to see what Paul had noticed.

Paul felt them crowd in beside him but never took his eyes off the diver, who had now turned over on his side and was rocking as the spasms of his body affected the controls of the suit.

The CEO stared in shock. "What's happening to him?"

"Has to be some kind of seizure," Paul replied.

As other employees in the lab became aware of what was happening, they rushed to the glass.

"Do you have a safety diver?" Paul asked.

"Yes, of course," Pradi said.

"Get him in the water."

Even as Paul spoke, a splash broke the surface up above. The safety diver, clad in a normal wetsuit with a small tank on his back, had pulled his mask on and dropped backward into the tank.

He twisted around and aimed himself for the bottom, venting air from his buoyancy compensator and kicking hard with his fins.

As this took place in front of them, a man with straw-blond hair rushed up to them. "We should call nine-one-one," he said. "There's no medic here today."

"Yes," Pradi said. "Of course. Call immediately."

As the blond man grabbed the nearest phone, the safety diver descended in front of the audience. He was halfway down and still heading for the bottom, but to Paul his movements seemed almost slow and lazy. The powerful leg kicks he'd begun with were becoming weaker and less pronounced. His dive angle was no longer vertical.

Soon the diver's legs stopped altogether and his arms made only feeble movements. He flattened out and began drifting across the tank.

"What's happening to him?"

There was no way to know. "This is no accident," Gamay said.

"We need to get up there," Paul said.

"The stairs," Pradi said, pointing to a door off to their left. "That's the fastest way."

Paul took off running with Gamay following right after him. They pushed the door open and raced up three flights, with Paul taking them two steps at a time.

Bursting through the door at the top level, Paul emerged into a world of chaos on the pool deck beside the tank. Several people were staring down into the water, with one man trying to communicate with the divers using a headset. Beside them, another man was heaving an oxygen cylinder up onto the backup diver's shoulders.

"No," Paul said. "It might be the air in the tanks. It may have been tampered with."

"Who are you?" the diver asked. "And what are you talking about?"

"Both divers went down without a problem," Paul said. "Both ended up with a problem. It has to be the air."

The backup diver had the regulator in his hand. He was about to take a test breath. He held it away from his face and vented some of the gas. It was colorless and odorless like oxygen should be, but an odd white residue appeared on the mouthpiece as the gas streamed out. "What in the world . . ."

They didn't have time to figure out what it was, but no one wanted to touch it.

Paul kicked off his shoes and got rid of his NUMA windbreaker. He stepped onto the deployment shelf, a section of the deck that sat several inches below the surface level like a very wide first step of a swimming pool. Gamay stepped in beside him.

"I'll go for the guy in the hard suit," Paul said.

"I'll get the safety diver," Gamay said.

Without another word, Paul grabbed a spare

weight belt and dove headfirst into the tank. Kicking hard and aiming himself straight down, he plunged toward the bottom.

The tank had a maximum depth of eighty-five feet and Paul felt every bit of it as the pressure built in his ears. He cleared them twice and then once more, but he had to do it carefully because he would need every bit of oxygen his lungs could hold.

Having spent years snorkeling and scuba diving, Paul was well aware of how fast the pressure would build and exactly what he would need to do when he reached the bottom. His only mistake was not grabbing a mask or pair of goggles. His unshielded eyes' blurred view raised the level of difficulty.

He found the diver in the hard suit easily enough—though the man looked like a beige rock on the bottom of the tank until Paul drew close— the problem was finding the buoyancy control for the suit.

Dropping the weight belt that had helped him descend so quickly, Paul grabbed on to the diver's suit. Lifting him was easy enough, but swimming to the surface while dragging the man would be impossible. The suit was set to negative buoyancy. It would be like swimming to the surface with a fifty-pound barbell strapped to one's back.

Squinting in hopes of sharpening his vision, Paul saw a trio of extruded symbols on the front of the chest plate. Running his hands over them, he found a valve and twisted it to the right. The dump valve allowed water to be forced out of the suit's buoyancy tank with compressed air.

The fluid was cleared in a matter of seconds, followed by a rush of bubbles. Immediately the suit began to rise. Paul shut the valve, grasped the lift points on one side of the torso of the man's suit and pushed off the bottom.

He and the man moved upward, but not nearly fast enough, considering the pressure that was building in his chest. Paul kicked hard but the progress remained slow.

Suddenly, another diver appeared. It was the backup diver who had been on the verge of inhaling the contaminated air. He'd done a free dive like Paul. He grabbed the other side of the suit and began to kick with everything he had.

Gamay had taken the plunge seconds after Paul, swimming down to the midpoint of the tank to get the original rescue diver. Her job appeared easier in that this diver was at a shallower depth, but as she arrived, he began to have convulsions.

She grabbed the diver around the chest, but he shook free, his muscles contracting in spasms. She grabbed him a second time, taking an elbow to the ribs in this round but holding on tight.

Like Paul, her first instinct was to inflate his buoyancy compensator, which she was able to do quickly. Kicking her legs in rhythmic fashion, she propelled them both upward, breaking the surface and inhaling a deep breath of fresh air.

Flipping over onto her back, she pulled the diver toward the deck like a lifeguard rescuing an errant swimmer. She dragged him to the deployment area and up onto the shelf, where two of Hydro-Com's personnel pulled him from the pool. They laid him on the deck while a female employee removed his mask.

"Get his regulator out," Gamay said, climbing out of the pool to assist.

"I can't," the woman replied. "He's clamped down on it."

Somewhere in the back of her mind Gamay remembered that seizures often resulted in broken teeth and chunks bitten from the afflicted's tongue because the jaw muscles tightened uncontrollably.

"Massage his jawline and the side of his neck," she said. "Try to relax the muscles."

They did as directed and the clamped teeth soon relaxed. The woman pulled the regulator away and leaned forward to apply mouth-to-mouth.

"No," Gamay said. "You might transfer whatever poison affected him to you."

The woman pulled back and put an ear to his chest. "It's all right," she said, "he's breathing."

Just then, Paul broke the surface with the buoyant hard suit. Paul was gasping for air and coughing as he fought to move it toward the shallow deck. Even with the help of the other diver, the bulky suit was too massive to push up onto the shelf.

Normally, it would be winched out of the water using a pulley system, but the only way to get the man out quickly was to use brute strength.

Gamay rushed over and grabbed one of the shoulder handles, leaning back and lifting as Paul and the other diver pushed from below. She strained with all her might, but the suit was just too heavy to pull clear.

Just as she was ready to heave backward, another figure appeared. It was the blond-haired man who had suggested they call 911.

"I'll help," he said, grabbing the other handle. "Ready?"

Gamay nodded. They pulled together. Paul and the other diver pushed. The combined effort was just enough. The suit came out of the water and slid forward onto the deployment shelf. It came to a stop, lying faceup in ten inches of water.

The blond man dropped down and unlocked the clamps holding the top and bottom of the suit together. When the last clamp was released, the suit came apart. The top half was pulled off.

The diver lay inside, eyes closed, face blank and pale.

"Help me get him out," the blond man said.

Gamay reached under one shoulder and helped slide the unconscious man free. She assisted the blond man in lifting him from the water and laying him on the deck. His body was limp, his head lolling to the side like a rag doll's.

"He needs oxygen," Gamay suggested. "Do you have any that isn't connected to the dive station?"

"We have medical oxygen at the first aid station," someone shouted.

"Get it. Hurry."

Two small green bottles were produced. Each had a sealed swath of printed tape around the valve.

"These should be uncompromised," someone suggested.

Gamay hoped so. One bottle was administered to each of the unconscious men, but neither seemed to be regaining consciousness.

By now, half the Hydro-Com staff had made their way to the pool deck. Even Pradi and Hiram Yaeger were seen standing on an observation deck above the tank.

As the recovery gave way to triage, Gamay pulled back. The rescue was over. The next chapter in the men's lives would depend on the speed and ability of the medical response. The sound of an ambulance siren wailing as it raced into the parking lot was reassuring.

Stepping to the background, she found Paul at the fringe of the crowd. Someone handed them towels, which they used to dab their faces and wrap around their shoulders.

"So much for our nice little trip to Silicon Valley,"

Gamay said, leaning into her husband. "Looks like we were needed after all."

Paul nodded, but his face was more grim than proud. "This wasn't an accident," he said. "We'd best be on our toes."

CHAPTER 23

Hiram Yaeger watched Paul and Gamay spring into action with great admiration. It had been a long time since he'd ventured out into the field and he'd almost forgotten how fast things happened, how quickly one had to act and how little information a field operative had to go on when making split-second decisions. It was a far cry from his world of analytics and data crunching back at NUMA headquarters. Standing beside the Hydro-Com CEO and watching the rescue unfold on the other side of the tank's glass wall, he'd felt almost useless.

Sunil Pradi felt worse. "I can hardly believe what I'm witnessing," he said. "Nothing like this has ever occurred here. We have safety protocols. Expert divers. And the best equipment."

Yaeger was tempted to tell him that it would all be all right, but that wasn't yet clear and he doubted very much that it would be. The two divers remained unconscious even as the paramedics arrived with a pair of wheeled gurneys. "Someone tampered with the oxygen or put a nerve agent on the masks. You're going to need to get the FBI in here."

"FBI?" Pradi said. "No, no, no, I'm afraid that's out of the question. We can't afford this kind of publicity."

"You don't have a choice," Yaeger informed him. "This is a crime scene. Those men might die."

Before the CEO could respond, a nearby elevator pinged. The doors opened and a woman with short black hair and glasses came toward them. She had a printed ledger in her hands and a sharpened pencil lodged above one ear.

She walked up to them, surprised by all the commotion. "What happened?"

Wherever she'd been, it wasn't an area with a view of the tank.

"A terrible accident," Pradi said, trying to maintain his preferred narrative.

Yaeger didn't bother to correct him. Up on the pool deck, the paramedics were on the scene attending to the injured men. Vitals were being taken. More oxygen administered.

"I should come back," the woman said. "This isn't a good time."

"No, no," Pradi said, sounding thankful to have some routine business decision to make. "What do you need?"

"I've been looking over the safety protocols in

preparation for Mr. Yaeger's visit." She nodded toward Hiram, obviously aware of who he was. "And I hate to say it but something odd has come up."

Pradi sighed heavily. "Hiram, this is Sabrina Lang, my security chief. I had hoped you two would meet under different circumstances."

Yaeger shook her hand. "Ms. Lang."

"People call me Bree," she said.

"Show us what you've found," Pradi said. "And please tell me it's not a breach of the source code."

"No," she said, stepping over to the nearest workstation. "Nothing like that. Nothing going out. But I have found something in the system that shouldn't be there."

She set the printed pages down on a table beside the computer. There were lines and lines of code in tiny print on the left side and a flowchart-style diagram on the right.

"This is the firewall protocol," she said, taking the pencil from her ear and circling one section of the code. "And this," she said, circling a second batch of code, "is the initiator for what we call the anti-siphon module."

Hiram understood it intuitively. "The firewall prevents anyone from tapping in. The anti-siphon module prevents anyone from sending data out, keeping it from being moved or copied from one computer to another."

"Even within the building," she explained.

"What happens if you need to transfer some

data?" Hiram asked. "If, say, two different departments are working on the same project?"

She adjusted her glasses. "The anti-siphon module will query the master control computer and double-check all permissions. It will only allow the transfer of any data when the sharing has been preapproved. All transactions of this type are logged in the master control unit."

Hiram nodded. He'd seen systems like this before though not usually with an internally protected, air-gapped system. It was quite impressive.

"So, where's the problem?" Pradi asked.

"Here," she said, circling another section of code.

Hiram knew the printed lines were only the first batches of code for each program, which would have millions of additional lines.

"This batch has changed the procedure," she explained. "All internal requests for permission have been directed into a new, unnamed module before being passed onto the anti-siphon module. And I can't make heads or tails of what this is or where it came from."

"Is it interfering with the system?" Pradi asked. "Copying data?"

"No," she said. "In fact, in every test I ran it simply passed the data along to the anti-siphon module and allowed the system to do its job properly."

"Let me see the code," Hiram said. "The entire code."

They moved to a nearby workstation, where

Sabrina logged in and brought up a display of the interloping code.

"May I?" Hiram asked.

Hydro-Com's security chief stepped out of the way and let Yaeger at the computer. Studying the data, Hiram scanned downward, looking for something in the lines of code. After a minute or two he ran a query, asking the computer to perform a specific type of operation. It revealed a new command prompt.

"I've seen this before," Hiram said. "It's a very advanced hacking technique. It sets up a virtual computer within your system without interfering with any normal operations. Once this program is activated, it makes a subtle change to the way your system operates. Mimicking the permissions and commands coming from the master control module by intercepting the sharing request and granting permission before the request ever reaches the anti-siphon module."

Pradi stiffened. "Can you tell when this module appeared in the system?"

"No, it's not apparent," Sabrina replied. "Whoever did it covered his tracks. It may have been in place for weeks or even months, lying dormant until the hacker finally decided to steal something."

"Fabricated permissions?"

"Copied from previously granted authorizations," Hiram explained. "But because the master control computer never sees the request and doesn't actually process the data, there's no record of the transfer. It's like robbing a bank but only stealing money that was never reported as being deposited in the first place."

"That's what I was afraid of," Sabrina said.

Pradi clenched his jaw ever tighter. "This is a dark day," he said. "Can you ascertain what's been queried?"

She shook her head.

"We don't need to wonder," Hiram said. "It has to be the source code for your server units."

"All may not be lost," Sabrina said. "Even if the permissions have been faked, the code could still be transferred only internally, from one computer in this building to another. Someone would have to physically smuggle it out. And the scanners would pick up any data storage device before it could be taken out of the building."

"Is everyone scanned?" Hiram asked.

"Even me and Ms. Lang," Pradi replied. "No exceptions."

"A zip drive could be swallowed," Hiram suggested. "It might sneak in that way."

"We've tested that theory," Pradi said. "The millimeter wave scanners pick up any silicon or metallic device even when hidden in a body cavity. More importantly, the source code couldn't be smuggled out on a zip drive. It's a huge program. Billions of lines of code. It wouldn't fit on ten zips. You'd need something larger. Something like a multiterabyte hard drive at the very least. And no one is swallowing one of those."

That narrowed it down. "How many hard drives do you have on-site?"

"Two hundred and ninety-three," Sabrina told him.

"Might want to check on them," Hiram said. "I expect you'll find that one has gone missing."

The security expert's face tightened. She stepped to the keyboard and ran a new query. The responses started coming in department by department. The progress bar filled rapidly as every workstation was accounted for.

All but one.

"Where's that unit located?"

"Sublevel three," she said. "Down in the testing department."

"Get security down there," Pradi ordered. "I want that whole department locked in."

"I wouldn't bother," Hiram said. "It won't be anyone from the testing department. Whoever hacked you is far too smart to use his own machine. It has to be someone else. Someone with access to the whole network. And someone with a plan to get it out of the building."

Hiram's mind raced while the CEO protested. "The entire building is locked down to insiders as well as outsiders."

"What about emergency exits?"

"No," Sabrina said. "They're hardwired to open

only if an alarm goes off. They're also monitored by camera. You couldn't use one without being seen in person and on camera."

"I'm guessing the windows are sealed shut," Hiram said.

"Double layers," Pradi said. "Bulletproof and alarmed. They don't open or break."

It seemed impossible for someone to get the hard drive out of the building; there was certainly no way to do it without being noticed. Unless . . .

The answer hit Yaeger like a thunderbolt. He looked over to the pool deck. The paramedics were gone. He glanced in the other direction. They were rushing to the exit, pushing the two gurneys and the injured men in front of them. In a moment, they'd be out the door and onto the bridge that led to the parking lot. And there was little chance they'd be frisked and scanned along the way.

"Hold on, there," Hiram shouted.

The paramedics ignored him, taking a ramp down toward the front door.

Hiram turned to Pradi. "Tell your security team to stop the paramedics."

"Why?"

"Because the hard drive is on one of those gurneys."

CHAPTER 24

As Pradi dialed the front desk, Hiram raced along the walkway and down the ramp, coming within view of the security checkpoint.

The two guards had stepped out from behind their desks, blocking the path. The paramedics were slowing only in the slightest.

"Gentlemen," Hiram shouted down to them. "Which hospital were you planning on taking these men to?"

The lead paramedic turned around and focused on Hiram. "Excuse me?"

"Which hospital?" Hiram repeated. "Which emergency room?"

The man offered a wry smile, looked as if he were about to reply and then reached beneath his jacket, pulled out a 9mm pistol and fired several shots in Yaeger's direction.

Yaeger dove out of the way, hitting the floor, as the bullets shattered the railing. He landed on the deck, with little cubes of safety glass raining down on him.

Down below, a pitched battle developed between the guards and the men impersonating paramedics. The guards had the better position, with the marble-clad podium between them and the paramedics, but they couldn't fire at will at risk of hitting the men on the gurneys or someone else inside the building.

As everyone took cover, Paul and Gamay raced up to Hiram and crouched down beside him.

"Great catch," Gamay said, brushing some of the glass from his hair. "They were almost out the door."

"They'll probably run like the wind now," Hiram said, getting to his feet. "We need to get down there. We didn't come all this way to protect the source code only to let it get stolen out from under our noses."

He took off running, racing headlong down the ramp toward the lobby.

"What's gotten into him?" Gamay asked.

"Action fever," Paul said, getting to his feet. "Come on. We can't let him chase after them all on his own."

Hiram had gotten ahead of them and was nearing the bottom of the ramp when the gunfire surged once again, quickly rising to a crescendo.

Not wishing to be spat out into a cross fire, Hiram came to a halt and leaned against a support pole for cover. Paul and Gamay crowded in beside him.

"This is how I imagine the shoot-out at the O.K. Corral," Paul said.

The paramedics had rushed the exit, trading shots with the guards while using the gurneys—and the injured men on them—as shields. They raced through the metal detector and the millimeter wave scanner, unleashing a furious barrage of gunfire at the podium as they passed by.

The security guards were forced to duck and cover. By the time they popped up, the paramedics had escaped out the front door and out onto the bridge to the parking lot.

Hiram, Paul and Gamay sprinted to the guard station. Both security officers had taken hits. One man had a bullet wound to the right shoulder while the other had been hit in the leg. He was applying pressure to it, but it was bleeding badly.

Hiram handed the phone to the less injured man. "You'd better get a real ambulance out here," he said, before asking, "Might I borrow your gun?"

The guard looked hesitant but handed it over. Hiram checked the safety and took off running, heading out the front door.

The cantilevered bridge had a slight peak in the middle. Yaeger raced up it and reached the top. He spotted the fake paramedics at the other end, piling into the ambulance. One of them rushed around to the driver's-side door while the other jumped in the back, slamming the double doors behind him.

Knowing he would never reach the ambulance in

time, Hiram assumed a shooter's stance, aimed the pistol and fired at the ambulance.

Whatever he might have hit, the shots did nothing to stop the vehicle. The engine roared, the tires screeched and the vehicle took off in a cloud of blue smoke. The wheeled gurneys were left behind like so much discarded junk, but only one of them still had a patient on it.

Hiram lowered the gun and sprinted for the rental car. He had the keys in his hand before he reached the door and pressed the unlock button, accidentally popping the trunk at the same time.

He jumped in the driver's seat and heard the trunk slam shut behind him. Paul and Gamay had caught up once more.

Gamay jumped into the passenger's seat. "Didn't think we were going to let you play Lone Ranger, did you?"

As Paul climbed into the backseat, Hiram handed Gamay the pistol. "Here," he said. "You're the best shot in the department. I'll drive. You shoot."

"Or," Paul suggested from the back, "we could follow them and call in the local police once we know where they're going."

Hiram put the car in reverse, backed out of the spot and slammed the transmission into drive as he stomped on the gas. "That does seem more logical," he admitted. "Hard to think clearly when your heart is in your throat."

Mashing on the gas, Hiram aimed the rental car

across the parking lot and out onto the road where the ambulance had just gone. They accelerated onto the deserted private drive that fronted the Hydro-Com campus. By the time they got up to speed, the ambulance was half a mile ahead, kicking up a trail of dust.

A little farther on, they reached an intersection with the state highway.

"He's turning east on Route 257," Gamay said. "That goes inland toward the mountains and the redwoods."

"Maybe you'll get to see them after all," Hiram suggested.

"Not too many exits on that road," Paul said. "The police should have no trouble setting up a roadblock or deploying those spike strips."

"There's just one problem," Gamay said, checking her pockets for the third or fourth time. "All our phones are in a locker at Hydro-Com."

Hiram glanced at Paul in the mirror and at Gamay. "Guess we have to do this ourselves."

With his foot to the floor, Hiram piloted the shiny new Ford at a breakneck pace. The ambulance stayed ahead of them, but the gap was closing. The road was rising and they began to catch up with small pockets of sightseeing traffic. That might have favored the smaller car, but whoever was driving the ambulance got the brilliant idea to turn the lights and siren on.

The cars on the road pulled dutifully out of its

way, allowing the ambulance to speed through at a blistering pace. To make matters worse, they pulled back onto the road before Yaeger and the Trouts could race by.

"That's cheating," Yaeger said as he swerved around yet another slower car.

He blasted the horn and flashed the lights, hoping to give the other drivers the impression that another emergency vehicle was approaching. It worked to some extent, but a few angry gestures still came their way. And at one point they nearly forced a pickup truck off the road.

As Yaeger drove, Gamay put on her seat belt. While Yaeger didn't have a chance to do the same, he figured that just gave him more incentive to avoid a crash.

Another straightaway loomed and the Ford began to make up for lost ground once more.

"Did you two notice that they got rid of both stretchers but that one of them was empty?" Gamay asked.

"I did," Paul said. "Who'd they leave behind?"

"The guy I rescued—the safety diver."

"I guess one hostage is as good as two," Hiram commented.

"Or maybe he's not a hostage," Gamay replied. "The man I pulled out of the water was as stiff as a two-by-four, fully seizing. They had to relax his jaw to get the regulator out of his mouth. But the guy Paul plucked off the bottom was limp once we got him out of the dive suit. Even at that point, it struck me as odd that their symptoms were different."

Paul grinned. "Good job, Sherlock Trout. You think the hard suit diver was in on the theft?"

"Easiest way for him to get out of the building without being questioned."

"That would explain something else," Yaeger added. "By the time I got over the bridge, he was already off the stretcher and in the ambulance. They were only out of sight for a few seconds. It seems to me like it would have taken a bit longer to load a fully grown man into the ambulance without using the gurney."

He swerved around yet another car and they started onto the curvy section of the road where it climbed more steeply. The Ford gained more ground with each switchback, but as they neared the crest of the ridge the back doors of the ambulance opened and the gunman in the paramedic's uniform opened fire.

Hiram swerved, but several bullets tore into the hood and two others blasted craters in the windshield.

Gamay opened her window and tried the almost impossible task of firing accurately at the vehicle in front of them.

"That never works in the movies," Paul said from the backseat.

They reached a right-hand curve and the ambulance swung wide, using the opposite side of the road and the shoulder to negotiate the bend. As the road straightened out, the gunman pulled the back doors shut. Whether it was a result of Gamay's shots or his own desire not to be flung out of the speeding vehicle, no one knew. But at least they weren't being fired on anymore.

Hiram hammered the throttle once again. A long left bend led to another sharp right as the road dug into a fold in the hills. "Tight curve coming up," he said. "I think I can clip his back wheels. Paul, you better strap yourself in."

The ambulance driver was doing the best he could to set himself up for the ascending right turn, but the big rig was too heavy to take it at full speed. The brake lights came on and he slowed and swung wide a second time.

Hiram darted to the inside and cut back toward the emergency vehicle. The nose of the Ford caught the back end of the ambulance, knocking it sideways. The ambulance leaned heavily, a cloud of smoke erupting from the tires as the rear wheels broke loose.

The vehicle slid onto the high side of the road and looked as if it might hit the rocks beyond, but the tires regained traction suddenly and the ambulance darted across the roadway at a forty-five-degree angle, flying off the edge and into the shallow ravine beyond.

It tumbled several times, taking out a couple pine trees and a clump of bushes, before hitting bottom. It came to rest forty feet below the road, lying on its side. Steam poured from underneath the hood and one of the front wheels continued to spin.

Hiram pulled the Ford to a stop and Paul and Gamay rushed from the car without saying a word.

Hiram had every intention of joining them but found his hands locked onto the wheel with an iron grip that he seemed unable to break.

He exhaled slowly, releasing a breath he'd been holding for what seemed like hours. With deliberate care, he peeled one hand off the wheel and put the car in park. Then, for good measure, he set the parking brake, shut off the ignition and removed the keys.

Feeling his heart pound in his chest and hearing the blood rushing through his ears, Hiram decided quite correctly that adrenaline was not something to casually mess around with.

Across the road, Paul and Gamay had reached the edge of the ravine. They scrambled down the embankment, sliding on the loose soil.

As they reached the wrecked ambulance, they found that one of the so-called paramedics had been ejected from the vehicle and thrown against a tree. Paul dropped beside him to check for a weapon and then a pulse. He found neither.

Leaving the dead man, Paul inched toward the cab. He peeked over the sill into the driver's compartment. One look was enough. He turned to Gamay and shook his head.

Gamay nodded. Two down, one to go.

Clutching the pistol, she crept toward the back end of the ambulance. The sound of movement brought her to a stop. With the gun held upward and close to her chest, she kneeled and took a quick look inside.

The hard suit diver, the man Paul had saved from the tank, was lying on what had been the side wall of the ambulance. He was pinned awkwardly by equipment that had tumbled down on him. With the strength he had left, he stretched to reach for a pistol that had fallen beside him.

Gamay stepped in and snatched it away. "So much for your drug-induced seizure. I hope it was worth it."

"They make billions and give us the scraps," he said. "A six-figure income gets you a one-bedroom apartment out here."

"So, to get back at them you planned to steal the source code and sell it," Gamay suggested.

He started coughing, eventually spitting up blood. He was fading fast. "You think I came up with this? I'm just a diver." His eyes glazed over as he spoke. His head fell back and he stared past her. "Hate to tell you," he whispered, "but you've got . . . the wrong . . . guy . . ."

Back at Hydro-Com, the real first responders had finally arrived. And despite his earlier protest, Sunil

Pradi had called his legal counsel and told them to get in touch with the FBI. In the meantime, he was determined to salvage any evidence he could find. He spoke with Sabrina Lang.

"Would you take me to the machine that's missing the hard drive?" he asked. "We need to store it somewhere safe until the FBI's forensics team can examine it."

"Of course," she said. "I think that's wise."

They crossed the room and took the elevator down to the lowest level of the building. A key card got them through a secured door and into the testing department. Once inside, Pradi switched on the lights. To his great shock, someone was standing in the darkened room.

"What are you doing down here?" Sabrina asked.

The blond-haired man offered a befuddled look. "I, umm . . ."

As the man fumbled for an answer, recognition dawned on Pradi. "You called the ambulance," he said. "You're part of this."

The blond man seemed saddened. "I really wish you hadn't remembered that."

He produced a small, almost toylike gun, aiming it at the CEO.

Sabrina took a step toward the door.

"Don't," the blond man ordered. "This may be a 3D-printed gun made here on-site, but the bullets are the store-bought, lethal variety."

She stopped in her tracks.

Pradi found his temper rising. "How dare you," he snapped. "How dare you betray us."

The blond man responded by firing the gun twice, hitting Pradi in the chest both times. The CEO dropped in a heap.

Sabrina rushed forward. But it was a poor risk. The shooter fired again, hitting her in the stomach. She crumpled to the floor, landing awkwardly and clutching her midsection.

With both of them down, the blond man made his way to a workstation near the far wall. Using a quick release lever, he opened the computer tower and removed the hard drive. He placed it in a silvery static-free bag, which he sealed with two layers of tape.

"I'm fairly certain my friends didn't get away," he said to the dying CEO. "Too bad. But you know the first rule of computer school. Always back up your work."

He held up the second hard drive, onto which he'd loaded the source code.

Pradi grasped the man's ankle, but he shook loose and fired the last bullet from his small weapon into Pradi's heart. The CEO went still.

With both the CEO and the security chief motionless on the floor, the blond man reached down and yanked their ID badges from around their necks. He stuffed them in his pocket before heading to the exit, calmly switching off the lights and stepping out the door.

He took the elevator up to the roof, where he sealed the hard drive in a second waterproof bag. This one black instead of silver.

He tossed it into the shallow rooftop pool and watched it float toward the waterfall near the front of the building. Dusk had come and gone. The black bag floating in the dark water would be invisible now.

With the package on its way, he pulled out the ID cards, snapped them in half and tossed them into the pool. They sank to the bottom and remained there.

With everything going to plan, the blond man went back into the building. Having already given his statement to the police, he was allowed to leave. He made his way out, submitting to a pat down and calmly allowing himself to be examined by both the metal detector and millimeter wave scanner.

Clearing the door, he went across the bridge and entered the parking lot, using the walkway that ran beside the canal. He soon reached the drain where the water was sucked back in and recycled through the system. The black bag was caught on the grate. Too large to fit between the gaps, it bobbed and turned in circles as the water swirled underneath.

With a quick swipe of the hand, he scooped it up, tucked it under his arm and continued toward his car.

Because he'd taken their ID tags, Sabrina Lang and Sunil Pradi wouldn't be found for over two hours. By then, Pradi would be long dead, Lang in a coma and the blond man safely aboard a private jet, sipping champagne and bound for Hong Kong.

CHAPTER 25

TAIWAN R.O.C.

The bad news reached Kurt and Joe as the **Sapphire** docked in Taipei.

"Someone got the source code out of Hydro-Com," Kurt said, reading the report. "The CEO was killed. Looks like an inside job."

"What about Hiram and the Trouts?"

"They're okay," Kurt said. "They were out of the building chasing someone else when it happened."

Joe nodded. "Things continue to get more dangerous. We'd better be ready for anything."

Kurt considered that sound advice. He put the report away. "Hungry?"

"I could eat," Joe said. "What do you have in mind?"

Kurt stood and grabbed a ball cap. "We have to link up with a CIA asset who's going to help us. He's suggested we meet at one of the night markets downtown. From what I remember, we'll find some of the best food on the island down there."

"Spicy food, clandestine meetings in dark, crowded streets," Joe said. "You have my interest. Let's go."

Leaving Winterburn, Stratton and the other crew members on the **Sapphire,** Kurt and Joe made their way into the heart of Taipei, arriving in a bustling area filled with people, music and the aroma of various savory dishes being cooked up at dozens of small shops and kiosks.

Globe-shaped yellow lanterns hung above the crowded streets, while boutiques selling trendy clothes and near-perfect knockoffs advertised their wares with neon signs of red, purple and blue.

"Not bad," Joe said, enjoying the buzz of activity. "A little bit of Times Square and Mardi Gras all wrapped up in one."

"The night markets are a big draw here," Kurt said. "This one attracts the most tourists, so we won't stand out like a pair of sore thumbs."

Despite Kurt's promise of food, the first order of business was to meet up with their contact, a man by the name of Steven Wu. They found him standing in front of a store that sold Hublot watches and cotton candy, an odd product mix if ever there was one.

Greetings were made, passwords exchanged. Kurt asked the obvious question. "Can we talk here?"

"We should be okay," Wu told them. "If we

walk and talk, it'll be far too chaotic for anyone to eavesdrop."

"What if we walk and talk and graze?" Joe suggested.

"Sure," Wu told him, "though I usually advise people not to come to the night markets hungry. You'll end up trying a little bit of everything."

"My plan exactly," Joe said.

Kurt had spent several months in Taiwan during his time in the Navy and had been there many times during his years with NUMA. He found it to be one of the most vibrant places in the world. Filled with energy, as if everyone who lived there was racing to get ahead, rushing to live as much life as possible as fast as they could. With the ever-present specter of China marching in one day and shutting the party down, he couldn't really blame them.

"What have you heard about this auction?" Kurt asked.

"Believe it or not," Wu said, "it hasn't been kept all that secret. In fact, you'll probably end up seeing representatives from several governments bidding alongside the more nefarious factions. Not to mention the assistance of several less than scrupulous banks."

"How's a group like CIPHER pull that off?"

"False pretenses," Wu said. "Officially, the auction covers the proposed sale of an African mining venture, which is to be transferred lock, stock and tailing-filled barrel."

Neat trick, Kurt thought. "Is that going to make this easier or more difficult?"

"Both. It means more competition. But at least you won't be in a dark room surrounded by thugs and dripping rainwater. You'll be in the lap of luxury."

"Really? Where?"

Wu turned. "Up there."

He pointed back down the street toward Taipei 101, the tallest building in Taiwan and one of the tallest in all the world. It stood like a neon monolith against the black sky.

Kurt studied the tower and said to Joe, "Things are looking up."

He turned back to Wu. "Tell us more about CIPHER. How did they get involved in this and what are we looking at in terms of security?"

"There's not too much to tell," Wu said. "They're a new player in this environment and they're different. Think of them as an amoeba, hackers without a firmly defined structure. More like a five-headed monster than a single entity."

"How does that work?"

"There's no real boss, just a decentralized group that votes on which schemes to attempt and which to reject. Aside from the funding, each of the five cells are compartmentalized and disconnected from the others. It's made them hard to penetrate. But it's also kept them relatively small, in the grand scheme of things."

"Until now," Joe pointed out.

"Until now," Wu agreed.

"Any idea why they suddenly took on bigger game?"

Wu shrugged. "It's a little hard to parse the tea leaves, but the intel suggests a turf war has blown up between one of CIPHER's leaders, a man named Degra, and a group on the mainland run by a British expat named Emmerson."

"We know about Emmerson," Kurt said. "Seems like the wrong guy to mess with."

"What can I tell you?" Wu said. "Ambition can't be caged. Like fighters trying to step up a weight class."

"Worse consequences than a knockout here," Kurt suggested.

Wu nodded in agreement. "Degra seems to be aware of that. He's been busy adding some muscle to the group, bringing in hired guns to beef up security. You'll see plenty of them at the auction, which I don't need to tell you adds another wild card to the deck. The guys they've brought on are from the street. Not exactly cool customers. If something goes off the rails, they're more likely to shoot up a whole room than to pick and choose their targets carefully."

Kurt filed this info away. All in all, he'd rather deal with trained professionals than wild-eyed gunmen. Their actions were easier to predict. "I'd say it's a bad idea to get in the middle of something like this, but that's what we're just about to do."

Joe scowled. "Remind me to update my life insurance."

Kurt laughed, then turned back to Wu. "Will Degra be running the auction?"

"He will," Wu said. "I've sent over a link with some photos. But you should be able to recognize him by the white streak in his black hair. If the plan is going to work, you'll need to talk to him directly, get inside his head. Whatever you do, don't try to shake his hand. He's a notorious germophobe."

"Good to know," Kurt said. "Now, assuming I can get his attention, what's the plan?"

Wu pulled out what looked like an old-fashioned flip phone but was actually a high-capacity portable drive. "To make those servers operate Degra needs the source code. This device contains a sample that his technicians can evaluate and verify. Give it to him, have him plug it in somewhere for them to study."

Kurt glanced at the palm-sized device. "Let me guess—the source code isn't the only thing on this drive."

"Correct," Wu said. "It also contains a program known as a tunneling worm. Think of it as a super-advanced Trojan horse or virus. While Degra's people examine the code, the worm downloads itself onto their system and starts jumping from computer to computer in search of information about the servers, bank accounts or anything else we might use against him."

"These guys are hackers," Kurt said. "Don't you think they might be on the lookout for something like that?"

"They'll never find it," Wu insisted. "No matter what they use to search, they won't be able to pick it up."

Kurt was not convinced.

"Trust me," Wu said, "I have a master's degree in programming and five years chasing hackers and I couldn't find it with any of the tools at my disposal. I don't know where it came from—aliens or some sixteen-year-old genius in Pasadena—but there aren't ten people in the world who could spot it and none of them are members of CIPHER."

True or false, that was all they were going to get out of Wu. Kurt put the device in his pocket and looked back at the towering building off in the distance. The sides of Taipei 101 were glowing pale blue while the spire at the top was lit up like a neon orange spike. The glow illuminated the low clouds and patchy fog drifting in from the sea.

Kurt turned back to Wu. "And if they're smarter than you think they are or they already have the source code, then what?"

Wu looked grim. "There's not much we can do to help you. There's one way up to the top and two ways down. But if you can't use the elevator, that first step is a doozy."

CHAPTER 26

TAIPEI 101

Kurt and Joe arrived in the lobby of Taipei 101 around midnight. Entering by special invitation, they bypassed the mall on the lower levels and made their way to a bank of high-speed elevators.

They were met by a pair of security guards in uniform who worked for the building and a man wearing a shimmery olive-colored suit who was apparently CIPHER's official security chief. A pair of equally well-dressed compatriots stood nearby.

This group checked their credentials and escorted them to one of the high-speed elevators, which Kurt and Joe entered alone. It rose quickly, picking up speed as it went.

"Must be the express," Joe said. "My ears are popping."

Kurt's were as well. "Did you see if those guys were armed?"

"You mean the overdressed security team in silk suits?" Joe said. "Weapons bulging under every jacket."

Kurt had thought as much, but Joe had the better view. "CIPHER obviously decided to secure the ground floor as well as the ballroom. Not sure if that's a good sign or bad."

After thirty seconds the car slowed, stopping smoothly without any noticeable bump. The doors opened to reveal a large foyer with a white marble floor and matching walls. Orchids in ceramic pots added a splash of color.

Kurt stepped out of the elevator. To the right, a pair of broad-shouldered men stood beside a rectangular table draped in red velvet cloth. A second layer of security. Less nattily dressed than the men downstairs. But just as well-armed.

Beyond stood a folding screen decorated with traditional Chinese artwork. And beyond that, delicate glass sculptures created by a renowned Taiwanese artist.

Before they could go any farther, Kurt and Joe were given electronic wristbands that had the smooth surface of a touch screen. "Enter the room, tap the wristband and your attendant will explain the rest."

Kurt nodded and walked around the screen and entered the ballroom. Though he kept an expressionless face, he found the ballroom impressive. It took up most of the ninety-third floor, with views of the city through windows on three of the four sides. A small catering station blocked the view on the fourth.

A chandelier made of colored glass flowers hung over the center of the room. Other lights were barely lit, creating a soft violet glow. On the far side of the chandelier was a dance floor backed by a low stage. Instead of a band or DJ, the stage was occupied by several enormous video screens, each of them over a hundred inches across.

Images of oversize construction equipment played across the screens: backhoes, excavators, dump trucks that would make a city bus look like a child's toy. These gave way to photos of rooms filled with gold bars and photos of smiling workers in hard hats and tattered clothes. Finally, a series of charts and graphs appeared, bragging about the yields from the various parts of the mine.

"These guys are playing the mining card all the way to the end," Kurt noted.

Joe shrugged. "Maybe you buy the computers and they throw in the mine for free."

"I wonder what NUMA would do with a gold mine?" Kurt asked wryly, before switching the subject. "Did you get a count?"

"Seventy or eighty," Joe said, having scanned the people milling about and done his best to tally rapidly. "I'd say it's split evenly between CIPHER's people and the bidders. And that's not counting the tuxedoed staff working the bars and carrying trays of champagne."

Kurt grinned. "The most important people in the room."

"And least likely to cause a problem," Joe replied.

They walked toward one of the well-stocked bars. "Let's meet up with our attendant."

Kurt tapped the wristband's curved screen. It lit up with a green glow. A reed-thin man appeared beside them seconds later. He spoke slightly accented English. "My name is Chen," he said. "How can I be of service?"

Their cover was deliberately murky, but with enough digging it would reveal links to a California-based corporation that had been a bitter rival of Hydro-Com. Years of litigation told the story. Nasty press releases filled with sordid accusations added a dash of color. The lawsuit and the rivalry were legit. But if the plan was going to work, Degra and CIPHER needed to make the connection on their own.

"First things first," Kurt said, "we'll need something stronger than champagne." He gazed over at the bottles lined up on the back side of the bar, looking for just the right beverage. "A bottle of the Speyside Sherry Cask Single Malt should do, for starters."

Chen looked unnerved. "The whole bottle?"

"And whatever he wants," Kurt said, pointing to Joe.

"Ice water," Joe said. "Still, not sparkling."

"Also," Kurt added, "if you'd show us to our booth, we'd like to make our initial bid."

Chen turned to the bartender, snapped his fingers and pointed to the bottle of 130 proof Speyside Single Malt. It was placed on a tray with two lead crystal tumblers and two carafes, one filled with water, the other with ice.

"Please follow me," Chen said.

He led them across the room to a booth aligned with the windows on the north side of the building. Curved couches, privacy walls and gauzy indigo drapes hanging from the ceiling offered a sense of intimacy.

Kurt sat down on one side of the booth. Joe sat on the other. Chen placed the items from the tray between them. "Be advised, the first round of bidding will commence in ten minutes."

Kurt nodded and Chen left.

"That's a thousand-dollar bottle of whiskey," Joe said.

"Too bad we won't be drinking much," Kurt said, pouring himself an extra-full tumbler.

"Your definition of **much** might need adjusting."

Kurt left the glass untouched and moved a flickering candle up beside the bottle. The caramel glow of the light through the whiskey added to the ambiance. "Darker than a Manhattan steak house in here."

"Nice and private," Joe said.

Kurt shook his head and pointed to the wristbands. Taking out the tablet computer they'd brought, he activated a jamming program the CIA had installed. The program detected Wi-Fi and other short-range radio signals. Sure enough, it picked up signals from the bands and also from a pendant lamp hanging over the table.

Once these local signals were detected, the computer began jamming. A second program used the tablet's speaker to create a buzzing sonic wave that was barely audible to the human ear but would prevent any microphones from picking up their voices.

As Kurt looked around, he had no doubt the Chinese and Russian contingents were doing something similar. All part of the game.

With that settled, Kurt logged into the offshore CIA account and linked it to the escrow account that CIPHER set up for the auction.

As he prepared their first bid, Joe sat back, looked around. Most of the attendees were retiring to other booths around the room. He saw no sign of a master of ceremonies. "Think we'll get to meet this Degra guy in person?"

"Not right away," Kurt said. "Doubt he'll show his face until he's separated the contenders from the also-rans."

From where Kurt was sitting, he could see the big screens at the front of the room. The photographs were gone and a digital clock counting down to the initial bidding had taken their place.

An auctioneer stepped onstage. "The bidding is about to begin," he said. "Please remember this is a multiround process. At this time, there are sixteen bidders. In each of the first three rounds, the four lowest bidders will be eliminated. The highest offer at the end of each round will be the lowest acceptable bid—the reserve, if you will—for the following round. Only the final four groups will have a chance to bid on the full property. No partial offers will be accepted."

The auctioneer stepped away. The clock hit zero and the bidding began. Kurt jokingly entered a bid of one dollar.

Joe shot him a look. "This isn't **The Price Is Right.** You don't win if everyone else goes over."

"Just testing the system," Kurt said.

There were only three minutes for the first round of bids. As the time went on, a graph appeared on the screens up front. It displayed sixteen separate lines showing who had bid and how much. As time went by, they moved up as they moved to the right just like a bull stock market chart.

All the lines rose, except the line for bidder number eight, which remained stuck at one dollar, and bidder number fifteen, who had yet to bid at all.

"Someone's using my trick," Kurt said, craning his neck around to see if he could tell who it was.

It was no use. Most of the groups had their privacy curtains drawn and those that didn't were chatting anxiously.

The time passed quickly, with the bidding eclipsing ten million dollars with only a minute left. Sixty seconds later, most of the bids had passed twenty million.

"Tricky little setup," Joe noted. "Everyone wants to keep the price down but no one wants to lose out on the next round."

"Cunning," Kurt said.

An additional twist had occurred in the last thirty seconds when the screens intentionally blanked. Another tactic designed to instill some panic in the potential buyers and drive up the price.

Kurt considered the upward slope of the lines and the effect this final little spur to the flanks had. Not wanting to miss out himself, he typed in thirty million dollars. After double-checking that the commas were in the right places, he changed it to forty.

Joe raised an eyebrow.

Kurt shrugged. "It's not my money."

The clock hit zero and round one of the auction closed.

There was no big announcement as to who had won and who had lost. Just a return to the softer lighting and photos of the mining operation. Eventually, Chen came to their booth. "I'm pleased to announce you've been approved for the second round."

Kurt nodded, raised the full glass of Speyside to Chen and smiled as he walked off.

While Kurt had a good view of the screens from his position, he couldn't see much of the ballroom. Joe's angle was better. "Anything happening?"

"Various other attendants stopping by the other booths," Joe said.

"Anyone leaving?" Kurt said.

"One group," Joe replied.

"Can you tell who they are?"

"Based on their clothing and some utterly spectacular haircuts, I'd say they're North Korean."

Two other groups left while Joe watched. Both groups looked to be made up of Europeans. If a fourth group had been booted out, Joe didn't see it.

The auctioneer returned to the microphone and announced the next round. At this point, the highest bid from the previous session was revealed. To Kurt's surprise, someone had outbid him by a wide margin.

"The starting bid is forty-nine-million U.S. dollars," the auctioneer said. "No bids below that number will be accepted. If it remains the highest bid after this second round, the auction will be deemed complete and the consignment will be awarded."

"Thought you might win that," Joe said, taking another sip of water.

Kurt had thought they might too, but it didn't matter. "Just need to get in the final four so we can ask a few specific questions."

The second round went much like the first, but by the end of the two-minute window, bidder number fifteen had pushed the price to seventy million dollars.

Joe pointed out the obvious. "You realize CIPHER could put any number they wanted up there and we'd never know if it came from a legitimate bidder or their own keyboard."

"I can think of one way to check," Kurt said. He typed in ninety-five million and one.

At the end of the second round, the auctioneer announced that the leading bid was indeed ninety-five million and one.

"They may still have their own bidders," Kurt admitted. "At least until round four. But at that point they won't risk getting stuck with the highest bid."

Several other groups were ushered out and an intermission of thirty minutes was announced. "Now," Kurt said, "let's see if we can have a word with our host."

He shut off the jammer, tapped the wristband and summoned Chen. When the attendant dutifully arrived, Kurt asked him a question. "How much would I have to pay for some legitimate inside information?"

"I have no such information," the attendant assured him.

"But if you knew someone who did?"

"No amount of money is worth my reputation," Chen replied.

"Understandable," Kurt said. "You have my respect." He took out a business card and wrote a single word on it. "Would you deliver this to the host for me? Not the auctioneer, mind you, the host. Tell him I'd like to talk about the source code."

CHAPTER 27

In no time at all, one of the men from CIPHER arrived at Kurt and Joe's booth. He looked nervous. Kurt offered a hand. Between the man's monochromatic hair and his willingness to shake Kurt's hand, Kurt knew he wasn't dealing with Degra.

"Sorry," Kurt said, "but I need to speak with someone in full authority."

The man hesitated, spoke into a lapel-mounted microphone and gave in. "Come with me."

"No," Kurt replied. "I need him to come speak with us. Here, at our booth."

The man looked uncomfortable. He relayed Kurt's message. Words flew until finally the man with the microphone moved off and a thin figure with a white streak in his dark hair appeared. He stopped a few feet from Kurt and came no closer.

Kurt glanced at Joe. "Might be a good time for you to admire the view."

Joe got up, offered his seat to Degra and went for a walk.

Degra looked at the seat but remained standing. "I'm told you want to speak about something."

"The source code for the stolen computers," Kurt said. "It was to be installed when the Vector units reached California. Since they never made it there, they currently lack everything but the most basic operational system. In other words, they won't do what any of your buyers want them to do."

Degra shifted on his feet, but he didn't buckle. "I assure you, the source code is in our possession and will be fully transferred—along with the machines—to the highest bidder of this auction." The man smiled wolfishly, revealing a gap in his teeth that seemed to line up with the white streak in his hair. "Which would give your employers the very thing they've been after for the past five years, so I suggest you tap that IPO money for all it's worth."

Degra had performed his due diligence, which played into Kurt's hands. "In that case, why don't you prove it to me?" Kurt asked. "Share a portion of the code that I can check against the records I have on file? But before you answer, you need to understand I have the ability to verify the programming even if no one else here does."

Degra's thin face turned sour. His eyes narrowed and his brows pinched together. He obviously understood the two-way trap Kurt had set for him.

If he refused to share a sample of the code, he was all but admitting he didn't have it. And if he risked sharing a fabricated section of code—and Kurt was able to determine it was false—he would lose not only his highest bidder but possibly others should Kurt make a scene as he walked out.

The icy veil cracked. "I might remind you there are plenty of bidders here who would gladly take the servers without the software. The Russians and Chinese, for instance. They can most certainly develop their own operating system. Or simply pirate the original program at a later date. It's the physical architecture of the servers and the silicon chips inside them that they're most interested in purchasing."

Finally, a breakthrough. CIPHER didn't have the code. Which meant Kurt had the leverage he needed.

"I'm sure they'll be plenty happy with the machines alone," Kurt admitted, "but they'll pay far less. And you'll be in their crosshairs if you deceive them. Trust me, they're not going to come looking for you with arrest warrants and notices from Interpol."

Degra fumed. For a minute, it seemed like he might even snap. Kurt was threatening his payout, his entire scheme. But he held it together. After all, a moment of violence right now might cost him two hundred million dollars later. "You must have some reason for this line of questioning. So, why don't we skip the rest of the banter and get right to it?"

Kurt slid the portable drive unit from his pocket and placed it on the table. "You need the code. I have the code. But it's going to cost you more than money."

Kurt imagined the rapid chain of thoughts going through the man's mind. Hydro-Com's bitter rival sued for theft of intellectual property. Of course they had the code. They would have done anything to get it.

Degra tore his eyes away from the portable unit. "Assuming I believe you, what type of exchange might you be interested in?"

Now came the tricky part. Kurt had to drive a hard bargain or it would seem like a trap. But asking for too much would blow the deal. "We get two of the machines for nothing. You sell the rest to whomever you want. We get fifteen percent of the sale price funded directly from here as the sale closes."

Degra was once again looking at the device on the table. He was practically salivating. "My people will need time to verify your claim."

Kurt put two fingers on the drive unit and pushed it across the table toward Degra. "The password is CIPHER," he said, glancing over at the ticking clock on the screen. "You have twenty-six minutes."

CHAPTER 28

While Kurt conversed with the man from CIPHER, Joe made a grand tour of the ballroom. Like anyone supposedly wandering aimlessly, his first stop was the nearest unobstructed window.

Standing with his hands behind him, he studied the view to the west, where the Tamsui River appeared like a black snake slithering through the brilliantly lit city. Clouds were blowing in as a weather front approached. Rain was in the forecast but not until the morning.

Aware that he was being watched, he feigned boredom, glanced back toward Kurt and Degra and then moved on.

Passing the various booths, he noticed half of them were empty now, while the remainder were packed with men and women plotting strategy. He couldn't approach close enough to hear their whispered conversations, but he recognized some of the nationalities. In one booth, he saw three men with pale Caucasian faces. Probably Russian.

A few booths down, a group of Chinese in expensive suits were posing as businessmen from Shanghai. But they sat ramrod straight, suggesting they were military men or intelligence agents from Beijing.

By the far wall he saw a group of Middle Eastern men. Iranian, probably. He was surprised that they'd remained in the bidding. Then again, oil money was flowing once more.

Turning away from the Iranians, Joe arrived at the bar. Another group stood nearby, conversing quietly. This team was harder to place. Three men and a woman. They were Asian. And if Joe heard right, they were speaking Mandarin, with fluid postures and almost casual demeanors. The men wore dinner jackets with no ties. The woman had on a burgundy-colored pantsuit.

As Joe watched, the woman glanced at the electronic boards, which had just changed over to indicate the third round of bidding would be starting early. Joe studied her features in the reflected light.

"You've got to be kidding me," he said under his breath.

As she turned his way, Joe looked off in the other direction. Attempting to be nonchalant, he leaned on the bar, angling his body so the woman could see only his shoulders and back. He ordered a shot of Don Julio tequila and gazed off toward the windows.

It was all for naught. As the bartender poured the liquor, someone approached him from behind. The hint of jasmine-scented perfume told him who it was.

He spoke without looking her way. "What in the world are you doing here?"

"I'm tempted to ask you the same thing," Yan-Li said. "This is an odd place to find an oceanographer. That said, there are those who think NUMA is a front for the CIA."

"Actually," Joe said, "we're part of the Justice League of America. Superman, Batman and Wonder Woman will arrive at any moment."

Joe caught her smile in the reflection of the mirror behind the bar. The same innocent smile she'd often reacted to his jokes with whether they were good or bad. It faded quickly. A moment of light in a sea of dark emotions.

"Is Kurt with you?" she asked.

"He is," Joe said.

Her posture softened. "I'm glad to hear it," she said. "I was . . . I was worried."

"About Kurt?"

"I thought something might have happened to him," she said, "that's all. He takes such risks."

Joe put his hand on his shot glass. "Seems like we're all doing that these days. Now, what are you doing here?"

"I don't have time to explain," she said. "But you and Kurt need to leave. You need to get out of here as soon as possible."

"These people stole American technology," Joe said. "We're not leaving till we get it back. Even if we have to buy it. A little demeaning, I admit. But in the end, it's just business."

"These people aren't businessmen," she snapped. "They're murderers."

"They're not choirboys," Joe replied. "But they're not going to hurt people who are trying to pay them millions of dollars."

She appeared frustrated by his logic. She sighed and fidgeted. "Please," she said. "Just leave."

The sound of desperation reverberated in her voice. No bravado. No demands. Just simple pleading.

Joe turned toward her. She was intense, on edge. He could see that she didn't feel safe despite her words. "If someone is forcing you to do this, just come with us," Joe said. "We'll get you home."

"I have no home," she said coldly. "They've taken it from me. If I leave now, I'll never get it back."

Joe didn't quite follow.

"I've said too much already," she insisted. "Please go. If you stay, things will only get worse."

She left without another word, departing as smoothly as she'd arrived, with the perfume lingering for several seconds before it too was swept away.

Joe stared at the shot of tequila in front of him.

He exhaled, lifted the glass and knocked it back. Life can never just be easy.

Returning to the booth, he found Kurt sitting with one leg crossed over the other. He appeared relaxed and smug. Everything going better than planned.

Joe slumped into his seat, ready to ruin the mood.

"You look like you've seen a ghost," Kurt said.

"I have," Joe replied. "And something tells me she's going to be a problem."

CHAPTER 29

On the far side of the room, Yan-Li and her entourage were gathering. Yan was fighting with her emotions, trying to decide if the sudden appearance of Kurt and Joe was a blessing or a curse.

She briefly considered asking them for help. Assistance so close at hand was not something to toss away without a second thought. But Emmerson's men were hovering, as they'd been ordered. And even if she escaped their clutches, it would mean disaster for her mother and children. Ultimately, that was all that mattered.

"We need to move up the timetable," she announced.

The leader of the group stepped forward. He was a wiry man of modest height with muscular forearms and long, spidery fingers that suggested a powerful grip. They seemed to be in constant motion and most certainly would strangle her if she tried to cross her new master.

Emmerson had called him Guānchá, or the Watcher. Whether that was a joke or a warning, it certainly told her his function. He hadn't let her out of his sight since they'd met, casting intense and suspicious glances her way anytime she moved too quickly or too far away.

"Why would we move now?" Guānchá asked. "There are still too many people here."

The plan was to wait until the last round of bidding and move against Degra during the final phase, when everyone's eyes would be on their own bids and the dwindling time left to enter just one more.

"Because American agents are going to interfere if we wait," Yan said.

"The man at the bar?"

He'd clearly seen her speaking to Joe.

"Yes," she said. "I know him. He works for their government. He won't be alone. We move now or we'll lose the opportunity."

A low grunt signaled Guānchá's understanding. He spoke to the other men in their party. "You know what to do," he said. "Get in position."

"I'll make contact with Degra," Yan said. "When he steps out of view, I'll subdue him. Make sure you're close by when I act."

The men nodded. Two of them left the booth,

headed toward the front of the ballroom and the elevators.

Yan-Li watched them go and left the booth in the opposite direction, heading for the stage. Guānchá and a man named Zhu trailed behind her, blending in with the crowd.

With her heart beating over a hundred times a minute, Yan did what she could to compartmentalize the situation. She had a task to complete, that's all.

She spotted Degra in the crowd. At first, she thought he was headed for the stage, but he passed it without a glance, striding briskly toward the back room, bumping into someone in his haste and not bothering to even turn to acknowledge the incident or apologize. He's distracted, Yan thought. And angry. That could play to her advantage.

She glanced back at Guānchá to make sure he'd seen her and changed course.

Degra pushed through the door into the back room, where a storage and staging area had been turned into the auction's command center. Three men stood back there, two hired guards and one of Degra's most trusted technicians, a hacker who called himself Ferret.

Ferret's job was to monitor the guests in the ballroom and the highly encrypted links each of the bidders was using. Just to see what he might glean from their systems. He had two laptops working in front of him.

Degra stopped at Ferret's desk. "New task," he said, holding out the drive Kurt had given him. "Analyze the program on this unit. I need to know if it's legit."

"What's it supposed to be?" Ferret asked.

"The operating system for the Hydro-Com servers."

Ferret looked surprised. "We've been trying to break into Hydro-Com for weeks. How did you get this?"

"One of their competitors handed it to me," Degra said while pumping sanitizer from a bottle on the desk onto the palms of his hands. "They want to trade the code for two of the machines and a large commission."

"Pricey," the man said.

"Not if it's genuine," Degra said. "Run it through the strongbox and look for anything that might cause a problem."

Ferret pulled out a third laptop from underneath the desk. While the strongbox had multiple systems designed to look for viruses and Trojan horses, it was also air-gapped. And without any mobile communications power, it couldn't be used to introduce a virus into their network.

Opening the laptop and booting the operating system, Ferret began the analysis. "It's a huge program."

"It should be."

"Even if we overclock the CPU, it's going to take a while to examine."

Degra didn't have a while. "Do what you have to," he said. "I need an answer before we start the next round."

Ferret offered a look that suggested that was impossible but went about attempting to make it happen anyway.

Degra let him work, turning away and heading for the exit. He put a hand on the door, pulled it open and came face-to-face with a vision in burgundy.

Yan-Li stepped boldly into the room. Instead of pretending she was lost, she demanded attention. "My employer would like to make a preemptive bid. Five hundred million and you end the auction now."

The look on Degra's face was pure shock. "You need to leave here," he said. "If the other bidders get wind of this . . ."

"I will be heard," she demanded, blocking the exit.

Degra reacted with incredible speed, lunging toward her and pinning her against the wall using his forearm. A stiletto knife appeared in his hand. He snapped it open and pressed it under her chin.

"Choose your words carefully," he said. "You have thirty seconds."

He had her pinned to the wall with her arms down. She was shaking with adrenaline but clear-headed. Her own weapon was already in her hand. A needle-tipped pen.

She thrust it forward and up. It punctured his shirt

and went deep into the layer of muscle around his abdomen. As she thrust it into him, her thumb slid forward, depressing a plunger on the side of the pen and injecting him with a rapid-acting anesthetic.

He pulled back, grunting. "Foolish witch . . . I'll have you fed to the . . ."

He never finished the sentence. His eyes rolled back, his legs buckled and he crumpled to the floor in a heap.

"Thirty seconds was more than enough," she said.

As Degra hit the ground, his men reacted. The technician in the corner stood up, nearly knocking one of the laptops over, while the two guards rushed toward her.

Two soft pops from a well-silenced gun went off in rapid succession and both men fell to the floor. One had been hit in the heart, the other between the eyes.

Yan-Li turned to see that Guānchá and Zhu had entered the room behind her.

Guānchá pointed toward the man with all the computers, holding up a finger until the man froze in place. As the tension faded, Guānchá smiled and then shot him in the chest.

The bullet put the man on the ground, but he was still writhing in pain. To finish the job, Guānchá stepped forward, grabbed the man by the neck and snapped it with a violent twist.

Yan shivered, imagining him using the same ferocity against her. She turned to Zhu, considering the task at hand once again. "We need to get moving. The freight elevator is in the back. Tie and gag him."

Yan helped Guānchá drag the dead men behind one of the desks in the corner while Zhu bound Degra's hands with a zip tie and hoisted the unconscious man onto his shoulder in a fireman's carry.

With Zhu carrying Degra and Guānchá right behind her, Yan led them into a dark, narrow hallway, heading for the service elevator. Reaching the far end, she pressed the up button and the waiting began.

The car was seven floors away. And unlike the high-speed expresses servicing the lobby, this one was a local and slow.

Just as it began to descend to their floor, all hell broke loose in the ballroom behind them.

CHAPTER 30

Shouting and gunfire rang out from the express elevator vestibule at the front of the ballroom. As the remaining crowd turned toward the disturbance, a man in blood-soaked clothing crashed through the folding screen, knocking one of the delicate crystal statues to the floor.

The shattering glass stunned everyone. But when the lights went out and the ballroom was bathed in staccato flashes of machine gun fire, everyone dove for cover.

After an initial spate of chaos, CIPHER's hired guns began firing back. Like all non-Hollywood combat, there was far more confusion than clarity. Glass wall panels soaked up shots, cracking and spidering in all directions. Bullets hit the chandelier in the middle of the room, lopping off its petals and dropping them to the floor in colorful crystalline explosions. Someone pushed a fire escape door open to start the exodus, setting off the alarm and adding flashing strobes to the madness.

Veterans of many firefights, Kurt and Joe dropped to the floor at the first sound of gunfire. Rolling beneath the table and lying flat against the marble tiles, they analyzed the scene.

"And it was all going so well," Kurt said.

A couple stray bullets zipped past.

"This must be what Yan was trying to warn you about," Kurt said. "Could have used a bit more notice. And some details."

"Something tells me she's not in charge," Joe said. "But who is she working for? And why?"

"Has to be Emmerson," Kurt replied. "CIPHER stole the Vector units out from under them. Who else would have any reason to turn this violent?"

"Makes sense," Joe said. "But what's her connection with him?"

"Other than they both live in Hong Kong, I can't think of one."

He scanned the ballroom. With only the emergency lights and the glow from the city coming in the windows, it was hard to make out much of anything. The flashing strobe lights didn't help. "Do you see her out there?"

Joe squinted. "Nope."

"What about Degra?"

"That's another negative," Joe said. "But if she's working for Emmerson and he wants those computers back and Degra is the only one who knows where they are . . ."

Joe didn't have to finish. He and Kurt were on the same wavelength. He crawled out from under the table and sheltered by the side of the booth. The fighting near the front of the ballroom had settled down into potshots and angling for position. "We need to find them."

"Looks like her people are trying to blast their way to the elevators in hopes of making an escape," Joe said.

Kurt shook his head. "Yan would know that's a dead end. She'd have seen CIPHER's people downstairs. I'm calling that misdirection."

"Get everyone looking at the front of the house and sneak on out the back—is that what you're suggesting?"

"That's how I'd do it," Kurt said. "I'd rule out the fire escape too. Hard to get a hostage to walk down eighty-five flights of stairs."

Joe nodded. He'd studied the plans of the building in case they needed their own escape routes. "There is a freight elevator in the back but it covers only the top quarter of the building. While it won't get you to the ground, it'll get you past the blockade. Or take you up top if you have something else in mind."

"Nice," Kurt said. He stood up and grabbed the whiskey bottle and a cloth napkin off the table. "Lead on."

Kurt followed Joe across the floor until they came to the staging area at the back of the ballroom.

Joe nudged the door open and glanced inside. "Empty."

They pushed into the room, quickly discovering the bodies of the three men piled up in the corner. "They've definitely been here."

"Look," Joe said, pointing to one of the computers.

Kurt glanced at the laptop. The portable drive he'd given Degra was sticking out of the main USB port. "Leave it," he said. "It's still running. Maybe it'll find something. Now, where's that elevator?"

"Down this hall and back around to the right," Joe said.

This time Kurt took the lead, with Joe a few steps behind. As they made the final turn, Kurt noticed a light at the end of the hall, a vertical column of illumination that was narrowing as the elevator doors closed.

He rushed forward, saw Yan-Li's face and dove to the side as she raised a pistol and fired.

His last-minute dodge took him into a stack of silver-plated serving trays. They went flying, clanging against the wall and across the floor in an off-key symphony.

With the elevator door closed, the hall went dark.

Joe rushed over to Kurt to help him up. "Still think she's not acting of her own accord?"

"More than ever," Kurt said. "She missed me by a mile."

———

Inside the elevator, Yan lowered her pistol and turned toward Guānchá. "We're not going to have much time on the rooftop. Did you call in the extraction team?"

"Of course."

"How far off is the helicopter?"

Guānchá glanced at the time. "Three minutes."

Yan looked up at the numbers on the panel. This elevator wasn't an express like the ones that had brought them up from the ground floor. In fact, it seemed interminably slow. At the same time, waiting three minutes on the open roof sounded like an eternity.

Back in the ballroom, the firefight in the elevator vestibule had settled into a stalemate, with the two groups trading shots while remaining undercover.

The two men Guānchá had sent to secure the elevator had done their job, making quick work of CIPHER's security team and holding their position against the reinforcements. To boost their chance of success, they'd flipped the heavy table on its side, dropping behind it and using it as a shield and a position to fire from. That had kept them safe. But as the seconds ticked past, they began to worry.

The plan—as they knew it—was for them to take the elevator lobby, attract CIPHER's men and then once Yan-Li had captured Degra, she, Guānchá and

Zhu would take out CIPHER's reinforcements from behind. If that didn't work, the backup plan was to use Degra as a hostage, forcing CIPHER's gunmen to stand down and allowing the whole group to escape the building safely.

Neither of these things appeared to be happening. Guānchá and the cavalry had not arrived to shoot CIPHER's men in their collective backs nor had there been any sign of a cease-fire suggesting Degra had been captured.

The first of the two men, whose name was Gesh, spoke his fears. "Something's gone wrong. They're not coming."

The second man agreed. "We need to get out of here."

"Cover me," Gesh said. He moved sideways, firing several shots into the ballroom and punching the button for the elevator as he reached the wall.

Seeing Gesh exposed, one of CIPHER's men popped out to take a shot. But the man behind the table fired first, triggering a burst from his machine-pistol and riddling the target with several direct hits.

The man staggered backward and fell. Gesh dove back behind the table. He hit the floor as a wave of return fire came from the ballroom.

He covered his head as the sharp, thudding sound of bullets hitting the table assaulted his ears. Thankfully, the table was made of thick wooden planks laid over a metal backing. Each shot splintered the wood and punched a circular dent in the steel. But so far, no bullets had forced their way through.

"I'm almost out of ammo," his partner shouted. "Where the hell is that elevator?"

Gesh looked up at the display on the wall. Glowing blue numbers indicated where each of the elevators was and what direction it was moving. The last elevator in the row was coming up.

"Slide the table back," Gesh said, grabbing onto one side. "The elevator is almost here."

Working together, they pulled the heavy shield backward, moving deeper into the lobby until they stopped next to the door of the approaching car.

A quick glance back toward the ballroom told them that the lobby was still empty, with CIPHER's men remaining hidden but not yet brave enough to charge.

Gesh fired once again for good measure. "Come on," he said, urging the elevator car to arrive quickly.

A soft ping.

The doors opened.

And a hail of bullets poured forth from within.

Gesh and his partner were hit with multiple rounds before they could even move. They fell without getting off a shot, winding up on the floor, sprawled out with trickles of blood leaking from beneath them.

CIPHER's ground-floor security team stepped from the elevator, quickly surrounding the dead men. The man in the olive-colored suit shouted across the room. "All clear. Get the lights back on."

The switch was found. The overheads flickered to life. The ballroom's illumination came up seconds later.

The place was wrecked and nearly empty except for CIPHER's men and a few guests and staff who had been injured or too scared to run for the stairs.

One of the other hackers came running forward. "Degra's missing. Ferret and the others are dead."

No one wanted to be there now. The police and the Army were probably on their way. But if anyone could answer their questions, it would be Degra. And having a few assailants to hand over to the police would help deflect any blame.

"These men were with the group from Macau," the security chief said, studying the dead men's faces. "There were five people in that group, including the woman in burgundy. Where is she now?"

The technician grabbed the laptop that had been knocked from the overturned table. It was linked by Wi-Fi to the wristbands. A quick scan was performed.

"Back of the building," one of his men said. "Freight elevator. Heading for the roof."

The man in the olive suit turned around. The main elevators at Taipei 101 were the fastest elevators in the world. They went all the way up to the observation deck. "Let's meet them at the top."

CHAPTER 31

The freight elevator jerked to a stop and Yan-Li slipped out the doors before they'd even fully opened. They'd come to the hundred and first floor, seldom visited, off-limits to the general public, where the management stored cleaning equipment, supplies and tools.

Yan stepped forward, found the exterior door and cracked it open, looking around for any sign of trouble. She saw the surface of the rooftop and the curved wall of the circular platform that made up the higher deck. Directly ahead lay a white crane that was used to lower the window-washing platforms. Other than that, the roof looked empty.

She stepped forward. The night air was heavy and humid with the threat of rain. A layer of mist drifted past, tinted orange from the glow of the illuminated spire above.

"It's clear," she called back, waving the others forward.

Guānchá came first, then Zhu, still carrying Degra over his shoulder like a sack of flour. The hostage was beginning to stir, groaning and moving one arm sluggishly. Yan hoped he'd be securely bound in the helicopter before the anesthetic wore off.

"Where's the helicopter?" Zhu cried out.

"Quiet," Yan demanded. She listened closely. The sound of rotor blades could be heard in the distance, coming in from the west. The noise grew louder and more thunderous. A landing light came on, piercing the mist with an arrow of light. It swung around, playing across the central column that held the building's lighted spire, bathing the rooftop in a brilliant glare. Yan held a hand in front of her eyes.

"Can't touch down," the pilot's voice called out over the radio. **"I repeat, we can't touch down. Move to the corner of the roof. We'll put one wheel on the edge and you'll have to climb in."**

Yan-Li rolled her eyes at the request. Move to the edge of a fifteen-hundred-foot building and climb up on the mist-slick wall. Hop from there into a helicopter balancing on the edge while the downdrafts swirl around you. Sure, she thought. No problem.

She clenched her teeth and stepped forward, kicking off her high heels and fighting her way into the wind as it whipped at her slacks.

The pilot was good. He eased the helicopter in close, putting the big machine exactly where he said he would. Its right-hand wheel touched the ramparts of the building while the lethal blades sliced the air within mere feet of the central spire.

Yan crouched at the edge of the wall. Turning back, she urged Guānchá and Zhu to hurry. "Come on," Yan shouted.

Guānchá moved out of the shadows, handing Yan the radio and stepping past her to climb up on the wall.

Its surface was wide and sturdy but slick with condensation. Guānchá tested the footing and reached for the helicopter, grasping a handle on the door and pulling himself in.

Safely inside, he turned and yelled to Zhu. "Hand him over to me."

Zhu stepped forward. But before he reached the wall, a brace of small-arms fire tore into the side of the helicopter, stitching a trail from the doorway up to the cockpit.

Yan heard nothing, but she saw sparks fly as the jacketed bullets punched holes in the helicopter's sheet metal. She dove to the wet rooftop as the helicopter peeled away, diving from its perch.

Zhu took several shots in the back and stumbled forward, almost heaving Degra over the wall in the process. Instead of falling to his death, Degra hit the wall face-first and slumped against it.

Dragging him to her position as a hostage, Yan took cover behind the metal stanchion that held up the window washer's crane. Checking her pistol, she got ready for what seemed like the last stand.

She was now trapped alone in the northeast corner of the building with a fifteen-hundred-foot drop at her back and CIPHER's foot soldiers closing in from the front.

CHAPTER 32

The sound of their own footsteps pounding metal stairs echoed off the concrete walls as Kurt and Joe raced up the fire escape toward the roof. They pushed open the door at the top, breathing hard but ready to take the fight to whomever they found.

The roof was empty but not silent.

"That's a helicopter," Joe said.

Kurt heard it as well. "This way."

They worked their way across the roof. The northeast corner came into view just as the helicopter began taking fire. It dropped away and vanished into the night, leaving several figures cowering behind a crane at the edge of the roof. They were trading shots with a group hidden around the curve of the building. "Looks like Yan and her friends missed the last flight out."

The sound of the helicopter faded rapidly.

Whatever payoff Emmerson had promised the pilot, it likely wasn't enough to fly into a combat zone.

"Something tells me he's not coming back," Joe said. "If we get Degra out of her hands, he'd owe us a giant favor. We might even be able to get him out of here to better accommodations. The kind provided free by the CIA."

Kurt was thinking the same thing. Number one rule when an operation goes sideways—grab the asset and get out. And this operation had gone about as sideways as it was possible to go. "Great idea, but we need to get CIPHER's men out of here before we offer our assistance." He pulled the cork out of the liter of Speyside. "Any chance you've got a light?"

Joe produced a Zippo lighter that he carried with him everywhere. "And I thought you were saving that bottle to make a toast."

"Who says I'm not?"

As Joe held the lighter, Kurt threaded the napkin down into the whiskey. It turned a dark amber color as it soaked up the heated 130 proof alcohol. "This has to be the most expensive Molotov cocktail in history."

"I figured you were warming it next to that candle for a reason," Joe said.

"Heat makes the whiskey more volatile," Kurt said. "More fumes mean a bigger explosion."

Joe lit the napkin. As it burned, Kurt eased around the curve of the building, hugging the wall, until he spotted CIPHER's men hiding behind some equipment.

The architecture of the roof, the position of the crane and the fact that Degra was still a hostage had brought the fighting to a standstill. Threats and demands were now being exchanged, punctuated by the occasional potshot.

"I count three of them," Joe said. "Let's hope they don't have any more in reserve."

With the napkin burning brightly, Kurt lobbed the thousand-dollar bottle of alcohol in a towering arc. It flew upward and dropped silently, smashing against the rooftop between CIPHER's men, exploding outward in a ball of liquid flame.

CIPHER's men scattered, covered in various amounts of burning whiskey.

Kurt rushed forward, tackling the nearest member of CIPHER's team and slamming him to the deck. To put him out of action quickly, Kurt pounded his head against the rooftop several times.

The second gunman was spinning and whirling, trying to put out the flames. He was arching his back, attempting to peel off his burning coat, when Joe body-slammed him to the roof.

The wet decking doused most of the flames, but Joe still offered his assistance. "Let me help you with that." He pulled the man's coat up and over his head. Before knocking him senseless with a right cross.

The remaining gunman was CIPHER's security

chief, the man in the olive-colored suit. He'd avoided the flames, having spun away from them, and was now looking around for the source of the attack.

He spied Joe and brought his pistol on target.

Joe dove to his left, combat-rolling behind the curved wall as bullets ricocheted off its concrete.

As the man fired at Joe, Kurt rushed toward him, launching himself into the man's midsection and driving the crown of his head upward into the man's chin.

The man in the olive suit didn't know what hit him. His head snapped back and he slammed into the roof as Kurt came down on top of him. He went out like a light, limp and unconscious.

As Kurt grabbed the pistol he'd dropped, Joe rushed up to him. "Nice tackle," Joe said. "Fifteen-yard penalty if this were the NFL."

"Sometimes unnecessary roughness is necessary," Kurt replied. "You pick up anything in the lost and found?"

Joe held up the pistol he'd taken from one of their foes.

"Good," Kurt said. "Now comes the hard part."

He turned toward the crane at the corner of the roof. Only now did he realize that just Yan-Li and Degra remained. He could see she was armed and that she was keeping the hostage in front of her as a human shield.

"Yan, this is Kurt," he shouted. "We can get you

out of here. But first you need to decide if we're friend or foe."

After several long seconds passed, a pistol came sliding across the rooftop toward them. Yan stood up slowly. "I don't know how you're going to pull that off but I trust you."

CHAPTER 33

Kurt picked up the handgun and stuck it in his belt.

"For a pair of guys who came in unarmed, we're starting to look like pistoleers," Joe said.

Yan helped Degra up. The anesthetic was wearing off. He remained groggy, disoriented and confused, but he could stand.

"What did you do to him?"

"Drugged him. Another five minutes and he'll start to be a problem."

Kurt turned to Joe. "Get him to the southwest corner and get him suited up. We'll be along in a minute."

"What about the rest of CIPHER's people?" Joe asked.

"There can't be many left," Kurt said. "And with half the Taipei police department heading this way, no one in the building with a criminal bone in his body will hang around for long."

"We probably shouldn't either," Joe noted, taking the prisoner and heading for the opposite corner of the roof.

Kurt figured they had a few minutes. The security teams would follow the standard procedure, honed to perfection in cities around the globe. First, they'd surround the building, setting up a perimeter. Then they'd enter in force, secure all the exits and clear the lower floors. Only when all that was done would they gear up and start ferrying officers to the eighty-fifth floor and the roof beyond.

As Joe left, Kurt turned to Yan. "How the hell did you get involved in this?"

She looked down, ashamed. "Emmerson took my son and daughter," Yan explained. "He has my mother as well. He says I owe him because of something my ex-husband failed to do."

In their time searching for Ching Shih's treasure, she'd told Kurt her husband was dead. "I thought you were a widow."

"I am," she said. "Now."

It finally made sense. "The man we found on the **Swift,** Lucas Teng, he was your husband?"

She nodded, tears welling up in her eyes. "He was involved in smuggling and piracy," she said. "He was taking that ship for Emmerson. CIPHER's people stole it out from under him. And now I have to pay for his failure. Emmerson won't let me go until he has the Hydro-Com computers in his hands."

Kurt felt for her. "Pirates and cybercriminals,"

he said. "You're not exactly keeping great company these days."

"My ex-husband's crew have been okay," she said. "I know they're criminals, but they know who I am and in the grand scheme of things they've been decent. Lucas was always decent even if he was a liar and a thief."

"You think they have your back," Kurt said. "Honor among thieves and all that?"

"I wouldn't go that far," she said. "But Lucas took care of them. So far, they seem willing to keep the faith with me."

That was something, Kurt thought. But not much. "What does Emmerson want with these computers? He's not a hacker, he's an old-school gangster."

"I don't know," she said. "To sell them, I guess. Like these people tried to do."

"Except he tried his best to keep the theft secret," Kurt said, "while CIPHER told the world about it to drum up interest."

It didn't add up, leaving Kurt with the feeling that Emmerson's plans ran deeper than anyone suspected. Still, as a new wave of sirens and horns echoed up from below, Kurt realized this wasn't the time or place for a full interrogation.

"We should be surrounded nicely at this point," he said. "Let's go."

He led her to the southwest corner of the building, where Joe had already opened an equipment locker and pulled out the items Steven Wu had positioned for them in advance. There were radios and handguns, even smoke grenades.

More importantly, there were backpacks containing BASE-jumping parachutes and harnesses to hook someone on for a tandem ride.

Joe had Degra in a harness and had pulled on his own parachute. He handed a backpack to Kurt and tossed a second harness to Yan.

Kurt glanced over the edge at the mass of vehicles and their emergency lights below. As he gazed downward, a thought occurred to him, a problem he hadn't considered earlier. He turned to Yan-Li. Moving in close, he asked her a question. "Do you still have an extraction team down there or was that helicopter your only way out?"

She looked up at him, her eyes wide yet soft. "There's a ground team," she admitted.

"Do you have a way to reach them?"

"A radio," she said.

"Call them," he said.

"Why?"

"Call them and tell them to stand by," he whispered. "But first . . . pick up my gun." He placed it down beside her as he tightened the straps on the chute.

Her eyes were wild with confusion. "I don't understand."

Kurt looked into her eyes. "What happens to your family if you don't show up with Degra?"

"I don't even want to think about it," she said.

"Then pick up the gun, call your team and take Degra to them."

"And what?"

"You tell me," Kurt said.

With that, he stepped away, turning his back on Yan and allowing her to do as he'd asked.

She hesitated, torn between what she wanted to do, which was leave with Kurt and Joe and find safety again, and what she had to do, which was anything and everything possible to save her family.

She grabbed the weapon and stepped up onto the platform. With her left hand, she racked the slide loudly, getting everyone's attention.

Kurt froze on purpose.

Joe and Degra did likewise, though out of genuine surprise.

"I'm sorry," she said loudly, "but I'm taking Degra with me."

Kurt turned slowly. She had the gun in one hand, the radio in the other. With the pistol aimed at them, she spoke into the radio, alerting her ground team.

Joe held on to Degra, who squinted as he tried to acclimate to the fog of the anesthetic. He seemed to understand what was happening but was powerless to stop it.

"Give me your chute," she demanded. Kurt handed her the tightly packed chute, which she slipped into and buckled.

Turning to Joe, she gave a new order. "Bring him to me," she demanded.

Joe looked in Kurt's direction. Kurt nodded. "Hook them up."

With the order given, Joe manhandled Degra up onto the platform, latching his harness to Yan's straps.

"Wait," Degra said. The first words he managed to force through the fog. "You can't do this." He twisted and turned but was now standing on the edge of a fifteen-hundred-foot drop. He grew very still, not wanting to fall.

"You know we'll come after you," Kurt said, mostly for Degra's benefit.

"You'll never find us," she said. "Not without help."

"You're right," Kurt agreed. "Not without help."

Without another word, Yan-Li pushed off, swan-diving forward and taking Degra with her.

Kurt stepped up onto the platform, looking down. The chute opened instantly. The paragliding wing snapped into shape. Yan and her prize soared outward, away from the building and toward the river.

"What was that all about?" Joe asked.

"Solving two problems and creating a third," Kurt said as he pulled on the tandem harness.

"I hope you have something to erase my memory back on the **Sapphire,**" Joe said, "because I really don't want to have to explain this."

"I'll do the talking," Kurt insisted. "Now, let's

get out of here before we have to explain it to the Taiwanese federal police."

Joe stepped up onto the platform, hooked onto Kurt and moved toward the ledge. "On one," he said. "Three, two, one."

As Joe uttered the last numeral, he and Kurt stepped forward, pushing off the building and falling through the dark. Joe deployed the parachute in textbook fashion. The harness pulled taut and they began to fly instead of fall.

With Joe controlling the wing, Kurt took the opportunity to study the world around him. He looked up at the wing above them, though it was matte black and hard to see. He glanced down and back at what must have been a hundred emergency vehicles clustered around the base of the tower.

As he'd expected, the building was tightly surrounded, which meant they'd face little trouble once they got beyond the perimeter.

As the building fell behind them, Kurt looked forward. They were heading across the city, making for an open-air park that Wu had told them to aim for. The ground seemed to pick up speed as they grew closer. Even with the high-efficiency wing above, they were dropping fast.

A stand of trees loomed ahead. They cleared it by several feet and raced across the open grass of the park. Joe pulled on the lines to soften the landing. Kurt lifted his feet. They skimmed the wet turf for a moment and slid to a stop.

Quick releases had them free of the chute in seconds. A small van raced over, cutting across the sprawling lawn. It pulled to a stop beside them, the side door already open.

Kurt and Joe dove in the back. Wu stomped on the accelerator and pulled away. Crossing the grass again, they raced onto the nearest street.

At this point, Wu turned to look back. Joe had radioed to tell him they were about to jump with CIPHER's leader in their custody, but a quick count of his passengers told him that hadn't happened.

"Where's Degra?"

It was a question they'd be asked repeatedly in the coming hours and days.

CHAPTER 34

NUMA YACHT SAPPHIRE

By the time Kurt and Joe returned to the **Sapphire,** the low-pressure system had rolled in. As a meteorological event, it wasn't much to speak of, just a steady, soaking rain that pelted the decks and streamed down the tinted windows of the ship.

Too bad, Kurt thought. If ever he'd have welcomed a torrential downpour strong enough to block the satellite signal, this would have been the day.

Instead, the system worked flawlessly and video links to the NSA and NUMA communications rooms were quickly established.

Rudi Gunn appeared on one screen, while the triumvirate of Anna Biel, Elliot Harner and Arthur Hicks appeared on the other.

"The incident is all over the news," Rudi said.

"Reporters are suggesting at least eight or nine fatalities, maybe more. Glad to see that you two are all right."

Kurt explained how Yan-Li and her crew used a firefight as a diversion and how he and Joe had tracked her and Degra to the roof, where they dealt with CIPHER's reinforcements in hopes of capturing Degra themselves.

That part brought praise for their bravery and quick thinking, but as Kurt explained how Degra ended up leaving with Yan, the goodwill faded away.

The initial broadside of disappointment came from all three agency directors. But Kurt noticed subtle differences.

After voicing shock at the outcome, Anna Biel of the NSA became still and aloof. The color had certainly drained from her face and the worry lines in her forehead had grown deeper. She didn't look happy but seemed content to let the others attack for now.

Arthur Hicks from the CIA's cyber division was bitterly disappointed, but he deferred to his boss, who was fuming over the outcome.

"Let me get this straight," Elliot Harner said. "You had Degra in your hands and you let this woman take him? In our parachute no less?" He shook his head in disgust. "I don't know whether to put this down to incompetence, stupidity or something worse. It sounds like you chose sympathy with this woman over the objective."

That was enough to stir up Rudi, who was launching into a vigorous defense of Kurt's character, when Kurt waved him off.

"It's all right," Kurt said. "Let him speak. Go on, Harner. Finish your thought."

As if he sensed a trap, Harner pulled back a notch. "The point is, you were sent in with a simple directive. You were given assistance and a plan to follow. There was nothing in that plan that suggested cooperating with a Chinese national who might be on Emmerson's payroll."

"She is on Emmerson's payroll," Kurt said. "She admitted as much. But I haven't gotten to that part yet. Let me guess. You knew that before we went in but chose not to share it with us."

Harner realized he'd said too much. "We connected her to Lucas Teng."

"And you didn't think that information might be worth sharing with us before you sent us into the lion's den?"

Sidelong glances from Anna suggested she wasn't happy about this development either. "The bottom line is, you had the asset in your hands and you let him go."

Kurt glanced at Joe, just a little forewarning that the lambasting was about to get worse. Might want to buckle your seat belt.

"I didn't let her take him," Kurt said coldly. "I told her to take him. In fact, I just about pushed her off the damned roof."

Kurt said this with clear eyes, looking straight into the camera, but it still caught every member of the videoconference off guard.

"Did she have a gun on you or something?" Anna asked.

"She did," Kurt admitted. "But I gave her that too."

A slight groan came through Rudi's microphone but nothing more. He'd known Kurt long enough to suspect he was laying the groundwork for something. He just hoped the payoff would be worth it because there was no denying how it looked at the moment.

"Have you lost your mind?" Harner said. He turned to his right, addressing the NSA director. It was still technically an NSA operation. "This is why I was against using NUMA in the first place. They're uncontrollable from the top on down. It's an entire agency of loose cannons. Always has been. Right since Sandecker launched it."

Anna gave him a look that said watch your tone with me, but she offered no defense of Kurt or NUMA. She turned back to the screen. "I'm expecting you to have a damned good reason for this. And I'm not interested in waiting any longer to hear it."

Kurt obliged her. "You sent us in with two options. Plan A. Convince Degra we had the source code and get him to plug the portable drive with the worm into one of his computers. Objective accomplished. It's in place, though who has that computer now and what they're doing with it I have no idea. Plan B. Even simpler. Make sure we were the top bidder and buy the computers back. But that obviously went by the wayside when Yan and her friends turned the place into a shooting gallery. That left us with the standard, unspoken Plan C. Grab the asset and get out of Dodge. Which we were in the process of doing until I saw two hundred police cars surrounding the building and realized this was about to blow up into a huge international incident."

"At which point you gave up and punted," Harner said accusingly.

"No," Kurt said. "I spiked the ball and stopped the clock."

The group fell silent, a sense of confusion mixing with the possibility that Kurt actually had a plan up his sleeve.

The NSA director took the conversation over. She spoke calmly and firmly. "Kurt, I'm going to need you to explain how you stopped the clock, which I take to mean you've bought us time that we otherwise wouldn't have."

"It's simple," Kurt said. "Degra's not some captured terrorist from a failed state without a legitimate government. He's a Chinese national, a citizen of the world's only other superpower. We can't just abduct him and put him in a safe house somewhere and sweat the truth out of him. We'd never get the chance. The second the Chinese know we have him—and, believe me, they would know already—you'll be facing unrelenting diplomatic and economic and legal pressure to release him."

Harner sat back and crossed his arms.

"The thing is, Degra knows this," Kurt added. "He also knows we're not going to torture him. At worst, he faces some sleep deprivation, long sessions of good cop/bad cop and maybe something like waterboarding."

"We don't do that anymore," Harner insisted.

"It wouldn't work if you did," Kurt insisted. "Not in the short amount of time you'd be able to hold him. All he needs to do is stall and keep it together for a few days and the Chinese government will force us to release him or start abducting our diplomats off the street as bargaining chips. In that scenario, the clock runs out. Degra wins. We lose. Game over."

"Degra's a criminal," Harner pointed out.

"A criminal who knows where the Vector units ended up," Kurt said. "They'd move heaven and earth to get him back."

The CIA director had no way to refute this logic, but he looked no happier. "Well, thanks to you they won't have to move anything. He's probably back in Hong Kong already."

"Almost certainly," Kurt said. "But in the hands of his enemy. A party not bound by the Geneva Convention, Chinese law or—as far as I can tell—any sense of morality and human decency."

"Emmerson," Anna said.

"Exactly," Kurt replied.

She leaned forward, looking interested, the color rapidly returning to her face. "According to your scheme, Emmerson tortures Degra in ways we couldn't even consider. He gets the location of the servers and what? How does that help us? They're still in the hands of criminals even if it's a different group."

"Because in this case we have an inside man," Kurt said. "Or, more accurately, an inside woman."

"Yan-Li," Anna said. "Of course."

Kurt nodded. The NSA director was now following in lockstep. She undoubtedly saw his whole plan, but he dutifully explained the rest. "Yan is trapped with Emmerson for now. Stuck doing everything he asks in hopes of getting her family back safely."

"Right up until the moment where he doesn't need her anymore," Anna broke in. "At which point, she and her family members become nothing more than liabilities that Emmerson will have every reason to dispose of quickly."

Kurt didn't disagree. "Yan knows that. She's too smart, too strong, not to see the truth. She knows we're out here and that we're after the computers. And she knows she can trust us. She'll bide her time and pick her moment and will reach out to us."

"And then?"

"I'll give you Degra, Emmerson and the Hydro-Com servers all wrapped up with a nice big bow."

The three rooms, separated by thousands of miles, went simultaneously quiet.

Anna nodded almost imperceptibly. It was a huge risk. But the risk had already been taken. And by NUMA, no less, not the NSA. Her calculations were simple. If it went bad, Kurt and Rudi would shoulder the blame. But if it went well, if somehow it worked out in their favor, there was plenty of glory to go around.

Still, she had questions. Beginning with how far Kurt had thought this through. "Why would she contact you instead of the Chinese authorities?"

"Because Emmerson has people up and down the ladder in the Chinese government. It's how he's survived for so many years. In her position, contacting the Chinese authorities is the same thing as talking to Emmerson himself."

Anna nodded once more. "And what makes you think he hasn't shot her and dumped her body in the ocean already?"

"Because he still needs her for the task at hand," Kurt said. "The Hydro-Com servers remain hidden somewhere beneath the waves. If they weren't, we'd have picked up a signal by now. Yan-Li is Kinnard Emmerson's diving and salvage expert. He doesn't have time to find a new one. And he'd be hard-pressed to find a better one even if he did. She's safe enough until those computers are in his possession or until they're beyond his reach."

"How sure are you of all this?" the NSA director asked.

"Looks like I've staked my career on it," Kurt said.

"I'd say so. But the fact is, you did stop the clock
and give us one more shot at winning the game. I
assume you have a plan?"

"I have a few ideas."

She turned and focused on Rudi. "It's your mission now, Gunn. Trust me when I tell you the blood
will be on your hands if this goes badly."

The participants signed off and only the NUMA
link remained active. Rudi took a moment to com-
pose his thoughts and then addressed Kurt and Joe.

"As usual, you two have climbed out on a very
long branch and sawed halfway through it before
looking to see what's underneath you. I'm honestly
surprised to find you're still in the tree. But since
I'm probably up there with you at this point, tell me
what you need to make this scheme work."

Kurt knew Rudi would deliver. "Intel regarding the whereabouts of Yan-Li's children and her
mother," he said. "If we rescue them, he loses all
leverage over her."

Rudi nodded thoughtfully. "I can get that.
Chances are, Emmerson has them tucked away in
Hong Kong. What else?"

"Yan said she was working with her ex-husband's
crew. While they're not honor students, they don't
look so bad compared to Emmerson and Degra.

They could be allies. Assuming we have something to offer them."

"Asylum could be arranged," Rudi suggested.

"I was thinking of something more appealing to people who consider themselves pirates," Kurt said.

"Money?"

"Treasure," Kurt said. "Lots of it. In the guise of Ching Shih's lost ship."

"The **Dragon**?" Rudi's eyes widened. "In case you've forgotten, treasure isn't finders keepers anymore. We can't just give a chunk of the world's shared heritage to a gang of hijackers and criminals because it suits our purpose."

"We don't have to give them the treasure," Kurt said. "There's a ten-million-dollar reward on offer to anyone discovering the ship's location. All we have to do is bring up proof of the wreck and the Chinese will pay handsomely, probably throwing in medals and commendations to the finders at the same time. What self-respecting pirate could resist becoming rich and legitimate in one quick move?"

Rudi didn't even try to answer. He'd given up fighting Kurt's intuition. Most likely, Kurt was right. Whether the Chinese would be so magnanimous was another question altogether, but that was for the pirates to weigh in their own minds. "There's still the matter of finding the ship."

"We were close before all this kicked off," Kurt said. "That wreck is either hidden in the bay at

Ki-Song Island or somewhere nearby. Paul and Gamay could pick up where we left off. If the wreck is where I suspect it is, they'll be able to pin down a location by the end of the week."

"And if it isn't?"

"Start emptying out the petty cash drawer and hope Yan's crew will switch sides on the cheap."

As usual, Kurt had simplified things greatly, relying on a healthy dose of optimism, faith and good fortune to fill in the blanks. It was a formula that had worked before.

"Done and done," Rudi said. "Now, how do we get you into Hong Kong, land of political unrest and ten thousand facial recognition cameras? It won't do you any good to walk in and have Emmerson and the Chinese government aware of your presence from the moment you land."

"I couldn't agree more," Kurt said. "Which is why we'll need the **Phantom.**"

CHAPTER 35

Joe stood at a computer panel next to the landing pad on the aft deck of the **Sapphire** as it ran south heading for the island of Ki-Song, where they'd abandoned the search for the **Silken Dragon.**

He squinted against the sunlight as what appeared to be a giant drone flew toward the yacht from the blue skies to the east.

"Air Truck approaching," a computer voice announced from the panel in front of him.

The Air Truck was a brand-new vehicle developed for NUMA by a group of engineers who insisted that pilots were superfluous. Much like the coming revolution of self-driving automobiles, aircraft equipped with cameras, radar, LiDAR and GPS receivers and other high-tech sensors were now flying themselves.

As a pilot Joe found it downright insulting, considering the Air Truck nothing more than a big, dumb remote-controlled plane with four fans attached to it. Still, he admired the solid-state battery packs that allowed the aircraft to fly five hundred miles on a single charge and plug into any outlet on any ship or power grid to recharge.

He pulled on a headset and transmitted a message to the passengers. "Stand by for autoland sequence."

Paul Trout's voice responded. **"Hope it's not a rough one. My back is already aching from being crunched up in this seat."**

Joe was happy to add another negative data point to his list of issues with the Air Truck. It clearly wasn't designed for tall people.

"This thing usually gets it right," Joe said jokingly, "but occasionally it flips over and dumps people in the sea. I'd hold on if I were you."

Gamay spoke next. Her tone suggested she was not amused. **"If anything of the sort happens, I'm holding you accountable, Joe Zavala. I'm not thrilled traveling across the ocean in a plane with no pilot to begin with."**

"Not my idea," Joe insisted.

Pressing a button on the remote panel, Joe activated the auto-land. Using eight different cameras and LiDAR, the Air Truck approached the **Sapphire** from the stern, matched its course and speed, lined up over its small helipad and descended gently. The truck even managed to adjust to the swells and the rocking motion of the boat.

With the skids down on the deck, the fans shut off, winding down much faster than a helicopter's rotor. In seconds, the machine drew still. The canopy slid back. Paul sat up straight for the first time in two hours, sighing audibly as he stretched.

He climbed out, followed by Gamay. Each of them carried a small duffel bag.

"Nice digs," Paul said, looking around at the yacht. "Last time I went out on a mission, Rudi sent us in a leaky trawler."

"She's a good ship," Joe said of the **Sapphire**, "though you'll find the staff grouchy and mostly unhelpful. Whatever you do, don't ask Stratton about the drones."

Kurt appeared a moment later, stepping through a door in the aft section of the superstructure. Hugs and handshakes were exchanged.

"Ships that pass in the night," Kurt said.

"Something like that," Gamay replied. "You two are heading into a hot zone, from what I'm told."

"Not sure how hot it'll be," Kurt replied, "but crowded, noisy and dangerous would be accurate."

"Better you than us."

Paul and Gamay went inside while Kurt and Joe climbed into the Air Truck.

Using a touch screen in the cockpit, Joe entered the coordinates of their destination and pressed start. He cringed. Flying an aircraft with a start button.

The fans spun up quickly and the Air Truck took off. It sped off to the east, heading for a NUMA supply ship carrying the **Phantom** in its hold.

CHAPTER 36

CHINESE TERRITORIAL WATERS
EAST OF VICTORIA HARBOUR

Water moved like black oil across the curved hull of the **Phantom,** sliding so cleanly that even when the vessel ran on the surface it appeared less like a machine and more like a minor swell in the fabric of the sea. Once it descended to any depth, the craft became virtually undetectable, invisible, making no sound, even resistant to detection by active sonar pulses.

A joint effort between the U.S. Navy and NUMA, each organization contributed different technologies to the finished project. Officially named **Phantom,** it looked more like a flattened, elongated turtle, sporting a wide, oval shape.

Designed for secret reconnaissance missions, the submarine had no dive planes or conning tower, no rudder or protruding propellers. It used water jets hidden deep within its shell for propulsion. It maneuvered by raising and lowering panels on the top and bottom of the hull and by vectoring the thrust from the water jets like a modern fighter aircraft.

Power was provided by a microreactor, the smallest nuclear power plant in the world, and it carried a suite of high-tech gear including its own stealth drone and sensitive scanners to intercept radio signals.

Kurt and Joe were mostly interested in its ability to get into crowded, shallow waters without being detected. Already quieter than any standard submarine, the **Phantom** had additional noise-canceling systems, including a quilted layer of gel-filled cells on the outside of the hull that absorbed and dampened active sonar pings.

As Joe guided the craft toward Hong Kong and Victoria Harbour, he detected a Chinese frigate on a training exercise. "We could run by them and give this underwater Frisbee a real-world test."

"Sorry, amigo," Kurt said. "I know you'd love to wring this thing out and see how it works, but we're under strict orders to avoid Chinese anti-submarine resources."

"Buzzkill," Joe said. "But I get it. This sub is as top secret as the computers that we're looking for."

"Which is why they stuffed three hundred pounds of explosives in the hull. So we can blow it to pieces if we're about to get scooped up in a net."

"Is that before or after we exit?" Joe asked.

"You know, they really didn't say."

"Let's hope it doesn't come to that," Joe said. "For now, I need to move into the channel. The bottom is coming up. Depth is going to be less than thirty feet in a minute or two. We need to get over into the dredged portion of the harbor or we'll be running too close to the surface."

Kurt nodded in Joe's general direction. "Just watch out for wreckage of the **Queen Elizabeth,**" he said, referencing the famed ocean liner that had burned and sank in the harbor back in 1972.

"If we run into that, we've gone way off course," Joe said. "The Chinese buried most of it under a land reclamation project."

Kurt laughed and turned his attention back to the screen in front of him. While Joe piloted the craft, he busied himself reviewing a raft of intelligence data downloaded to their computer prior to departure.

Emmerson owned quite a spread of properties throughout Hong Kong. But the largest and most isolated was a sprawling complex on the west side of an area formerly known as Junk Bay but now renamed Tseung Kwan O.

Junk Bay had once been the domain of shipbuilding and shipbreaking. As China's wealth increased and those industries moved to poorer nations, the area was redeveloped, sprouting glittering high-rise buildings, public parks and sports complexes.

The only remaining hint of the old world was Emmerson's industrial park, which took up the old shipbreaking yard and a massive seaplane hangar that had once belonged to the Royal Navy.

Emmerson bought the dilapidated hangar from the British government before they left Hong Kong in 1999. Since it needed to be torn down, he'd gotten it on the cheap. But instead of demolishing it, Emmerson had refurbished it, turning the hangar and the yard into a production facility, where he rebuilt aging military equipment for export to Third World nations.

"Reminds me of a junkyard where I used to scavenge old car parts," Kurt said, looking at the photos.

The sprawling open space was littered with defunct military apparatus, most of it being stripped for parts and valuable metals, some of it being rebuilt and upgraded for sale.

"Looks ex-Soviet or Communist bloc," Kurt said, "which would explain those pipeline welders that attacked me near the wreck of the **Canberra Swift.**"

Joe agreed. "That mini-sub they were operating from looked Chinese. But that doesn't mean we're going to find Yan's mother and her kids here. What makes you think this is the right place?"

"It's the most logical choice," Kurt said. "Out of the way and easy to secure. The kind of place where the presence of armed guards wouldn't arouse any suspicion. Beyond that, we have the intel Rudi got from the CIA."

"Bet he had to pry it out of Harner's clenched fist," Joe said.

Kurt figured the same, though Rudi hadn't mentioned it. "Turns out the CIA had this place under surveillance since shortly after the **Swift** disappeared. Apparently, Emmerson was an early suspect. They even considered the possibility that the **Swift** was hidden in the seaplane hangar."

"Not a bad thought," Joe said. "It's a huge building. Those segmented sliding doors span over four hundred feet from side to side. If you're into vaulted ceilings, here's a place with a hundred-thirty-foot clearance."

"It is pretty impressive," Kurt admitted, "but ultimately not big enough to hide a six-hundred-foot ship inside. Not even diagonally. Still, the early surveillance paid off in other ways."

He swiped through pages on the screen, sliding his finger to the left to reveal additional documents, stopping at one that was particularly helpful. "These photos were taken three days after the hijacking."

He held the tablet where Joe could see it. The images were grainy due to the distance from which they were taken but clear enough to show a pair of large men escorting three smaller figures toward the building.

In a series of shots, it was obvious that the diminutive people were being pushed forward, but their identities remained hidden by oversize gray sweatshirts with the hoods pulled up.

"Can't see their faces," Joe pointed out.

"Intentional," Kurt said.

"Looks like three kids."

"Two kids and one grandma," Kurt said. "Yan's mother is only four foot eleven."

Joe glanced at the photos once more and nodded. "That's something."

"Here's something else," Kurt said. "Some tech at Langley managed to get a track on Emmerson's men by cloning one of their cell phones. The man made several trips to a nearby pharmacy. A text indicated blood pressure and heart medications were to be picked up."

Joe shrugged. "It's stressful being a henchman in the syndicate these days. They really should have a support group."

"You'll get no argument from me," Kurt said. "But the prescriptions match the medications that Yan's mother takes. The kind of pills that get left behind when you kidnap someone from their home and don't want to go back to the scene of the crime."

Joe conceded the point. "Sounds like we're heading to the right place. What do we know about the building?"

"Strong security system, cameras, multiple guard shacks, not to mention gates, razor wire fences and junkyard dogs," Kurt said. "But that's on the land side. We'll enter from the water. The building juts out over the bay and it's basically a covered marina. That makes it more of a boathouse than an airplane hangar. The doors stop at the surface. We just swim up to them and under."

"Should I even ask about motion sensors?"

"Plenty of them," Kurt said. "But not on the bay side. Too much activity out on the water for motion sensors to work properly. From the waves alone, they'd be buzzing every ten seconds, let alone from boats, seagulls and flying fish. Cameras are likely, but they won't see us beneath the surface."

"Like your confidence," Joe said. "And once we're inside?"

"We find some out-of-the-way spot, shed our wetsuits and walk around like we own the place."

"I see," Joe said with a grunt that suggested the plan was hardly foolproof. He pulled at the collar of the cheaply made coveralls he was wearing. "Figured there was a reason we were dressed in these one-piece Elvis Presley jumpsuits."

"Elvis would never be caught dead in a jumpsuit without sequins or fringe," Kurt replied. "But you're right. We're not dressed like this for comfort. These match what Emmerson's people were wearing in the CIA photos. They should help us blend in."

"And just how many of Emmerson's men are we likely to encounter?"

Kurt glanced at his watch. It was late. After midnight. "Hopefully, very few. There are bound to be several men keeping an eye on the hostages. But other than that, it should be a soft target. Even if there are men and women working inside, they'll be mechanics and run-of-the-mill personnel. Not everyone will be armed."

"But some of them will."

"Naturally."

Both men fell into silence after this. They entered Victoria Harbour proper using the central trench of the dredged channel. This took them west, deep enough to avoid any issues with local shipping traffic.

Joe eased closer to the surface as he turned the **Phantom** into Junk Bay.

"According to the latest satellite photo, there's a small fleet of barges anchored outside the breakwater at the north end," Kurt said.

"Sounds like a good place to park without being seen," Joe replied.

Slowing the submarine to a crawl, Joe eased it between two of the barges, stopping at a spot between the hulking rectangular vessels. Still submerged, he deployed a motorized anchor that would burrow down into the mud. "Not much current here, but I'd rather not come back to find that our ride has drifted off without us."

The anchor bit in, twisting itself downward until the sub was held securely, fifteen feet below the surface.

"Let's gear up and get into the lockout chamber," Kurt said. "It should be an easy swim to get from here to the hangar."

CHAPTER 37

JUNK BAY, HONG KONG

Kurt and Joe left the turtle-shaped submarine by way of a dive lockout on the underside of the craft. They used rebreathers and wore full-face helmets with integrated communications gear so they could communicate. Instead of wetsuits, they wore a layer of clothing NUMA called shrink-wrap, which was basically a waterproof one-piece suit with no insulation.

It went over a person's existing gear, usually a wetsuit, to provide an additional layer of insulation or as protection from chemicals or other harmful elements in the water. Unlike regular dry suits, which were bulky and buoyant, the shrink-wrap version didn't add any buoyancy, at least not after one used an attached straw to suck all the air out, vacuum-sealing it to their body.

"Important parts of me are sweating in this suit," Joe said, testing the comm system and trying to get a laugh out of Kurt.

"Mine too," Kurt said. "Just keep swimming. The cool water helps."

They moved across the bay at a depth of ten feet, guided by a soft glow in the water spilling out underneath the hangar door that turned the dirty harbor water a greenish hue. As they closed in on their destination, a distinct pattern of stripes became noticeable where the light was blocked by a grate of vertical steel bars.

Studying the layout, Kurt got the impression that it was a giant lower jaw clenched shut until someone inside pressed a button that would allow it to fall forward. It was certainly obvious that the bars could be dropped to allow boats or seaplanes in and out, but in the upright and locked position the setup was well suited for preventing anything larger than a mackerel from slipping past.

"Didn't see this on that intel report," Joe said.

"No one dived down here to check things out," Kurt replied. "But I expected a barrier of one kind or another. All in all, this isn't too bad."

He unzipped the pack on his chest and pulled out a battery-powered saw. It had a thick cutting disc made of carbon steel encrusted with industrial diamonds.

Kurt switched it on. The blade spun up instantly,

quickly reaching four thousand rpm. Holding it against the first bar, Kurt cut into the corroded steel, grinding through it in a matter of seconds.

He made a similar cut several feet below the first and removed the length of steel, which he dropped in the silt down below. Before long, he'd removed four bars from the grate. The resulting gap offered plenty of room for a diver to pass.

As Kurt put the saw away, Joe eased up to the opening. "You realize the Chinese will have us shot for committing espionage if we get caught."

Kurt put the saw back in his chest pack. "Trust me," he said, "that pales in comparison to what Emmerson will do."

Twenty miles away, Yan-Li watched a demonstration of brutality that would have proven Kurt's words prophetic.

There, in the semidarkness of an unadorned storage room, in the lower levels of the Government House, Degra was on his knees. He'd been beaten, tortured and threatened almost continuously, but he'd yet to crack and tell them anything.

The longer Degra held his tongue, the more enraged Emmerson became. He was soon administering the beating personally, ignoring Degra's body and pummeling the man's face instead.

Degra's right eye was swollen shut. His face was a mesh of bruises and cuts while blood, saliva and mucus dripped from his busted lips and shattered nose.

"You thought you could steal from me," Emmerson hissed, leaning in close to the bloody pulp of a face. "You thought your little veil of anonymity would protect you."

He slapped Degra across the face, more to insult him than to hurt him any further. A spray of bloody spittle coated the wall. "You tap away at your little keyboards, thinking you have power, but like everything else in your world it's not real. And it won't help you here."

"My people will come for me," Degra insisted. "They know you have me, and they'll come for you."

"Oh, how I wish they would," Emmerson replied. "But unfortunately, they think the Americans took you. Which means they'll never find you here . . . with me."

Degra spat at Emmerson, marring his gray suit with blood and saliva.

Emmerson stepped back, wiped the spit off and plucked a hammer off the table. Lunging forward, he slammed the hammer down on one of Degra's outstretched fingers.

The howl of pain that came from the prisoner was barely human.

Yan-Li turned away as the hammer was lifted from the bloody mess that had been Degra's index finger. She held her breath, trying not to vomit.

"Nine more to go," Emmerson warned his captive.

"I assure you, each blow will hurt more than the last."

Even though Degra had threatened to cut her throat, even though he might have been the man who'd killed Lucas, it was still not part of Yan's makeup to watch a man be tortured. Desperate to see it stop, she blurted out the first thing that came to mind. "This is pointless."

Emmerson paused and turned her way. "Getting squeamish on me?"

Yan gritted her teeth. She tried to look stone-cold. "No," she lied. "But this is going nowhere. He's losing blood. He's becoming incoherent and numb. If you keep beating him, he'll go into shock. He'll die. And we'll be back to square one."

Emmerson raised an eyebrow. "We?" he said with a surprised tone. "Interesting. And just what would you suggest we do?"

She was surprised to have used the word **we,** even though her needs and Emmerson's were aligned in certain ways. But her own sense of reality was becoming blurred as exhaustion and desperation set in.

Perhaps she'd spoken subconsciously, hoping to curry favor with him. Perhaps it was a form of Stockholm syndrome arising in her tired mind.

She willed herself to think, breaking out of her stupor and trying to come up with something that would please Emmerson and get Degra to speak without more torture.

"He's a germophobe," she said suddenly. "He's afraid of sickness and bacteria and filth. You could use that against him."

"Interesting," Emmerson said, putting the hammer back on the table. "Very interesting." He turned to one of his men, speaking loudly so Degra would overhear. "Go to the cages. Bring us the rats."

The rats, Yan thought. The starving, feral, flea-bitten rats. They were probably half mad after being trapped for so long. The smell of them alone might convince Degra to speak. But if not, they'd soon start crawling on him, sniffing at him and gnawing at his wounds. His bloody face and fingers will smell like fresh meat.

The thought horrified her as much as watching Emmerson continuing the beating. "I can't be here for this. I can't watch this anymore."

"No need," Emmerson said. "We'll lock him in here alone and let time do the work. Between the stench of their filthy bodies, the sound of their claws scraping on the ground and the sharpness of their little teeth, he'll soon be begging for a chance to tell us where those computers are."

Emmerson led her out of the room with one last instruction to his guards.

"Let him scream a good long while before you call me. I want him broken before I come back down here."

They left the storage room together, Kinnard Emmerson keeping strangely close and Yan-Li wondering whether she'd set in motion a form of mercy or something more evil than a continued physical beating.

As if sensing the struggle, Emmerson smiled warmly. "Come with me," he said. "You've done well. You should be rewarded."

CHAPTER 38

After swimming beneath the hangar door and into the former seaplane base, Kurt was surprised by the amount of light filtering down through the water. Instead of a few left on for security purposes, it seemed like the large overheads up in the rafters were blazing.

"Stay low and slow," he said. "It's not as dark as I hoped."

They crept along near the bottom, careful not to stir up any sediment, heading for an area of shadow cast by a vessel resting above on the water.

Swimming beneath the hull, Kurt drifted upward. He placed a hand against the underside. He could tell right away this was not a normal craft.

The hull was a wide V shape, strangely ribbed on each side. It was clean and smooth, without a hint of nautical growth. It was also long and narrow. More cigar-shaped than any ship Kurt had ever seen.

He eased along the hull, looking for a rudder

or any sign of a propeller but finding nothing of the sort. About halfway down, he noticed a second shadow diverging from the hull at a sharp angle. In the distance, he saw another shape sitting in the water. It looked like a thirty-foot canoe, but Kurt recognized it as an outrigger pontoon.

Surfacing cautiously, he came up beneath the wing of an aircraft—which was parked with its tail toward the dock and its nose pointed out toward the doors.

Joe surfaced next to him, both of them hidden by the overhang of the aircraft's V-shaped hull.

"What is this thing?" Kurt asked in a low voice. Even though they were hidden and communicating by radio, something about being on the surface made him want to whisper. "Flying boat of some kind?"

Joe looked it over. Despite the limits on what they could see, he could tell it was something rare. High above, on a short wing at the front of the plane, were three jet engines mounted side by side. He had to assume three additional engines were mounted on the other side for a total of six. The thick wing that grew from the side of the aircraft was solid and stiff. The tail split in the middle, taking the shape of a broad letter Y.

"It's an Ekranoplan," Joe announced.

"Sounds like something from a science fiction movie," Kurt replied. "What, exactly, is an Ekranoplan?"

"A crazy idea the Russians came up with years ago," Joe said. "It's something like a flying boat, but it doesn't actually fly very high. It travels in ground effect, which is an area near the surface where the plane gets an extra cushion from air pressure underneath the wing and body. Ground effect allows this thing to move quickly and carry a tremendous amount of cargo. Much more than you could lift in a normal aircraft this size."

"This thing is massive," Kurt said, trying to get a sense of its full dimensions.

"Bigger than a 747," Joe said. "The Russians built a bunch of them in the seventies and eighties. The idea was to use them like fast ships, launching invasion forces in a type of seaborne lightning strike."

"I'm guessing Emmerson refurbished it for himself in the midst of his other work," Kurt said.

"And kept it here under wraps," Joe said. "Away from the prying eyes of our satellites."

Refocusing, Kurt scanned the hangar, trying to get a sense of the place. The interior was a vast, empty rectangle with docks on three sides and the formidable doors protecting the front. Despite the bright fluorescent lights shining down from up above, the overall impression was of a giant cave. The dark metal walls and murky water soaked up the light. Shadows cast from the tail and wings of the Ekranoplan added to the effect.

The only real color came from the yellow-painted

beams of a ceiling-mounted bridge crane used for carrying heavy equipment from the dockside.

So large was the hangar that even the monstrous plane didn't fill it. A couple center-console boats were docked on the far side with a pair of small delta-winged craft floating beside them.

"More Ekranoplans?" Kurt asked.

"I think they're skimmers," Joe said. "Short range, a little slow, but a lot faster than the fastest boat. Think of them as minivans with wings. Used to ferry personnel around like a ship's tender."

"With all this activity, it should be easy enough to blend in with the crowd," Kurt said. "But it's not going to help us find Yan's mother and her kids."

"Or maybe it will," Joe said. He was staring off toward the bank of offices that sat behind the dock farthest from them. "What do you make of that?"

Kurt followed Joe's gaze, spotting one of Emmerson's people carrying a tray of food and three bottles of water. He went up the stairs, along a walkway, stopping at the fourth door on the upper level. Using a key, he unlocked the door and stepped inside.

Joe offered his assessment. "Either the boss wants a midnight snack or that's where they're keeping Yan's family."

Back at the Government House, Yan-Li was ushered into the luxurious confines of Kinnard Emmerson's home. The difference between these accommodations and Degra's couldn't have been more stark.

She sat on a luxurious white couch covered in some rare hide of exceedingly soft material. Once she was comfortable, Emmerson offered her a glass of wine from a lead crystal decanter. She accepted it and reluctantly thanked him.

The wine was bold and smooth, of a brand and vintage she'd never be able to afford.

"Remember the deal I offered you back in your small apartment home in the Mid-Levels?" Emmerson said, pouring himself a glass and placing the stopper back into the decanter. "A small fortune for your help?"

"I remember," she said.

"That offer still stands," he insisted.

She studied him closely, trying to gauge his sincerity while recalling a proverb her mother often used. It's easy to promise the sun when you never intend to wake up in the morning.

"Why would you want me to join you now?" Yan asked. "You have Degra. You'll soon have the computers. Why not just let me and my family go? You don't need me anymore."

"Need you?" Emmerson laughed. "My dear, you should know by now, it's the other way around. Your attractive little face is all over the news in Taiwan. Your ex-husband has been identified as the man who hijacked the **Canberra Swift.** And you've been linked to the shoot-out and to Degra's disappearance. If I removed my protective hand, you'd be in prison before the day was out. And that's only if CIPHER's people don't find you first and cut you to shreds."

He shook his head like a disappointed professor admonishing a student. "I'm afraid it's you and your family who need me." He put a hand on her shoulder and gazed into her eyes. "You're not my prisoner anymore. You're my ward."

His touch and his words turned her stomach worse than the torture she'd been forced to watch. One part of her mind rebelled against what was obvious manipulation, but another, more calculating part realized there was some truth to it.

She would expect CIPHER's people to look for revenge where they could get it. Even if they didn't, the Chinese government could make her disappear without a trial if the wrong official decided she'd betrayed the nation.

She was trapped, tangled up in a web. It seemed the harder she tried to get free, the tighter and heavier the web became. Perhaps that's why she'd used the word **we** in the storeroom. Perhaps she truly had nowhere else to turn.

She took another sip of wine, hoping the alcohol would soon calm her nerves.

"It's not just my inherent generosity," Emmerson said with a straight face. "You've also proven yourself to be cunning, resourceful and discreet. I won't say loyal, because I'm not a fool. I know it's your family's fate that binds you to me. But I also know you could be an excellent asset in my world."

Her discomfort grew. "How would that work? Once these computers are recovered, how will I be of any use to you?"

"Not all my dealings are so nefarious," he insisted. His hand slid from her shoulder to her forearm. "I have legitimate businesses and pretensions to society like everyone else. You could help me in that capacity. Loan me a bit of your prestige and, in return, I could fund your research. And perhaps— from time to time—I'd require a favor or two." He shrugged. "Who knows? You may even come to appreciate me."

She wasn't sure if the favors he was referring to were going to be criminal acts or personal intimacy. Either way, the idea repulsed her. But she was getting better at hiding it. She decided two could play this game.

"I'm a big enough woman to understand what you're saying," she said. "Truth be told, I spent years suspecting Lucas was up to more than he let on. A woman knows these things about her husband. She notices mood changes and speech patterns. For a while, I thought he was having an affair. When I found out he was faithful in love but leading this double life . . ."

She paused as if reliving the past, but she was actually watching Emmerson's reaction. He was looking . . . interested.

"Instead of defending himself," she continued, "he asked me to join him. And for a moment—for just a moment—I considered it. The life of a researcher is dull and monotonous, for the most part. That's why I hunt for treasure. At least it's a thrill."

As she spoke, Emmerson sat across from her, sipping his wine, eyes sparkling, legs crossed at the knee. The torturer was gone, the aristocrat had returned. Even if a splatter of Degra's blood still marred his expensive shirt.

He topped off her glass and spoke. "I understand you've been studying the life of the pirate queen, Ching Shih," he began. "I'm quite familiar with her as well. As you obviously know, she faced a similar choice. It was her husband, Lord Cheng, who was the true pirate lord of the region. She was merely his consort and partner until he died suddenly. Ching Shih could have cowered and withered away. Instead, she took charge of the dynasty, building the most powerful and feared fleet this part of the world had ever known."

Yan knew all this of course. She also grasped how her situation was similar to the pirate queen's she'd so long studied . . . and how it was different. "I don't see myself as a pirate queen."

"Why not? Your husband's men do. They follow your every command."

"You said they'd betray me if push came to shove."

"And they will one day," he insisted. "But people can be more than one thing. It often depends on whether they're led properly or allowed to roam free."

She nodded and took another mouthful of wine. She'd eaten so rarely and slept so little, it was starting to hit her already. She fought to keep her thoughts clear.

"The point is," Emmerson added, "Ching Shih made her choice. Now you must make yours. I give you my word that once the computers are in my possession, I will release you and your family as I've promised. You'll be free. Your husband's debt satisfied. But what shall become of you?"

It was a rhetorical question meant to send her spiraling down the path of possibilities that inevitably led to focusing on the worst ones. She did her best to keep her mind from making those leaps. "I'll consider it," she said. "If I do accept, I'll need some guarantees."

"Of course," he replied. "First, let me give you a gift. Instead of returning to the city, you'll sleep upstairs tonight. There's a room at the end of the hall. It has a marble bath, a closet filled with designer clothes and a bed made up with silk sheets and the finest of pillows."

She looked at him nervously.

"Don't worry," he said, "the door has a sturdy lock. No one will be visiting you in the middle of the night. But while you rejuvenate, please think about my offer. Picture your children in the most prestigious of schools and your mother being attended to instead of working at her age. Imagine them protected from every danger while you fly off on expeditions the university could never afford to pay for. I can create that world for you. But you have to want it first."

"I'll need to sleep on it," she insisted.

"Of course," he said once again. "And what's more important for a deep, healthy sleep than saying good night to your children?"

Her eyes widened. "Are they here?"

"No," he said, disappointing her. "But you may speak with them."

She looked up. "I'd like that," she said a little too eagerly. "Will you give me the phone again?"

"I'll do you one better," he said, picking up a remote control and pointing it across the room at a flat-screen television. "I'll let you see them in living color."

The screen lit up. A communications link was quickly established. In a matter of seconds, the blank rectangle resolved into a crystal clear image. It displayed a spartan room in some industrial space. A mattress lay on the floor, along with a dirty comforter, several toys and a coloring book.

Yan's mother was there, her children in the background sleeping with stuffed animals beside them. They all looked thin and frail, but they were safe and alive.

The sight released a flock of butterflies in Yan's

stomach. She tried not to overreact, but it was all she could do to fight back the tears.

Emmerson handed her the remote. "Five minutes," he said in the tone of a dutiful parent. "After all, it's quite late."

Emmerson left, allowing her the illusion of privacy. Yan spoke quickly, almost breathlessly. She asked a half-dozen questions, begged her mother to wake the children. She spoke with each of them about things both mundane and important and found herself promising things would soon be back to normal.

When her daughter told her they were fine, Yan felt great pride in her strength. When her son said he'd had nightmares and wanted to come home, her heart shattered into a million splinters. The tears she'd kept at bay began to flow.

"Soon," she promised. "Soon."

Five minutes went by more rapidly than Yan could have imagined. When one of Emmerson's men came into the room to end the conversation, she almost lost control.

She harnessed her emotions and calmly said her good-byes, watched as the screen went blank. She stared at the darkness for a long, lingering moment and then followed one of Emmerson's servants upstairs to the luxuriously appointed room he'd had made up for her.

She took a bath, pulled on a pair of silk pajamas

that fit almost perfectly and climbed into the sumptuous king-sized bed.

Another wave of tears came crashing forth the moment she laid her head on the pillow. Despite every logical thought, despite all she'd suffered and risked, her tired soul could feel nothing but guilt and shame. Here she was, sleeping in the lap of luxury, while her mother and children slept on the floor of a dirty warehouse somewhere in Hong Kong.

But they are alive, she told herself. At least they're alive.

She cried herself to sleep, telling herself over and over that she'd do anything to save them, anything at all to keep them safe. Even joining Kinnard Emmerson, she thought finally, in his criminal world.

CHAPTER 39

After emerging from the water in a darkened corner of Emmerson's hangar, Kurt and Joe slipped behind a stack of equipment, peeled off the shrink-wrap and hid their dive gear.

Scouting around, they found a flatbed cart with several crates on it and used it as a prop to merge with the buzz of activity on the dock behind Emmerson's colossal floating aircraft. With knit caps pulled down tight over their ears, they crossed the dock, heading for the suite of offices on the far side.

"So far, so good," Kurt whispered. He kept his voice down as a precaution, but between the clang of equipment, the hum of a generator and the raised voices of men shouting orders to one another, there was little chance they'd be overheard.

"Agreed," Joe said. "But we're not going to get this cart up the stairs. How are we going to keep from being seen?"

"I have an idea," Kurt whispered back.

"Figured you would," Joe said. "So let me skip ahead and ask a pertinent question. How, exactly, are we going to get them out of here? We planned on sneaking them out of a quiet, empty hangar. That's not going to work with this place buzzing like a factory floor."

Kurt realized they'd have to adapt, but it all depended on what they found and where they found it. "Let's just get to the other side first. We'll figure that out later."

Pushing the cart along, they reached the far dock, where the boats and the small delta-winged skimmers were tied up. Moving along, beneath the walkway that fronted the offices on the second floor, they stopped near a door that was directly below the room where the food had been delivered.

Parking the cart next to the door, Kurt grabbed the handle and eased it downward. It was unlocked. Without hesitating, he pushed the door open and stepped inside. They'd found a storeroom filled with equipment and huge spools of cable.

Joe stepped in and Kurt closed and locked the door.

"Look at all this stuff," Joe said.

"What am I looking at?"

"High-capacity fiber-optic cable," Joe said, his hand on a giant spool of rubberized wire. Next to it he found a container filled with strange-looking tools. "These are automated splicing connectors for linking the cable together. Looks like Emmerson is going into the telecommunications business."

"Had a feeling he was up to something more than selling stolen goods," Kurt said. "First things first. We need to get upstairs to Yan's family."

"How would you suggest we do that?" Joe asked.

"By building a pyramid."

The first step was to construct a platform, which they accomplished by stacking crates on top of a table. The crates were spaced wide enough apart to put a desk chair on top of them.

"This would never pass an OSHA inspection," Joe said.

Kurt climbed the rickety structure and removed the dropped-ceiling panel. Nothing major stood in their way.

He tossed the panel down to Joe, pulled out the battery-powered saw and switched it on. It spun with an efficient electric hum, but the noise level rose as the blade cut into the ceiling.

"Better hope they keep up the racket outside," Joe said, moving toward the door and pulling a pistol from his coveralls in case they suddenly had company.

Kurt worked quickly, pulling out a bunch of insulation and cutting into the load-bearing panel above.

"Let's hope we're in the right spot," Joe said.

"Should be," Kurt replied. "I just hope I don't come up under someone's shoe."

He cut down and across and then up and back across the other way. As he connected the last incision to the first, the panel above him wobbled. Kurt handed the saw down to Joe before working the board loose.

It slid free and Kurt pulled it down while looking up. He spied the startled faces of two young children looking back at him. Yan's daughter, who was fourteen, had furrowed eyebrows and a stern gaze. She was the spitting image of her mom. Yan's son, who was ten, stared with wide eyes, astonished at what he was seeing. Behind them Kurt saw an older woman with a nervous look on her face. Yan's mother.

Kurt smiled and held his finger to his lips, hoping the universal shush translated across languages. "Don't make any noise."

Yan's daughter nodded. "Okay," she said in English. "Who are you?"

Kurt introduced himself and pointed to Joe. "We're friends of your mother. We work with her. We're going to get you out of here. But we need to hurry." He waved for them to come forth. "Send your brother down first."

The boy shook his head and backed away. Whatever Emmerson's thugs had threatened him with, he was afraid.

This was a bad development. Kurt pulled himself up and found Yan's daughter arguing with her brother in hushed but urgent whispers. "I promise, we'll keep you safe. But we have to move quickly."

The kid continued shaking his head and Kurt considered grabbing and tossing him down to Joe, but the last thing they needed was a ten-year-old screaming loud enough to draw Emmerson's heavies.

Needing a plan that didn't include gagging the kid, Kurt remembered Yan mentioning how her son loved old movies and pretending he was a character in them.

"It'll be like **The Great Escape,**" Kurt said. He began whistling the famous theme music to the best of his ability.

"**Great Escape,**" the boy said haltingly. "With Steve McQueen and Richard Attenborough."

Kurt grinned at the reference. He had a soft spot for anyone who loved old movies. "Don't forget James Coburn," Kurt said, picking the kid up and lowering him down to Joe. "If we're going to be characters from the movie, we might as well be someone who actually made it out."

Yan's daughter smiled and went next. Finally, Kurt helped lower their grandmother through the gap. She let go a little too quickly, but Joe caught her like they were an ice-skating duo performing a trick.

Now it was Kurt's turn. He swung his feet back over the edge and was just about to drop in when a key hit the lock on the door.

Damn, Kurt thought. We were that close.

The door pushed open and one of Emmerson's men stepped in casually. He froze, dumbfounded at the sight of a fully grown man sitting on the floor with his legs through what looked like a trapdoor.

While he didn't understand that particular vision, there was no mistaking the meaning of the 9mm pistol with a suppressor attached that Kurt had pointed at his heart.

Kurt saw the clarity on the man's face. With his free hand, Kurt waved for the man to finish entering and move across the room to the far wall.

Hesitation followed. A moment of indecision.

Don't do it.

The man grabbed for a gun that was tucked into his waistband, snatching it free with surprising speed.

Kurt fired two shots. The first shell hit the man's leg, causing him to stumble into the room instead of back out onto the second-floor walkway. The second shot hit his center mass.

The man fell onto a desk in the corner of the room. Other than a grunt, he made no sound, slumping flat and sliding off the wooden surface.

As he fell to the floor, the pistol dropped from his hand. It hit grip first and discharged loudly, shattering the office window with an errant shot.

So very close.

Kurt jumped up, grabbed the dead man's weapon

and glanced out the shattered office window. Several of Emmerson's men were looking up toward the second level. One of them was pointing right at the window. The shot came from up there, he imagined them saying.

Leaving the window, he came back to the square hole he'd cut in the floor.

"Sounds like we've lost the element of surprise," Joe said, looking up.

"We're about to," Kurt said. "Several of Emmerson's men are heading this way. Time for a new plan. I'm going to keep their attention focused up here while you get Yan's family out of here and back to the **Phantom**."

As Joe had mentioned earlier, that was easier said than done. "I suppose we could steal one of the boats, but we still have to get the hangar doors open to get out. Most likely, the controls are at the end of the dock. How long do you think you can occupy these guys without getting shot?"

"I have a few jokes I can tell," Kurt said, "but I wouldn't dawdle if I was you. Put your earpiece back in. Might as well stay in contact."

Joe wedged the earpiece into his right ear. Kurt did the same and stepped away from the opening and back to the window. He pressed himself flat against it, looking out at an oblique angle.

A couple of Emmerson's men were on the stairs, several more were rushing over from the concrete dock. "I've got five or six coming my way," Kurt said. "The rest are still working."

"We're ready to make a break for it," Joe said. "Give 'em something to think about."

Kurt intended to do just that. He unscrewed the suppressor from his weapon so it would discharge with the maximum noise possible and positioned the dead man's gun in his other hand. Squinting at the target, he opened fire with both guns.

The percussive blasts echoed through the cavernous building. The approaching men threw themselves flat against the stairs and the men on the deck took cover as well. But Kurt was not firing at them. He was aiming upward at the banks of lights in the rafters. With a handful of well-placed shots, he took out three of the nearby arc lights.

Shattered glass and glowing filament sections fell like embers across the dock. The section above the offices went dark as a wave of return fire came in his direction.

Kurt dropped to the floor, moved to the door and cracked it open, firing out the tiny gap he'd made.

There was a lull in the shooting. Orders were shouted across the dock. A high-intensity light was trained on his position. It lit up the second-floor walkway while leaving the lower level that much darker in contrast.

Kurt knew what came after being illuminated. He dove backward as a hail of bullets tore into the corrugated metal wall.

"I seem to have their attention," he said. "Make a break for it next time I open fire."

"When is that going to be?" Joe asked.

"In three . . . two . . . one . . ."

As Kurt traded fire with the men on the stairs, Joe cracked open the door that led to the newly darkened dockside. The trusty cart with its payload of wooden crates remained where they'd left it.

"Follow me," he said to the children. "Stay close and tell your grandmother we're going to one of those boats."

The gunfire had unnerved the kids. The boy seemed more frightened than ever, but his sister grabbed his hand and spoke to their grandmother. They pulled in beside Joe, ducking down low, as he pushed the cart across the darkened pier.

One of Emmerson's men spotted Joe, but instead of attacking, he shouted a warning, waving to Joe to back up and take cover. Joe stopped in his tracks and waved back. The man rushed off to join the fight against Kurt, having never seen the three escapees hiding behind the boxes.

Hoping not to draw any further attention, Joe changed course, weaving to the dockside and quickly reaching the first boat.

"Get in and hide," Joe said to Yan's daughter, asking her to tell the others. "Keep your heads down and don't make a sound."

The grandmother went first, helped by Yan's daughter. Yan's son hopped over the transom with ease. All three ducked down.

The small craft had an outboard motor, high gunwales to keep the spray out and a pedestal seat at the helm. The space between the center console and the side wall created the perfect spot to hide as long as everyone lay flat.

"I'll be right back," Joe said.

He left the cart and ran along the dockside toward the giant hangar door, finding the controls right where they belonged by the side of the door itself. There was only one problem. They were locked in the down position and Joe had neither a key card nor the password required to release them.

Up on the second level, Kurt was wondering about Joe's progress while trying hard to avoid getting shot to pieces.

He stuck his hand out the door, firing blindly down the catwalk at the men who were coming for him. Three quick shots and a retreat. He rolled away from the door as a hail of return fire tore into the office from several angles.

Light streamed in as punctures appeared in the door and the thin corrugated wall. The remains of the glass exploded out of the window frames. A drawer slammed open, releasing papers that fluttered around the room like feathers from a wounded bird.

Kurt pulled back farther, but the withering round of fire he expected did not come. He had something going for him that was even better than luck. Emmerson's men had to assume that Yan's mother and her kids were still in the room and they knew he would be enraged if they killed his valuable hostages.

Still, a charge would soon be launched. "How's it going down there?" Kurt called out.

"We've run into a snag," Joe said. "The hangar doors are locked down tight. I can't release them from here. Which means time for a new new plan."

A bullet hit the door. And another. They were clearly aiming for the hinges. A third shot took out the top hinge and the door swayed at an odd angle.

Kurt pushed over the file cabinet in the back half of the room and dropped down behind it for extra protection. "Whatever you're going to do, do it quickly. I get the feeling these guys are moving closer."

Guessing at their approximate location out-side the office, Kurt aimed toward the thin wall and fired off several rounds. Waiting a few sec-onds before firing again, he tried to conserve ammo, but he'd soon burned through everything in the dead man's gun and the last few shots from his own. He tossed the borrowed gun aside and replaced the magazine in his own weapon with his only spare.

He was more cautious with the rest of the ammo, triggering off shots sporadically, doing his best to space them out and give Joe time for whatever he had in mind.

CHAPTER 40

Joe's new plan took him in a different direction. He ran across the dock with his head down, trying to avoid getting shot. As he sprinted for cover, he looked like any other regular worker in the hangar. Just a man trying not to get hit by stray bullets.

But instead of taking cover, Joe climbed onto the ladder fixed to the wall. The one that led up to the enclosed booth where the crane operator sat.

He scaled the ladder with surprising speed, his hands and feet flying over the rungs. Reaching the underside of the small cab, he threw open the hatch and pulled himself up.

The crane operator turned as the hatch banged against the stops. The man had been watching the shoot-out down below. A bird's-eye view to the chaos.

He glanced Joe's way, said something in Mandarin and shifted forward.

Joe sprang from the top of the ladder and rushed the man, gathering his momentum and swinging a haymaker left hook.

The crane operator was knocked from his chair. He banged against the glass panel on the side of the booth, which kept him upright. His adrenaline surged and he lunged toward Joe in the constricted space, grasping at Joe's coveralls with one hand and clamping the other around Joe's neck.

The impact threw Joe back. He slammed against the rear wall of the cab. The crane operator pressed hard, trying to crush Joe's windpipe, but Joe's arms were free and a steam-piston blow to the man's gut knocked the fight out of him.

The crane operator doubled over, holding his stomach. Joe dropped a hammer of an elbow on the back of his head.

The operator crumpled to the deck. Joe looked around for something to keep him subdued. Finding a small electric fan that was plugged into a socket, he yanked it free, flipped the man over and hog-tied him with the cord.

Just to ensure that no one surprised him in a similar fashion, Joe shut the lower hatch and shoved the unconscious man's body on top of it.

"Now," Joe said to himself. "Time to make an exit door where there is none."

He climbed onto the seat and looked over the controls. He'd operated plenty of cranes before.

And even though the writing was all in Chinese, he had a pretty good idea which controls did what.

Looking out the glass, he saw the entire hangar below him—the small boats, the delta-winged skimmers, even the top of the Ekranoplan. As he studied the big plane, he noticed classic Russian designer touches. A random bulge here, an odd indentation there. The roof of the aircraft sported a couple hatches and mountings for machine guns—though Emmerson had clearly removed the weapons. There was a forest of antennas sprouting from the fuselage just behind the cockpit and a dark strip down the spine of the aircraft that appeared to be a nonslip surface for crewmen to walk on.

Quite a machine, he thought, turning his attention to the task at hand. He couldn't get the doors to open from up here, but he could make his own door.

He looked to the heavy load suspended on a platform beneath the moving trolley. He counted four pipeline welders, the same machines that had attacked Kurt days before. Each of them weighing several hundred pounds. That should do the trick.

Using a small joystick to move the load sideways and tapping a second control that operated the cable, Joe raised the platform and moved it toward the back of the hangar.

"Phase one complete," he called out to Kurt. "What's your situation?"

"Bad and getting worse," Kurt replied. "I took a quick look. They've finished building their battering ram and they're coming this way."

Looking over at the walkway, Joe saw that the men lining up behind the battering ram were only the first problem. A second group was using a ladder to climb up to the walkway on the other side of Kurt's position.

"They've got you surrounded," Joe said. "But don't worry, help is on the way."

"Just get the door down and get out of here," Kurt ordered.

Using the small joystick on the panel in front of him, Joe controlled the crane's direction and speed. He moved the load away from the walkway, let out a fair amount of slack and sent it back toward the second-level walkway at full speed.

The platform at the bottom of the cable picked up speed and momentum. Just as the trolley from which the load was suspended reached its maximum rate of travel, Joe began retracting cable.

The trolley hit the end of the track, banging against the stops, cushioned by large rubber bumpers. The heavy pallet continued to swing, accelerating as Joe pulled in more cable. The girders above creaked as they strained under the load. The men on the upper walkway who'd built the battering ram never saw it. A shout from below alerted them at the last second.

The men turned and scattered just as the

makeshift wrecking ball hit the walkway. Two of them jumped to safety, the rest were tossed about like bowling pins.

The surface of the walkway folded up as if it was made of tinfoil while the corrugated metal wall beyond caved in.

As the pendulum expended its energy and swung backward, the surviving men tumbled onto the dockside. One man clung to the pallet until it was over the water, falling with a splash.

Kurt felt the impact as the entire room around him buckled and swayed. The metal walls twisted, warping and releasing fasteners that pinged around the office like pellets from a BB gun.

"Well, that shook things up," Kurt said.

Stealing a glance out the battered doorway, he studied the carnage. Joe had wiped out the threat from the right side, but the men coming in from the other direction were still in place.

"Phase two beginning," Joe called out. **"Time to bust open the hangar door. Also, I'm definitely going to wrecking ball school when we get back home. You have no idea how much fun this is."**

Kurt could imagine. But the problem was, Joe's effort had gotten everyone's attention. Shouting and gunfire were now directed his way. Several men raced toward the ladder that led up to the control cab.

Kurt opened fire, scattering them and keeping the heat off Joe for a moment, but he couldn't do much more.

"Make a hole and get out quickly," Kurt said. "You've had enough fun for today."

"Love to," Joe said. **"But I'm not sure how I'm going to get down. You get to Yan's mother and kids. I'll bust the door down so you can escape. They're hiding in one of the boats."**

Kurt didn't much like that idea, but he lost any chance to argue the point when two of Emmerson's men peered around the door.

Kurt fired once, brushing them back and buying himself some time.

They flinched, ducked out of sight and gathered themselves for an assault. Whipping around the corner, knocking the door off its remaining hinge in the process, they opened fire with everything they had. They shot high and low and all around.

Orders be damned, they riddled the office with bullets. Blasting the filing cabinet, the desk and the mattress. Anything a man might try to hide behind.

Feathers flew from the comforter as bullets ripped it, stuffing exploded out of the mattress, sparks jumped from the metal walls.

After shooting up the place for a good ten seconds, they stopped.

The smoke cleared without any sign of movement. Feathers drifted down.

The two men stepped into the room. They found

their dead comrade and the overturned filing cabinet. They saw the mattress, the ratty comforter and children's toys on the floor. But they found no sign of the prisoners or the man who'd been shooting at them just moments before.

CHAPTER 41

Kurt had dropped through the hole he'd cut in the floor and reached up and slid the comforter across it to hide his escape. It settled as gunfire reverberated above him.

"I'm clear," he said to Joe. "Get yourself out of there."

Joe's response told Kurt he didn't see much chance of getting out. **"Yan's mother and children are in the first boat. Suggest you get to it before they figure out your disappearing act."**

The shooting had stopped above him. He heard footsteps from men in heavy boots. Even with the deception, it wouldn't be long before Emmerson's gunmen discovered his escape route.

With no time to argue, Kurt raced to the boat, slid on his hip and hopped over the edge of the dock into the boat.

He found Yan's mother and the two kids curled

up inside, all of them shaking with fear. He released the aft line and crawled forward to the bow where the line was tied off.

Above him, the heavy pallet was swinging. It brushed across the dockside, forcing several people to dive for cover, and swung the other way, clipping the tail of the Ekranoplan.

Emmerson's men were now focused on Joe. They raced toward the ladder, shooting upward at Joe's position before scattering as the huge pendulum swung toward them again.

Kurt got the impression of a giant trying to fight off ants or King Kong on the Empire State Building attempting to swat at the biplanes buzzing around him. Every fiber in his body told him not to leave Joe, but at this point there was very little he could do except act as a distraction.

Moving back to the center console, Kurt raised the motor so the prop was only half in the water and fired up the engine.

The outboard sputtered to life, Kurt gunned the throttle and the boat took off in a curving arc, spraying water from a rooster tail and sending a bow wave crashing over the dock.

"I see you've finally made it to the boat," Joe said, his voice breaking up a bit through the earpiece. **"Get ready to head for the door. I'll make you an opening."**

Kurt drove the boat like a madman in the tight

quarters, turning a hard circle, driving with one hand and manipulating the throttle with the other. As Emmerson's men took notice, some of them began firing his way.

Kurt spun the wheel, weaving in one direction and back in the other. He sped toward the Ekranoplan, swerving hard at the last minute and sideswiping the big flying boat as he finished the turn.

His move filled Emmerson's men with a new fear, that he might be trying to blow up the plane kamikaze style, which would turn the hangar into a blazing death trap. Some of them fired at him, only to realize they were missing and punching holes in the aluminum skin of the fuel-filled craft.

Kurt circled back, safe as long as Emmerson's crown jewel plane was behind him. At least, that was the case until a figure popped out of a hatch on top of the fuselage and started shooting down at him.

Reacting quickly, Kurt sped under the tail, looping around in a tight arc, just in time to watch Joe's final act of demolition.

With Kurt's antics giving him a brief respite from attack, Joe had time to swing the pallet into a new position.

He moved it away from the hangar door and then back toward it. As he'd done before, he allowed the line to go slack, causing the payload to pick up momentum. This time he aimed for the surface, letting out more cable at the last second.

The trolley stopped. The pallet whipped forward, dropping to the water and skipping just as it hit the door. The resounding boom echoed inside the hangar like a gigantic drum. The thin door stood no chance against the battering ram, which punched a jagged hole in it, knocked it off its tracks and brought the left half crashing down in sections.

Kurt saw the door fall, spun the wheel and shoved the throttle forward.

Knowing he needed a ramp to get over the submerged barrier without ripping the guts out of the boat, he aimed for a floating section of the door.

"Hang on," he shouted.

He timed it almost perfectly. The boat skipped off the floating door, which pushed it upward, causing it to skid across the barrier with only a glancing blow instead of a jarring thud. The skeg guard in front of the prop took a pretty good hit, but the thick wedge of steel did its job, protecting the propeller from damage.

The boat landed flat and straight. Kurt turned right, heading south and away from the barges and the **Phantom.** When he'd put a decent amount of distance behind him, he turned east for the shore and finally looped back around toward the rusting barges to the north.

Yan's mother said something Kurt didn't understand so Yan's daughter translated. "What about your friend?"

"We're going to go back for him," Kurt said. "But first we have to disappear."

Joe knew Kurt wouldn't abandon him, but he also knew he was now the number one target for everyone left in the building. It was time to get out if he could.

He rolled the body of the semiconscious crane operator out of the way and opened the hatch. Looking down, he saw men climbing up the ladder. The nearest man extended a pistol and fired.

Joe slammed the hatch shut and shoved the half-conscious man back on top of it. That would hold it for a while. But time was running out.

He considered the options and there was really only one. If he couldn't go down, he had to go up.

He stepped up onto the panel, pushed open the hatch and pulled himself up onto the roof of the cab. Leaning toward the wall, he grabbed for a handhold.

The ladder continued upward to the overhead rail system, Joe knew, so that some poor mechanic could go up there to repair it.

"Looks like I'm the poor mechanic," Joe said. He started to climb, moving quickly and never looking down. He considered jumping in the water, but from this height he'd end up embedded in the mud at the bottom.

Shots began to ping around him. One hit up high and another several feet below. They were bracketing him. And though it wasn't easy to fire accurately at such an angle, especially with handguns, it would take only one lucky shot to ruin Joe's day.

Nearing the roof, Joe climbed up onto the yellow track that supported the trolley. Working his way along it, he put the beam between himself and the bullets heading his way.

He shimmied farther, slipping at one point on the well-greased track. Finally, he reached the trolley, locked in position after his last act of destruction. He studied the cables that led from it to the platform now submerged in the water by the hangar door. They led down at a forty-five-degree angle.

A little steep, Joe thought, but better than nothing.

He pulled the sleeves of his coveralls over his hands, doubling up the fabric to protect his palms. Grabbing the cable, he swung from the yellow crossbeam and began to slide.

Emmerson's men fired at him, but Joe was committed. He relaxed his grip, sliding faster and faster. As he raced down the cable, his hands started burning from the friction. The steel tore the fabric of the coveralls and dug into his leg, gouging a diagonal wound.

He let go all at once, dropping the last thirty feet and hitting the water with a thunderous crash. As he plunged, he stuck his arms out to slow himself down before he hit the muddy bottom fifteen feet below.

Flexing his legs, he absorbed the last of his momentum and held still. He was uninjured, though his boots were stuck in the muck. He twisted one leg free and then the other. Employing the breaststroke, he swam underwater in the direction of the hangar door.

Even with his eyes open in the murky water, Joe could see very little. He felt his way along and held his breath. The exhausting hand climb and the slide down the cable had taxed his body, leaving his muscles screaming for oxygen.

He bumped into part of the collapsed door, swam across it and found the subsurface barrier. He pulled himself over, sucking in a huge gulp of air as he broke the surface.

Now outside the hangar, Joe swam arm over arm, heading for the rusting barges and the hidden submersible.

Unknown to Joe, he'd been seen.

And while Emmerson's regular workers had endured about all the madness they could take, those who were charged with keeping the hostages knew their fate would be grim if they didn't capture someone to take the blame for all the damage.

Four of them jumped in the remaining boat. One man untied it while another rushed to the helm. The last two steadied themselves at the bow and stern, weapons in hand, as the boat raced from the dock.

CHAPTER 42

The men hunting Joe reached the underwater grate and turned the boat sideways, waiting impatiently for it to drop. As the correct button was pressed on the dock behind them, the barrier fell away.

The man at the console engaged the throttle once more and the boat surged out into the darkened bay, all eyes looking for the escaping swimmer.

"Anyone see him?" the driver called out.

Near the bow, one of the men fumbled with a portable light, eventually getting it switched on and aiming it out over the water. It cast a bright but narrow beam that illuminated the surface for about two hundred yards.

He swept the light from side to side, looking for any sign of the swimmer or the stolen runabout but found nothing.

"He must have gone farther out," one of them said.

"He's not going to swim across the bay," the helmsman insisted.

"Well, he'd be a fool to swim back to shore on our side."

"What about the barges?" one of the gunmen asked.

The helmsman looked toward the collection of silent hulks. They were nearly invisible in the dark. And not all that far away. Of course.

Working the steering wheel around, he brought the power up slowly, setting course for the silent anchorage.

The beam of light settled on something up ahead. One of the gunmen fired off a burst. His shots bracketed the target, raising tiny splashes that caught the light. A second burst did the same, but there was no reaction from the water.

The helmsman eased the boat up beside it. Instead of a bullet-riddled body, they found a pair of coveralls, hastily shed by the escaping swimmer and floating on the water supported by a few pockets of air.

"Keep looking," the helmsman ordered. "He can't have gone too far."

The men looked in various directions now, scanning back and forth. One of the men caught a splash of white foam. "There."

All eyes turned. The spotlight zeroed in. Compared to the dark coveralls, the man's wet skin shimmered in the glare.

The pilot gunned the engine and turned toward the escaping swimmer. The men in the front of the boat took aim, but the spotlight had given them away.

The swimmer arched over like a dolphin, diving and kicking hard. He was gone even before the men opened fire.

"Stop shooting," the helmsman ordered. "You're just wasting ammunition."

He shut the motor off and they drifted, listening as much as watching. The men were hair-trigger, waiting for the kill shot. And waiting. And waiting.

"Maybe you hit him?" one of them said.

"He would have floated to the surface."

The helmsman knew better. "He's a diver. He's obviously got strong lungs. But he's not a fish. He can't stay down forever."

Joe had swum deep and found the bottom. Using his legs, he'd pushed himself along, a much more efficient method of propulsion for a human than swimming. He kept his arms slack except for balance. Kept the rest of his body as calm as he could. But with each compression and extension of his legs, he used up more oxygen. His chest began to ache, his diaphragm tensing as his lungs demanded more oxygen.

One more push, he told himself. Then one more. And just one or two more after that.

Finally, he could take it no longer. His chest felt like it might explode. He pushed off the bottom for the surface, exhaling a stream of bubbles as he rose.

He broke the surface farther from the boat than anyone could have expected.

It was not far enough.

"Over there."

The spotlight swung around once more. The swimmer had almost reached the barges.

"Shoot him," the helmsman ordered.

The men took aim, but before they could fire, the boat lurched sideways. It rolled and tilted forward.

One of the gunmen tumbled out into the water, the other fell forward, knocking over the man with the spotlight. Only the helmsman remained standing. He grasped the wheel, spun it in the direction of the tilt and pushed the throttle forward. The outboard revved and turned. The propeller broke free of the surface and was spinning fast and incredibly loud.

The helmsman looked aft. The entire stern had lifted from the water. The outboard itself had been pushed upward and to the side. It was as if they'd run aground, but they were still moving, even picking up speed. Looking over the side, he realized why. The boat had been lifted onto the curved back of what appeared to be some great dark sea creature. It was driving them forward at an ever-increasing speed.

The helmsman looked ahead. The steel wall of the nearest barge appeared in the spotlight. They were surging toward it.

"No," he shouted helplessly.

While the beast dropped down at the last second, the small fiberglass boat was rammed headlong into the resting ship.

The bow splintered. The rest of the boat rolled with the impact, slamming hard against the barge's rusted flank.

The helmsman was ejected from his seat and thrown against the hull. He ended up in the water, desperately trying to remain conscious and keep from drowning. He lost track of the others, forgot about the man they were chasing and sank to the bottom without any clue as to what had caused their destruction.

A short distance away, Joe Zavala watched the spectacle with no doubt as to what had just occurred. He cheered as the fiberglass boat was crushed and waited patiently as the **Phantom** swung around and surfaced beside him.

As the water flowed off the turtle-shaped hull, Joe climbed aboard. He noticed damage to the gel packs, caused by the runabout's hull and propeller. He wondered how badly it would affect the acoustics or the speed.

Moving to the center of the hull, he rapped on the hatch. It opened seconds later and Kurt popped his head out. "Did someone order a water taxi?"

"About time you got here," Joe quipped. "Thought I was going to have to swim back to California."

"Is that why you're half naked?"

"Coveralls were weighing me down."

Kurt got out of the way and Joe dropped down into the craft, shutting the hatch behind him. He was short of breath, bleeding from his hands and wearing only his shorts, but he beamed at the sight of Yan's children and mother huddled behind the command chairs.

Kurt threw him a towel and relinquished the driver's seat. "You have the con."

Joe dried off as best he could and settled into the command console. "And you win the Oscar for best imitation of an angry whale."

"Your King Kong imitation wasn't half bad either," Kurt replied. "Care to take us out of here?"

"With pleasure," Joe said. "What course would you like me to set?"

"The same way we came in," Kurt said. "Get us into the channel and head for international waters."

At that exact moment, Kinnard Emmerson was in the study of his mountaintop estate with the blond man from Hydro-Com. A nautical chart of the western Pacific lay on a table. Long, thin lines of various colors crisscrossed the map in all directions, bunching up as they neared landmasses.

"These are the international fiber-optic trunk lines," Emmerson explained. "The submerged cables are color-coded by type and ownership." He pointed to some additional markings. "These are depth gradients."

The American nodded. "I know what they are," he said. "I can see several locations that would work, but we need help. That visit from NUMA cost us our diver. You're going to need someone who can work below a thousand-foot depth. Any shallower, the splice will be too easy to spot."

Emmerson knew that. It was half the reason he'd kept Yan around. "Don't worry about it," he said. "Just figure out which location offers the maximum chance of success. I want access to U.S.–China communications."

The blond man looked up. "I thought you wanted to place these all around the world?"

"In time," Emmerson said. "But you defend your own hill first, then you take others."

The man looked back at the chart, zeroing in on the main U.S.–Hong Kong trunk line, looking for a spot at the right depth but away from the shipping lanes.

Emmerson let him search, turning his attention to Guānchá, who had just entered the room.

"We have a problem," Guānchá said. He held a cell phone out to Emmerson. "It's the men at the hangar."

Emmerson felt the American glance his way. "Keep looking," he said to the American. "I want a location before morning."

Stepping away, he took the phone from Guānchá. "Yes. What is it?"

The voice on the other end spoke in a full panic, shouting and breathless. The statements were unintelligible.

"Slow down," Emmerson demanded. "Tell me what's happened."

"Men came in here," the caller said, more calmly. "They took the prisoners. They almost destroyed the place. We're lucky they didn't blow up the plane."

The hangar. Yan's family. His leverage. Emmerson felt a band of pain across his forehead.

"Who came in there?" he demanded. "Were they CIPHER's people?"

"No," the man on the phone said. "Caucasians. European or American. Just two of them."

"Two men broke into the hangar and took the hostages out from under you?" Emmerson snapped. "By themselves? How could you let this happen?"

"They had guns. They surprised everyone."

Emmerson rubbed his temple. He didn't bother pointing out that a dozen men at the hangar were armed as well. "How did they get inside? I ordered the hangar locked down."

"We found diving equipment," the man told him. "Modern gear. Good stuff."

Emmerson began to suspect who the culprits might be. "What did these men look like?"

He put the phone on speaker as the intruders were described. Guānchá listened and nodded. "The men from the auction."

Emmerson knew them as members of NUMA. He'd had them investigated after the skirmish over the wreck of the **Swift.**

"NUMA." He grunted. They had become more than a thorn in his side. If they were willing to swim right up to the door of his stronghold and bring the fight to him, they had to be considered a grave threat. "How did they escape?"

"They took one of our boats, but we found it nearby. They must be onshore. Should I alert our friends in the police?"

Emmerson considered the idea for a moment and decided against it. The men from NUMA wouldn't escape on foot. That would put them in his domain. Where police and cameras and their very European looks would work against them. Instead, they would play to their strengths. That meant a ship or a submarine.

"Don't bother with the police," he said. "Just secure the building. And have the aircraft inspected. We need it ready to fly in the morning."

"What about the Americans?"

"I'll take care of them."

Emmerson hung up and dialed the number of a highly placed friend in the Ministry of State Security. Explanations were offered. Promises made. Appetites whetted. When enough had been agreed upon, a second phone call was placed. This went out to the naval garrison on Stonecutters Island.

Orders were soon given, the likes of which had never been issued in Hong Kong before.

"A top secret American submarine has infiltrated Victoria Harbour and been used to kidnap three Chinese citizens. That submarine is to be found and either captured or destroyed. Under no circumstance is it to reach international waters. As an additional incentive, the unit that succeeds in accomplishing this mission will be richly rewarded."

Gunboats and other patrol boats were launched without delay. Anti-submarine helicopters were fueled up and readied as their crews were roused from their slumber.

Two anti-submarine frigates outside the harbor were ordered into position to intercept. An unnamed submarine chaser with the pennant number 805 sailed from the dock with only a skeleton crew.

These efforts were reported to Emmerson, who offered his sincere appreciation and stressed his desire to be continuously informed.

He hung up the phone, concerned but confident.

And pleased with himself for allowing Yan-Li to talk to her mother and children earlier that night.

Had he waited to play that card, he would have lost his chance, as he was quite certain they'd all be dead by morning.

CHAPTER 43

With Joe in the left seat of the **Phantom,** Kurt turned to Yan's mother and her children. They were in the aft section of the craft, draped in towels.

"We're going to make our way out of the harbor and meet up with some friends once we clear Chinese waters," he said. "It's going to take a while, so get as comfortable as you can."

Yan's daughter translated for her grandmother while Yan's son stared at Kurt. The fear seemed to have returned.

"New movie," Kurt said. "Jules Verne, **20,000 Leagues Under the Sea.**"

The boy grinned. "Kirk Douglas and James Mason."

"Exactly," Kurt said. "Only without the giant squid."

Pulling on a set of headphones, Kurt began to

manipulate the passive-sonar system, listening for anything the computer might not have picked up. He heard turbulence coming from the port quarter. It showed up on the monitor as an unknown. No matter which direction the submarine pointed, the bearing of the signal remained constant. That could mean only one thing. The disturbance was coming from the **Phantom** itself.

"We're leaking noise," Kurt said.

"The forecheck you put on the guys in the runabout tore up part of the soundproofing. Shouldn't be a problem unless someone gets right on top of us."

"Famous last words," Kurt said.

They completed the turn to the east and continued down the main channel. "Five miles to deeper water," Joe said. "Twenty minutes, at this speed."

Kurt was listening intently. The harbor was coming alive. Ships moving everywhere. "A lot of activity for this time of night."

"Could it be the harbor that never sleeps?" Joe asked.

Kurt didn't think so. He zeroed in on the pounding reverberation of a fast patrol boat racing toward them, skipping over the waves. It soon overwhelmed the background clamor.

"Target approaching from dead astern," Kurt said. "High velocity."

"Tracking us?"

The merging courses on the plot suggested it was

on an intercept heading, but it was moving too quickly and violently to notice them.

"Negative," he said. "Just rushing to head us off at the pass."

"You'd better be right," Joe said. "We don't have a lot of room to maneuver here."

The sound of the churning props crept in, a background harmony to the thud, thud, thud of the hull slamming across the surface. The boat passed overhead without slowing, continuing on at full speed.

Kurt swung the sonar array to the east, picking up pinging in the distance. Through the headphones, it sounded faintly like a bell.

"New problem," Kurt said. "Someone's dropping sonar buoys across the outer leg of the channel. Trying to cut off our escape."

Joe looked grim. "I'd say not to worry, except that we're not as quiet as we were coming in. And with the gel packs ruptured, a direct ping would probably give us away."

As Kurt considered that, another sound from the outside world found its way in, this one muffled but distinct. "Helicopter joining the party," Kurt said. "He's trailing something. Probably a sonar array or a mag."

Joe pushed them deeper toward the bottom of the channel, but he couldn't risk hitting bottom and getting caught in the mud. "This is as low as I can go."

"Full stop," Kurt ordered. "Turn our good side to the north."

Joe cut the power and pivoted the **Phantom** as it coasted to a halt. Both men held their breath as the sonar array passed a couple hundred yards north of them. The pinging of the emitter sounded sharp and clinical. It grew louder, closer and higher-pitched, probing like an invisible searchlight.

It swept over them and began to fade as it continued to the east.

Joe looked Kurt's way but said nothing. Kurt was pressing the headphones to his ears, trying to tease every last bit of information out of them. Without looking at Joe, he spoke quietly. "Turn us around. We need to find another way out."

CHAPTER 44

On board the Chinese helicopter it was anything but quiet. The howling engine, churning rotors and open side door made it impossible to hear even the loudest shout. The men inside wore helmets with noise-canceling headsets embedded in them. They spoke by intercom or communicated with hand signals.

"What do you have?" the commander asked his sonar operator.

"Something there," the sonarman replied. "In the channel."

The commander squinted at the screen that displayed a visual of the sonar returns. He saw nothing. "Where?"

The man pointed to a blur in the corner. To the commander, it looked like an error in the processor, like pixels dropping out on a cheap TV. "It's nothing."

"The channel should be featureless," he explained.

"It should give us a smooth return. This could be a small craft."

"Or garbage dumped from a ship."

"It's definitely something," the sonarman said.

The commander looked again. He saw no other blurs on the screen. He pressed the intercom switch connecting him to the pilot. "Take us around, we have a target bearing two-five-zero. Prepare to drop charges."

The idea of flushing out an American spy craft and capturing it brought on a wave of adrenaline. They'd be heroes of the People's Republic, feted and compensated handsomely.

"Charges ready," the pilot confirmed.

"Overfly their position and release on my command."

"No good," Kurt said, hearing a change in the helicopter's aspect. "They've found us."

"Give me a heading."

Kurt heard several splashes hit the water. They were to the north. Outside the channel. "Stay in the channel and take us down."

Joe aimed them for the bottom, hoping to be shielded from the blast. He leveled off as four explosions detonated in rapid succession.

The **Phantom** was hit by a shock wave and pushed forward and up. Its nose tilted toward the surface as it fluttered like a leaf in the wind.

Joe got control of the sub. "That wasn't too bad."

"Small charges," Kurt said. "Training charges. They'd clearly rather capture us than destroy us."

"Neither of those options sounds appealing to me," Joe said. "Remember what I told you would happen if we were caught and charged with espionage?"

The helicopter could be heard turning around once again.

"Get us out of the channel," Kurt ordered. "Go south and then west."

Joe pushed the throttle to the stops and brought the sub up out of the channel. He took them south, into the shallows, and turned west as Kurt had ordered.

Listening for a sign they'd escaped the dragnet, Kurt heard the tiny splashes of additional explosives hitting the water.

This time the explosions sounded farther off. The charges had settled into the channel before detonating. The shock wave was partially contained and well behind them.

"Keep heading west," Kurt said. "Full speed."

"Heading west takes us back into Victoria Harbour," Joe said.

"It's our only hope," Kurt said. "We need to run while there's still turbulence in the water to block their signal."

Joe brought the **Phantom** to full speed and kept them submerged. The flattened-turtle profile made it possible to move in the shallows, but they had no more than ten feet between the top of the hull and the surface, maybe half that between the keel and the slime of the harbor bottom.

Joe concentrated on the forward profiler that scanned the area ahead for obstructions or other impediments. He brought them up several feet at one point to avoid a sandbar and swerved right to avoid a concrete pylon not indicated on the chart. Moments later, they passed several automobiles half buried in the mud. "And I thought traffic in D.C. was bad."

"Must have fallen off a ferry," Kurt said, his ear cocked for the sound of pursuit.

"Anyone following us?"

"Patrol boats churning up the bay," Kurt said. "Helicopter still circling. They're making so much noise, I doubt they'd hear us if we had music blasting."

The forward profiler began to flash an alarm. A target was blocking their path. Long and thin and without an end on either side.

"Gas line," Kurt called out. "Don't hit it."

"Damn," Joe grunted.

There was no way to stop in time. All Joe could do was go up over the top and hope no one noticed.

They crested the surface, not quite flying but rising and settling and leaving a broad white wake like a giant swan touching down on a quiet mountain lake. As soon as they were clear of the pipeline, Joe pushed the nose over, taking them under and stabilizing their depth at fifteen feet.

He looked at Kurt. "I suppose there's always a chance they forgot to activate their scanning radar?"

Kurt had the headphones pressed to his ears. He shook his head. They'd been spotted once again.

CHAPTER 45

PRN SUBMARINE CHASER, PENNANT NUMBER 805

The captain of the 805 had been annoyed by the sudden orders at two a.m., thinking they were most likely someone's idea of a readiness exercise rather than a true emergency deployment. An American submarine in Victoria Harbour. The idea was preposterous.

Still, he roused his men and left the dock in record time. But even so, they'd left the slip at Stonecutters Island well behind the missile boats and helicopters that had sped off to the east. He was all but certain they'd reach the designated area only to be told the exercise was over.

With that thought in mind, the commander was mildly surprised when the helicopters reported contact with a target and began dropping charges. Surprise turned to outright shock when his radar operator reported a contact fleeing from the impact zone.

The radar track showed a craft appearing and then disappearing moments later, a solid indication something had been forced to the surface only to dive once again.

"Full sonar scan," he ordered. "Plot an intercept course."

"I have something," the sonar operator insisted. "Confirmed target, moving west at twenty-six knots. Four thousand meters and closing. It's heading our way."

The 805's commander allowed himself a smug grin. Sometimes being late to the dance had its advantages.

"Bring us onto a parallel course," he ordered.

"Should we load the mortars?" This from the executive officer, or XO.

The ship was equipped with six anti-submarine mortars capable of launching various charges.

"Put them on standby and arm the anti-submarine rockets," the commander ordered. "I want to hit them with our first shot, not chase them all night."

The XO looked at him and spoke quietly. "Shouldn't we try to force them to the surface as per our orders?"

The commander shook his head. "The Americans will never allow their top secret vessel to be captured. They'll either evade our attack and escape our pursuit or scuttle it with explosives of their own. Better we destroy them with one blow and pick up the wreckage afterward than risk them escaping."

The XO asked nothing more. He checked with the weapons officer to ensure the proper weapons were selected and armed. "Missiles on the rack," he said. "Units one and two armed and ready to fire."

Despite the orders and the chain of command, the XO and the weapons officer were both filled with nervous tension. The anti-submarine missiles were, in reality, rocket-launched torpedoes. They were normally used at longer ranges to drop homing torpedoes in the water in the vicinity of a distant target. Using them in the tight confines of Victoria Harbour was a dangerous choice. If they flew off course, they would hit the residential areas of Hong Kong in seconds. And if they hit the water as intended and found no submarine to chase, they might just lock onto a passing freighter, cruise ship or tanker. Or even the 805 itself.

"Launch unit one," the commander ordered.

At the touch of a button, the rocket fired, lighting up the deck of the darkened ship in a blinding glare. The missile leapt from its tube and raced out across the harbor to the astonishment of anyone who might have been watching from shore.

It tracked to the northeast, cleared the safety zone around the submarine chaser and turned sharply to the south. Three seconds later, the rocket motor cut out and the torpedo detached from the launcher.

It plunged into the harbor and went active almost immediately.

Inside the **Phantom,** Kurt picked up the roar of the missile being launched and the splash of the torpedo hitting the surface eight seconds later.

It seemed like the endgame scenario. The only thing in their favor was the distance—they were so close to the 805 that the rocket flew past them before circling around and dropping the torpedo into the water one mile from their stern.

The rapid pinging of the homing torpedo swept over them.

"I don't like the sound of that," Joe said.

Kurt couldn't tell for sure if the torpedo had targeted them, but the computer was certain. "It's on an intercept course. Let's hope the Navy's countermeasure system does its job. Launch the decoy, cut the throttle and make a hard right turn."

Joe reached over to the countermeasures panel, armed the **Phantom**'s decoy and pressed the launch button. A garbage-can-sized decoy was released. Its deliberately noisy propeller spun up rapidly while a pair of six-foot wings telescoped out from either side. They fluttered in the water, creating turbulence and reflecting sonar pings.

As the decoy went forward on the **Phantom**'s original course, Joe turned the submarine ninety degrees to the right, keeping the undamaged starboard side of the hull toward the incoming torpedo. If they had one remaining advantage, it was that the little sub could spin and turn like a UFO, turning at almost perfect right angles in the sea, the type of course changes that no ship or torpedo could match.

As Joe whipped the sub around to starboard, Kurt was nearly thrown from his seat. Yan's mother and her children grabbed for anything they could hold on to.

The homing weapon was closing fast, the sound of its propeller and sonar emitter audible through the hull of the submarine.

It raced by them without detonating, following the decoy and continuing to close the gap. Kurt would have liked to put more distance between them and the coming explosion, but there wasn't much they could do.

"Hold on," Kurt shouted, pulling off his headphones and watching on the computer screen as the two tracks merged. "This is going to be loud."

Loud was an understatement. The detonation felt like a thunderclap inside a small room. The **Phantom** rolled in the shock wave, being shoved in one direction and pulled back in the other.

It would have been much worse had the **Phantom** been a regular submarine with a flat steel wall on either side, but its streamlined, turtle-like shape allowed most of the energy from the explosion to pass over the craft instead of boring through it and impacting the occupants.

Kurt glanced at Joe. "This is our chance. Turbulence from the explosion won't clear for several minutes. Set a new course." He pointed to a spot on the navigation screen. "This is our target. Get us there and park in the mud."

Joe looked at the navigation screen, wondering why Kurt had picked that particular spot. He saw only a thin dotted line on the map, which meant nothing to him. Still, this was not the time for a discussion. He set course and coaxed the submarine along.

The crew of the 805 watched the plot of the torpedo merge with the suspected target. They felt the muted thud of the detonation and saw an eruption of whitewater a second or two later. Smoke and steam merged. Gravity took over and the sheets of water began to fall. Darkness and quiet returned, with only a growing circle of foam to mark the location of the explosion.

The commander bristled with confidence. He knew his torpedo had hit the target.

"Engines to one quarter," he ordered. "Swing wide and continue to scan. As soon as the turbulence abates, I want to find the wreckage of that submarine. Whatever's left of it."

He stood proudly on the bridge for the next three hours. But despite every effort and multiple passes by his ship, the ASW helicopters and even the anti-submarine frigates brought in from picket duty, they found no sign of wreckage nor any hint of the mysterious American submarine.

Dejected, the captain finally took a seat, lowering himself in beside the sonarman. "Have you heard anything?"

"Only this," the man said, switching the feed from headphones to speaker.

The captain tilted his head, trying to make sense of the dull grinding sound on the audio. "What is that?"

"Morning traffic in the Cross-Harbour Tunnel. Rush hour is getting underway."

The **Phantom** had spent the night half buried in the sediment directly over the Cross-Harbour Tunnel. Using the burrowing anchor and the vertical thrusters, Joe had screwed the craft down tight, like a tick in a deer.

The ships and helicopters searching for them had passed overhead half a dozen times, but the sonarmen on board had all trained in these waters. They knew the tunnels when they heard them. They recognized the long diagonal lines that appeared on the sonar display when the sound waves reflected off the buried tubes of concrete. Not one of them even gave it a second thought.

"One of your best ideas," Joe admitted as the fleet dispersed above them. "But we can't sit on top of this tunnel forever. How, exactly, do you plan to get us out of here without anyone noticing?"

"Easy," Kurt said. "Hong Kong is one of the busiest ports in the world. This little incident won't keep it shut down for long. Once it opens, we wait for the right ship to push off from the dock, move in underneath it and escort it to open waters like a pilot fish or a remora. If the Chinese have hydrophones monitoring the entrance to the harbor, they won't be able to pick us up with the rumble of a tanker or containership directly above us."

Joe tipped his imaginary cap and sat back, waiting for the right ship to come along. They passed up the first two ships before releasing the anchor and pulling free of the sediment when an empty tanker came past.

The tanker had the useful attributes of being big, noisy and slow. All things the wounded **Phantom** needed to hide its presence. The fact that it was riding high in the water, having unloaded its cargo, didn't hurt either. It gave Joe plenty of room to fit the **Phantom** between the underside of the ship's hull and the muck at the bottom of Victoria Harbour.

CHAPTER 46

GOVERNMENT HOUSE, THE PEAK

Yan-Li woke up to the kind female voice of one of Emmerson's servants delivering an exquisite breakfast, then pulling back a tall curtain, allowing the sunlight to stream into the room.

"Mr. Emmerson requests that you meet him downstairs in thirty minutes," the woman told her and left.

Yan looked at the meal and decided to eat. She needed to keep her strength up.

As she dug into the breakfast, she thought about Emmerson's offer. It bothered her that she was considering it, but how could she not?

Finishing the breakfast, she showered and changed back into her clothes, which had been laundered and pressed while she slept. "I'm a prisoner in a five-star hotel," she said quietly.

Leaving the room, she walked the hallway and

took the stairs. She found Emmerson waiting along with several members of her ex-husband's crew. Callum was front and center. He gazed at Yan suspiciously.

"It's time to finish the contract," Emmerson said. "Degra has surrendered the location of the computers."

A helicopter took them from the mountaintop estate and down to the industrial site next to the old seaplane base. Entering the hangar, Yan saw the Ekranoplan for the first time. Callum had described it while relaying the horrors of what had happened there after they'd been plucked from the sea due to the sinking of the **Swift.**

His description hadn't done it justice. And yet it didn't look ready to fly. Several mechanics were up on the top of the fuselage, repairing some damage and replacing part of the Y-shaped tail.

Looking around the hangar, she realized that was the least of the damage. "What happened here?"

Emmerson didn't miss a beat. "CIPHER's men broke in last night, either thinking they might find Degra and rescue him or to send us a message. They killed six of my men. I told you they'd be vengeful. Keep that in mind when you make your decision."

Yan nodded slowly. "What's the plan?" she said. "Where are we going?"

Emmerson nodded toward the submersible. "You and your men will take the submarine out to a vessel west of the harbor. I've already given Callum here the information. The ship was an old amphibious vessel. It has a deployment bay where you can dock."

As he spoke, two smaller delta craft taxied in from the bay. They had wings like manta rays or perhaps giant moths. Emmerson called them skimmers and explained that they worked by the same principle as the Ekranoplan. Yan watched as a dozen men best described as mercenaries boarded the two planes.

"Camouflage, body armor, assault rifles," she said. "Are we going to war?"

"CIPHER isn't going to leave the servers undefended," Emmerson insisted. "Not at this point. These men will deal with whatever defenses we encounter. You and your men will snatch the computers out from under them."

Yan was glad to know she wouldn't have to do any more fighting. She nodded in understanding.

"I'll meet you on the ship," Emmerson said. "Double-check your gear and be ready for an extended dive. You and your crew are about to earn your pay."

Emmerson moved off, with Guānchá joining him. They met with the armed men, engaged in a brief discussion and began boarding the skimmers.

Yan and Callum rounded up the rest of their crew and made their way to the mini-sub. As she walked the debris-strewn dock, she wondered why CIPHER's men would attack the hangar instead of

Emmerson's home. Stranger still, she wondered why they would wreck the place while leaving his crown jewel aircraft untouched.

She was no expert in the behavior of criminal gangs, but something about it didn't add up.

CHAPTER 47

KI-SONG ISLAND

Upon boarding the **Sapphire,** Paul and Gamay Trout had the impression they'd drawn the long straw.

"Yachting over cramped submarines any day," Paul had proclaimed.

By day three of the expedition, both he and Gamay were growing bored. Despite all the hoopla and glory surrounding the search for sunken treasure, ninety percent of the work was about as exciting as methodically searching a living room carpet for a missing contact lens.

They made continuous runs around the island and into the bay, trailing all sorts of different sensors. Ground-penetrating sonar, sub-bottom profilers, hypersensitive magnetometers. Everything in the shipwreck hunter's arsenal. But after scanning the entire bay, the approaches to and from it and an ever-widening swath of the waters around the island, they had nothing to show for their efforts.

Paul was fed up. "We need to go down and retrieve that blunderbuss that Kurt and Yan spotted."

"Blunderbuss?"

"Isn't that what it was called?"

"Harquebus," Gamay said. "Sometimes called a swivel gun because it commonly sat on a tripod so the heavy barrel could be turned and aimed."

"Harquebus. Blunderbuss. One bus is as good as another," Paul said. "Point is, we need to bring it up. It may tell us something."

Gamay felt the same. "Anything is better than another day of staring at a magnometer's squiggly lines."

They swapped out casual clothes for diving gear and waited as Winterburn eased the **Sapphire** up to the entrance of the bay.

From here, they would swim. With the GPS coordinates locked in, they dropped off the stern platform and moved slowly across the reef.

"Let's hope the tiger shark Kurt encountered hasn't hung around," Paul said.

"Do sharks eat Trout?" Gamay joked. "We're a freshwater fish, aren't we?"

"Not funny," Paul said. "And I'd rather not find out."

Using the GPS locator, they navigated to the outcropping of coral that Kurt and Yan-Li had hidden behind to escape attack. Drifting slowly across the bottom, they looked for signs of the artifact.

Gamay scored first, discovering the jagged, broken branches of staghorn coral that had been snapped off in the fight. "We must be in the right place."

"We are," Paul said. "Look at this."

Paul used his hand to sweep away some sediment, revealing the blackened portion of the reef covered by the invasive growth. Another discolored area lay a few feet away.

Gamay drifted to a spot beside Paul, holding her position with slight kicks from her fins. "Let's excavate this and bring it to the surface."

"I like it when you break the rules," Paul said with a grin that was magnified by the glass of his helmet.

Using their dive knives and small chisels, they chipped away at the coral and the sediment surrounding the weapon. Over the course of thirty minutes, they exposed the length of the barrel, the ornate trigger guard and the remnants of the mounting that allowed the weapon to sit on the tripod and swivel.

Paul wrapped it carefully and brought it to the surface while Gamay investigated the other area of invasive growth. Digging into it, she found another surprise. A brass telescope. She did the excavation work and wrapped it in a protective casing.

She surfaced a few minutes after Paul and was soon treading water beside the **Sapphire**'s swim platform.

"Look at this," she called out.

Paul reappeared with Stratton beside him. Gamay

handed the nautical relic to her husband and climbed aboard.

"I'll take your tanks," Stratton said.

"Thanks," Gamay replied, easing out of her dive harness while Paul unwrapped her discovery.

"Eighteenth-century brass telescope," Paul said, examining it. "There's a little bit of zinc leaching but not much, considering how long it must have been down there."

Gamay nodded. "Both of these artifacts are extremely well preserved. Let's hope they're actually as old as we suspect and not something dropped here a hundred years later."

CHAPTER 48

Later that night, Paul and Gamay set about studying the artifacts. Stratton and Winterburn stood by as interested observers, throwing out the occasional question or comment.

The first part of the process involved placing them in separate tubs containing different solutions that would prevent further oxidation or corrosion while at the same time dissolving the concreted salts that had adhered to them.

After several hours, detail work began. Using tiny picks and brushes, Paul and Gamay meticulously cleaned the deposits from the surface, revealing an ornate pattern on the handle of the harquebus and a series of Chinese characters on the brass casing of the telescope.

They also discovered something they hadn't expected. Hardened gray sediment packed into the barrel of the swivel gun and the hollow tube of the telescope.

Gamay found it annoying and sticky. Paul, the geologist, found it subtly interesting. "This isn't regular sediment," he said, removing a small amount and rubbing it between his fingers. "It's volcanic ash."

"That's an encouraging sign," Gamay said, "since the **Silken Dragon** vanished in a volcanic explosion."

"Looks like Kurt's optimism is proving correct," Paul said.

Gamay nodded. "The wooden portion of the harquebus shows signs of charring," she added, "as if it was exposed to flames that were quickly quenched."

"Which is what we'd expect of wood that was hit with volcanic heat and dumped in the water," Paul said. "Or . . ."

Gamay shot him a look. "Or what?"

Paul answered her question with a question. "Tell me what the diary said about the volcanic eruption again?"

Gamay turned on a nearby laptop and brought up the translated information from Ching Shih's diary.

"'The **Silken Dragon** cannot escape the bay,'" she read. "'Snared in the claws of coral, she is devoured by the smoke and fire and a downpouring of molten lava from the mountain. A fitting end for such traitors.'"

Paul nodded, thinking about the phrase. "Very exciting. But we haven't found any volcanic rock," he said. "Just the reef and the sediment and the ash.

If the eruption included molten lava, we should find outcroppings of it here and there, especially where the current has removed the silt and sand."

"What are you getting at?" she asked suspiciously. "And if you tell me this is the wrong island, you're sleeping on the couch tonight."

"Not the wrong island," Paul said, "the wrong observation. Ching Shih basically told the world that the **Dragon** was consumed as a punishment. Poetic justice, in her mind. But she was miles away. And her observation may have been self-serving. Either as a divine warning to those who might cross her or because she didn't want anyone coming back to the island to look for what she thought was rightly hers."

"Like saying 'fire and brimstone,'" Gamay suggested.

"Brimstone would actually be more accurate," Paul said. "Because it's a synonym for sulfur, which is commonly present in volcanic eruptions."

"You realize I was agreeing with you," Gamay said, narrowing her gaze at him.

"Right," Paul said. "Sorry, got off track. Anyway, the point is, no volcanic rock, no lava, no fire and brimstone."

"Then how did this harquebus get charred?"

"Superheated ash or pumice," Paul said. "The very stuff we dug out of the telescope. And if that's the case, we'll never find the ship where we think it's supposed to be."

"Where would we find it?" she asked, feeling as if she was losing the thread.

"Deeper down," Paul said. "Covered by a thick layer of ash. Like the city of Pompeii."

Now she began to see. "How deep?"

"Sections of Pompeii were buried under twenty feet of ash. There may be parts yet to be excavated that are buried even deeper."

Gamay found this news less uplifting than Paul. "The sonar will never pick up anything buried that deeply. And considering how little iron there was on a ship of that era, I wouldn't count on using the magnetometers either."

"There has to be something we can use," Paul said.

They brought Stratton back into the conversation. He thought for a minute. "We have a high-bandwidth sub-bottom profiler," he told them. "It's not designed to look for buried treasure. But if the sediment was laid down evenly, anything large enough trapped underneath should appear as a density fluctuation. Like the almonds in a Hershey bar."

Paul and Gamay shared a glance. Anticipation.

Stratton did his best to douse their expectations. "That's if the old wooden ship didn't burn before it sank."

"The stock of this swivel gun is hardwood covered with oil paint," Paul said. "If it didn't burn, the ship with water-soaked planks wouldn't have time to burn either. At worst, it would lose its masts and top deck."

"We still can't take the **Sapphire** into the bay," Winterburn said. "Too big."

Gamay turned to Stratton. "Can you rig up one of the drones to carry it?"

"Sure," Stratton said. "I think we still have one left that Kurt and Joe didn't ruin."

CHAPTER 49

NUMA HEADQUARTERS, WASHINGTON, D.C.

Rudi Gunn was working late when the intercom buzzed and the voice of the night receptionist came over the speaker. **"Anna Biel here to see you, Mr. Gunn."**

Rudi didn't get many visitors, certainly not this late at night. He glanced at his watch. "Tell her I'll meet her in the . . ."

The door cracked open and Anna Biel leaned in through the gap. She had a pair of Starbucks cups in her hands, steam curling out the sipping vents in the plastic lids.

"Never mind," Rudi told the receptionist.

"Sorry for the intrusion," the NSA director said, "but you don't get to the top by waiting your turn."

Rudi took a cup and waved for her to take a seat. "Not to sound ungrateful," he said, "but we have four coffee machines on this floor and an all-night cafeteria downstairs."

"So do we," she replied, "but it's easier to add a shot of the good stuff to something in a paper cup. Don't you agree?"

Raising the cup to his face, Rudi could smell a hint of liquor in the brew. "In that case, I accept." He took a sip and asked the burning question. "Are you here for moral support or to deliver bad news?"

"The former," she said. "I assume you haven't heard from your men since the Chinese shot up Victoria Harbour."

"No," Rudi admitted, "but we're not worried yet. If the Chinese had Kurt and Joe, they'd be parading them through Tiananmen Square by now. And if they'd sunk the **Phantom,** video of the wreckage would be all over the evening news."

"Our thoughts exactly."

"Are you worried that the Chinese will start pointing the finger at us for the incursion?"

"Not really," she said. "Not publicly anyway. They can't risk admitting that a small American craft evaded an armada of their anti-submarine forces in what's basically a pool in their own backyard. Without wreckage to prove they've succeeded in beating us, they'll stick to the terrorist story."

Rudi raised his cup. "Here's to Chinese prudence."

She joined Rudi in the toast. "It still leaves us wondering what happened to Kurt and Joe. Eyewitness accounts suggest multiple depth charges were dropped and at least one anti-submarine rocket was fired in their direction. Just because the Chinese didn't find any wreckage doesn't mean they got out alive. Damaged submarines have a habit of limping along for a while only to fail before they make it home."

"Obviously, that's a concern," Rudi said. "But the **Phantom** is a sturdy craft. Even if the hull cracked suddenly from some underlying damage, Kurt and Joe would almost certainly manage to get out. They're experienced divers and cool under pressure. I can only assume they're avoiding the most obvious places the Chinese might look, like a NUMA support ship or any American naval vessels in the area."

"But you're not actively looking for them?"

Rudi shook his head. "Can't mount a search effort without leading the Chinese toward them or admitting we were responsible for the incursion in the first place."

"Hell of a pickle to be in," she said. "You have my sympathy."

"Save it," Rudi said. "I expect we'll hear from them again before too long, even if they call collect from some out-of-the-way island resort that they've drifted to on a life raft."

"I like your confidence," she said. "And then what?"

"And then we do our best to get a message to Yan-Li, letting her know her mother and children are safe."

Anna took a sip of coffee. "That's no small order,

considering that Emmerson isn't likely to give her access to email, phone or texts at this point. How do you plan to pull it off?"

Rudi didn't have an answer, but he had faith that they'd come up with something. "We're still working on that. Worst comes to worst, I'll hire a sky-writing team to buzz across Hong Kong scribbling **Call Kurt** along the horizon."

Anna smiled at the notion, then turned serious again. "Let's just hope Kurt reappears in time to answer the phone."

CHAPTER 50

NUMA YACHT **SAPPHIRE**,
KI-SONG ISLAND, SOUTH CHINA SEA

Paul stood with his head bowed, ducking to fit himself into the darkened sonar room with Stratton. Gamay and Winterburn were monitoring the results up on the bridge. All of them were straining to see the readout from the sub-bottom profiler.

"You have something there," Paul said, calling out to Stratton, who was guiding the drone. "Bring it back over that last section."

Since the yacht was too big to maneuver safely in the shallow, coral-filled bay, they were patrolling the entrance like a picket ship on blockade duty. Meanwhile, the small drone was zipping around the bay in a circular pattern.

The first pass at a shallow depth, scanning a

wide area, had revealed nothing. A second pass at a slightly deeper depth with a narrower focus had also come up empty. But the third pass turned out to be the charm—even though the drone was forced to dodge growths of coral and scan the bottom in narrow slivers instead of wide swaths.

At such close range to the seafloor, the transmissions from the sub-bottom profiler were more concentrated. They gave a clear picture of the various layers of sediment piled on top of one another.

Everything was smooth and uniform until suddenly it wasn't. Stratton had turned the drone around and passed over the anomaly a second time.

"Definitely something buried there," Stratton said.

The next pass showed it again. But they were now too close to see all of it.

"Pull up a little," Paul suggested. "Come at it from this angle, along the main axis."

Stratton maneuvered the drone into position and put another five feet of water between the sensor and the bottom. On this pass, everything became clear as a cigar-shaped object appeared on the screen.

After several additional passes, the computer stitched the images together. The target was two hundred feet long, sixty feet wide.

"It's a match," Paul said, checking the size against what they knew of the treasure ship. "It's either the **Silken Dragon** or someone has played a fantastic joke on all of us."

Stratton gave him a high five and let out a triumphant shout of joy.

Paul hit the intercom button and called the bridge, where Gamay and Winterburn were watching on a remote monitor. "We've found it," he called out. "It's down there and it appears intact. Preserved in the sediment just as we expected."

Gamay's response was unexpectedly flat. **"We've found something too. A craft approaching us from the north. Think you might want to get to the stern and check it out."**

As Gamay spoke, Paul heard the engines cut. Why Winterburn would stop the ship at the approach of a mysterious craft, he couldn't say, but he didn't much like the idea.

"Stay here," he told Stratton. "Be ready to erase everything in case we get boarded by claim jumpers."

Stratton nodded, set the drone into station-keeping mode and scribbled the coordinates in barely recognizable chicken scratch in the middle of a doodle-filled notepad—just in case he needed to wipe the computers.

Paul ducked out of the compartment and raced back through the ship, heading for the stern. He glanced out the salon windows as he went, but he saw no sign of a ship on either side. It had to be approaching from dead astern.

Pushing open the aft doorway, he stepped out onto the platform.

Fifty yards aft of the ship he saw a black disc-shaped craft bobbing in the sea. The highest point of its hull was only five feet above the waterline. It looked like a UFO that had gone for a swim.

Paul blinked twice as the hatch opened. Instead of little green men, he saw a familiar figure emerge.

Kurt had a thick layer of stubble on his face. "Permission to come aboard," he said loudly. "I've got two crewmen that were promised grilled cheese and ice cream and another who is owed a hot bath and a glass of wine."

The kids popped up on the deck, followed by their grandmother.

"I don't know," Paul replied. "You might try to steal the treasure out from under us."

"Treasure," Kurt said. "Did you find some?"

"Not some," Paul replied. "All of it. The entire ship and its contents are buried in forty feet of ash."

With the **Phantom** in tow and Yan's family members well fed and resting, Kurt and Joe joined Paul and Gamay in the communications room.

"We're certainly glad to see you," Gamay said. "But why come all the way down here? Surely the **Phantom**'s control ship was closer."

"We figured the Chinese would be watching it, which meant more submarine chasers between us and them," Kurt said. "By coming this way, we made half the journey in Vietnamese waters. Much safer."

"Besides," Joe added, "we wanted to see how you were getting on. So, let's hear it. What have you found?"

Paul unrolled a poster-sized version of the high-resolution scan depicting the buried ship. The image left Kurt speechless.

"The detail is incredible," Joe said. "You got this with the sub-bottom profiler?"

"Stratton found a way to narrow the beam and get more detail," Paul said.

"Gold star for Stratt," Joe said.

"What about the artifacts?" Kurt asked.

"Ask and ye shall receive," Gamay said. She placed the meticulously cleaned harquebus on the table. "We have to put these back in the tank ASAP, but I thought you'd like to see it in person."

Kurt, who was a connoisseur of ancient weapons, gazed at the detail of the silver filigree around the stock of the ancient gun. It was still white with salts, but the worst of the concretion and oxidation had been carefully removed. "Stunning condition," he said. "Definitely eighteenth-century workmanship."

Gamay nodded. "But wait. There's more."

She brought over a second object wrapped in cloth. Placing it on the table, she unrolled the flaps of the cloth, revealing the telescope she'd uncovered a few feet away.

Like the harquebus, the telescope was exquisitely preserved by the airless environment of the volcanic ash. And now cleaned, it looked as if it might have come from a shelf in some antiques store.

"Amazing," Joe added.

"Incredible," Kurt said.

"Here's the best part," Gamay said, pointing out the engraved characters. "The first two are symbols for luck and wealth. The last two match the name of someone found in Ching Shih's journal. Zi Jun Chu, or Master Jun."

Kurt recognized the name. "Jun was the owner of the **Silken Dragon.** The man who stole the treasure from her in the first place."

"This telescope belonged to him. It proves beyond any doubt that the wreck under the ash is the **Dragon,**" Gamay said.

Kurt sat back. They'd finally accomplished what Yan-Li set out to do nearly three years earlier. If there was any justice, the effort would help to save her.

"Let's put a call in to Rudi," Kurt said. "It's time to make our next move."

The video call to Rudi went far better than the call from Taipei. Rudi was so thrilled to learn that Kurt and Joe were alive—and that the **Phantom** hadn't fallen into the hands of the Chinese—that he never even mentioned the words **international**

incident nor did he ask for details regarding the damage done to the fifty-million-dollar prototype.

"Now that we have her mother and kids safely stashed away, we need a way to reach her without Emmerson knowing," Kurt said.

"We've been working on that," Rudi said. "The problem is, she's vanished. CIA had eyes on her for a time, but she was never out of Emmerson's sight. She was seen at his estate and at the seaplane hangar the day after you busted the place up. Since then, she's dropped off the grid."

"That tells me Emmerson is making his next move," Kurt said. "Degra must have given up the location of the servers."

"Which is when we hoped Yan might put in a call," Rudi pointed out.

Kurt was not dismayed. Things were moving a little faster than he'd hoped but they still were following the course of events he'd expected. "Emmerson isn't going to blurt out any more information than he has to. He'll keep the location close to the vest until he has no choice but to share it."

Rudi pointed out the obvious flaw. "It won't do us any good if she contacts us at the last second or so close to the event that we don't have a chance to intervene. And I hate to bring this up, but if she recovers the computers for him and he does away with her, we're back to square one: trying to buy the computers from the criminals who stole them."

"I don't think Emmerson would sell them," Kurt

said. "That was all CIPHER's doing. Emmerson is up to something else."

"Like what?"

"Couldn't say. But Joe and I found a storeroom full of high-tech splicing equipment and high-bandwidth fiber-optic cable in the seaplane hangar."

"Not the residential stuff either," Joe added. "We're talking huge spools of heavily insulated commercial-grade cable."

Gamay jumped in. "The divers in Silicon Valley were practicing deepwater splicing techniques for mating the Vector units with submerged fiber-optic cables. That can't be a coincidence."

"Sounds like Emmerson wants to link these computers together," Kurt said. "But to what end?"

"Has to be some form of hacking," Paul suggested.

"That would explain the conflict with CIPHER," Joe suggested. "We've been working on the assumption that it was CIPHER muscling in on Emmerson's turf, but maybe we had it the wrong way around."

"All of which still leaves us in the dark regarding Emmerson's ultimate plan," Rudi said. "I'll run this by Hiram and see if he can read the tea leaves for us."

"Where is Hiram?" Kurt asked. "Figured he'd be on this call."

"He's still out in California," Rudi said. "He's spent the last five days digging into Hydro-Com's data, trying to pull out anything that might help. I'm sure he'll appreciate the info you've uncovered. In the meantime, you two should get some rest. Not sure when the next shoe is going to drop but it'd be best if you're ready when it does."

CHAPTER 51

Sabrina Lang awoke to the beeping alarm of the IV pump, which was signaling it had run out of fluids. The nurse came in, silenced the machine and checked her blood pressure and other vitals.

"How are you feeling?"

They asked that question every time they came in. Sabrina really had no answer. Physically, she was still dealing with the pain of the gunshot wound, but the meds knocked that down to a dull ache. Mentally, she was numb. She almost wished she was still unconscious. She knew Pradi was dead, even though they refused to tell her. She knew the breach of Hydro-Com's security system was partially her fault, even if it was so cunningly accomplished.

"I'm fine," she muttered unconvincingly.

"You don't sound fine," the nurse said. "But I'll take your word for it. Are you up for a visitor?"

"Who?" she said. She'd already seen her parents and she wasn't interested in seeing any more lawyers or special agents from the FBI or colleagues from Hydro-Com.

"A fellow computer geek," Hiram Yaeger said, poking his head in the doorway.

To her surprise, seeing him brought a smile to her face. "Sure," she said. "I'd hug you, but I'm hooked up to all these tubes and wires."

The nurse waved Hiram in. "I told you to wait in the hall," she said, scolding him. "But considering that's the first smile we've gotten out of her since she woke up, I'm going to let it slide. You have thirty minutes."

Hiram stepped into the room and pulled up a chair. He'd remained in California partly to see if he could find anything in the Hydro-Com database that might lead them to the computers and partly so he could keep checking on the injured security chief.

He felt partially responsible for her injuries. If he hadn't raced off chasing the diver or if he hadn't shown up to begin with, she might never have been injured. The fact that she was young enough to remind Hiram of his own daughter, who was in grad school down the road at Stanford, only made him feel more protective of her. "I'd ask if you're feeling okay, but I'm sure you're sick of that question by now."

"Thoroughly," she said.

"So instead, I'll ask for your help," he replied. "We've learned a thing or two about the men who stole the Vector units, but it's not what we expected. I was hoping you might be able to guess what they're really up to."

"You need my help?"

"As much as I know in general, I don't know what these servers are capable of," Yaeger admitted. "No one outside Hydro-Com does. And with Pradi gone and your lead programmer on the run with the source code, there's no one else around who knows them better than you."

"I might dispute that," she said, "but I'll do what I can to help. What have we learned?"

Yaeger explained who Emmerson was and about the three-way struggle between CIPHER, NUMA and Emmerson for the Hydro-Com computers. He explained what they knew about CIPHER's plans to sell the machines and why they thought Emmerson had something else in mind. "What can he do with those computers that would be worth more than selling them?"

"He could link them together," she said. "If they were set up to operate in a parallel fashion, he could build a tremendously powerful supercomputer. It would be an order of magnitude faster than the fastest existing machines out there, but it would require a whiz of a programmer . . . Which, of course, he has now."

Yaeger had considered that. "But how does that benefit him? Supercomputers are good at studying the intricacies of nuclear explosions and modeling the universe in seventeen dimensions. Universities and governments use them. But I fail to see how such a machine would be of value to a man like Emmerson."

She nodded and adjusted the hospital bed so she could sit up higher. "He could process Bitcoin and other cryptocurrencies," she suggested. "I read recently that the mining of crypto uses more electricity than the nations Finland, Denmark and Sweden combined. Because the Vectors can be self-powered by tides and currents and don't require intricate cooling systems, they could mine and process crypto transactions much more efficiently than the currently existing server farms. That was actually one of the original ideas behind the project."

"How much wealth could he generate that way?" Yaeger asked.

"Difficult to say," she replied. "Depending on the price of the various currencies, of course, it would probably add up to several million dollars per month."

It sounded like a lot of money, but CIPHER had been looking at a five-hundred-million-dollar payday for selling the machines. The idea that Emmerson would choose to grind out income on crypto mining while shunning a half-billion-dollar one-time offer didn't sound likely. Yaeger figured that wasn't it.

"There has to be something your Vector machines can do that no other computer can accomplish. Something that would be of more value to a crime lord than a regular corporation or government."

Sabrina leaned back, her eyes drifting, as she pondered Hiram's question. It required a different way of thinking, different inputs and information. As a security specialist, she was trained to think like a hacker, like a criminal. It was the only way to stay ahead of the black hats.

An answer finally came to her and she refocused on her visitor, smiling once again.

CHAPTER 52

The phone on Rudi Gunn's nightstand chirped to attention. Rolling over, Rudi opened one eye and glanced at the screen. He saw Hiram Yaeger's name and answered immediately.

"Ivy Bells," Yaeger announced without saying hello.

Rudi propped himself up. "It's a little early for Christmas carols but hum a few bars and I might recognize the tune."

"It's not a song," Yaeger told him. "It's the code name for an intelligence operation our Navy pulled off during the Cold War."

"Operation Ivy Bells," Rudi said.

"Exactly," Yaeger replied.

Rudi was wide awake now.

"Early seventies," Yaeger continued, "middle of

the conflict. The Russians were using the Sea of Okhotsk as a private lake for testing submarines and developing new missile technology. They had an ICBM site on the Kamchatka Peninsula and they were in the process of developing submarine-launched anti-ship missiles. Despite all the activity in the area, our intelligence agencies could pick up only sparse radio chatter and nothing of major importance. This led them to conclude a subsurface cable had been laid between the peninsula and the mainland."

Rudi recalled some of the particulars. "The Navy went out and found the cable using a modified attack submarine."

"The USS **Halibut,**" Yaeger said. "It had been fitted with the most advanced electronic gear of the time, a deep-sea lockout system for saturation divers and protective skids that allowed it to touch down on the seafloor without damaging the hull. After sneaking past several Russian patrols, divers from the **Halibut** placed an electronic collar on the cable. The collar recorded all the information passing from one side to the other without interrupting it. Because the Russians assumed the cable was secure, the communications weren't encrypted. And because it was the analog era, the Navy had to record the information on tape and send people back to get it and change out the tapes."

Rudi recalled hearing about it from an old Annapolis buddy years ago. The adrenaline-filled missions were some of the most highly guarded secrets of the Cold War. Even the sailors on the submarines were given cover stories in case they got captured. "The recordings were brought back to Washington," Rudi recalled, "where the CIA could analyze them and listen in on unfiltered top secret Russian communications. It was, as they say, an intelligence coup."

"Exactly," Yaeger said. "And I think Emmerson's planning something similar, only in a twenty-first-century internet-based style."

"We don't have any military cables in the Pacific," Rudi said. "And neither do the Russians or the Chinese."

"Emmerson isn't a military man," Yaeger countered. "He's a civilian. He's after civilian—that is, commercial—information. Things he can use to make money or leverage power."

"Go on," Rudi said.

"The world runs on data these days," Yaeger began. "Corporate reports, financial information, blueprints, technical diagrams, chemical formulas. All this information is in constant motion, flying around us every second of every day. It moves markets, makes and destroys fortunes, lifts some nations to the heights of power while consigning others to the dustbin of history. In the twenty-first century, information is worth more than all the gold, oil and Bitcoin combined. And since the world's economy is linked, the vast majority of data crosses borders repeatedly, racing around the globe on a web of fiber-optic cables that span the world's oceans."

"Not via satellite?" Rudi asked.

"Common misconception," Yaeger insisted. "Despite hundreds of communication satellites in orbit, less than one percent of all data travels through space. The rest of it—billions upon billions of megabytes per day—travels underwater in shielded cables like the ones Kurt and Joe found stored in Kinnard Emmerson's hangar."

Rudi saw where Yaeger was going. "And using that cable and Hydro-Com's servers, Emmerson is going to tap into the flow and drink from the firehose."

"Just like the Navy did with Operation Ivy Bells," Yaeger said. "Only in this case, there won't be any tapes to retrieve because he'll have the Hydro-Com servers sitting on the bottom of the sea stealing the data and delivering it to his fingertips at whatever computer terminal he uses to access the news of the world."

"That explains why he needed the source code but never looked for a buyer to take the machines off his hands."

"Precisely," Yaeger said. "It's also why he tried to fake the destruction of the **Canberra Swift,** because he wanted everyone to assume the computers had been obliterated, allowing him to splice them into the network without anyone knowing they still existed."

"Pretty shrewd," Rudi admitted. "I'll assume that

the ability of the Hydro-Com machines to operate underwater plays a part in this."

"You assume correctly," Yaeger replied. "With a regular server, the hack would have to take place on land, which is far easier to spot and eliminate. But the Hydro-Com units can operate at great depth, functioning independently by drawing power from the currents and the tides. He can place them in any ocean around the world, splicing them into whatever trunk line he chooses to attack."

Rudi had more questions. "How does this hack actually work? Operation Ivy Bells was the equivalent of a deepwater phone tap, but today's systems use pulses of light. Emmerson can't overhear them, he'd have to see them."

"There are really only two ways for him to accomplish this," Yaeger said. "Through the utilization of a beam splitter or by installing a shunt loop bypass."

Rudi sighed. "Layman's terms, Hiram. It's two a.m. here."

"Of course," Yaeger said. "A beam splitter divides the light, reflecting a small portion off in one direction while allowing the rest to pass. Beam splitters have been used in hacking before, but they're problematic for Emmerson because they would cause a noticeable drop in signal strength. Which would be a sure giveaway that there's a problem with the cable or that a hack is taking place."

Rudi understood that. "And the second method," he said. "This loop bypass. How does that work?"

"In this type of operation, the fiber-optic cable is cut in two places and a bypass loop is spliced into it. This loop takes the full signal and funnels it through another device that reads and copies the data before being sent back to the main line. The data arrives at the far end in full strength but in fractions of a second late. Think of it like a detour on the highway," Yaeger added. "You're still driving at highway speeds but you have to take the long way around and therefore you arrive later than planned."

"I get it," Rudi said. "But light travels at one hundred eighty-six thousand miles per second. Are we really going to notice a delay?"

"A detour of even a single mile would throw off the arrival of the data packets," Yaeger insisted.

Rudi accepted this. "Which means Emmerson would have to put the machines right next to the trunk line, something he's able to do because Hydro-Com machines were designed to operate at great depth."

"That's right," Yaeger said. "In fact, he can splice them directly into the submerged cables because the Vector units are equipped with their own signal boosters. This makes it possible for the data to arrive at full strength with virtually zero delay, rendering the hack impossible to detect."

A few choice words came to mind, but Rudi kept them to himself. "The entire planet's information at his fingertips and the world's second-largest economy at his back to buy that data from him."

"Yep," Yaeger said, uncharacteristically succinct. "He'll have access to industrial secrets, governmental communiqués, profit reports that move the markets. Not to mention illicit texts and emails sent between people having affairs or engaged in otherwise compromising behavior. Anything sent between the two nations or regions on the cable."

"You forgot to mention cat videos and dating profiles," Rudi joked.

"Those too," Yaeger said, laughing.

Rudi grew serious again. He thought there might be a catch. "Isn't all this data encrypted?"

"Of course," Yaeger said. "But with eight of the most powerful computing systems in the world at his disposal, none of it will stay encrypted for very long."

Rudi sat back. The combination of information to sell and leverage would make Emmerson one of the most powerful men in all of China and, for that matter, the rest of the world. He'd be the closest thing to omniscient the world has ever seen.

"**Semper magis,**" Rudi said, recalling Emmerson's family motto. "Always more."

"Trust me," Yaeger replied. "If Emmerson gets these machines, there won't be any more."

CHAPTER 53

CABLE-LAYING SHIP OCEANIC NAVIGATOR

The **Oceanic Navigator** was an ungainly ship from any angle. It looked front-heavy and awkward, with a superstructure pushed all the way forward to the bow and a midships section given over to a giant drum around which thousands of feet of fiber-optic cable were wrapped. The stern housed a forest of cranes and curved metal bands called tensioners that allowed the cable to be safely lowered to the seafloor.

Yan-Li's trip to the vessel had been uneventful, if not tedious and slow. After reaching the ship, the mini-sub had been hauled aboard with a crane and covered with tarps. Similar precautions had hidden the skimmers near the stern of the ship.

Since then, they'd traveled southwest at the ship's top speed for seventeen consecutive hours. The tension and the monotony had driven Yan outside for some fresh air.

She stood near the port rail, where several plastic chairs had been screwed to the deck to keep them from going overboard and a sign that sarcastically read **Crew Lounge** had been affixed to the wall.

It wasn't much of a lounge, Yan thought, but there was enough of a breeze to make it pleasant.

Leaning over the rail like any passenger on a cruise ship, Yan gazed at the horizon. She felt a sense of freedom for the moment. At least until Kinnard Emmerson and Guānchá appeared.

Emmerson left Guānchá at the door and stepped toward her. "I was told you wanted to see me."

She took a deep breath and looked him in the eye. It was time for a leap of faith. "I accept your proposition," she said. "I doubt it means the kind of luxury and glory you've promised, but it's better than the alternative."

He accepted this without any fanfare as if it were a foregone conclusion.

"But first," she added, "I want to speak with my children."

"Do you, now?"

"I do," she said firmly. "I have no illusions about what we're trying to do. CIPHER's people will be on full alert after what happened with Degra. Not everyone who goes into this is going to come back. I'd like to see my children's faces and tell them how much I love them. Just in case I'm not one of the lucky ones."

"You have very little to worry about," he insisted. "The men I've brought on will deal with what's left of CIPHER. You'll simply have to steal the computers while the combat is going on above you."

"Nevertheless," she said, "I want to make that call. Things can go wrong. I had to fight my way out of Taipei. I might not be so lucky this time."

He sighed, pursed his lips and shook his head. "Afraid not. I want you properly incentivized to survive and succeed. Let me be clear. When I have what I want, you'll get what you want."

She'd fully expected this response. In fact, it would have thrown her off had he reacted in any other fashion.

She pressed him. "Even you can't be sure we'll succeed."

"You'd better," he replied coldly. "If you ever want to see your children again, you'd better not fail me as your husband did."

The velvet glove was off, the iron fist out. She tensed up, pulling back and stiffening at his change in tone, but it was all for show. In fact, she hadn't felt this free since before she'd encountered Emmerson in her apartment two weeks prior.

"I'll do my best," she said, sounding subservient.

He reached out and touched her arm. It made her skin crawl. "I know you will," he said.

With that, Emmerson turned and left. Guānchá

eyed her for a second and then retreated back into the ship with his boss.

Yan was left alone at the rail.

She turned back to the sea, staring out at the endless blue waves, suppressing a smile. She was certain now. Emmerson no longer had her son and daughter or her mother. Someone had stormed the hangar and taken the hostages away. But it wasn't CIPHER because they'd have burned the place to the ground and blown Emmerson's precious aircraft to confetti.

The joy and relief she felt grew in waves to the point where she couldn't contain it. The grin began to force its way out, like sunbeams breaking through the clouds.

Who would come in from the sea and storm a fortress like Emmerson's hangar just to rescue an old woman and a couple children, she wondered. Who could possibly hope to pull off such an audacious act? Who would even try?

"Who indeed," she whispered to the wind.

Shoving her hands into the front pocket of her pullover, she touched a small device. She'd found it in her dive bag. A memento from her time with Kurt and Joe. A parting gift Joe had given her on a lark. He'd even said all she need do is twist the top and they would come running. She hoped against hope that his little quip would come true.

Without pulling her hands free, she twisted the top until it clicked. Now all she needed to do was get it into the water.

With a deep breath, she steeled herself to act. She wrapped her palm around the device and tensed her core. Pulling her hands out of the pocket, she faked a yawn, stretching her arms out behind her over the rail, at which point she flicked it overboard with a snap of her wrist.

The tiny device flew outward from the hull, hitting the water twenty feet away. It plunged downward for a couple seconds, then rose as its natural buoyancy took over.

By the time it reached the surface, it was caught in the ship's bow wave and being drawn back along the hull. It was pulled into the ship's wake, swept under and spat out once more, reappearing a hundred feet behind the ship.

At this point, the device was all but invisible, especially since Yan had destroyed the flashing strobe that might have given it away. But its L-band signal was broadcasting at full strength just as it was designed to do.

Yan only hoped that someone at NUMA was listening.

CHAPTER 54

**NUMA HEADQUARTERS,
WASHINGTON, D.C.**

On the top floor of the NUMA building, the night shift in the Remote Sensing and Communications department was puzzling over a mystery.

"There it is again," Lexi Fields said. She pointed the eraser end of her number two pencil at the blip on the screen.

Lexi was a new hire at NUMA, fresh out of Caltech. She still got excited every time something unusual happened. Which was rare in her department.

Lee Garland, director of the department, stood over her shoulder, studying the screen.

"What are we looking at?" Lexi asked.

"It's a dive recovery beacon," Lee said. "But

the location doesn't make any sense. It's got to be a glitch."

Lexi shook her head. "I've run every diagnostic possible. It's a legitimate signal. A weak signal," she added, "but it's not a ghost or a malfunction."

"What field team is it coded to?" Garland asked.

She looked down the list on a pop-up menu. "Kurt Austin. Whoever he is."

Lee chuckled. "You really are new, aren't you?"

"Today's my eighth day," she said proudly. "Still haven't been assigned a parking spot though."

"Well," Lee said, looking at the blinking icon on the computer screen, "something tells me this might expedite your parking credentials. For future reference, when you find something in code for Kurt Austin or Joe Zavala, consider it a priority. Especially if it doesn't make any sense."

Garland picked up the phone and dialed Rudi Gunn's extension. "Hey, Rudi, this is Lee down in Remote Sensing. We're picking up an odd signal that I thought you might want to know about."

"What kind of signal?" Rudi asked.

"A diver's locator beacon."

"An emergency beacon?"

"No," Lee said. "Just a standard locator signal designed to help us find someone finishing up a drift dive or caught out in bad visibility."

"What's so odd about that?" Rudi asked. "All our teams use them."

"This one is registered to Kurt Austin," Lee explained. "And unless he's gone missing again, it's a long way from where he's supposed to be."

Charts of the South China Sea contained more overlapping territorial claims than any other body of water on the face of the earth.

Within minutes of receiving the encrypted satellite message from Washington, Kurt and Joe were poring over one such chart.

A quick glance revealed intersecting lines emanating from China, Taiwan, Vietnam, Malaysia and the Philippines. In certain cases, the claims of three or four countries crossed the stretch of water or chain of small islands. Some of which were only reefs or rock formations that spent half the time submerged.

"Your average diplomat could make a lifetime career out of trying to untangle this mess," Joe said.

"Dozens have," Winterburn said, joining them at the navigator's station.

Kurt reached toward the bulkhead and switched on an overhead light. With better illumination, he was able to see the fine print indicating the fractional intervals of latitude and longitude.

Picking up a fifteen-inch parallel ruler and an old-fashioned set of brass dividers to calculate the distance between several points of reference, he marked a spot on the chart. "This is where the Remote Sensing team picked up the recovery beacon."

"Nothing out there except open ocean," Joe replied.

"Are you sure you know how to use those things?" Winterburn said with a grin. "With all the new-fangled equipment you two run around with, you may have forgotten basic navigation."

Kurt allowed a smile to crease his face but said nothing. He double-checked his calculations and stood back. "The spot is correct," Kurt said. "I have to assume the chart is correct also."

"I don't want to be grim," Joe said, "but what if they tossed her overboard?"

Kurt doubted that. "It'd be a lucky thing to get thrown overboard with an emergency beacon in your pocket. More likely, this is Yan telling us something. But what?"

"Maybe that's where the servers are hidden," Joe said.

"If so, we're too late," Kurt replied.

"We should at least be able to figure out what ship she's on," Winterburn suggested.

Joe got on a computer terminal and dialed up the AIS system to see if there were any ships nearby. "I've got three ships in the area, but backtracking shows none of them passed within ten miles of the signal."

"We're not going to find Emmerson running with a beacon on," Kurt said.

"I wonder if Rudi could ask his new buddies at the NSA to get a satellite over the area," Winterburn said.

"Already in the works," Joe said. "But they take a little time to reposition. We won't have anything for an hour or two."

Kurt doubted they had a few hours to wait. He racked his brain for a way to anticipate Emmerson's move and beat him to the punch. "Assuming she's with him and they're on a ship, their point of departure would be Victoria Harbour or somewhere nearby."

He grabbed the ruler once again, placing one end over the western passage out the harbor and the other next to the marked locator beacon. He drew a line through the two and then down the chart.

"And assuming they're in a hurry and traveling in a straight line, it would lead them . . . here."

Putting the ruler aside, he studied the map. The new line didn't cross anything directly, but it came within ten miles of clearly indicated land.

"Badger Island," Joe said, reading the map. "It's less than eighty miles from here."

"That's a stroke of luck," Kurt said.

"Not sure I'd call it good luck," Winterburn countered. "Badger Island is disputed territory. Vietnam and China fought a series of skirmishes over it in the nineties. When we started this search for Ching Shih's treasure, we were warned not go anywhere near it."

"What happened there?" Joe asked.

Winterburn adjusted his glasses. "The Chinese asserted a claim to the island in 'ninety-two. After a few years of bickering, they decided to drop the negotiations and just build a settlement there. Turns out, Vietnam had beaten them to it, erecting a small outpost, building a harbor and manning it with a hundred soldiers or thereabouts. The Chinese got angry and attacked with a fleet of gunboats. Two dozen Vietnamese were killed in the bombardment while the Chinese lost one of their boats to rockets fired from the island. A cease-fire of some kind was reached. Both sides agreed to abandon the island without relinquishing their legal claims. Since then, it's been uninhabited and in limbo."

Kurt stood up straight. "An island devoid of law or sovereignty upon which no one from any nation is allowed to set foot. Could there be a better spot for a group of international criminals to hide something the whole world is looking for?"

It was a rhetorical question. No one in the room doubted that CIPHER had chosen it as their version of Treasure Island. Nor did anyone doubt that Emmerson and Yan-Li were heading right for it.

"I'll get the **Phantom** ready to move," Joe said.

Kurt nodded. "I'll gather up what we need to make it worth the trip."

CHAPTER 55

Kurt and Joe left in the **Phantom,** leaving the **Sapphire** behind. They'd briefly considered using the Air Truck, but knowing the Vector units were hidden underwater and aware of the obvious need to approach the island without being seen, there really was no other choice.

As they traveled north, the **Sapphire** turned in behind them, following at a distance. The idea was to stay close enough to offer help should it become necessary yet not so close that it would raise the alarm on the island or Emmerson's ship.

As the **Phantom** closed in on the island, Joe brought them to the surface so Kurt could launch the **Phantom**'s stealth drone. The radar-resistant drone had wide, flat propeller blades that generated less lift than regular fan blades, but they were much quieter. They allowed it to hover unobtrusively. A thousand feet up, the drone was inaudible to the human ear.

The first pass showed little activity. "All quiet on the island front," Kurt said.

"Anything suggest where they might be keeping the servers?" Joe asked.

The island was five miles in length but only a few hundred yards across. Jungle covered the lowlands while a ridge of volcanic rock formed the spine of the island, cresting two hundred feet above the sea at its highest point. A half-moon-shaped bay protected by a reef was the defining feature of the northern side of the island while the southern side was more jagged, with a deeper drop-off and a small harbor guarded by a crumbling stone breakwater.

"The only hot spots I'm picking up are near the harbor," Kurt said. "A pair of dilapidated Quonset huts and a couple vehicles with warm engine bays."

"The harbor is a good possibility," Joe said. "Flat bottom and easy access. Protected from the waves."

Kurt had to agree. Zooming in on the dock, he found something else that supported that idea— a single large piece of machinery that looked shiny and new. "What do you make of that?"

Joe leaned over and studied the screen. "Telescoping crane," Joe said. "It's about the right size to lift those servers."

"Head for the harbor," Kurt said. "I'll get my gear."

Kurt emerged from the **Phantom** a quarter mile from the stone breakwater. He wore a black wetsuit and used a rebreather once again so as not to give himself away with a trail of bubbles. A night vison headset, integral to his dive mask, worked far more effectively at the shallow depths around the harbor than the **Scarab**'s system had in the deep, dark water around the wreck of the **Swift.**

Kicking firmly, he eased past the breakwater and propelled himself into the sheltered harbor. He wore a pack on his chest filled with explosives and towed a second pack with additional charges. All the weight made for a slow approach.

The first thing to come into view was the outer end of the concrete dock. Tucking in against the wall of the monolith, Kurt continued forward, eventually spying a pair of glowing lights that would have been invisible without the night vision assist.

He continued his approach, aiming for the pinpoints of illumination and arriving beside a long octagonal cylinder that he recognized as one of the missing Hydro-Com Vector units.

This was the first time Kurt had seen them in person. They were larger than he'd imagined. He swam alongside, running his hand across the carbon-fiber panel that made up the outer pressure hull. It had a rough texture like a pebbled wall. He stopped as he reached the glowing control panel and a bank of LEDs that cast the water in blue-white radiance.

Leaving the control panel, he moved to the center ring extending from the casing. This ring held the turbine blades that rotated around the unit, capturing energy from the passing current and changing it to electricity that powered the server.

It was an elegant design, a technological marvel. One he almost felt bad about destroying.

Grabbing a handhold, he pulled the towed pack of explosives in close and set it on the bottom. Opening the pack, he removed the first charge from the stack inside.

These were the same fire sauce charges they'd used down on the wreck of the **Swift.** RDX and thermite, designed to destroy with four-thousand-degree heat and a concussive shock wave.

Kurt placed the charge and set the timer. As it began to count down, he swam to the second unit and did the same, syncing the detonations to within a second of each other.

With the two charges beginning their count-downs, he moved on, eager to place the rest of the explosives. He passed the tail end of the second Vector unit and paused.

Drifting in a state of neutral buoyancy, Kurt scanned the bay. He adjusted the night vision to full power in hopes of picking up the slightest hint of another lighted control panel. He saw nothing but mud, the concrete wall of the dock and the keels of a few small boats.

The other servers were nowhere to be found.

CHAPTER 56

Yan-Li sat in the familiar confines of Kinnard Emmerson's refurbished mini-sub. It was more crowded than usual. Along with the members of her ex-husband's crew, Guānchá and several of Emmerson's men were packed into the space. They would go into the water together, Yan and her people to grab the servers, Guānchá and his men to deal with any resistance.

Trailing behind the mini-sub were four other divers. They rode on propulsion pods—or sleds, as Yan called them. They were slowly losing ground to the submarine but caught up when the sub reached the edge of the bay and came to a halt, allowing Yan and her team to egress.

Emerging into the darkened water, she took one of the machines, while the other divers rode double and a few stragglers swam using only their fins.

They moved across the shallow bay, looking for a cave where Degra insisted the computers were hidden. She half expected to find nothing—a last, vengeful trick from a vanquished foe—but moving along the rock face, she spotted an entrance.

Yan glanced at her watch. They were right on time. Somewhere north of them Emmerson's commandos were hitting the beach in the skimmers. Another minute or so and they'd be on foot, ready to fight.

The plan was a simple one. Emmerson's mercenaries would engage CIPHER's men near the harbor on the far side of the island. Her team of divers—all unarmed because Emmerson refused to give them weapons—would go after the Vector units hidden in the cave.

CHAPTER 57

On the far side of the island, Kurt surfaced near a crumbling section of the dock where chunks of concrete had broken off and fallen into the bay. With his head above the water, he could hear the rumble of the generator up on the dock.

"Joe, do you read me?"

"Soft but clear," Joe replied. **"You've finally learned how to use your indoor voice."**

"Seems like a good time to try it out," Kurt replied. "Unfortunately, we have a problem. I found only two servers in the harbor."

"Could they have shipped the others out already?" Joe asked.

"Possible," Kurt said. "But according to Rudi, they've heard nothing to indicate a sale has gone down. After what happened in Taipei, the market understandably dried up for a bit."

"The only other place they could be is on the far side of the island," Joe said.

"In the bay," Kurt noted.

"Anywhere else and they'd risk the wave action driving them onto the coral," Joe said. **"No one wants damaged goods."**

Kurt fully agreed. "It'll take too long to swim back out to the **Phantom** and circumnavigate the island. I'm going across on foot. Meet me over there."

"Will do," Joe said.

Kurt slipped back under the water and swam for the shoreline opposite the dock. Finding a gap in the rocks, he left the water and settled down among the foliage to organize himself.

He pulled off his fins and mask, stuffing them in the pack with the explosives. He needed to get up a two-hundred-foot slope and over to the other side of the island. And he had to bring the dive gear and sixty pounds of explosives or it wouldn't be worth making the trip.

He packed things in as tightly as he could, double-checked that his earpiece was still working so he could communicate with Joe and set off at a diagonal, intending to climb the hill in a switchback fashion.

He'd gone about fifty yards when an explosion lit up the jungle with a brilliant orange glow. Flames raced upward, illuminating wide, drooping leaves, thin bamboo stalks and a large number of squawking birds flying in all directions to escape the heat.

As the initial flash faded away, Kurt saw the

skeleton of an old flatbed truck burning in the distance. Panicked shouts and gunfire followed. Kurt couldn't tell who was shooting at whom, but there were men running through the foliage and tracers crisscrossing the darkness.

He dropped to the ground and moved in behind a fallen palm tree. "Big problem here," Kurt said to himself. "The Montagues and the Capulets have decided to finish their war between me and the other side of the island."

CHAPTER 58

Yan paused near the entrance to the cave, releasing her sled, which drifted down to the sandy bottom. Using hand signals, she waved Guānchá and his men up. She pointed inside the cave and made a pistol with her fingers.

It was time for them to do their job.

Guānchá nodded. But instead of swimming boldly forward, he gestured for her to lead the way. Apparently, she would be going with them.

Using only her fins to propel herself, Yan-Li swam into the throat of the cave with Guānchá and his men behind her. They didn't dare use any illumination, but a soft glow from up ahead told her they were in the right place.

At the end of the narrow tunnel, she found the wider grotto they'd been promised. The water was clear, calm and tinted blue from the glowing panels on the Hydro-Com servers. She hugged the wall, staring at the nearest machine. It was hooked to an auxiliary cable that led upward. She heard the hum of a generator reverberating through the cave. That would play to their advantage.

She held her breath to avoid exhaling a cloud of bubbles, swam toward the server and got behind it. Guānchá and his men followed.

She pointed to the surface, he nodded and they went up together.

Yan emerged as quietly as she could. The hum of the generator grew as her ears cleared the water. She saw it on the rocks to her left. Across the way, about as far from the noisy generator as they could get, two of CIPHER's men were sitting on overturned crates, playing cards. Assault rifles leaned against the wall next to them. A bottle of liquor sat at their feet.

Guānchá saw them also. But before he could fire, shouting echoed through the cave.

Yan looked up. High above, perched on a rope ladder that led to a gap in the top of the cave, was a third man. He appeared to have been climbing in or out. Either way, the view from above had allowed him to spot the intruding divers.

He shouted and twisted, attempting to retrieve his own weapon while holding on to the ladder.

Guānchá aimed up at him, pulled the trigger three times and knocked him from the ladder. He fell forward, crashing into the water a few feet away, but his shout had alerted the men on the rocks.

They tossed over their game and grabbed for their

weapons. Cards went into the air. The liquor bottle shattered as one of them kicked it in his haste to move out of the way. And gunfire rang out as the men shot into the water.

Yan dove deep, evading bullets that left bubble trails in the gin-clear liquid. Reaching the bottom, she ducked in behind the casing of the nearest server.

Up above her, Guānchá and his men were kicking furiously, trying to turn and shoot and avoid being killed at the same time. One of them slumped suddenly, rolling over facedown in the water. Blood trailed from his body as his weapon slipped from his hands and sank to the bottom. Yan swam from her position, racing to pick it up.

With the pistol in hand, she swam to the entrance of the cave. She surfaced in the shadows. Thoughts of killing Guānchá and Emmerson's other men raced through her mind. First, they had to deal with CIPHER's gunmen.

She looked around, spotting them near the rocks by the generator. She aimed at the rumbling device and pulled the trigger several times. Fuel spilled, a fire broke out. One of the men moved to get away.

He didn't get far. Guānchá shot him in the back.

His partner took a different tactic, kicking the burning machine off the rocks and into the pool of water.

It released a cloud of steam when it crashed in the water and spread burning fuel across the surface.

The fire raced toward Yan's position. She dove

back under, swimming downward once again. This time a bullet grazed her arm, cutting the wetsuit and slicing her skin.

The cold salt water soothed it, stinging at first and then numbing the injury. She looked up as a quick chattering sound reverberated as one of the submachine guns went to work.

The cave fell silent. The battle was over.

Surfacing cautiously, Yan-Li looked around for other signs of danger. She found none. If ever she was going to attack her captors, this was the moment.

The water swirled behind her. A long, bony hand touched her shoulder and Guānchá pulled her around to face him. He spat out his regulator as his free hand reached for her pistol.

"I'll take that," he said, wresting the gun from her grasp. "You get to work loading the machines on the floats."

The weapon had been a fleeting chance, nothing more. Her better odds lay with NUMA. She would do her job loading the servers and getting them ready to be towed out to the submarine. She planned to work slowly, giving them every possible minute to arrive.

CHAPTER 59

**NUMA OPERATIONS ROOM,
WASHINGTON, D.C.**

Back in Washington, Rudi Gunn, Anna Biel and a pair of staffers sat in the NUMA operations room watching the mission unfold in real time. On one screen, they saw images from the **Phantom**'s drone. On a screen next to it, they had a wider view encompassing the island and the waters around it that came from an NSA satellite transiting the area.

For the better part of twenty minutes, the room had been utterly quiet with only the hum of the ventilation system and the occasional scratch of a pen on paper breaking the silence.

The mission had been going off without a hitch. Until everything fell apart all at the same time.

The drone video showed flaring explosions rupturing the quiet night. Gunfire tracers could be seen flying through the jungle in multiple directions. The rapid back-and-forth audio between Kurt and Joe gave them the play-by-play account.

But that wasn't the worst of it.

On the satellite screen, a flashing icon appeared to the west of the island.

"What is that?" Rudi asked, squinting at the image.

"The satellite is picking up a new heat source entering the area," the NSA staffer said. "Type or origin unknown, but the course is confirmed. It's heading for the island."

The flashing red dot continued forward, a red line trailing out behind it showing the direction from which it had come.

"Too fast to be a ship," Rudi said.

"Direct the satellite to zoom in," Anna said.

The staffer redirected the cameras, tightening the focus on the new intruder. The island vanished. The lines representing Emmerson's ship and the **Phantom** vanished. All that remained on-screen was the sea and the newly discovered threat.

Up close, the image resolved into a pair of distinct and familiar outlines.

"Helicopters," Rudi said.

A recognition code appeared beneath the two images as the NSA's system matched the infrared signatures with recognized patterns from its catalog.

"Mi-26 Halos," Anna said, reading aloud the subtitle.

"Russian heavy-lift helicopters," Rudi noted. "Where did they come from? There aren't any Russian ships in the area."

The NSA staffer tapped away at his computer searching the NSA database. "The most likely point of origin is a spot on the Vietnamese coastline, a rural area one hundred and sixty miles to the west."

This complicated matters. "ETA for the helicopters?" Anna asked.

"Eight minutes," the NSA staffer said.

"What's the countdown on those charges?" Rudi asked.

The NUMA staffer gave him the bad news. "Fifteen minutes and change."

Anna looked at Rudi. It was still technically NUMA's mission, but the executive branch would prefer to avoid an international incident. "I'm not interested in blasting two fully crewed Russian helicopters out of the sky today."

Rudi understood. A lot of bad things happened in the clandestine world, but in general the operators were professionals. We didn't kill their people if it could be avoided and they didn't kill ours. It's just how the game was played.

Rudi looked at the NUMA staffer. "Put me in touch with Joe."

A few buttons were pressed. A line was opened.

"Joe, this is Rudi. There are two Russian helicopters inbound to pick up the stolen servers. Do

everything in your power to keep them from landing and loading."

Joe sat in the command seat of the **Phantom,** listening to Rudi's order and mulling over his options.
He briefly considered leaving the **Phantom** and
swimming to reset the timers on the explosives. But
as he studied the footage from the drone, he could
see a group of CIPHER's men assuming a defen-
sive position around the dock while the telescoping
crane dipped its beak into the water to lift the first
of the servers from the harbor.

At the very same time, Kurt was trapped in the
jungle, caught in the cross fire between CIPHER's
and Emmerson's people.

Keying his microphone button, he called out to
Kurt. "What's your status?"

"Trying not to get blown up or shot," Kurt replied. **"But I'm pinned down with zero chance of
getting across the island."**

Two problems, one solution, Joe thought. "Ping
me your location. I'm sending the drone."

"What for?" Kurt asked, following through on
Joe's request.

"Air superiority," Joe said, tapping the drone's
command console and ordering the craft to perform its automated landing sequence a few yards
from Kurt's position.

The drone moved toward Kurt and began descending. "I trust you still have explosives left," Joe said. "If you can spare a couple, I should be able to scare off the Russians and make a path for you to get across the island and over to the bay."

"Sounds great," Kurt said. **"If you can drop me a cold beer while you're at it, I'll put you in for a commendation."**

"Sorry," Joe said. "No beverages on this flight. But I can give you some intel on where the shooting is coming from."

Joe paused to check the visual. The infrared view showed two dozen men spread out in various spots. Some of them between Kurt and the water, others between Kurt and the ridge that ran down the center of the island. "Assuming you want to go straight across, I'll have to chase some of the newcomers out of your way."

"In case you forgot, that drone is unarmed," Kurt said.

"For the moment," Joe said. "Get three charges ready. Set the timers for thirty seconds, forty seconds and five minutes. Load the short-fused charges in the left claw and the long fuse in the right. Don't mix them up."

"Thirty, forty and five minutes," Kurt repeated, **"left to right. What, exactly, are you planning to do?"**

"I'm going to blast a path through the forest with

the first two," Joe said. "And then I'll use the last one to scare off our visitors from Moscow."

Joe watched on the monitor as the drone approached Kurt's position. It buzzed some foliage, using its cameras to find a level spot and touching down five feet from where Kurt had taken cover.

Kurt's frame appeared on camera. Moving quickly, he attached the charges to the gripping claws that hung beneath the body of the drone.

While Kurt attached the charges, Joe toggled the screen to the satellite feed from Washington. The Russian helicopters were proceeding on course. They were either unaware of the firefight or under orders to continue on despite the obvious combat.

"Charges are set," Kurt said. **"Get this thing airborne."**

Joe took command of the drone and ordered it to climb away from Kurt's position. It rose up slowly, heavier now and less maneuverable. For a moment, the whisper-quiet blades were a definite detriment.

"Come on, baby," Joe said, urging the machine skyward. "Just a little higher."

As it cleared the trees, someone began shooting at it. Joe saw tracers off to the right and immediately pushed the control stick to the left.

Moving away from the combat zone, the drone continued to climb while the number of seconds on the timer continued to drop.

Joe turned the drone back toward the attacking

group. He brought it in on the flank of the battle-field, weaving back and forth and hitting the release button on the left claw as the timer hit twenty-seven.

The two charges fell, the drone rolled to the right and sped off. The first charge erupted in the jungle, louder and brighter than the earlier explosions. The thermite spread across the tree line, setting fire to palm fronds and bushes while sending the nearby combatants running away from the scene.

The second charge went off ten seconds later, chasing anyone with sense even farther along.

"Coast is clear," Joe said. "Keep the blast zones to your right and you'll be unimpeded all the way to the top."

Kurt was already on the move. He swung wide, avoiding the flames and the acrid odor of the burning thermite. Emerging from the foliage, he raced onto the rocky slope and up toward the crest.

Having thirty pounds less to carry helped him make the ascent, but he no longer had enough explosives to blow up all the servers even if he found them.

Scaling the last twenty feet, Kurt came out on the top of the ridge and paused. The half circle of the bay shimmered in the moonlight a hundred feet below. It was an oddly tranquil sight, considering the war taking place on the far side of the island.

Crouching down and moving cautiously, Kurt

scanned the water, looking for any sign of activity. Not a single boat marred the surface of the bay nor were there vessels of any type out beyond the reef where the breakers were crashing.

Kurt was not dissuaded. The Vector units had to be nearby. There was simply no other place left on the island to hide them.

CHAPTER 60

Down in the grotto, Yan and her team had attached a float to each of the servers, inflating the bags until the big octagonal machines were in a state of neutral buoyancy. They came off the sand and hung motionless as she adjusted the volumes of air.

One had too much buoyancy and kept rising toward the surface. Another continued to sag since its yellow bag had sprung a small leak.

She dragged the process out, even suggesting they look for the two missing units, as they'd only found six of the eight machines. Guānchá vetoed that idea and his patience for anything but swift progress was soon spent. Yan decided not to risk antagonizing him and got things started.

Using raw muscle power, she and her people maneuvered the units into position and pulled them across the cave and into the tunnel. They may have been weightless, but they remained bulky and hard to move.

The first two were the most difficult. Yan directed them herself, taking them through the tunnel to the bay outside. The airbags proved adept at snagging the roof of the tunnel while the servers themselves liked to twist as they emerged from the exit, scraping the walls, their ends banging on the loose rocks.

Once they reached the bay, things got easier. Using towropes, they were linked to a pair of the powered sleds. After testing the security of the arrangement, Yan sent them onward and then returned to the cave.

With more space to maneuver, they guided the rest of the machines out one by one.

With the last of the servers out in the bay, Yan hooked up the second train. This one had four cars; four servers pulled by two sleds. It would be slower than the first, all part of her effort to delay things and create more time for help to arrive.

She climbed on the right-hand sled and put one of her people on the left-hand machine. Everyone else, Guānchá and Emmerson's men included, would have to swim.

CHAPTER 61

Back in the **Phantom,** Joe was busy piloting the drone. He saw that the Russian helicopters were now over the harbor, preparing to land and take on the servers. He noticed that CIPHER's people had lifted the Vector units out of the water with the telescoping crane, where they'd been placed on wheeled dollies.

Joe checked his watch. The explosives that the drone was carrying still had a full minute to cook. He suddenly wished he'd asked Kurt for less time.

By now, the first helicopter was moving toward the dock. As it closed in, the **Phantom**'s frequency-hopping scanner picked up radio chatter between the Russian pilots and CIPHER's people on the ground. The back-and-forth was rapid, clipped and tense. It gave Joe an idea.

He switched his transmitter to the Russian frequency and began to speak. "Russian helicopters approaching Badger Island," he said, trying to sound vaguely Chinese. "You are approaching sovereign territory of the People's Republic. Turn around immediately. Do not land or take on cargo."

"Who is this?" a laughing Russian voice replied. **"You sound about as Chinese as my babushka."**

Joe looked at the drone video. The helicopters were coming in with lights blazing. He had forty seconds before the drone's charge would detonate.

"Turn around immediately," Joe said. "This is your final warning."

"I'm sorry, Amerikanskiy," the Russian said. **"We are taking your computers and there's nothing you can do to stop us."**

"We'll see about that," Joe said.

He took over control of the drone and buzzed the dock as if he were on a strafing run. Some of CIPHER's people fired at the drone, others dove for cover.

After overshooting the dock, Joe turned the drone around and brought it back in for a second run. This time he aimed for the servers, hoping to blow them off the dock and back into the water. As the timer hit five seconds, he released the last of the charges.

By chance, it skipped off the boom of the telescoping crane and detonated in the air above the dock instead of between the octagonal cylinders.

The blinding flash lit up the harbor. Plenty bright to get the Russians' attention.

The lumbering helicopters broke off their approach, scattering in opposite directions. One flew off to the south and the other to the north, both climbing and making evasive maneuvers.

Joe was disappointed that he hadn't hit the target, but he hoped the fiery blast might be enough to get the Russians to abandon the attempt.

He watched as the helicopters circled around out in the distance. After what he could only assume was a conversation implying court-martials and free accommodations in Siberia if the pilots didn't retrieve the cargo, the helicopters began approaching the dock once more.

"Very impressive, Amerikanskiy," the Russian said, far less jovial now. **"Let's see you do that again."**

Joe only wished he could. He was out of explosives, but he still had the drone.

He sent it racing toward the lead helicopter, aiming for the cockpit and switching on the spotlight in the nose.

The first pass took the pilot by surprise. The pilot broke formation, before circling back around.

Joe's second attempt at playing chicken was less effective. The big helicopter remained steadfastly on approach and Joe was forced to turn the drone away or watch his only weapon splatter against the armored windscreen like a plastic bug.

As he swung wide, the Russians opened fire, unleashing a punishing stream of 7.62mm shells from a four-barreled rotary gun mounted on the side.

Joe immediately climbed and curled over the top

of the helicopter, saving the drone from destruction but well aware that he wouldn't likely get that lucky again.

The lead helicopter continued toward the dock, reaching the far end as CIPHER's men pushed the first server toward it.

"Do not take on that cargo," Joe called out. "It's been booby-trapped and will explode long before you reach home."

This time there was no response.

"Listen to me," Joe said. "I'm a pilot myself. I'm trying to warn you, do not load anything aboard your craft."

Silence told him it was useless. So Joe sent the drone on a suicide run, racing for the dock and the men pushing the server along on the wheeled cradle. He aimed for the group on the right side, coming in head high.

Three of the four men dove out of the way. The last one held his position but ducked. The cart skewed in their direction after they stopped pushing.

"Enough of this," the Russian shouted over the radio.

When Joe turned the drone back around, it was obliterated by a hail of bullets from the mini-gun.

Joe could no longer see the battlefield. But he could see the timer on the computer screen. He'd fibbed a little about the countdown. "I'd get away from that container if I were you," he called out. "You have three . . . two . . . one . . ."

As Joe uttered the last number, the explosives Kurt had placed on the servers went off. Towers of fire raced up from the two machines and CIPHER's men were thrown from the dock into the sea.

For a brief moment, the harbor was lit in a swaying, drunken glow. It faded quickly, darkening to orange and then to red embers and black smoke.

Joe no longer had the video feed from the drone, but he had access to the satellite view. He tapped the screen and brought up the image.

He could just make out the shattered wreckage of the Hydro-Com machines on the dock. He could see a few of CIPHER's men swimming away from the fires. Others were running back toward the Quonset huts. Most importantly, the big Russian helicopters were turning away, undamaged and empty-handed.

As Joe pumped his fist to celebrate, he heard an odd call over the radio.

"Na vashe zdorov'ye," the Russian said. **"To your health,** Amerikanskiy. **I drink a vodka to you tonight."**

The gruff pilot clearly realized that Joe had saved his life and the lives of his crew.

"Make it a double," Joe suggested.

He turned his attention to the radio controls, switching back to the satellite channel. "Russians heading home without any presents," he announced proudly. "Now to go help Kurt."

———

As Joe was leaving the harbor and beginning his circumnavigation of the island, Kurt was moving along the cliff that overlooked the bay. He'd finally spotted something that didn't belong.

Staring intently into the bay, allowing time for his eyes to adjust and focus, he noticed something that suggested the bay wasn't as empty as it appeared. A thin sheen of air bubbles floating on the surface at the base of the cliff. Too widespread and too uniform to be natural, the streaks caught the moonlight, creating lines that pointed directly at the cliff wall.

He picked his way along the bluff to a spot above the effervescent streak. Only now did he see the entrance to the cave that was cut back into the rock. Invisible from the air—and, by the looks of it, only accessible by boat—it was a brilliant choice to hide the servers.

Kurt was thankful that he'd found the entrance. Unfortunately, he obviously hadn't found it first.

He could tell by where the foam was appearing and dissipating that a group of divers had just left the cave. They were on their way out into the bay.

He called Joe on the radio. "Think I've found the servers," he said. "Emmerson's people are stealing them from a cave in the south side of the bay. Unfortunately, I'm too late to stop them. They must be headed for that cable ship. See if you can get in position to cut them off."

"On my way now," Joe replied.

That was good news. Bad news came as Kurt heard movement in the bushes across from him. He wasn't sure if it was CIPHER's people or Emmerson's. But it didn't much matter since he had no friends on the island anyway.

He ducked and scrambled out of the way as gunfire rang out. Several shells whistled by. Others blasted chips out of the stone to Kurt's right. The only safe direction took him down toward the very precipice of the cliff, where he dropped into a gap in the rocks.

Muffled voices drifted from the brush. Another burst of gunfire rang out, but it was wide and high.

Cover fire, Kurt thought. He was right. The next burst was followed by a thud and the sound of something metallic clinking and tumbling down the rocks toward him.

He didn't need to see it to know it was a grenade.

There was only one way out. He raced for the cliff, leaping from the edge as the grenade went off behind him.

CHAPTER 62

Kurt hit the water at forty miles an hour. The explosion behind him added an unintended but welcome assist that helped him clear the rocks directly below the cliff.

He landed boots first, plunging through twenty feet of water before his momentum slowed. Rather than push toward the surface, he found his regulator, cleared it and placed it in his mouth.

Sucking oxygen from the rebreather, he remained on the bottom, calmly pulling his mask from a pocket and sliding it over his face. After clearing the mask, he was rewarded with the gift of sight.

He activated the night vision and began peering around. Out in the bay he could see a group of figures moving slowly away from the wall and toward the depths. Not only were there several divers in the formation but there was a train of the Hydro-Com servers linked together in single file. He could see the inflated lifting bags on top and could just make out the powered sleds ahead of them struggling to pull the load.

Steeling himself to give chase, Kurt reached into the chest pack, where he'd stuffed his fins. He pulled them out, preparing to slip them on his feet, when he was hit from behind. An arm went around his chin, pulling his head back. A knife flashed toward his exposed neck. Kurt threw his right arm upward, catching the wrist of the hand that held the knife and forcing the hand to open wide.

The attacker pulled Kurt's mask off. Kurt shoved his elbow backward into the man's gut. He spun and twisted, still grasping the man's wrist.

In the dark, all Kurt could make out were blurred shadows of silver and indigo. The diver attacking him was large but not particularly quick. He didn't understand leverage and probably hadn't experienced much underwater combat.

Kurt drew him close and brought a knee up into his midsection. The diver curled up from the blow, temporarily stunned. Kurt ripped the man's mouthpiece out and kicked hard. He got on top of the diver and drove him down toward the bottom.

The man pulled the knife free and slashed at Kurt's face, cutting his air hose and releasing a torrent of bubbles.

Kurt knocked the knife free and held the man down. It was a contest of holding one's breath at this point, one that Kurt knew he would win. The man stretched for the knife, but Kurt knocked it farther out of reach.

The diver reached up and tried to grab Kurt's throat, but Kurt extended his arms, which were longer, and pressed the man into the sand.

The man's hand flailed and fell, bubbles flowed from his mouth. His eyes stared sightlessly into the deep.

Kurt held him in position until he knew his attacker was dead, grasped the man's regulator and took a deep draw of oxygen.

This was one of Kinnard Emmerson's men. He wore a hooded black wetsuit with a silver tank on his back. His mask and regulator were basic, without any night vision gear or communications equipment. All of which meant Kurt hadn't been seen or heard. The fact that no one had doubled back told him as much.

Kurt took the man's tank, harness, mask and fins. Slipping out of his ruined rebreather and leaving his high-tech mask behind, Kurt took off on a furious swim, using every ounce of strength he had left to catch the dead man's fleeing companions.

CHAPTER 63

Yan-Li didn't know that Kurt and Joe had arrived on the scene. Nor did she know about the Russians or how the battle had gone on the far side of the island.

All she knew was that the caravan she was leading had cleared the reef, finally arriving at the mini-sub. The plan was to secure the servers to the sub and tow them the rest of the way to the waiting **Oceanic Navigator.**

She came aboard and shed her diving gear. The mini-sub began to move, with the other divers back on the sleds or clinging to the two ropes tethering the servers.

"Keep our speed at one quarter," Yan said. "No more. Otherwise, we risk losing everything we just worked so hard to get."

Guānchá, who had also come back aboard, eyed her suspiciously. "That will take forever," he said.

He turned to the helmsman. "Take us up to half speed. Those computers aren't going anywhere."

They moved faster now, but still no better than four to five knots.

"What about the divers?" Yan asked. "Your people and mine?"

"They'll have plenty of time to catch up while we load the computers."

Yan couldn't argue with that. So she didn't. She found a seat, drank some water and wondered if all her hopes were in vain.

Coming around the south side of the island, Joe was moving much more swiftly than Emmerson's refurbished mini-sub, now with one propulsion unit dangerously overheated. He made it past the angled point where the rocks jutted out like an outstretched claw and made a beeline for the resting cable ship.

With no drone, he had to rely on the satellite image coming from Washington. But even that was starting to drop in quality. "What's happening to the feed?" he asked. "Did you guys forget to pay the phone bill?"

"We're losing coverage," Rudi replied. **"The satellite is in orbit. We can't just park in one place. It's heading around the curvature of the globe."**

Joe could see that the view was getting flatter

and taking on some distortion. It was like looking through a wavy pane of glass. "How long before we lose it completely?"

"Sixty seconds."

"Any sign of Kurt?"

"Negative," Rudi said. **"We lost his signal after the last explosion. No contact since."**

"Do you want me to double back and look for him?"

"Also negative," Rudi said. **"If he's alive, he'll be heading for that freighter. And if he's gone, you have to finish the job on your own."**

Joe understood. "I'll ram that ship's stern and set off the scuttling charges if I have to. She may not go down, but a bent rudder and a warped propeller shaft will keep her from getting away."

"Consider that as a last resort," Rudi said. **"But you should be well ahead of the divers Kurt reported. All you have to do is keep them from hauling the servers aboard."**

That sounded easier, Joe thought. "Give me one last look at that freighter before we lose the satellite. A close-up if you can."

Rudi and the NSA team quickly obliged. The satellite's powerful lens and high-definition camera zoomed in on the ship. It was just sitting there, venting steam but going nowhere. As the satellite focused on the stern, Joe saw that a crane had been deployed. A group of men milled around beside it. There was no sense of urgency. No sign they were worried about escaping from the area or that anything of importance was about to happen.

It should have told Joe he could ease up as well, that he was well ahead of Emmerson's divers and could wait to ambush them like a state trooper waiting behind a billboard with a radar gun. But the crew of the cable ship seemed almost too relaxed. As if their work was already done.

He strained to see what he might be missing, but the satellite went over the horizon and the image went dark.

"We've reached the rendezvous point," Guānchá announced. "Take us up." The dive planes tilted upward. Water was forced from the tanks. The submarine rose.

Yan-Li grabbed a handhold as the mini-sub breached the surface. She was numb and exhausted.

"Open the hatch," Guānchá ordered, looking right at her.

She got up from her spot and climbed the short ladder to the circular hatchway. Unlocking it and turning the wheel, she felt the hatch release and pushed it open. The cool night air streamed in. It gave her a little life.

She climbed up through the docking collar and popped her head out for a look.

The freighter wasn't there. She turned from point to point. The ship was nowhere to be seen.

She remained baffled until a strange roar announced the arrival of something else. She looked to the north as the sound of jet engines grew louder and closer. Cruising toward her across the waves, she saw Emmerson's Ekranoplan. His monster of the sea. Repaired and now here to collect them, one and all.

CHAPTER 64

The Ekranoplan taxied toward Guānchá's submarine, pivoting its stern in that direction as it approached. Lights came on beneath the tail as the great aft door began to descend, offering a ramp on which to load their cargo.

The servers were detached from the mini-sub, towed toward the ramp and hooked to lines that led up into the cavernous fuselage. Winches engaged and the train of servers moved slowly forward.

Hitting the ramp, they began to rise, stopping here and there as adjustments were made and the flotation bags removed. It was a slow, meticulous process. One that was repeated with the mini-sub.

Now that the cargo was safely on board, Yan climbed out of the submarine. Guānchá and the rest of the crew followed her. Feeling forlorn and useless, she found a dark place in the plane to wait out the journey.

She watched as the divers on the propulsion units

surfaced. They came aboard one by one, their machines hauled up the ramp and strapped here and there. But as the space was filling up, time for help to arrive was running out.

She looked out toward the island. It was a mere silhouette against a matte gray sky. No sign of the battle could be seen. No activity of any kind.

At long last, a boat appeared. A ribbed fast boat with several men on board. As it came close, Yan recognized Emmerson sitting front and center.

Transferring the flag, she thought. How perfect.

The boat came right up on the ramp and was quickly hauled on board and secured at the aft end of the cavernous aircraft.

Emmerson got out and went forward, passing her without a word as he made his way to the cockpit to give orders.

The pitch of the engines began to rise. Emmerson's divers moved past as well, heading for the better accommodations up front. In the confusion of loading and the rush to depart, no one counted the dead or worried about those left behind. They just hurried to get the work done and get the plane moving.

Yan barely noticed. She was staring out the aft end of the plane as the ramp rose into place. It came up slowly, seawater draining from all sides, as it relentlessly narrowed the gap between the outside world and the prison inside the aircraft.

She was tempted to make a break for it. But to what end? They could easily shoot her from the aircraft or run her over or leave her there to die of exposure. She held her ground, shuddering as the door locked with a heavy metallic clang.

The plane was already moving, picking up speed and turning into the wind.

Yan found a place to sit, collapsing against the wall and sliding down to the floor. She was devastated. She'd been so sure that rescue would come, so certain that Kurt and Joe would arrive to save the day.

Even if they'd been late, they could have followed the freighter. They could have tracked it and disabled it. They could have boarded it and taken control. But this monstrous aircraft of Emmerson's would not be tracked or intercepted or boarded. It would scream across the East China Sea that night and have them back in Hong Kong by morning.

And there, she was quite certain, her life would end.

CHAPTER 65

Without the drone and the satellite feed, Joe was temporarily blind. But he could still hear. He activated the sonar system, listening for any sound of an approaching vehicle.

The hydrophones were damaged from the explosions in Victoria Harbour and the static coming through the headset was unrelenting. But even with all that, Joe was able to pick up the sound of something approaching.

It wasn't the quiet hum of a submersible's electric propeller or even the rumbling turbulence in the water that towing a half-dozen automobile-sized servers would cause. It was more of a high-pitched buzz, like someone running a lawn mower in the backyard.

Zeroing in on that direction, Joe turned the **Phantom** and brought it closer to the surface. The submersible didn't have a traditional periscope but did sport a small photonics mast, which held cameras and other sensors.

Training the cameras toward the oncoming vibrations, he switched to night vision mode and spotted the two small aircraft coming his way.

"The skimmers," Joe said under his breath. They were the same ones he'd seen in Emmerson's hangar in Hong Kong.

They came in low across the water, settling down directly between Joe and the anchored ship. In the air, they were quite nimble, but they wallowed on the water like overloaded rafts.

Joe turned his attention to the cable ship. Activity was picking up at the stern. The cigarettes were gone, the men were manipulating the crane into position while unspooling lengthy orange hoses. The color told the story.

"Fuel lines."

The first skimmer moved in toward the stern of the ship. The mechanical arm reached out toward the nearest skimmer. Instead of hoisting the plane aboard, it grasped the aircraft and held it steady. With the crane locked on, one of the freighter's crewmen bravely hopped onto the floating aircraft. He stood on the wing and worked with one of the orange hoses, plugging it into a port on the right side.

"I've got two small amphibious planes docking at the stern of Emmerson's ship."

"**Must be his expeditionary force returning,**" Rudi said.

"Returning but not staying," Joe said. "Looks like they're stopping by for a splash of gas."

"**Any sign of the servers?**"

"Not yet," Joe said. "These things are too small to carry them. They're more like minivans with wings."

"**Still, that's good news,**" Rudi said. "**The rest of the force might be with you soon.**"

That was reasonable, Joe thought, but wrong. "I don't think so. In fact, I think they're already long gone."

"**How do you figure? If another ship had come into the area, we'd have seen it approaching hours ago.**"

"Not if that ship was a jet-powered transport that was flying in the surface effect zone," Joe replied. "Remember that Ekranoplan Kurt and I saw in Emmerson's hangar? I'm betting he used it to swoop in, grab the servers and exit stage left before anyone noticed. The only reason this freighter has been hanging around is to fuel up these skimmers."

Rudi muttered something over the open line that might have been a curse. "**That's bad news any way you cut it,**" he then said. "**He could be halfway to Hong Kong by now.**"

Halfway was a stretch. Hong Kong was six hundred miles away. Fully loaded, the Ekranoplan might be good for a top speed of two fifty, maybe two seventy-five. And that didn't include all the time to load up and get airborne. Still, there was no chance of stopping Emmerson before he got to Chinese airspace and the sanctuary of home.

Unless he wasn't going home.

Joe took another look at the skimmers being fueled up at the stern of the freighter. They were short-range craft, heavy and slow, designed to travel in ground effect just like the Ekranoplan. They couldn't make Hong Kong from this distance, not even with full tanks. Their destination had to be closer.

Rudi's voice came over the headphones, interrupting Joe's train of thought. **"In light of this new information, it's probably best for you to leave the area. Head back to the island, make a recon of the bay, see if you can find Kurt. If he's been injured, he'll need help. And if he's been killed . . . Well, either way, it's important that we get him off the island before either the Chinese or Vietnamese investigate."**

"Kurt's not on the island," Joe said. "If he was, we'd be picking up his signal. He went in the water, which tells me he's probably with Emmerson. Either as a stowaway or a prisoner."

"And Emmerson is on his way back to China."

"Except I don't think he is," Joe said. "Not yet. These skimmers are short-range. They can't reach Hong Kong from here. They'll need to refuel one more time at least. Or better yet, be picked up by something bigger and faster."

On-screen, the first skimmer was being fueled, the second still patiently waiting its turn.

An idea hit Joe, an idea he loved and hated all at the same time.

"I need the Air Truck," he told Rudi. "Contact the **Sapphire** and have them launch that big, dumb remote-controlled plane to pick me up. I'm going to follow these guys when they leave."

CHAPTER 66

Kinnard Emmerson sat in the cockpit of the Ekranoplan as it took off and left Badger Island behind. Turning in his seat, he checked with the navigator. "Any sign of pursuit?"

The Ekranoplan had a Russian countermeasure system that Emmerson had updated. It included forward-facing antennas and infrared sensors designed to alert them if they'd been painted by radar or if another plane or missile was approaching from behind.

"Nothing, sir," the navigator replied. "The board is clear."

Clear. He liked the sound of that. They were clear of the island, clear of the menace from CIPHER, clear of the never-ending interference from NUMA.

Emmerson almost shouted in celebration, but that wasn't his style. He gave the navigator a stern look. "Keep an eye on things. I don't want to be surprised."

As the navigator nodded, Emmerson undid his seat belt and got up. He stepped back through the cockpit door into the insulated crew compartment. Guānchá stood there, along with the blond man from America and Yan-Li, who'd been brought forward for a little tutorial.

The American was explaining the next task to her. He had a length of fiber-optic cable in his hands and the K-shaped tool. "This splices it," he explained. "It's important to make sure the two lasers are lined up correctly. You'll get a green indicator when the cable is in the right spot."

Yan nodded and the man continued. "Just close the two ends when you get the green light. A cold laser does the cutting and polishing. The splice is nearly instantaneous."

"I see you two have met," Emmerson said. He looked at Yan. "I assume you understand this process."

"A child could do it."

"Not twelve hundred feet below the surface."

"So that's the final task," she said.

"Final task?" he repeated. "I thought we were partners."

"Partners get a say in things," she said, unable to hold back her acid tongue.

Emmerson arched his eyebrows and gently shook his head. "Not in this firm."

Yan felt a sense of helplessness and anger boiling up inside her. She held his gaze for a moment and then spoke. "I'll hook your computer into the line," she said. "But I will do nothing more until my family is safe and sound back home."

He nodded. "Fair enough."

Only the slightest pretense remained, with both of them trying to use it to their advantage.

Emmerson reached into his pocket and pulled out a stack of booklets the size of international passports. "Go brief your people," he said. "And give them these."

"What are they?" she asked, taking them from his hand and noticing that each one was sealed with metallic tape on which holograms had been imprinted.

"Numbered account booklets," Emmerson said. "Payment for services rendered. Which has been withheld until now."

Yan studied the passbooks more closely. They were very impressive, including computer chips for verification and covers embossed with the name of a Malaysian specialty bank.

He reached into a separate pocket and produced one more. "Your husband's share. It's yours now. You've certainly earned it."

Yan took the final booklet calmly. She recognized it for what it was—one last incentive to lure them across the finish line.

"Don't lose those," Emmerson warned, grinning like a man telling a witty joke. "They're numbered accounts. They'll be paid to the bearer."

Yan recognized a masterstroke when she saw it.

Like Emmerson had just served for game, set and match. How, after all this, could she ask the others to back her and mutiny against the man who offered them riches?

She tucked the booklets in a pocket. "I guess we're not going to Hong Kong."

"We most certainly are," he corrected. "But after we finish the job."

CHAPTER 67

NUMA YACHT SAPPHIRE

The **Sapphire** was plowing its way north when the orders came in. Gamay got the call and ran to get Paul and Stratton.

"Rudi wants us to strip the Air Truck of excess weight and send it to pick up Joe," she told them.

"Excess weight?" Stratton asked.

"Everything except lifesaving gear," she said.

"What about Kurt?" Paul asked.

"He didn't say," Gamay replied. "He did say as soon as humanly possible."

Racing to the top deck, they surrounded the odd-looking craft and slid open the cockpit doors. With great speed, Paul and Gamay pulled tools, equipment and the removable seats from the craft. While they lightened the load, Stratton sat in the cockpit readying the Air Truck to fly autonomously. He finished punching in the coordinates and climbed out with a hand from Paul.

"That's everything," he said.

"Not so fast," Winterburn said, rushing up to them. He had a hard plastic case in his hands. Inside was a loaded pistol and a spare magazine. "More lifesaving equipment."

He placed it inside, strapping the case under one of the seat belts.

While Paul slammed the canopy shut and the group stepped back, Stratton went to the remote-control panel at the side of the helipad and hit the start button.

In a matter of seconds, the craft had been run through its preflight check and powered up. The four lifting fans went to full speed and the Air Truck took off, launching into the air like a dragonfly springing from a rock in the river.

It went north, picking up speed. Once the wings provided enough lift, the rear fans rotated to a vertical position, becoming pusher propellers and driving the craft forward. So configured and accelerating to maximum speed, the Air Truck vanished into the night.

CHAPTER 68

Yan left Emmerson and made her way out of the insulated crew compartment into the noise-bombarded cargo hold. She walked like a zombie, passing the first group of servers and squeezing past the mini-sub that took up the mid-section of the plane.

Passing the remaining servers, she arrived near the tail end of the craft, where her men had gathered.

She studied their faces. They appeared subdued instead of euphoric. She had no knowledge of what they'd witnessed from this very spot only two weeks earlier. But she sensed their pain. After all, they were still trapped in Emmerson's hands, indentured servants with no legitimate future. Such circumstances had a way of grinding one's soul to dust.

She considered withholding the bankbooks. But if she did and Emmerson exposed her, he'd alienate them from her. A final insult and triumph in one.

"I have some news," she said loud enough to be heard over the howling wind and whining engines.

She gathered them close and pulled out the books. "From Emmerson," she said, dropping them onto the covered bow of the ribbed fast boat.

The pirates looked at the books and glanced around at one another. For a group long motivated by money, there was an odd hesitancy. Eventually, one of them reached forward, plucking a book from the pile. The man broke the seal and looked at the information. His face was a mask without emotion.

Another member of the crew reached in and took his pay. And, one by one, all six surviving pirates collected their shares.

Callum was the last to pick up a bankbook. "There's one left," he noted.

"It was meant for Lucas," Yan said.

"You should take it," he told her.

She shook her head. "No. You take it. Divide it up among the crew."

Callum stared at the bankbook but never touched it. As he waited, a voice called out from the shadows behind them.

"Don't waste your time," the voice announced. "Even if those accounts are real, none of you will live to see a penny."

The group turned toward the intruder. Yan-Li was no exception. She gazed past her men, staring intently at Kurt Austin as he emerged from the shadows like a ghost.

CHAPTER 69

Callum stepped toward Kurt hastily, but Kurt was ready for an aggressive maneuver. "Take it easy," he warned. "I'm on your side."

"Who the hell are you?" another of the pirates asked.

"Keep your voice down," Kurt suggested. "I'm a friend of Yan's. And if you want anything out of this besides a watery grave, you'll listen to what I have to say."

Yan was shocked by his arrival, nearly overcome with emotion. It took a second for her to find the words. "How did you get here?"

"Who is he?" Callum demanded.

"Kurt's a friend of mine," she said firmly. "He's an American who works for NUMA."

Callum obviously recognized the agency's name. "You're the one who interfered at the wreck site."

Kurt offered a disarming smile. "**Interfered** is a pretty strong word. Especially considering that I was there first and the computers were already gone. But you're right. That was me. And now I'm here to offer you a way out."

"We have a way out," one of them insisted, holding up the passbook.

"Do you?" Kurt said. "And when do you get access to that money? After you dive to the bottom of the sea and hook Emmerson's computers into the fiber-optic trunk line. Do you really think he's going to be here waiting for you when you return to the surface? Do you really think he's going to let the only people in the world who know what he did—and where he did it—live to tell the tale? Have any of you even read **Treasure Island**? After Captain Flint buries the treasure, he kills the sailors who help him so he'll be the only one who knows where it is. Emmerson is going to do the exact same thing."

They stared at him blankly. He let them stare. He needed them to think. He needed them to see it for themselves.

"How would he get rid of all of us?" another of the pirates asked.

"Any number of ways," Kurt said. "He might have you shot when you swim to the surface or just fly away and leave you treading water until you drown or die of exposure or get eaten by a shark."

"We're not going to be treading water," Yan said. "We'll be using the sub."

"So much the easier. Seven birds with one stone. You go down and hook the computer into place. He sabotages the sub and you're never seen again."

The group became agitated, partly because they knew Kurt's scenario was likely, partly because they didn't want to believe it. Small discussions broke out. Murmurs flowed like electricity.

"Quiet," Yan said as the voices rose. "One of you go check the submarine. Look for anything that might be sabotage."

A man nodded and moved off. A second man joined him.

"It's not going to be something obvious," Kurt pointed out.

"You better hope it is," Callum insisted.

Kurt shrugged. He would wait.

Yan looked his way. "While we're waiting, how about you tell us your plan?"

"Simple," Kurt said. "We take the plane by force. Fly back to Da Nang and turn Emmerson over to the authorities."

That suggestion went over like a lead balloon.

"They have all the guns," Callum pointed out. "And we'd have no way to get home once the Vietnamese government impounds this thing."

"My people will pick us up," Kurt said.

"And then what? Do we get to choose between an American prison and a Chinese one?"

"Something much nicer," Kurt said. "A ten-million-dollar reward. And, most likely, a sudden case of amnesia with the Chinese authorities regarding your previous activities."

They looked at him as if he'd lost his mind. Kurt turned to Yan-Li. "Tell them what you were searching for prior to Emmerson drafting you into all this."

"Ching Shih's lost treasure ship," she said, "it's part of our cultural heritage. The leadership in Beijing has offered ten million dollars to whoever finds it. I've been trying to locate it for a long time. Kurt spent the summer helping me. We're very close."

The pirates appeared far more impressed by this story. They may not have known what **Treasure Island** was or who Captain Flint or Robert Louis Stevenson were, but they knew their own legends well. Ching Shih was a hero to the people of China, as were pirates and smugglers in particular. The legend of her stolen treasure ship was also well known. Every few years, someone would find some broken pottery or old bronze statue and claim to have discovered it, all to great fanfare but nothing more.

Kurt let them think about the treasure and the reward and then added the finishing touch. "Friends of mine have taken over the search since we were called away. They've found the wreck."

He pulled his phone from a waterproof pocket.

After turning it on and entering his passcode, he handed it to Yan. "Scroll through the pictures," he suggested. "You'll find all kinds of treasures in there."

She opened the photo app and began sliding her finger sideways. The first dozen photos were pictures of sonar scans and images from the sub-bottom profiler. Next came the artifacts Paul and Gamay Trout had recovered.

"Master Jun," she said, reading the ancient Chinese script.

Kurt nodded. "The ship is there," he said. "Buried under forty feet of ash. It will be perfectly preserved when it's finally excavated. The find of the century. And as of right now, only a handful of people know where it is and none of them work for the Chinese government. If you help me take this plane from Emmerson, we'll sail away. Leaving you to discover the wreck and reap all the fortune, fame and glory."

The men started discussing the idea. They used hushed whispers this time, a sign that Kurt was winning them over.

Across from him, Yan continued sliding through the photos. Finding one that almost brought her to tears. Her mother and her children standing on the deck of the **Sapphire** with Kurt's arms around them.

She breathed in sharply and looked up at him, her eyes glistening. "Please tell me this isn't a trick?"

Kurt knew what she was looking at. "They're real," he insisted. "Taken twenty-four hours ago on the deck of the **Sapphire**."

She stared at the photo a moment longer, lost in the eyes of her children and fighting back tears. "Thank you," she said. "Thank you."

Kurt nodded and Yan scrolled back to the photos of the artifacts. She handed the phone to the other pirates and they passed it from palm to palm, studying the images. The pictures were sharp, the detail impressive, but none of the pirates had enough knowledge to guess whether they were being tricked or not.

"Do you trust him?" one of them asked.

"More than anyone I know," she said firmly. "Certainly more than I would ever trust Emmerson."

That seemed to satisfy all except one.

"Well, I don't trust him," Callum said loudly. "He's an American agent who'd tell us any lie he could think up to get his way. But I don't really give a damn if he's lying or telling the truth. Emmerson murdered two of our brothers and it's time we paid him back."

As Callum finished, he threw the bankbook to the floor in disgust. "I'd rather die trying to kill Emmerson for what he's done than live to spend his money."

Kurt hadn't expected this. It was welcome. In a close quarters brawl, revenge was a far better motivator than money.

And if Callum's stand wasn't enough, the two pirates who'd gone to inspect the mini-sub returned. They held a pair of black cylinders in their hands.

"We found these," one of them said. "They were hidden in the submarine and set to explode."

They held out a pair of charges with illuminated LEDs showing a countdown clock stopped at 0073.

Kurt didn't mention that the explosives were his or that he'd placed them while hiding in the submersible after the Ekranoplan took off. He hadn't actually intended for the charges to be found, considering them just as insurance in case Yan's people weren't willing to come over to his side. But between Callum's words and the newly discovered explosives, the pirates were now primed to fight.

One after another, they tossed the bankbooks down. In classic pirate fashion, they'd thrown their lots in together. And now it was time to mutiny.

CHAPTER 70

Joe was running on the surface, five miles east of the cable ship, when a signal on his control screen told him the Air Truck was approaching.

He brought the **Phantom** to a halt, turned on the exterior lights and left his chair. Climbing out the hatch, he saw the red and green navigation lights of the pilotless craft coming his way.

Shutting the hatch, Joe waited as the Air Truck eased in above the sub. With all four fans now back in their vertical positions, the machine hovered overhead. The floodlights on the underside came on, illuminating the **Phantom** and the green water around it.

With a more accurate view of its target, the Air Truck adjusted position a bit and lowered a weighted line from the open space in the belly of the craft. It dropped directly down to Joe. He barely had to reach to grab it.

Impressed with the automated maneuvering, Joe

admitted that his disdain of the craft might have been a bit hasty.

Wrapping his arm around the line, he stepped onto the hook, getting one foot firmly in place and wedging in the other above it.

He pulled himself close and began swaying as the cable was retracted. It rose smoothly, the entire ride surprisingly stable. Because the Air Truck used four counter-rotating fans instead of a single large rotor like a helicopter, the air beneath it didn't swirl like a man-made tornado. This allowed Joe to travel upward without the need for a guideline to keep him from spinning like a top.

He was pulled up into the gap between the two booms where the cable stopped. Joe stepped off the hook and onto the rear shelf that Kurt and Yan had climbed onto when escaping from the shark. From there, it was a short crawl to the cockpit.

He opened the aft hatch and climbed inside, making his way to the pilot's seat. He grinned as he found the care package Winterburn had left him. He put it in the copilot's seat and tapped the glass touch screen of the control panel, which lit up brilliantly.

Finding the comm system, he contacted the **Sapphire.** "I'm in the truck," he said. "Go ahead and release the controls so I can show you guys how a real pilot flies this thing."

Paul's voice came back sounding strangely robotic. **"I'm afraid I can't do that, Joe."**

"Very funny, HAL."

"No, seriously," Paul said. **"I can't do it. I'm waiting for Stratton to key in the command."** There was a slight pause. **"He says you'll have full control . . . now."**

As soon as Joe had command of the machine, he tapped the touch screen and moved the virtual controls to full speed. The nose dipped and the Air Truck shot forward with the type of acceleration a helicopter couldn't possibly attain.

Glancing back, Joe saw the **Phantom** fall behind him. The **Sapphire** would be along in a couple hours to take it under tow. He doubted anyone would find it between now and then.

With the Air Truck picking up speed, Joe reached over to the configuration panel. At eighty knots, he switched the rear fans into propulsion mode. The machine picked up more speed, soon maxing out at a hundred and sixty knots.

Glancing at the navigation display, Joe double-checked the course. He'd watched the skimmers fly off ten minutes before. They'd gone almost due east. He set his heading to match.

He guessed their maximum speed at a hundred and ten knots, give or take a few for wind. They might be fifteen miles in front of him, a distance he could make up in half an hour.

"Easy-peasy, mac and cheesy," he told himself.

All he had to do was follow them to wherever

they might land, take on Emmerson's army by himself and find and rescue Kurt.

He stole a quick glance at the pistol. He hoped Winterburn had the sense to pack him plenty of ammunition.

CHAPTER 71

Kurt felt a subtle tilt in the deck of the Ekranoplan. It was followed by a change in volume of the high-pitched engines. "Sounds like we're about to make a pit stop."

Yan-Li explained. "Emmerson wanted to get the server spliced before we flew back to Hong Kong." She looked at her watch. Daylight was almost upon them. "Figured he'd want to do it at night. But what do I know?"

Kurt understood. "He probably worked out all the satellite schedules and found himself a gap in the surveillance coverage, a brief window when he could act unobserved. This is going to be our chance."

Plans were made, traps rigged. While Emmerson's men still held all the weapons, the pirates had the element of surprise. Kurt gave only one piece of advice. "Act normal until Yan gives the signal. Just go about your business until Emmerson's men are spread out and lulled into a false sense of security."

The group dispersed, moving to different places in the crowded cargo hold. Yan climbed on top of the mini-sub, standing near the orange docking collar. Kurt moved to a stack of oxygen cylinders a few yards forward of the submarine. The rest of the pirates gathered in the back of the plane in different spots.

The Ekranoplan slowed further and the keel hit the water. The deceleration was powerful. Those who weren't holding on struggled to remain on their feet.

The big duck was now back in the pond, coasting to a stop. It slewed around, pointing its nose into the swells as it lost its final bit of momentum. It wouldn't be long now.

Kurt waited, his eyes down, his hair tucked under the knit cap. His plan was to be leaning over, checking the oxygen cylinders with a pressure gauge when Emmerson's men came into the hold.

The door to the crew compartment opened. Emmerson's men filed out. Kurt was pleasantly surprised by the numbers. Five men, including the big guy he'd seen in Taiwan, plus a blond fellow who looked like a California surfer. Finally, he saw Emmerson himself.

It was shaping up as a fair fight.

They moved toward the aft end of the hold, slipping by the Hydro-Com servers and approaching Kurt's position. As they came near, Kurt heaved an oxygen cylinder onto his shoulder, obscuring his face. They passed him without a second glance.

Looking back, Kurt noticed that two of Emmerson's men remained by the forward door. As he considered what to do about that particular problem, Emmerson called to Yan, who was up on the skirt around the submersible pretending to inspect the dive planes.

"It's time," Emmerson called out, his voice booming louder than the idling engines outside.

Yan looked toward him, meeting his eyes. "Yes," she said. "Yes it is."

She turned, intentionally knocking a lead weight off the edge of the submersible. It fell ten feet and banged against the metal deck, the sound reverberating throughout the cabin.

The act was both a distraction and a signal. Emmerson, Guānchá and the blond man glanced that way. At the same time, two of Yan's people stepped aside, revealing Callum beside a pair of oxygen cylinders that had been hooked to a pipe.

Callum threw both valves open simultaneously and they blasted high-pressure air into the tube. A length of metal had been packed inside, bolstered by a wad of cloth. It launched from the tube like a harpoon, flying toward Emmerson but careening off course and striking the blond man in the chest.

He fell to the ground, clutching at his sternum.

Emmerson gawked, frozen by the incident.

Guānchá reacted quickly, drawing his pistol and firing at Callum.

Callum dove behind the submersible as bullets ricocheted off the hull.

Up on the submersible, Yan dropped to one knee and grabbed the dive belt that she'd pulled the lead weight from. Twisting her body to maximum torque, she slung it at Guānchá. It hit him in the neck and shoulder, knocking him off-balance and causing him to discharge a shot into the deck in front of him.

As soon as he had regained his balance, he spun and took aim at Yan, but she was already racing over the top of the sub. As two shots hit the ceiling above her, she jumped down on the far side.

Emmerson's reserves realized what was happening. They came rushing forward, pulling out their own weapons and charging into the fray. As they raced by Kurt, he twisted his shoulders suddenly, swinging the oxygen tank into the path of the onrushing men. The nearest man took the brunt of the impact. He went down as if he'd been clotheslined, landing flat on the deck with a shattered nose and concussion that left him motionless.

His partner was more fortunate, receiving only a glancing blow that knocked him off course as he ran forward. He crashed into the nose of the submarine, used it to stabilize himself and turned toward Kurt, raising his gun.

Kurt was already on him. He knocked the pistol aside with his left hand and slugged the man in the jaw with a right cross. The man dropped, sprawling out as Kurt grabbed his weapon off the deck.

By now, Emmerson had recovered from his initial shock. He and Guánchá were backing up, firing off shots here and there, retreating toward the cockpit. Two of the pirates raced to stop them but were cut down in a hail of gunfire.

As the men fell to the deck, Emmerson and Guánchá reached the bulkhead wall, ducked out the door and slammed it shut.

Kurt and Yan dragged the bleeding pirates back behind the submarine. Callum joined them.

"Now what?" Yan asked.

"We could rush them," Callum suggested. "We have the numbers now. And the guns."

"Some of the guns," Yan said. "Who knows what they have up front. If they see us coming, they'll shoot us right through the wall."

All eyes turned Kurt's way.

"I'm done making this difficult," he said. "Get the back door open and push the boat out. I'm going to blow up the damned plane."

CHAPTER 72

Emmerson fell into the cockpit, reeling at the reversal of fortune. He berated himself for not keeping a few of the mercenaries with him or waiting on the skimmers to return from the island before departing, but that would have meant sitting in the danger zone for too long and possibly missing the window in the satellite coverage that he needed to place the first Vector unit. It was simply not in the plan.

But now what? He could hardly fly back to Hong Kong fighting a rearguard action on the aircraft as he went. And if he left the pirates behind, he risked exposure.

"Get us moving," he ordered. "I want this plane traveling at full speed as soon as possible and I want you to maneuver back and forth sharply until everyone in the hold is battered to a bloody pulp."

The pilots hesitated for only a second and then

pushed the throttles to the fire wall. They had no desire to be killed by the rampaging pirates either.

Near the tail end of the aircraft, Kurt heard the engines howl as he was resetting the timers on the explosive charges and placing them where they would do maximum damage.

At the same time, Yan was gathering up the injured men and helping them into the ribbed inflatable boat, which they'd pushed up to the edge of the locked ramp.

It was Callum's job to get the ramp down and the door open. He stood at the panel, recalling what he'd seen Emmerson's man do weeks ago. First, he disarmed the lock, then he released the safety lever and finally he pulled the main handle down, moving it from closed to open.

The hydraulics powered up. The latches released and a crack of light appeared between the clamshell doors. Dawn had arrived, the sky was pink and the sea a deep blue.

All of a sudden, the doors froze in the half-opened position, jerking to a sudden stop.

"What happened?" Yan asked.

Callum turned back to the control panel. The indicator lights were neither red nor green. They'd gone dark.

"They've shut off the hydraulics," he said. "They must have pulled the circuit breaker in the cockpit."

All eyes went to the opening. It was far too narrow to slide the boat through.

"We're trapped," Yan said.

The plane was moving now, making a wallowing turn into the wind so it could start its take-off run.

Kurt looked around. They had to act before the plane got off the water.

He spotted a ladder on the wall near the stack of oxygen tanks he'd been pretending to inspect. It led up to the roof, which, in Joe's words, resembled the deck of a ship.

"See if you can find a manual override for the hydraulics," he said. "I'm going to break into the cockpit and have a word with the pilot."

Yan glared at him. "You said that was a bad idea."

Kurt grabbed one of the explosive charges, leaving the second one in position in case he failed in his quest. "I said rushing the door is a bad idea. Going up and over the top should work just fine."

Kurt moved to the ladder and scaled it quickly and unlocked the hatch above. Putting his shoulder into it, he forced the hatch upward and back, fighting the wind the whole time. Clearing the opening, he found himself behind a low windbreak and next to an empty gun mount, which had once sported a heavy-caliber weapon.

He began to move forward, squinting in the rushing air. They were definitely picking up speed. He needed to hurry. He ran forward, covering a third of the distance in a low crouch before dropping to his hands and knees.

He was amidships, with the huge Y tail far behind him, the stubby wings directly beneath him and the forward-mounted engine pylons fifty feet ahead. He needed to keep going.

He flattened himself against the aircraft's roof, shimmying along using his elbows and feet in a modified version of the old Army crawl. The ribbed design of the airframe gave him some grip, the aging nonslip coating a smidgen more, but he was rapidly approaching the point where he'd be unable to hold on.

He pressed tight to the aluminum skin, pulling even with the screaming engines. He winced as the earsplitting wail assaulted him from both sides, rattling his teeth and reverberating through his skull.

Lifting his head almost caused a disaster, as the wind tried to pull him from the fuselage. He slammed his face back down and angled his body to the right side, heading for the antenna nest halfway between the cockpit and the engine pods.

He was two feet away from the protruding antennas when the Ekranoplan lifted free of the ocean. The slipstream vanished for a moment, blocked by the rising nose. It came howling back with a vengeance as the aircraft leveled off.

The renewed gust nearly shook Kurt free. His right foot slipped, and he slid backward several inches. He flattened his leg and ankle against the roof, using the entire side of his dive boot for more grip. A last-second reprieve, he thought, but the battle with the wind would soon be lost.

In desperation, he lunged forward, grasping the base of the nearest antenna. Wrapping his hand around it with an iron grip, he pulled himself forward. Grabbing a second antenna, he managed to drag himself into the center of the small forest of protuberances.

Turning to a more advantageous position, he wedged his feet against a third antenna, this one a wide, stubby blade.

Thank god for the ethos of Russian design, he considered. If this was an American plane, these would all be hidden inside a streamlined bubble.

The wind whipped his face. His hair felt as if it were being pulled out by the roots and his eyes watered to no end. They were airborne now, doing over a hundred knots.

He would obviously never make it to the cockpit. And there was no way to go back.

He looked around. He had one more card to play. If his next move didn't work, he'd have to choose between being blown off the plane or hanging on until the charge he'd left down below detonated and tore it apart.

In the aft section of the fuselage, Yan-Li was still looking for a way out. There had to be a way to open the doors manually. "Look for an override," she said to Callum. "Some kind of manual release."

The two of them scoured the back of the plane. Yan didn't speak or read Russian, but she could guess what some of the icons painted on the old fuselage walls meant. She soon found a panel that had an emergency icon on it. She pulled the door open, finding a long lever that reminded her of a jack used to lift cars.

"This is it."

Grabbing the lever with both hands, she pulled with all her might. At first, it wouldn't budge. But as she leaned back and worked it one way and then the other, it began to move. The next stroke was easier, as was the next after that.

The manual hydraulic lever probably hadn't been oiled in years. Still, with great effort she got it moving. Callum came to help and they took turns working the pump.

Glancing to the aft door, she saw it opening farther, but just a few inches at a time. "Faster," she said. But Callum was slowing down, giving up.

"It's too late," he said, nodding toward the opening in the doors and the sea beyond. "We're flying."

With his left hand still grasping the antenna and his feet wedged in firmly, Kurt reached into the pack and pulled out the last explosive charge in his possession. Cradling it against his chest, careful not to let it get blown away, he thumbed the timer button, clicking it repeatedly and dropping it all the way down to :02. Then, for good measure, he bumped it up to :04. This wasn't the type of pass one wanted to rush.

With the timer set, he glanced over to his right and back. The engine pod was there, maybe twenty feet behind him. The pylon was so stubby that the first engine in the bunch was right up against the fuselage. All he had to do was get the explosive outward about ten feet and the wind would do the rest.

Knowing he couldn't extend his arm into the wind without being pulled from his perch, he tested a twisting motion, found that it worked acceptably and looked back at the explosive charge.

Blinking until he could see clearly for a second, Kurt pressed the start button.

The timer went from :04 to :03 to :02. Kurt twisted his body and flung the charge out at a forty-five-degree angle. The wind took it instantly and Kurt never saw it again. It flew backward and sideways as he buried his face against the fuselage and grabbed the base of the antenna with both hands.

He'd hoped to get the second or third engine in the multiengine pod—the farther out, the better—but the first engine gobbled it up before it got there.

His timing was near perfect though. The explosive went off as it hit the inside of the cowling, blowing the engine apart from within.

Shrapnel from the first engine tore into the

second one while the shock wave twisted the entire pylon, causing the third engine to chew up its own fan blades. A hundred-foot trail of fire and molten sparks flared from the back end, lighting up the morning like the world's largest Roman candle.

Kurt felt the blast wave but was insulated from most of the explosion by the rushing wind and the fact that the charge detonated inside the cowling.

Peeking under a raised elbow, he looked back to see a trail of smoke and fire marring the sky behind them.

With a twist and a groan, the number one engine tore away, flipping back along the fuselage and nearly hitting the tail before vanishing behind them and dropping into the sea.

The plane began to shudder, yawing to the right, pitching upward and slowing.

Kurt held on with a white-knuckled grip. He'd thrown his best punch and landed a knockout. The only question now was, would he survive the aftermath?

CHAPTER 73

All Emmerson felt was a muted thud, but the wall of red and yellow warning lights on the engineer's panel concerned him and the plane starting to shake terrified him.

"What's happening?" he demanded.

The pilots didn't answer. They were too busy trying not to crash and die.

"Starboard engines are out," the navigator said. "Fire detected. Cut the fuel. Shut down the port side."

While the copilot shut off the fuel supply, the pilot manipulated the wheel and the rudders, exhibiting strong hands and quick feet. With no power and a fire burning on the starboard side of the plane, he had only the rudders to guide them now. He pushed and strained and twisted his body, deftly keeping the nose straight as the plane slowed down.

As the aircraft neared the water, he pulled back hard on the controls, flaring at the last second and carving a near-perfect landing on the sea.

Emmerson was stunned. "What are you doing? Get us airborne."

"This plane isn't going anywhere," the pilot said. "Ever again."

Eliminating the pirates in back was no longer an option. Escape wasn't looking too likely either. Emmerson undid his seat belt, grabbed his pistol and prepared to fight to the death.

He was furious, but they still had some advantages. The first being that he and Guānchá were used to killing, while the holier-than-thou Water Rats were not.

"We have to kill them the old-fashioned way," he told Guānchá. "Face-to-face."

Guānchá nodded, reloaded his pistol and stepped through the cockpit door.

Emmerson was ready to follow him when a radio call came over the speaker. **"This is Skimmer 1,"** the voice announced. **"We see the smoke. Are you all right?"**

Maybe escape was possible after all. Emmerson grabbed the pilot. "Get the skimmer down here. Tell him to come and pick us up."

CHAPTER 74

Yan-Li felt the explosion and dropped to the deck as tumbling engine parts and shrapnel punched a dozen holes in the fuselage. Though there was no major fire, the acrid smell of burning kerosene poured in.

A wave of euphoria surged through her body. Kurt had somehow done what he'd promised to do. She turned to Callum. "Get the boat in position."

Callum and the others pushed the boat onto the rollers in the center of the ramp. Yan went back to the hand pump, working it as her arms and shoulders threatened to cramp up. Eventually, the doors opened wide enough for the ramp to fall with the aid of gravity.

It splashed into the blue water behind the aircraft and the boat slid down the rollers into the sea. Yan exhaled and let go of the lever and slumped over for a second.

Straightening up, she stepped toward the ramp,

ready to run down it and into the beckoning water. She was ten feet from freedom when something sharp hit her in the back of her leg.

The echoing pop of the gunshot seemed to come afterward as she landed face-first on the metal decking. She was stunned by the impact, confused by the burning sensation in her thigh and very aware of the taste of blood in her mouth where she'd bitten her tongue.

She heard heavy boots on the deck behind her. She lifted her hand and waved for the men to get out of there, to get away before anything else happened.

They refused. Callum swung the boat around but gunfire from above and behind her chased them off.

With great effort, Yan rolled over. Guānchá was standing there. Thirty feet behind her, half hidden by the nose of the submarine.

She glanced up at him, wanting to look him in the eye when he fired the last shot. She wanted him to know that even though he'd finished her, she'd likewise destroyed him and his boss.

And then something else caught her attention. A glowing LED just to Guānchá's right. Exactly where Kurt had placed it.

She started to laugh at her would-be killer. Laughing so hard it unnerved him. He looked down just as the last of the NUMA explosives went off at his feet.

Guānchá vanished in the explosion. Yan was pushed toward the tail. Her clothes and hair were singed by the heat. She found herself at the edge of the ramp only yards from the embrace of the sea. Smoke and fire swirled around her. She got to her knees and began to crawl, but the deck started to tilt the wrong way. The aircraft, broken in the middle, was taking on water amidships, sinking in the center with both ends rising toward the sky.

CHAPTER 75

Kurt had managed to hold on as the Ekranoplan made its emergency landing. As it slowed and began to drift, he got to his feet and raced toward the nose of the aircraft. Finding his pistol, he pulled open the emergency egress hatch at the top of the cockpit and pointed the weapon down into the green and gray space.

He saw three empty seats, debris on the floor and an abandoned headset. There was no sign of Emmerson or the pilots.

Still on top of the plane, he moved to the port side, away from the smoldering engines. Looking down over the side of the plane, he noticed an open hatch. A rope ladder had been dropped from it, the bottom rung only six feet above the sea.

Kurt looked out through the swirling smoke to the ocean beyond. A hundred yards from the plane, he spied three figures clinging to flotation pillows and swimming for all they were worth.

He saw one of the skimmers touching down on the water nearby. The men swam toward it.

"Has to be Emmerson," Kurt said to himself.

Planting his feet, he'd raised the pistol, but a buzzing, grinding noise racing toward him from behind set off alarm bells in his head. He spun around in time to see the other skimmer racing toward him, then dove to the side, landing flat on the rooftop just in time to avoid being decapitated.

As the noisy craft flashed over the top of him, Kurt opened fire, pulling the trigger as rapidly as he could.

Rolling onto his side, he tracked it as it flew off. A thin line of smoke was trailing from the aft. It darkened and thickened and then there was a burst of flames.

The craft turned back to the east, rolling slowly to one side and nosing over into the sea. It seemed to happen in slow motion. Just a small white splash and a growing circle of foam.

Getting to his feet and turning back toward the craft that had stopped to rescue Emmerson, Kurt raised the pistol. It was no use, he'd fired his last shot. "Emmerson," he muttered in disgust. "I can't believe you're going to get away."

"Did you say something, buddy?"

Kurt was shocked by the sound of a voice in his

ear. He was shocked that the earpiece still worked and had somehow remained in place. He looked up to see the Air Truck racing in from the west.

"Joe?" he called out. "Can you actually hear me?"

"Loud and clear," Joe said. **"Is that you on top of the airplane?"**

"Who else would it be," Kurt said. "How'd you find us?"

"I'd tell you it was the mile-long smoke trail you left me," Joe said. **"But I've actually been following these skimmers for the last hour. It's been a fun ride, but the battery is getting low. Hang on, I'll come in and pick you up."**

"Negative," Kurt said. "Use whatever juice you've got left to stop Emmerson from escaping. He's in that other skimmer."

"Are you sure?" Joe asked. **"I don't really want to leave you on a burning plane."**

"Don't worry," Kurt said as the Air Truck sped past. "I'll be fine."

The very next instant, things became the opposite of fine as the explosive charge Kurt had planted inside the fuselage went off and the plane folded up like a broken straw.

Kurt was knocked off his feet. He landed flat on his back, lost his grip on the empty pistol and felt the angle of the world change drastically beneath him. As the plane bent in half, Kurt slid down the rapidly steepening grade, coming to a stop at the bend in the middle. The aluminum was hot and soft from the thermite.

Kurt knew that was a bad sign. He pushed himself up with his hands, attempting to get to the edge. But the skin of the aircraft split and a chasm opened up beneath him, swallowing him whole.

CHAPTER 76

Unaware of the explosion, Joe turned toward the skimmer to the north. The machine was already accelerating and lifted off the water before Joe could reach it. It quickly sped up to its maximum velocity. And though it couldn't outrun the Air Truck, it still had several advantages.

For one thing, it was made of aluminum instead of plastic, making it unlikely that Joe would get the better of even a glancing impact if he tried to side-swipe the machine. Another advantage was that the skimmer had wings instead of fans. If Joe lost even one of the four fans, the Air Truck would become instantly unstable and probably flip over and crash.

Seeming to recognize this fact, the pilot of the skimmer swerved toward Joe as soon as he moved in close.

With quick fingers on the control panel, Joe turned the Air Truck away from the danger. It banked hard and all but jumped out of the way before leveling off.

The pilot of the skimmer pressed the attack, turning hard toward Joe once again.

The second attempt to knock him out of the sky was just as fruitless. But this time Joe went up over the top and dropped back down on the far side of the charging machine. He was tempted to shout **Olé.**

The Air Truck was so agile and maneuverable, Joe felt as if he was toying with the ponderous skimmer.

"This is like racing a minivan in a souped-up Corvette," he said to himself.

Inside the skimmer, Emmerson wasn't taking the situation so lightly. He shouted at the pilot, to no end. So when it became clear that the aircraft could go no faster, he turned to the mercenaries. "Unless you want to spend the rest of your lives in an American prison, you have to eliminate that aircraft."

The armed men, three of whom had been injured in the fighting on Badger Island, looked less than pleased by the request. But they understood the gravity of the situation. They clicked off the safeties on their weapons and nodded.

———

As Joe maneuvered into position, the skimmer came at him again. But instead of trying to smash its nimble pursuer, it pulled up beside him with the side door thrown open.

Joe knew what was coming next. He peeled away to the right as a commando inside fired at him with an assault rifle.

"Dangerous minivan," he said, revising his earlier assessment and reaching for the pistol on the passenger's seat.

He managed to open the case and put his fingers on the semiautomatic weapon. But just as he got it in hand, another hail of bullets from Emmerson's plane forced him to take evasive action.

He was thrown about inside the cockpit and almost dropped the gun. "If ever I needed this thing to fly itself," he said, "now's the time."

A calm female voice replied from the control panel. **"Please say course and destination."**

Joe was shocked. Stratton hadn't told him about this feature.

"Aircraft detected in your vicinity," the voice continued. **"Please turn left forty-five degrees for collision avoidance or activate formation flying mode."**

"Formation flying?" Joe said.

"Formation flying mode activated," the voice said. **"Please state formation: side by side, echelon right or echelon left?"**

Joe could hardly believe his ears. "Echelon right,"

he said. "Put us in second position. Forty feet off the right wingtip."

As the autopilot took over, the Air Truck slowed suddenly. It snapped to the right with a violent twist that had the seat belt digging into Joe's lap. Straightening up, it sped forward, hitting full speed in seconds.

It was whiplash-inducing. But when Joe looked up, they were racing in just behind the skimmer's tail and off its right wingtip, matching its speed and course in a tight echelon formation.

The skimmer turned hard, attempting to get away, but Joe's computer reacted so fast the picture never changed.

"My apologies to the world of RC enthusiasts," Joe said, gripping the pistol and switching off the safety. "This is fantastic."

The skimmer turned hard again, this time cutting toward Joe, but the Air Truck adjusted instantly. The fans pivoted and the vehicle twisted and banked, punishing Joe with more whiplash but never breaking formation.

Reaching up, Joe grabbed the canopy's emergency release bar. Pulling hard, he slid the canopy back. The wind roared in. The sound of the fans suddenly deafening.

With a two-handed grip, he leveled the pistol at the skimmer's engine compartment and opened fire. He blasted away until smoke began to pour from the cowling.

The skimmer turned away and the Air Truck followed.

"End formation flying," Joe said.

The computer didn't respond. It was following the smoking aircraft, which looked like it was about to roll over and hit the drink.

"End formation flying."

The wind was too loud. The microphone couldn't pick him up.

The skimmer flipped on its back and nose-dived. Joe slapped his hand against the control panel, slamming every button he could find. The autopilot disengaged and Joe turned away from the impending crash site, pulling up and to the right.

He caught a glance of Emmerson in the small plane, his face a mask of rage and horror behind the cockpit plexiglass. Then the burning skimmer plunged nose-first into the sea.

"That was a close one," he said. "Maybe automated flying is not that great after all."

Joe got the craft under control and brought it back around. There was no sign of survivors below, no one bobbing in the sea waiting for rescue. Just wreckage, white foam and the nose of the small craft disappearing beneath the waves.

"No one could have survived that," he told himself.

With the battery indicator critical, he turned back toward the Ekranoplan. As he grew close, he was shocked at the condition of the craft.

What had been a magnificent example of engineering and ingenuity was now a shattered hulk. It was broken into four pieces and sinking from the middle.

The tail slid under the waves first, dragging the right wing down through a spreading circle of unburned kerosene. The nose was pointed upward and sinking as dramatically, air and spray venting from the cockpit windows and open emergency hatches.

It disappeared from view, leaving only floating debris and several men on a ribbed inflatable boat poking around as if they were looking for survivors.

Circling the wreckage, Joe saw no one swimming for safety or clinging to any of the floating debris. Just small fires and slicks of kerosene.

The battery light went from solid red to flashing red. The fans dropped to half power and the computer voice returned. **"Autoland sequence engaged."**

There was little Joe could do except sit there as the Air Truck settled onto the ocean. The body touched first and then the fans, which stopped the instant they slapped the water.

He sat there quietly as waves lapped at the side of the craft. The machine was now a very expensive canoe for which Joe didn't have a paddle.

The men in the boat idled over toward him. "NUMA," one of them said.

There was no way to deny it, the logo was plastered

on the side of the vehicle in thousand-point font. Joe nodded. "And who are you?"

"Water Rats," the man said. "My name is Callum."

The pirates. Better them than more of Emmerson's people.

"Is Yan-Li with you?"

"She was," Callum said. "And your friend with the silver hair."

Joe looked around. There was no sign of either colleague.

Joe used the last of the battery power to alert the **Sapphire** of his position and situation. He told them he'd linked up with the pirates and then reported Kurt missing and presumed lost.

It was a moment Joe never believed he'd see. Even with all the risks they took. "I really thought he'd have made it out," Joe said sadly. "I shouldn't have left him behind."

He leaned back in his seat, closing his eyes. Opening them only as a rumble in the water attracted his attention.

He glanced around. Foam was appearing in a circular formation thirty yards from where he floated. It spread and widened, turning the surface white. An object appeared in the center of the circle, breaching the surface and settling and displacing a large wave.

Joe recognized the mini-sub, its wide, flat hull, off-white paint job and orange docking collar unmistakable.

It was possible, he thought, and even likely that the sub's natural buoyancy had ripped it free from the wreckage of Emmerson's aircraft. But that would have required it to be buttoned up and watertight.

"I wonder . . ." Joe said.

The top hatch popped open. Kurt emerged from the sub and stretched in the sunlight. Reaching down, he helped another passenger up out of the machine, a woman with long dark hair whom Joe recognized as Yan-Li. Her leg was bandaged and she seemed unable to stand, but she was smiling.

"Hope we didn't scare anyone," Kurt shouted.

"How did you . . ." Joe said. "I mean . . ."

Kurt laughed. "I bumped into Yan as the plane was sinking. We tried to swim out, but we couldn't get free. The only option left was to hide in the mini-sub. We figured sooner or later someone would come down to inspect the wreck and we'd ask for some assistance. But the plane broke apart when we hit the bottom. We were jarred loose and up we came."

Joe grinned. "Good to know your patented Kurt Austin luck hasn't run out." He turned to Yan. "Glad to see you. I always say it's hard to keep a good woman down. In your case literally."

She grinned despite the pain. "Nice to see you too, Joe."

"And Emmerson?" Kurt asked.

Joe beamed. "Happy to announce he's been put out of business . . . permanently."

That brought a smile to every face. Yan looked over to Callum and the other pirates, then turned back to Kurt and Joe. She began slyly. "Now, about the treasure . . . When, exactly, can my new colleagues and I announce 'our' discovery?"

CHAPTER 77

KI-SONG ISLAND
THREE WEEKS LATER

"Yan-Li, come here."

Callum's voice sounded desperate, but it might have been the warbled distortion of the underwater communications system. Yan-Li lowered her tape measure onto the sand where she was measuring an exposed timber and pushed herself off the seafloor. The water visibility was incredibly clear, nearly ninety feet, and she could observe the entire wreck site. There were others working nearby, clad in bright orange wetsuits like hers. Two divers from the Republic of Vietnam were probing the bottom with stainless steel rods while two members of her own team, including Callum, operated a vacuum hose at the far end. He was on his knees slowly sweeping the vacuum across the seabed. He didn't appear to be in trouble.

She made a scissor kick with her fins and propelled herself over a large aluminum grid that had been laid over the site. This was the true beginning of the excavation. They'd removed eighteen inches of silt from a large rectangular area around the ship and burrowed a few test pits. They still had a lot more to dig and plenty of shoring up to do before exposing the bulk of the **Silken Dragon,** but they'd begun the task and were already finding small artifacts.

Callum was working within one of the grid frames and had excavated a shallow hole in the packed sediment. Yan approached and hovered over him, noticing that he was working the vacuum with a remarkable level of caution and restraint.

He had good reason to be careful. Now that he and the other pirates were officially part of the expedition, they had a potential share of the Chinese reward money waiting for them, not to mention official government documents that cleared them of any wrongdoing for their previous endeavors. A modern pirate amnesty, Yan thought, similar to the one Ching Shih had arranged for her people at the end of her pirating career.

"Are you all right?" she asked.

"Yes," Callum replied with an eager look in his eyes. "I felt something smooth under the sand."

As the vacuum gobbled up loose sand and small pebbles, she noticed a white object emerge at the bottom of the resulting cavity. It was flat, smooth and shiny. A blue pattern was visible on one side in the shape of a floral sunburst. Callum gradually exposed the object as a small plate made of porcelain. He pried it gently from the sand and passed it to Yan.

"Is it anything?" he asked.

She held the plate close to her mask. Ancient shipwrecks in Southeast Asia nearly always contained unique pottery that could be instrumental in dating the vessels. Yan-Li was well versed in antique Chinese porcelain and she trembled as she turned the plate over. On the bottom was a square hand-painted symbol, the **zhuanshu,** or archaic seal. It was a reign mark typically reserved for imperial wares. Yan recognized the marking as the seal of Jiaqing, an emperor of the Qing Dynasty who ruled from 1796 to 1820. The exact same period in which Ching Shih sailed the seas.

After carefully placing the plate in a mesh bag numbered with a grid location identifier, she turned and patted Callum on the shoulder. "This is a great discovery. You may have just helped identify the **Silken Dragon** and earned the team ten million dollars."

"Thanks. And thanks for not going back on your word."

She was across from him now and could see his face through his helmet. "You didn't abandon me to Emmerson when he was trying to break me as much as use me," she said. "You and the others stood together. Lucas would have been proud."

Looking into his eyes, she could see that this meant as much as anything to him. He grinned at her and went back to work.

Yan-Li turned and initiated her ascent. Looking up, she saw her two children snorkeling on the surface with Kurt and a smile came to her face. Kurt and Joe had just arrived on the **Sapphire,** ostensibly to help with the excavation. Both men had instead spent their time entertaining her kids.

She surfaced alongside her children, who swarmed around her.

"Kurt said he would teach me to dive tomorrow," her son gushed.

"Me too," her daughter added.

"Aren't they a little young to be wreck-diving?" she asked Kurt.

"It's never too early to start recruiting some NUMA explorers," he said with a laugh. "Did you find anything?"

She showed him the porcelain plate. "It's Qing Dynasty. Same as Ching Shih."

"Almost as good as a ship's bell," he said.

"I can't wait to show it to Dr. Zhou."

"Come join us on the **Sapphire** for lunch when you're finished. Joe's about to treat the kids to some mac and cheese with a side of tamales."

She turned and swam to a large Chinese research

ship that was officially overseeing the excavation in partnership with the Vietnamese government. The project's chief archaeologist, Dr. Zhou, was equally impressed with the discovery. Leaving the porcelain plate to a team of onboard conservators, Yan-Li swam over to the **Sapphire** moored nearby.

A lunch feast had been spread across a folding table on the stern and her kids were knee-deep in bowls of macaroni and cheese. Kurt handed her a dry towel and a chilled bottle of sparkling water as she climbed aboard.

"With service like this, I may not return to the Chinese ship," she said.

"And you haven't even tasted Joe's tamales yet," Kurt replied, pulling up a chair for her.

"I'm so glad you and Joe were able to return for the excavation. I felt awkward initiating work on the site without you."

"We had a few loose ends to tie up with Mr. Emmerson's inventory."

"You were able to recover the Vector servers from the wreckage of the Ekranoplan?"

"Yes. They all survived intact and appeared operational."

Joe arrived with a platter of hot tamales still in their corn husks.

"Those look great," Yan said.

"My grandma's recipe. The best in all the land."

Kurt gazed at nearby Ki-Song Island. "By that, I take it you mean Vietnam."

"Very funny. Somewhat less funny is the fact that Rudi just called and is waiting for us to chat on the video line."

"Excuse us," Kurt said. He took a quick bite of one of the tamales as he followed Joe inside the salon. "Your grandmother knew what she was doing."

"She claimed my grandfather could wrestle a bull after eating these."

"Sounds just like what we need before facing Rudi."

Gunn was waiting patiently on the video screen, formally dressed in a blue suit and yellow tie. "Sorry to intrude on lunch, Kurt, but I just returned from an intelligence briefing downtown and wanted to share the good news with you two."

"You've decided to give us the **Sapphire** and the rest of the year off?" Joe asked.

"No. As a matter of fact, you owe me twelve hundred dollars. And I'll grant you three days of leave until your next project assignment."

"What's the twelve hundred for?" Kurt asked.

"It's a bill from the CIA, for a bottle of whiskey purchased in Taiwan on the government's account. I hope it was good."

"It was smashing, actually. A necessary expense that helped get Degra out of the building."

"Part of the reason for my call," Rudi said. "The NSA has awarded you both a commendation for your aid to the country."

"How much cash does that involve?" Joe asked.

"None, I'm afraid. And, since it's the NSA, you don't even get an ugly wall plaque. But you will get a nice letter in your employment file. The intelligence agencies are pleased that there have been no repercussions from your assorted actions. The Chinese believe Kinnard Emmerson's disappearance was attributed to the accidental crash of his aircraft and suspect nothing more. Degra was found alive, but he'll spend the rest of his days in jail, along with the surviving members of CIPHER. And I can report that the five Vector units have safely returned to the U.S. after your stealth salvage work following Emmerson's crash."

"Five Vector units?" Joe said. "We recovered six units intact, which we transferred underwater to a Navy submarine."

"Indeed." Rudi turned as someone off camera spoke to him. "Excuse me for a moment."

Joe glanced at Kurt, who just shrugged. Rudi reappeared a minute later holding a paper in his hand.

"I just received this note from Hiram. He says Dr. Zhou, the archaeologist on your little venture, has notified the Chinese authorities that they have positively identified the **Silken Dragon** based on an harquebus, a telescope and a Qing Dynasty plate recently recovered. He is requesting that the ten-million-dollar reward be authorized to Yan-Li's consortium."

"That's terrific news," Joe said.

"Wait a minute," Kurt said. "That plate was just recovered twenty minutes ago."

"Was it?" Rudi said.

Joe looked at Kurt quizzically. "You don't mean . . . the sixth server?"

"Tell me they didn't," Kurt said to Rudi.

"As I told you, there officially is no sixth server. After further analysis, the National Security Agency has determined that there were, in fact, only five Vector units aboard the Ekranoplan when it went down."

"I see," Kurt said. "And that extra octagonal section of aircraft wreckage we placed gently on the seafloor next to the Navy sub?" he asked.

"It has a new home. A nice quiet spot on the seabed, somewhere deep and dark, with a steady current and an international fiber-optic trunk line nearby." Rudi leaned forward in his chair. "Of course, you didn't hear that from me."

Kurt shook his head. "In that case, Rudi, you better requisition us some new stationery."

"And why's that?" he asked with a knowing smile.

"Because I have a feeling Joe and I will be corresponding the old-fashioned way from now on. With pen and paper."

ABOUT THE AUTHORS

CLIVE CUSSLER was the author of more than eighty books in five bestselling series, including Dirk Pitt®, NUMA Files®, **Oregon** Files®, Isaac Bell®, and Sam and Remi Fargo®. His life nearly paralleled that of his hero Dirk Pitt. Whether searching for lost aircraft or leading expeditions to find famous shipwrecks, he and his NUMA crew of volunteers discovered and surveyed more than seventy-five lost ships of historic significance, including the long-lost Civil War submarine **Hunley**, which was raised in 2000 with much publicity. Like Pitt, Cussler collected classic automobiles. His collection featured more than one hundred examples of custom coachwork. Cussler passed away in February 2020.

GRAHAM BROWN is the author of **Black Rain** and **Black Sun**, and the coauthor with Clive Cussler of **Devil's Gate**, **The Storm**, **Zero Hour**, **Ghost Ship**, **The Pharaoh's Secret**, **Nighthawk**, **The Rising Sea**, **Sea of Greed**, **Journey of the Pharaohs**, and **Fast Ice**. He is a pilot and an attorney.